Z: Beyond the Xingu

by
Diana Ashley

Maps © Rand McNally, R. L. 09-S-61
Front cover and interior photographs by the author
Author photograph by Larry Ashley

For PHF

with admiration

From your sister

across space and time

PART ONE

The Seduction

FAWCETT, PROLOGUE
London, 1924

He stood well over six feet and his cap, concealing baldness, made him appear even taller. The housekeeper answered his knock and ushered him into a dimly-lit foyer. She took his coat and his cap, but deliberately ignored the wooden case he held; this he shifted from one hand to the other as he removed his coat.

"This way, please," she said, and motioned toward the arched entrance to a parlor. "Watch your step."

Indeed; the room was almost completely dark. With cat-eyes she led him to a chair beside a sturdy table, and as he carefully took his seat he discerned the figure of an elderly man sitting opposite. The housekeeper quietly withdrew.

"Good evening, sir," intoned a friendly voice.

"Good evening, Mr. Haddock. Thank you for seeing me on such short notice."

"Quite all right. Now, what have you brought?"

His visitor placed the box on the table, opened it, and removed a figurine, an idol ten inches high carved of black basalt. In the semi-darkness the plaque on its chest could not clearly be seen, nor the band around its ankles, both engraved with a number of characters. "Here." He pushed the figurine forward on the table, and Haddock groped before him until he had the article firmly in his hands.

"Well!" he exclaimed immediately, with a little laugh.

"Ah, you get the effect, as everyone else has! Describe to me what you're feeling, please."

"Ah... it would best be described as an electric current, I think."

"That's what most people say; some of them have been forced to lay it down, in fact."

"It *is* quite a buzz!" Mr. Haddock hesitated, then sighed deeply. "And now, sir, if you will bear with me for a few minutes... "

The two fell silent, and soon the old gentleman began to write rapidly in the gloom.

Fawcett sat quietly staring from the window of his bedroom, but seeing nothing, trying to contain his rising excitement. Then he picked up a pen and opened the old leather notebook.

September 1, 1924

So many times in recent months I've turned to this journal or my memoirs, finding comfort in expression as the funds for my Amazonian expedition failed to materialize. With every year that I've watched myself grow older, self-doubts have compounded one upon the other. Yesterday, my birthday, I gazed in the mirror at my fifty-seven-year-old body and wondered, after a few years of easy living and struggling to stay fit, if I can once more carry forty pounds on my back day after day.

But I will! Finally, most of the financing has been arranged. We leave for South America in a few weeks and I'll not have another chance to write until we're aboard ship, as there are myriad details to take care of. I am like a madman— but a happy one!

Packing for this trek is at once simple, yet challenging. Since there will be only the three of us, Jack, Raleigh, and myself, carrying our own supplies most of the time, we're carefully considering each item. For instance, we're debating whether or not to take a 22-calibre rifle; it could be useful if game is available— which so often is not the case— but one begrudges the weight of it. More powerful firearms could be dangerous, as it's wiser to leave large animals alone; and any human enemy who's serious about killing you will do it with a silent dart before you even suspect he's near.

Without question, however, the figurine will go with me. When Sir H. Rider Haggard gave it to me he could tell me only that it was found by the British Consul, O'Sullivan Beare, in the ruins of a lost, ancient city in Brazil; he could supply no more details. But I've already determined fourteen of its twenty-four characters are found separately on pieces of ancient Brazilian pottery, which convinces me it isn't a fake. None of the experts at the British Museum were able to shed any light on its origins, saying they'd never seen anything quite like it, and were particularly flummoxed by its strange current.

Therefore I've taken it to several psychometrists who've told me much more than the archaeologists could. I'm impressed by the concurrence of the readings each one independently gave, knowing nothing about me (or the idol) in advance. This fact alone provides powerful evidence. In addition, their accounts of the idol's history tend to agree with archaeological and geological data I've unearthed. I've recorded, elsewhere, a summation of these readings. Suffice it to say, it seems more than happenstance that the idol has found its way to my keeping, and now I shall take it back where it belongs.

Bringing it along is more than foolish superstition; its inscribed symbols could match others we might uncover in scattered ruins or in City Z, itself– our goal. Of course, I could merely bring a paper copy of the characters. But if the city I seek is still occupied, the inhabitants plainly do not want to be found; the idol itself may in some way help us gain entrée.

I suppose this does sound fanciful, so I'm willing to admit the object might serve as a sort of talisman for me; as if it can lead us, one might say, to its home...

But I make no apologies for my theories and methods. Those who have never experienced what I have been through, or seen what I've seen in the wild godless places, where one's arrogance in the face of the unexplainable is like a shield of smoke that soon disappears and leaves one defenseless... Those smug, safe chaps are saying I've lost my reason, but never mind. A hundred years ago the radio would've sounded like sheer magic; so why is it modern science cannot credit even the possibility of psychometry? In the Orient they're many years ahead of us, in this respect.

Thanks be to Heaven my dearest Cheeky not only understands but is in full accord. Only ten of our twenty-four years of marriage have been spent together, and our marriage, our family life and finances, have been sacrificed to my quest... which some think vainglorious; "Fawcett's Folly," they'll no doubt call it, if I fail.

For the past few years I've occupied myself with the organizing of my notes, journals, sketches, and photographs, and tried to make sense of the time spent in South America. Stepping back to view it as a whole, I can trace the path that led me to this point. But on the day of Jack's birth, I could never have imagined twenty-one years later he and I would embark on such a formidable mission.

What I've seen with my own eyes is compelling enough to justify every sacrifice and every risk; I can only hope that in the end my loved ones will still agree.

FAWCETT, CHAPTER 1
SOUTH AMERICA
Ceylon, India 1903

Perspiration soaked her thin cotton sheets and the young woman writhed in pain and terror. Someone, lithe and dark, leaned over her and mopped her brow, speaking to her soothingly, with pity. "It's going to be all right, you'll see, soon you'll be holding a beautiful little one in your arms."

But the midwife's words barely registered with the pale woman, who sank in a boiling sea of confusion and misery, unable to breathe in the heat and unable to believe there would ever be a happy outcome. The sound of repetitive chanting drifted into the room as it had for all the hours she'd struggled, using its rhythms to focus her mind.

Dimly she then saw the round, crinkled face of her maid, Susan, hovering over hers. "Yes, mum, she's right, the first is the worst, you know, but all will be well. Breathe slow and deep!"

If only she could. She gasped, then fell into a pit of agony; but she would not allow herself to cry out, not even once... The bungalow was so small, he would hear her, and worry...

The tall, lean man paced in the parlor of the bungalow, repeating the umpteenth gesture of smoothing the hair that wasn't there. Drops of perspiration trickled into his open collar. His friend stood watching him in helpless sympathy.

He paused in his pacing. "It's too quiet in there," he mumbled. "Is that normal? Something isn't right. I– "

He was interrupted by the sound of a feeble, tremorous cry, and the hard lines of his face crumpled into a crooked smile; tears stung his eyes but he blinked them back. He dropped into a chair heavily and lowered his head in prayer: Now, if only she is all right... His friend sat on the arm of the chair, his hand on the new father's shoulder, comfortingly. And they waited.

"Major Fawcett?" He hadn't heard the woman's light footsteps. Her plump, pink English face was smiling. Thank God! "Why don't you come in now, for just a moment."

He was through the doorway to the bedroom like a shot. "My dear!" he exclaimed, and rushed to her bedside. She looked pale and exhausted but was grinning like the Cheshire cat and holding a tiny bundle.

With his long arms he enveloped his wife and child, kissing her forehead and trembling with joy. "Are you all right? I didn't hear a peep, I was so worried... "

"That is because everything was fine," she lied, "rather uncomfortable, but proceeding well."

"Most women scream the house down, I believe; I thought you had died."

"Oh, posh! " she laughed weakly, and winced, making a mental note to avoid laughter for a while. She wanted nothing more than for everyone to leave her alone, and take the baby with them, so she could blot out the world and the lingering pain with blessed sleep. Then she looked again at her son's wrinkled, strange little face, and felt her breasts weep for him. "Little Jack," she said, her soft voice full of weariness.

"Jack," her husband echoed. A boy. He silently vowed his son would have all the affection he himself had been denied. He thought of his childhood in Torquay, on the English Channel, and the parental coldness that had driven him to withdraw into himself; of his school years at Newton Abbot and the canings that reinforced his reserve. Army life had further hardened him. It would not have been his career choice; there were several academic fields which suited him better, but as a second son, he was offered few options.

But as he looked at his wife he felt the present was ample compensation; though married scarcely two years she had, with her warmth and spirit, done much to thaw him. As much as anyone could, he thought. He was a loner still, a maverick straying from the common path.

He looked closely at his son, scarcely able to believe his own happiness.

"Does he look like me, do you think?"

"Yes, Puggy," she murmured, fading into overwhelming drowsiness. "He is exactly like you..."

Spike Island, Ireland, early 1906

Jack, three-years-going-on-thirty, sat on the rug at his mother's feet, arranging the spools in her thread box by color: first blues, then greens, yellows, orange and red, and finally he sat puzzling over spools of purple and brown.

Nina looked up from her sewing now and then to watch him with interest. He certainly was a "different" child; everyone said it. Even his birth had been surrounded by odd events: First of all, the local Buddhists had paid her husband a visit, telling him he would have a son who would be born on May 19, a full month past Nina's due date; what's more, they insisted, "He will be an advanced spirit." After Jack was born— on May 19, to the sound of their chants— crowds of Buddhist believers came to spread flowers about the grounds and celebrate the great event.

For a boy so small, he was immensely gentle and protective with the kitten he had begged for persistently. She thought he'd be a good brother to the coming child, soon to be born.

"Where's Daddy?"

"He'll be home soon."

"I'm bored." He had just learned the phrase. She wasn't sure he understood its meaning; he said it whenever his father had gone out.

"So am I, love." Nina adored children but she wasn't very good at being pregnant. She liked doing many of the things men did, wearing pants, riding, arguing politics and such— which had led Fawcett to dub her "Cheeky", a nickname that stuck— and the condition of gestation was quite a slap-down for her. But another baby would be worth it all, she knew.

Jack suddenly sat straight. "My daddy!"

"I think you're right."

She heaved herself from the chair and went to the door as quickly as her awkward, heavy body allowed. Her husband rushed in, face flushed and eyes shining. He kissed her generously and, she perceived, there was something conciliatory in his manner. He scooped Jack up in a big bear hug.

"Well! You have news, I can see!" She couldn't help but smile at his obvious excitement, though her heart was beginning to pound with dread.

"Sit down, my dear, I'll tell you all!" He led her to the large, plush chair and settled her, placing Jack beside her, but he could not sit down and walked the floor as he talked. The summons from the President of the Royal Geographic Society had come just as he had thought he could stand the monotony of his army career no longer. Neither of them had wanted to leave Ceylon the year after Jack was born, and for him the life of an artillery officer in a home station, namely, Spike Island, County Cork, was beginning to feel like prison. Then out of the blue had come an offer which made his blood race.

"Cheeky, we're going to Bolivia!"

"Bolivia— "

"Yes, and I've you to thank! You helped me learn surveying, and finally, all the hard work we did together is about to pay off!" He paused a moment, remembering how the War office's promises that his laborious training would result in boundary survey work had begun to seem hollow. But now... "Who would've thought my chance would come through the Royal Geographic Society?"

"I'm thrilled, darling, but now tell me exactly— "

"Oh yes, yes; well, there is disagreement among Peru, Brazil, and Bolivia concerning their boundaries in the rubber country, and with the price of rubber as fantastic as it is now, this dispute could wind up in warfare. They need an unbiased referee, and Bolivia has asked the Society to recommend an army officer to undertake this demarcation. Since I'd completed the Society's boundary delimitation course with 'great success', he told me, he thought of me for the job!" He stopped, grinning widely, his usual reserve quite vanished.

His pleasure made her happy, as always, but in her heart she knew she wasn't going anywhere, at least for a while. She felt the baby kick, as if reminding her of her biological limitations. "This is wonderful news, I know how dull it is for you here; for me, too..."

"This shall take care of our boredom, I expect! And you know how I've loathed army life, in general; but perhaps it's all been worth it. Cheeky, you should see the map he showed me; the best map the Society currently has, and yet it's full of blank spaces in large areas of Bolivia because so little is known of it all. This is a great deal more than boundary work; it's exploration!"

"It sounds— risky, darling."

"No doubt there's some risk, of course, but I wouldn't worry, really." He was glad she hadn't heard the President's warnings: disease, murderous savages, poisonous insects and reptiles... But in Fawcett's mind these obstacles were nothing compared to his present grind of meaningless work, which challenged no part of him and yet bled his spirit drop by drop, day by day, as his life slowly passed by.

Now his imagination raced with visions of the vast, unknown wilds, dark jungles where Spanish and Portuguese conquerors had roamed; but his wife's question jerked him quickly back to present realities.

"Well, what is the first step, then?"

"There's much to be done; besides arranging my release from my post here— which could take some weeks, knowing the Army— I must find an assistant and make travel arrangements for the two of us." He knelt before Cheeky and took her hands in his. "We must go on ahead, my dear; but as soon as possible I'll have you and the children join me in La Paz."

Little Jack interrupted. "Where are you going, Daddy?"

"Far away, to the biggest woods in the world!"

"I want to go."

"You have to stay and take care of Mummy and your little sister or brother who's coming, remember?"

"A brother," Jack said firmly.

Fawcett and Nina glanced at each other and smiled.

"Oh, very well. Before too long we'll know if you're right!" He turned to his wife. "And you'll have much to keep you occupied until I can send for you all. Don't worry; our separation won't be a long one."

*

The voyage to South America afforded Fawcett a breaking-in period of sorts, a buffer between the genteel civilization he had known and the rough, ruthless new world of his future. England and its forms and proprieties began to seem static, even moribund, compared to the struggling vigor of New York, the first stop on his itinerary, Panama, and eventually, Peru.

He was accompanied by a young assistant named Paul Chalmers. The two men left the luxury ship Kaiser Wilhelm der Grosse in New York and boarded the S. S. Panama, a dirty Government ship loaded with "Diggers", bound for work on the Panama Canal, as well as various white-collar workers, adventurers, sourdoughs from the Klondike, Texas Rangers, gunmen from south of the border, railroad men, prostitutes, and college boys out on a lark.

Major Fawcett could empathize with the boys; standing at the rail of the Panama, watching New York City recede in the morning mists, he didn't feel exactly like a 39-year-old man with a family in England. He reckoned he looked the picture— bald for many years, bearded, the ends of his generous brown mustache neatly and tamely waxed— but he felt suddenly young, terribly vital. Trimming his beard that morning in New York, he was brought to a pause when he noticed his eyes in the mirror: Normally a mild steel-grey, at times they snapped to life with a greenish cast, and they were snapping now. He needed the stimulation of this life-change more than he had consciously realized.

Poor Cheeky, he had thought soberly; her misfortune to fall in love with a man who can't be satisfied to collect his meager Army paycheck and go home each day to putter in the garden until suppertime. His long, narrow face with its equally long, thin nose stared back at him. Lines between his arched brows bespoke intensity, echoed in the piercing eyes. It's hard for the leopard to change its spots, he reflected, but in truth, he felt torn between the warmth of home and Nina's arms, and the exhilaration of the unknown. It was as if two separate men possessed him, competing for dominance. But only a driven man could've born the farewell from little Jack, and from a loving wife blinking back tears as she laughed and held up their new, tiny son, Brian, for a last look as his father's ship pulled away from the dock.

Now, as he stood again at a ship's rail, he wished she could be at his side, and he hated the joyous little part of him that felt as free and young as the swaggering college boys.

From the port of Cristobal, then known as Aspinwall, they journeyed overland by rail to Panama City, eagerly taking in their first sight of the tropical forests of the Americas: the impenetrable tangle of scrub, dangling lianas, mosses, huge buttressed trees... and, in the railway stations, the stacks of black coffins which testified to the effects of fever, rife in the area.

Panama City served to introduce both men to Latin America: charm and color mixed with overpowering odors and lack of sanitation; crowds of insects thronging an abundance of humans, including scantily clad females. By the time they had boarded the Chilean ship which would at last take them to South America, their British reserve had been thoroughly shaken, all for the best, no doubt.

Fawcett and Chalmers stood on deck as the port of Guayaquil, Ecuador came closer, but when the ship steamed up the Guayas River to the wharves, swarms of mosquitoes quelled their excitement.

"Damn!" cried Chalmers. "I've never seen anything like this! They're in every nook and cranny of the ship!"

"Well, it's not hard to see why Yellow Jack is endemic; the place is filthy. Reminds me of Malta."

Chalmers clawed at the bites on his arms. "There's only one thing to do, if you have no objections, sir; I think I'll have a bit of gin with the fellows. A little anesthetic seems called for, I'd say."

"Oh, yes, go right ahead, Chalmers."

"Won't you join me? I know you don't often imbibe, but— "

"No, thank you; I have a feeling we're in for a great deal more of such infestations. Might as well get hardened to it. I'm going to get back to my Spanish grammar study, if it isn't too noisy. But go, enjoy yourself. We'll be out of here and on to Callao soon enough."

Once free of the Guayas River they were again met by the fresh Pacific air, and soon enough Salaverry Port came into view, then Callao. Fawcett wrote constantly in his journal, describing everything he saw, heard, and smelled:

Arequipa, May 23, 1906

Chalmers and I were brought down to earth, literally and figuratively, when we at last disembarked at Mollendo, a place made shabby and grim by outbreaks of both fire and bubonic plague. We boarded the first train out for

Arequipa, munching oranges, bananas, limes, chirimoyas, and grenadillas as we rolled past, first, sugarcane fields and then snowy white sand dunes. But soon true snow could be seen in the distance: the lofty peak of El Misti, the slumbering volcano with its intermittent, smoky warnings that it lives, and will wreak havoc on nearby residents at whim. But survivors of El Misti's tempers continue on, thumbing their noses at life and death by building their homes of glistening white lava blocks.

We spent only one night in Arequipa, a city of fine shops, green fields, and other assets; the next day we went by train to the port of Puno, on Lake Titicaca, the highest navigable lake in the world.

As the train climbed for Puno, we were treated to our first glimpse of llamas and vicuñas, both shy but dignified relatives of sheep. And upon our arrival at the famous lake, we were dumbfounded to see an ocean-going steamer.

"Imagine," Fawcett had exclaimed as they boarded, "What it took to bring this steamer up here, 12,500 feet above sea level! Neither the lovely women of Arequipa and Panama— yes, I noticed them— nor the llamas can compare to this! Why here," he clapped Chalmers on the back, "You can be seasick and altitude-sick at the same time!"

Chalmers laughed, but with a certain pique, since Fawcett, damn him, never appeared to suffer from either malady. It almost seemed as if he were far too fascinated by his surroundings to have even a moment for common illnesses.

When we had crossed the chilly lake with its Island of the Sun, ruined, legendary birthplace of the Incas, and its native reed rafts sliding silently by in the pale haze, we stepped onto Bolivian soil and into a train bound for La Paz. But first we stopped at Tiahuanaco, where my lifetime interest in archaeology re-emerged; the place excited me tremendously. Those ruins are reputed to be the oldest in existence in the world, older even than the Sphinx. There is a legend they were built by giants; in fact, it's said that skeletons of giants have been found in tombs near Cuzco... and it makes one wonder, because who could have placed the gigantic boulders? And what genius could have carved them so precisely that they could have been joined without mortar, and one cannot insert so much as a knife blade between them?

Legend aside, I wouldn't attempt to guess how these structures were built. But I do believe Tiahuanaco was built on an island in a lake. Excavation may reveal several cities, built one upon another, as in Cuzco. There were apparently cataclysmic seismic upheavals, evidenced all over the continent, so the lake may have been lifted thousands of feet with the Andes, draining through a cleft near Illimani. Then a new lake could have formed, because there is no doubt that Tiahuanaco was submerged for a considerable time.

"I've heard," Chalmers had remarked as they stood among the ruins, "That one can dig around in these parts and still find obsidian arrowheads, perhaps even little gold relics. The museum in La Paz is supposed to have quite an interesting collection."

"Hmm, yes, gold... The conquering Spaniards were willing to risk anything for gold.." Fawcett pronounced the word slowly and softly, as if it were at once both reverent and obscene. "But though I understand the pressures of their society, I must say, the world could have learned much from the Incan civilization, my instincts tell me, if it hadn't been virtually destroyed."

The approach to La Paz by rail afforded Chalmers and me a grand, panoramic view of the city, situated at the bottom of a deep canyon. We looked down upon a foaming mountain stream, red-tiled roofs, and a colorful pattern of farm lands and gardens; presiding over all, as if in mockery of the city's many church towers were the snowy peaks of the Cordilleras to the east, reaching high above the Andean plateau which itself stood 12,000 feet above sea level.

We felt the altitude immediately. After settling into our hotel, we strolled the steep streets, enjoying the variety of human beings we encountered— when we weren't pausing to gasp for breath, that is. It was market day, and Indians were everywhere, having come in from their warm valleys to trade; their clothing, a kaleidoscope of bright, rainbow hues, was picturesque: The men in their ponchos, slashed trousers, and felt hats, appeared good-tempered and strong. But the cholita, or half-caste, women were truly spectacular, decked out in short, full silk skirts revealing a snowy froth of lace petticoats; silk stockings, laced boots, velvet jackets or bright shawls; and an array of jewelry and white straw hats worn at a jaunty angle completed the effect. I've written Cheeky a full description of the local fashions, in case she's interested!

"How lovely!" Fawcett had exclaimed as a pretty cholita passed by.

"It's a modern enough place," observed Chalmers as they continued their measured pace. "Even sophisticated, one might say."

"If you gauge that by the number of high-heeled pumps," Fawcett chuckled. "I've noticed quite a few foreigners here, and miners, too."

Chalmers had stopped. "Lord," he panted, "Even at this easy pace, my heart is racing; and I thought myself in good condition."

"You are, I'm sure. All newcomers feel the altitude, or so the hotel manager tells me. We should take it very easy for a few days until we've acclimatized. Avoid exertion, and, I might add— " Here he paused and shot a significant glance at his assistant— "Though I'm not quite a teetotaler myself, we should both abstain from alcohol for a while. It makes matters infinitely worse."

Chalmers sighed. "I imagine you're right. At any rate, I don't want to fall prey to mountainsickness; you'll surely think me a weakling then."

They gave up conversation; it was simply too difficult to both talk and walk the sharp inclines. But they took silent note of the ubiquitous prospectors, with their worn Stetsons and heavy shoes, and somewhat ominously emaciated and jaundiced faces, signalling the challenges of the deep, unknowable wilderness which now seemed to stare Fawcett and Chalmers right in the eyes.

Fawcett's first challenge proved to be one that, even with all the difficulties and dangers that would face him in the coming years, was the hardest thing of all for him to handle: patience. He was constitutionally unequipped to deal with "mañana", but he was about to learn how his impatience made matters worse. Nagging and prodding the Bolivian government for the money to outfit his expedition only resulted in a digging-in-of-heels which stretched into days, and then weeks. Next, Fawcett found himself in a rather nasty battle of wills over the amount he was to receive. He went to the British Consul in frustration, and the Consul attempted to set him straight.

"Major, you have to get the hang of using finesse, rather than pushiness, if I may say so, to get what you want; it's a matter of custom in these parts, a way of allowing people to save face, even."

"Well, I can't argue with what you say, because obviously my methods haven't been working."

"To complicate matters," the Consul continued, "The government resents your presence here, period."

"Oh? But it was the government that brought me here."

"True, but it was, remember, this dispute with Peru over rubber territory which essentially forced them to bring in a third, disinterested party— namely, you— to settle the boundary issue; although of course, they would prefer the line were run by a Bolivian engineer.

They may even decide to cancel your contract and delay running the line at all until tensions with Peru have eased. In the meantime, they're going to try to diminish your credibility as much as possible; after all, the boundary you establish may not suit them at all."

"I see." Fawcett was thoughtful. This business could be tricky, indeed. He could see he would have to smooth some ruffled feathers if he wanted to get anywhere at all. He had learned a valuable lesson.

After a tense and delicate session with Bolivian officials, by some miracle an agreement was reached which provided Fawcett with sufficient funds without too much discomfort for the officials. Polite and cordial relations seemed to have been reestablished, at least on the surface. He was finally handed £1,000 in gold from the Government.

"My, do I feel important with this weight of gold in my possession!" he joked to Chalmers. "Come, let's do a bit of shopping, shall we?"

At the end of the "shopping" spree, he felt somewhat less important; after settling their hotel bills and purchasing mules, food, and other supplies, his fortune was reduced to £800. Still, he was thrilled to the bone: At long last, on July 4, 1906, they were ready to explore the Beni.

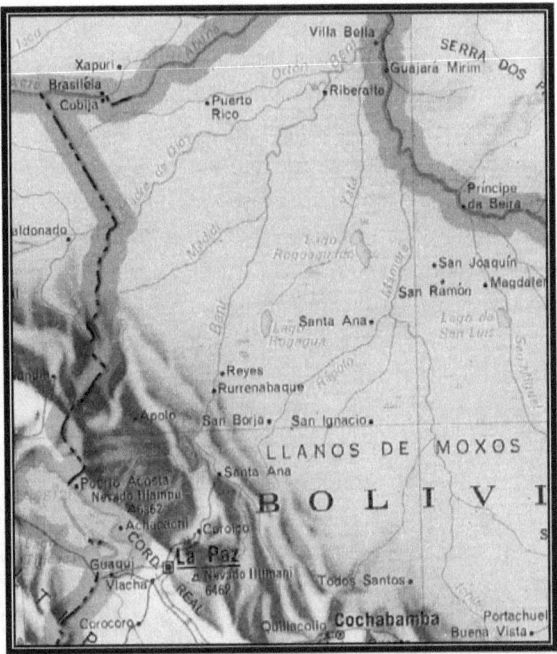

FAWCETT, CHAPTER 2
RIO BENI

Fawcett awoke from a deep sleep with the hairs on the back of his neck standing stiff. His body was suddenly rigidly alert, but his mind was dull and confused as he struggled to full wakefulness. Where was he, and why was he so terrified? That strange, unfamiliar smell— was that what had awakened him? He remembered he was in Bolivia, yes, in an open-sided hut on the Beni River... but what was that odor?

He turned his head toward the soft light of the candle-lantern; within arm's length from his hammock was a jaguar, watching the flickering candle, entranced by it. Fawcett froze. His gun lay within easy reach— no one in these forests slept without a gun at the ready— but he dared not make a move for it; the jaguar was too close. He lay perfectly still, trying to breathe quietly, hoping the animal wouldn't be aroused by the scent of perspiration which seemed to explode from his adrenaline-flooded body. For if it turned on him, he was finished; there would be no time to get off an effective shot.

There was nothing to do but lie as quiet as the dead.

He felt that even his eyes, open and staring, might somehow attract the attention of the animal and spur it to attack, so he closed them, and tried to calm his racing heart. Breathless seconds passed like hours, as he waited for the ominous, low growl of an enraged beast, praying not to hear it. After a few minutes, he had no idea how many, he could stand it no longer and cautiously cracked one eye. The hut was bathed in the gentle glow of the candle-lantern, as before, but there was no jaguar to be seen. It had left so quietly Fawcett's straining senses hadn't detected the merest sound. He drew a long breath and looked around; the hut was indeed empty of all life but his own and a few humming insects. He reached one tremorous arm out for his gun and cradled it to his chest. As his heartbeat gradually slowed to near-normal he began to wonder, dazedly, if there had been a jaguar there at all, or only a surreal vision.

It was at least an hour before he drifted into a fitful sleep, frequently awaking, his gun still clutched to his chest.

In the morning he joined Chalmers for breakfast in the home of an Englishman named Pearson, at whose rubber smallholding they had camped.

"Good morning, Major," boomed Pearson, "Please, sit down, help yourself."

"Good morning. Thank you."

"I say," remarked Chalmers, passing a pot of coffee, "You look a bit peaked; didn't you sleep well?"

Fawcett hesitated. "Not very. There was— I think— a jaguar in my hut. "

"A jaguar!" exclaimed Chalmers. "Why didn't you fire a shot, scare it away?"

"It was too close, I could've reached out and touched it. I couldn't gamble on being able to get my gun and fire before the beast got *me*. But I closed my eyes and it disappeared; I almost think I could've dreamed it..."

Pearson laughed. "Oh, I doubt that you dreamt it. They're quite common around here, and bloody dangerous. Though they can be tamed if you get one as a cub. I know a fellow at Reyes who has one, friendly as a dog; he's a great jokester, this bloke, and he's trained the jaguar to spring out at mule-back travellers on the trail. Of course, mules are more terrified of jaguars than of anything else, so they usually throw the rider and take off. The poor fellow is left sitting on his arse, staring at what he thinks is a wild jag! Ha! Ha! Can you imagine the feeling? Uh—well, yes, now I suppose you can, after last night! Ha!"

Fawcett had to smile, even if he didn't find the prank quite hilarious. Jaguars aside, he was remembering the mule he'd ridden out of La Paz only a few days ago. It seemed like weeks...

"El Beni" was the name of both a province, enormous and largely uncharted, and a river. To reach the area, Fawcett and Chalmers had needed first to traverse the Altiplano— the Andean plateau— then ride north to Sorata and cross the Cordillera Real. With pack mules and a drover they had left La Paz early on July 4 and set out across the rolling plain, in snow falling so thickly that visibility was twenty yards at best.

Fawcett pulled his alpaca-wool poncho closer around his body, regarding the garment with admiration as he did so. "This is a 'first' for me; the poncho, I mean. Quite practical item, I must say, eh? Wonderful protection against this driving snow, waterproof and warm... and the Indians use them as bed blankets, as well. Wonder why, though, the women don't wear them? Strictly a male article of apparel, I suppose..." Just then, the corners of the poncho fluttered in the wind, spooking Fawcett's mule. Before he could react, he found himself bucked from his mount.

Chagrined, he brushed the snow from his backside and glared at the mule. "Not everyone is so fond of ponchos, I see," he muttered, as Chalmers stifled a smile. Deliberately, Fawcett tied up the corners of the poncho to discourage their flapping about, and remounted.

They rode on. The wind grew ever stronger, until it lifted the men's ponchos and reached cold fingers underneath. "Ah, well, the good old English slicker has its uses, too," Fawcett conceded, turning in the saddle to draw the cold, stiff garment from his pack. He removed the poncho and was putting his arms in the slicker when his mule, rattled by the movement of crinkling fabric, bucked once more; Fawcett again landed hard on the ground, and yelped as the mule, bearing £800 in gold, darted away up the trail. The men stared at each other in helpless disbelief as the animal disappeared in the driving snow, listening to the maddening, diminishing sound of their gold jingling in the saddlebags.

Fawcett snapped to life and called back to the drover, cursing himself that his Spanish wasn't better as he struggled to explain what had happened. The drover then vanished into the whiteness which had swallowed the mule, calling for help from Indians who could be heard somewhere on the trail far ahead. But meanwhile, Indians to the rear, surmising the owner was farther ahead, had stopped the mule after it turned from the path and headed for home. Before long they brought the mule up the trail to Fawcett, who had mentally bade his money farewell. He was surprised to find the gold intact; the Indians didn't understand his surprise, nor did they understand the reward he gave them for their honesty.

"They could have so easily taken all of it," Chalmers commented, "Especially since it advertised its presence so audibly; they had plenty of time, and couldn't have been seen."

"Quite so, " replied Fawcett thoughtfully. "They could've kept the money *and* the mule."

They continued on, their mood now sobered a bit, pausing now and then to take coffee or beer at inns, or *posadas*, along the way. When night fell they stopped at another posada, hoping for a much-needed, good night's rest. But it wasn't to be.

"Lord in heaven!" exclaimed a disgusted Chalmers. "Each posada seems worse than the last! There's a competition, it seems, to be the filthiest, the coldest, the most unsanitary— "

"And the most dangerous," interrupted Fawcett, with a wry smile.

"Now, Major, surely those tales are *just* tales... "

"In Bolivia, I'm afraid, the stories are true. Particularly about the posadas ahead of us, along the Mapiri trail. Remember the revolting one we heard in La Paz, about a room in which many travellers died one by one and were each found to have strangely blackened bodies, as if they had been poisoned?" Chalmers' eyes had grown larger and he shook his head. "Well," Fawcett continued, "eventually the authorities discovered an *apazauca* spider, larger than the span of my hand, residing in the thatched roof. As the victim slept, the spider lowered itself down onto the poor devil, and with one bite dispatched him and was once again ruler of the posada!"

Chalmers swallowed. "No, I missed that story, apparently; thank you so very much for relaying it."

Fawcett laughed, but in truth he didn't rest any better that night than Chalmers. He blamed it on his aching muscles: *So soft we are,* he thought, *from our previous easy living; we'll harden up soon enough, I hope.* But he was also recalling other tales, such as one about the thieving half-caste landlord who knifed to death a total of forty sleeping travellers, and was later executed for it. *The farther we*

get from so-called civilization, he mused, *the greater the chance of any number of atrocities; out here, the reach of the law is limited. If Nature doesn't
get you, her "finest" creation, Man, will at least try.*

The next morning Fawcett and Chalmers crossed the Divide at approximately 14,000 feet, gazing with admiration at Lake Titicaca in
the distance, surrounded by and reflecting towering white mountains.
To the north, thousands of feet below them in a misty gorge, lay the
Mapiri River and the beginnings of subtropical vegetation.

It was during their descent on the narrow trail into the gorge, ma-
neuvering continual switchbacks, that Fawcett's new Mistress began to
exert her tender but terrible influence, to stealthily crawl into his soul
and make her bed there in a corner that had been waiting for her for
many years. At every bend of the trail a new vista awaited; the beauty
overwhelmed him, dissolving every hard fragment of his spirit, van-
quishing and buoying him at the same time. It was like falling in love
in the most helpless way possible. Chalmers expressed his awe more
volubly than usual, but Fawcett was a man struck dumb.

They moved deeper into the gorge and the vegetation increased.
They rode through strange, stunted trees, deformed by wind, into
eucalyptus and algarroba. They drank from a mountain stream, very
cold and so delicious that Fawcett couldn't stop drinking.

"Ahhh..." He breathed during a pause in his slurping, drops glistening in his mustache and running through his beard. "With such
water every day, one would hardly need food, eh?"

Down and down they wound until they had finally attained the
floor of the valley. They crossed the Mapiri on a suspension bridge,
and the trail turned upward to reach the little village of Sorata.

"Look, Major, there's a group waiting to greet us."

And so there was. After warm salutations from the townsfolk they
were given *chicha,* the native maize beer, thick and satisfying. A German resident offered them hospitality for two comfortable evenings
of superb food and wine and clean, safe bedrooms. They slept like
infants.

When they left the friendly residents of Sorata they faced a stiff
climb to a mountain pass at 17,000 feet, which could be fatal for
mules that were too heavily laden. They moved very slowly, and at
last made Ticunamayo, where, finding no indoors accommodations,

they were forced to bed down in the piercing, damp cold, sorely missing Sorata. Fawcett consoled himself with the thought that they were at least hardening themselves.

At Yani, once the site of a rich gold mine, Fawcett's Mistress decided it was time to expose him to another of her wiles. The two men passed the night at the Government rest-house where a local regaled them with this story:

Some years ago two Bolivian army officers, returning from the Beni, came into Yani late at night. In the doorway of one of the houses stood a pretty girl, smiling at them beguilingly. The two men tossed a coin to see which one of them would try his luck with her, and the loser stayed with the village headman. The next morning, the "unlucky" one returned to the house to fetch his fellow officer and was stunned to find a ruined house, rather than the perfectly whole dwelling they had seen the night before. He was even more shocked to discover his friend lying dead on the floor of the unoccupied ruin. The headman said the girl they had seen was a *duende*, a ghost, and that the house had been a ruin for many years. He knew nothing of the history of the place, only that the duende was occasionally seen by visitors, and never by the residents.

As Fawcett listened to the tale, which seemed mildly amusing to Chalmers, he found himself uncharacteristically ready to believe it. In fact, it gave him an odd feeling he could neither pinpoint nor describe. There was something about the area— the fringes of the Beni, Bolivia, South America, he wasn't sure when the feeling had begun— that struck him as inherently mystical in some way. He shrugged it off, or tried to; but it nagged at him, and it wasn't an altogether unpleasant sensation. He sometimes felt as if, just below his ability to hear, someone was speaking to him, and the subliminal message was both eerie and seductive.

The only thing other-worldly to Chalmers was the terror of the precipitous trails they were forced to endure. These narrow tracks were beyond imagination, and the bones of dead animals lying at the bottom of great drops testified to the reality of the danger. As sure of foot as the mules and llamas were, nonetheless, one slip meant the end for both animals and humans. Treacherously loose boulders and gravel made up the trail, which twisted above deep chasms.

"I've never prayed so much," Chalmers confessed, his brow beaded with perspiration as they made their way along a meager ledge cut in the rock face of a mountain. "Why in *bloody* Hell does this infernal beast insist on walking at the outermost edge of the trail?" He looked over the bulge of the mule's side and saw no earth, no trail, only hundreds of feet of empty space below him. One bit of loose rubble, he thought...

The Major, he noticed, was relatively calm. Nervous in the beginning, a sort of distant tranquility, or perhaps fatalism, had eventually settled over Fawcett. It may even have been a form of meditative will, as if the power of his resolve could keep his mule on firm ground.

"Our host in Sorata cleared up that mystery for me," replied Fawcett. "He said that, for one thing, if they scrape their load along the inner wall of the trail, it hurts their backs; for another reason, this can throw them off balance and right off the trail! They aren't so stupid."

Call it resolve, prayer, the skill of the mules, or luck, they made it through each tortuous mile without incident. From time to time they encountered Indians from the rubber estates, carrying considerable loads on their backs but making the ten-day trek with only coca leaves and lime for sustenance. They appeared strong, though somewhat drugged and mentally torpid.

Below them as they descended the eastern side of the Cordilleras was a blanket of cloud, pierced by mountaintops. At 13,000 feet they dropped below the timber line, then down and down into the cloud where the air was warm and there were cabbage palms and magnolias. From this subtropical zone they dropped still more, into the tropics. Here the forest was thick and the air hot.

When they rode into the settlement of Mapiri they found the entire population, some fifty or sixty souls, drunk as lords. There was a fiesta going on, and the Governor sat doddering on a doorstep, watching those citizens who were still upright dance, after a fashion, to sounds which only approximated music. Most of the other residents lay unconscious, but one fellow, lying in a gutter with bottle still in hand, had obviously been dead for some time judging by the degree of decomposition. There were about fifteen dirt-floored huts thatched with palm leaves around a muddy clearing— the Plaza— and a crumbling hut with a leaning cross above it: the Church.

In this charming village Fawcett and Chalmers arranged transport down the river aboard a *callapo*, or balsa raft, piloted by six Lejo Indian raftsmen who were well stoked on *cachaça*, a sugarcane liquor and true firewater if ever there was any, capable of rendering a sane man perfectly mad. All the villagers who were ambulatory lurched down to see the Englishmen off, laughing and screeching; something about the hilarity put Fawcett a bit on edge, and he correctly inferred they were in for a wild ride. He had heard, in Sorata, of the sudden river floods caused by heavy rainfall in the mountains above. Without any warning at all, a wall of water advances downriver, crushing into matchsticks any vessel unlucky enough to be in its way. Many river travellers died in this fashion.

But this week it was not their destiny to be swept away by tons of rainwater; the river demons, and the Indian raftsmen, were having too much fun terrifying them out of their skulls with the rapids, whirlpools, and ominous rocks. Chalmers was white as a sheet, and even Fawcett was only barely aware of the magnificent forest speeding past them, and the flamboyant trees, with their brilliant red-orange blossoms and populations of parrots and macaws; the red sandstone cliffs, and narrow gorges.

They spent their nights sometimes in trading posts where they were fairly comfortable and well-fed, and sometimes camping on beaches, where they were devoured by sandflies and mosquitoes, drenched by rain, and alternately baked in humid heat and chilled to the bone.

They were now on the Beni River, and though there had been several minor mishaps along the way and a few crates of valuable surveying instruments lost, the raftsmen were gradually sobering up and the river was sometimes peaceful. Fawcett and Chalmers could only count their blessings and gaze around them at the splendid scenery, until they floated one day into the port of Rurrenabaque. Fawcett's face became long with disappointment.

"I'd say they use the word 'port' loosely, in reference to this place," he remarked dryly to Chalmers. "On the map the name is in capitals, for mercy's sakes, and I had hoped to see at least a few attempts at permanent architecture. But this barely qualifies as a settlement." As the raft was tied he looked at the mud beach, covered with garbage, and the small cluster of roughly-made huts of split bamboo with palm-thatch roofs. It was beginning to sink in how very wild the river country was, how far away from anything resembling civilization they truly were. He would have laughed bitterly, indeed, if he had known then that Rurrenabaque would come to look like a roaring metropolis to him.

*

The two weeks that Fawcett spent in Rurrenabaque gave him time to think, and these thoughts led to a very glum mood. He was beginning to think he must have been mad with boredom in Spike Island to have done something so rash as this. The import of what he was in for was becoming clearer: cut off from the world in an area rife with malaria, beriberi, and espundia, to say nothing of menacing insects and animals, not the least of which was his fellow man; with three years of crushingly difficult and dangerous work ahead... and no easy way to take the occasional break in a better climate, with civilized society.

He began to keenly miss his wife and children, but he now realized it was not possible to bring them to live in La Paz as he had planned. The salary that had looked so good back in England now seemed inadequate, in light of the relatively exorbitant costs of living in La Paz; even if he had been able to locate housing for his family, an almost impossible task, he could not afford it. And many aspects of La Paz, he knew, made it completely unsuitable for an Englishwoman on her own. Even if it were not, there was little sense in bringing them there, when he would have such great impediments to reaching them for visits. From deep wilderness, it would take at least five or six weeks of hard and hazardous journey to reach La Paz, and even much longer, as the traveller often got stuck for weeks in some outpost waiting until a raft happened along which was going where he wanted to go, or until mules were available to cross the Altiplano.

He couldn't even expect to keep in contact by mail, as letters would find their way to him only after long delays, if at all. He drew a deep sigh; he was sorely tempted to quit and return to England. What madness this was!

He wasn't sure exactly what kept him there, in the end. It could have been many things: his natural reluctance to give up, the responsibility to carry out his contracted duties, his curiosity, sheer stubbornness... or something else that influenced him below the surface of conscious reasoning; for though he was presently viewing everything with distaste and homesickness, the pull of destiny held him in place.

And Bolivian Independence Day held them both in Rurrenabaque. They were anxious to move on to Riberalta, where surveying instruments which Fawcett had requested from the Government were supposed to be waiting, brought out by a General Pando. From Riberalta Fawcett would proceed to map the Acre and Abuná rivers. But the holiday interfered, meaning as it did that days of drunkenness would be followed by days of after-effects, in which no one would be able to accomplish anything.

But as luck would have it, after many mañanas two Customs officials from La Paz arrived and were impatient to get to Riberalta, also. They must have been men of some influence, because very soon a craft called a *batelón* was found which would transport all of them. Fawcett, a talented amateur yachtbuilder himself, looked askance at the heavy, 40-foot vessel, its keel hewn from the trunk of a tree.

"Clumsy-looking thing," he commented with distaste to Chalmers. "Obviously designed by some foreigner who knew little about these rivers and even less about design. I'd rather have the balsa raft, by far. Those seams must be difficult to caulk, it's bound to leak like a sieve. It draws about three feet, quite inappropriate for these waters, and the freeboard is no more than four inches! Pah!"

He proved correct. Though the crew bailed constantly, they could not keep up with the influx of water and it was soon necessary to beach the boat and repair its seams. They were late arriving at Pearson's place, where they had been told they would find hospitality, and all four men were tired. As they sat slumped over the evening meal Pearson, delighted to have company, blathered on about the Barbaros Indians, reputed to be savage terrors.

"Everyone in these parts is scared to death of 'em. They use palmwood bows that are anywhere from five to ten feet long, and the arrows are about the same size. Of course, if they're at war, they tip them in poison. Even the women and children carry spears. Oh," he chuckled, "perhaps I shouldn't say that *everyone* is afraid of them... We have a fortune-teller, a clairvoyante, who lives 'way out in the woods. Has a crystal globe, looks exactly like a witch, the complete picture. But everyone around here consults her at some time or the other, and no one would fool with her, not even the Barbaros; they respect her greatly. Would you like to go pay her a visit? She's an herbalist, as well, and she can fix you up with a love potion." He winked at Chalmers. The Customs officials, who spoke passable English, smirked.

Chalmers gave the man his best don't-be-ridiculous look, saying, "I think not, but thanks... "

Fawcett hesitated. Then he said, "No, she sounds interesting, but— we can't take any detours right now."

Chalmers gave him a sidelong glance, surprised he hadn't laughed outright at the very idea.

"It's raining," Fawcett remarked. "Seems to be coming down hard. I thought we were in the middle of the dry season."

"Eh, yes, but it's the new moon," said Pearson, walking to the doorway. "At the full or new moon we can get very heavy rain, this time of year. Then when it quits the *surusu* will blow, so damned cold we'll even find a bit of ice in the mornings, sometimes!"

Thunder rumbled across the sky, and the cloudburst increased in intensity until rain was falling as solid water. Fawcett had never seen anything like it. As the men watched the twilight storm, the river began to rise rapidly, until the batelón was suddenly swept onto its side and into the trees with a crash.

"The baggage!" shouted Fawcett, racing out into the deluge. Chalmers, Pearson, and the officials followed, and the men struggled to save the crates and cases which were about to be swept away. They managed to save it all, and as they secured everything well away from the water the rain diminished as suddenly as it had begun. Wearily they slopped back into the bungalow, and when the rain stopped, Pearson took them to the group of rough huts where they hung their hammocks.

"Sleep well!" he had called, but of course, he couldn't have anticipated Fawcett's jaguar.

In the freshness of the morning they prepared to leave, Fawcett yawning as they loaded the baggage back onto the boat. The river had returned to its usual level, but on its banks lay a snarl of vines, small branches, half-drowned snakes and enormous bird-catching spiders, all washed up by the flood.

Pearson looked at the tangle of snakes and called, as they pushed away from the bank, "Good luck to you, gentlemen! And by the way, watch out for poisonous snakes, they're more abundant than jaguars. Hee, hee!"

"Thanks," Chalmers muttered under his breath, but he knew the man wasn't kidding. They had already been warned that the Beni was home to a fearsome variety of venomous snakes, including rattlesnakes, the dread bushmasters, and anacondas up to twenty-five feet long.

After twenty tedious, slow days drifting down the river, gazing into a forest scene which looked exactly as it had the day before, and the day before, they would have almost welcomed a boatload of snakes to break the monotony. As it was, the men kept their eyes peeled for monkeys and tortoise eggs, which made up the main portion of their diet. They fought off sandflies and camped each night on the east bank, since they were told savages abounded on the west side.

"The Barbaros are very fierce," declared one of the Customs officials. "But they have reason. Employees of the rubber estates have treated with them with cruelty. They look upon the Indians as mere wild animals, and their slaving raids into the Indian villages amount to atrocities. Recently a Swiss and a German from a rubber barraca near here captured all the men from a village, and killed most of the women and children. They either dashed the little ones' brains out against trees, or they found it amusing to throw babies into the air and catch them on the points of their machetes."

"Such a revolting affair," agreed the other official. "But the Government is never able to prove anything or do anything about it."

Fawcett was silent, but Chalmers arose with an exclamation of disgust and moved to the edge of the boat. He mopped his brow. "What a place! We're far removed from any sort of civilization I've ever known. And it's so bloody *hot*; I feel drained, every day." He looked overboard at the relatively cool waters, and began to remove his shirt.

"What are you doing?" asked one of the officials, his eyes wide.

"I'm jumping in, of course; haven't seen any crocodiles hereabouts." He smiled at them over his shoulder.

"Stop! I wouldn't advise it, truly. There are electric eels that can paralyze you!"

"I know. I'll keep a sharp lookout for them."

"No, no, you mustn't," pleaded the other man. "It isn't just the eels; there is the *candiru* to reckon with." He shivered. Chalmers looked at him quizzically. "It's a nasty little fish about this long," the man's fingers showed a length of two inches, "And it is covered with tiny, back-swept barbs, and it will enter any opening of your body it can find. Then it is hell to remove, because of the barbs. Many people die in agony due to this fish."

"It's the truth," put in Fawcett. "This is the little fish the doctor at Rurrenabaque was showing me, the one he had taken from a man's penis."

Chalmers stood with his shirt in his hand and looked once again at the tempting waters. Then he heaved a sigh, expressed a heartfelt profanity, and slowly pulled his damp shirt back onto his body. What a place, indeed.

"Here's something to entertain us," the official exclaimed. He was fetching one of the mailbags he and his companion were to deliver to residents of Riberalta.

"Now what are *you* doing?" asked Fawcett in horror as the man broke open the seal and started rummaging through the bag.

He tossed a newspaper to Fawcett and a periodical of some sort to Chalmers, and continued to sift through the mail. "It's all right; everyone in Riberalta shares reading materials anyway, they would not mind."

Fawcett struggled for a brief moment with his sense of propriety, but as his mouth formed another protest, his craving for reading matter exerted itself. The newspaper he held was in English, and that proved impossible to resist. "Oh, well," he murmured, leaning back and opening the paper.

On August 28, moving at their stately speed of three miles per hour, the batelón glided into Riberalta. This almost-town stood at the junction of the Beni and Madre de Dios Rivers, and boasted of, in addition to a good number of huts with ugly corrugated iron roofs, the adobe headquarters of the Suarez Brothers' rubber concern.
It was 110° in the shade.

Fawcett was nagged by guilt, since most of the newspapers and periodicals they had pirated were lost by this time, and he was well aware of the long wait from one delivery to the next in these parts, sometimes three months or more. But he was distracted by an introduction to General Pando, who had come down to meet the boat. He was a man of imposing intelligence who had explored Bolivia extensively and who could offer much useful information. Unfortunately, the first report he gave wasn't something the Major wanted to hear.

"No, I'm sorry, Major, your instruments are not here; but you'll find them in Cobija, not to worry."

But Fawcett was worried, and his face showed it. He would believe in those instruments when he saw them.

"A boat will take you up the River Orton to Porvenir," General

Pando continued, "And from there, there is an overland trail to Co-bija and the River Acre."

"How long would you estimate this work to take, General; that is, plotting the Rivers Acre and Abuná, including travel time and all?"

"Oh, easily two years, I'd say; there are many difficulties involved."

"Two years!" Fawcett exclaimed. Secretly he was thinking, not on your life! But as the days passed and he discussed the area and the task in more detail with the General, who proved very knowledgeable, indeed, he slowly realized that the two-year estimate had actually been conservative; two and one-half was more like it, almost the entire length of the contract. The Acre, he learned, had not only been ex-plored, it was dotted with rubber barracas for most of its length. Still, the official surveys must be made.

As usual, Fawcett was champing at the bit to get on to Cobija, but things moved as slowly in Riberalta as elsewhere in South America, it seemed. When he realized the condition of most of the inhabitants, he decided that in this area, at least, there was an excuse: Fully ninety per cent of them were diseased. Beriberi and consumption were common, as were a plethora of other ailments, many of which were undiagnosable. Health was a rarity, the well person the exception.

"And is it any surprise, considering their diet?" commented Chalm-ers. "A bit of moldy rice— if they're lucky— and that dried meat, what do they call it, the stuff we saw that was full of maggots?"

"Charque," answered General Pando. The three men shared a meal made up of the best of the food which was imported to Riberalta and selections from Fawcett's stores. "That's about all they can afford, since things here cost ten times as much as they would back in civili-zation. But, you know, there's game in the forests, and rivers, and fruit for the picking, but they don't seem to have the energy to bother."

"Sort of a downward spiral, I'd say," remarked Fawcett. "Then add drink into the mix, and there you have it. Almost everyone appears to be in the grip of alcohol, not that I completely blame them, living as they do in such isolation, with brutality and death all around them."

"You paint a pretty gloomy picture, Sir," said Chalmers.

General Pando refilled Chalmers' wine glass. "Oh, it's accurate enough, unfortunately. The forest itself isn't an unhealthy place; dis-ease seems to come from the so-called 'civilized' villages, our little cen-ters of self-indulgence! The Indian tribes that live in out-of-the-way areas, keeping clear of the villages, are quite healthy."

Everywhere they turned, life was cheap in the South American wilderness. As if Nature weren't challenge enough, the rubber barons reigned supreme with simple and ruthless laws of profit and expediency. All that mattered was to get the rubber downriver to market, and almost all labor was based upon slavery of some kind or another. Some slaves were captured outright and dragged off either to work or be beaten to death; other workers were hired for a salary, then trapped into ever-increasing debts, as it was necessary to purchase everything they needed at exorbitant prices from the rubber firms. If anyone had tried to leave without paying his debts, he would've been brought back and beaten. In this way, they remained forever in debt, and freedom was only a concept. Once a man became a rubber worker, he could expect to live only an average of five more years. But he was replaceable, hence the continuous slave raids on the Indians, and even the breeding of children for the slave market. All the while immense profits floated downriver to the waiting arms of owners and managers.

Fawcett and Chalmers languished for almost a month in Riberalta, giving them plenty of time to hear about the ways of the rubber world. But they busied themselves studying Spanish and learning all they could about the Acre and its environs. Too, they had spent the requisite amount of time wining and dining some of the locals, who were as starved for fresh faces as they were for a taste of the seldom-seen goodies in Fawcett's food stores. In due time, on September 25, they found themselves once again stepping into a batelón, accompanied by ten Ixiamas and eight Tumupasa Indians.

"Close those ends tightly, there," Fawcett ordered some of the crew, as they draped both ends of the boat's palm-leaf shelter with mosquito netting. Dan, a young army officer of mixed Scot and Bolivian blood who was going along as interpreter, hastened over to supervise the men. A steersman made up the remainder of the party, and he pushed away from the bank amid farewells from the various friends Fawcett and Chalmers had made.

Soon they entered the River Orton, a course as quiet and sluggish as most of the men aboard; all but Fawcett had enjoyed one last drinking session the night before, and today were the worse for it. Dan was moody and lethargic, and Chalmers was roused to foul temper by the swelling numbers of insects which descended on the batelón.

"They're driving me mad!" He swatted uselessly at the masses of bugs swarming around him. "The sandflies, and those bloody little bees... Look at me, I'm covered in blood-blisters, every inch of exposed flesh itches and burns with them— "

"Stop scratching, they'll become septic." Fawcett handed out head-veils to Chalmers and anyone who wanted them. "Put this on, my man, and try to stay calm. We're all in the same condition." Day and night, the insects never let up, worsening as they continued. It was a particular hell for Fawcett, who had to bare his hands and face in order to take survey observations.

Days passed in relentless, smoldering heat and monotony. It was as the Major took a reading one afternoon that he heard the distinctive, rising call of the *seringuero* bird. "Ah," said Dan, who was at last beginning to come to life; "Rubber trees are near. I think this little bird eats parasites from the rubber trees; at any rate, it's always near them, and the rubber gatherers listen for its call when they're searching for the trees. That's why the rubber workers are called seringueros, of course!"

A sudden lurch threw all standing off their feet. "Damn! Not again!" yelled Dan, and the steersman issued a curse in his own language. They had hit another snag, one of those treacherous, hidden ends of branches or submerged tree trunks. Once more they would have to bail the already leaky boat furiously, and stop to repair the gouge with estopa caulking. They pulled the boat ashore at an abandoned rubber barraca, and while the crew worked on the gash Fawcett and Chalmers gathered papaws and other fruit from the overgrown plantation. The crumbling, cane barraca already looked as if it were a part of the jungle which was rapidly overtaking it; before too long, one would be hard pressed to detect any signs men had ever been there. Once the daily battle to hold back the forest had been given up, it moved in quickly.

As they walked back to shore, looking carefully for snakes, Chalmers eyed the water with desire. "I'd give anything, almost, to take a cooling swim now and then. But if it isn't eels and candiru, it's piranhas! I wouldn't even dare to dangle my feet, with all the bloody little blisters I'm sporting. I'd draw them from far and wide."

Fawcett clapped him on the shoulder sympathetically; it was a damned miserable trip, no doubt about that, and both Chalmers and Dan were showing signs of strain. Generally Dan was a cheery enough fellow, but the other day Fawcett had had to give him a sharp dressing-down. It seemed everyone on the batelón had needed that, for afterwards, all the men seemed to try a little harder and complain a bit less. Chalmers, like most of the others, was quite young, and he couldn't blame them if things got to them now and then.

The only thing breaking the tedium was the occasional barraca they came upon, where they usually stopped to take a meal. In general the residents, thrilled to have company, were as hospitable as they could possibly be. At Trinidad the group spent a couple of days with General Pando's niece and her husband, who lived in relative luxury compared with anyone in Riberalta. The travellers were entertained like kings, dining very well indeed, but the *pièce de résistance* was the hostess' offer of English reading matter. Fawcett and Chalmers fell upon the stack of magazines and books like Crusaders upon the Holy Grail.

"Ah, what a feast," sighed Fawcett as they stretched out amid piles of periodicals on the veranda. Chalmers knew he was not referring to the dinner, good as it had been.

"I'll say it is, I don't even mind reading between the termite holes."

Fawcett laughed. He was busily devouring every word of the advertisements.

Forty-three dismal, insect-ridden days later, they arrived at Porvenir, a small outpost consisting of two huts. The Ixiamas took the batelón back downriver to Riberalta, while Fawcett's party, retaining their eight Tumupasa Indians, made the twenty-mile overland trek with the help of cargo mules sent from Cobija.

When they rode into Cobija Fawcett and Chalmers knew immediately they had reached a new low. It was a surprisingly miserable village, for Cobija's position on the Acre and its elevation of less than eight hundred feet above sea level allowed for an uninterrupted navigable course to the Madeira River, then on to the mighty Amazon herself and the Atlantic Ocean, making Cobija a river port of some consequence. Brazilians and Bolivians had fought bloody battles over it, until at last Bolivia had prevailed by burning the Brazilians out. When Fawcett now arrived some three years later, he and Chalmers found skeletons still lying here and there.

He also found his instruments, such as they were.

"Blast all hell!" he exploded. "Where are the chronometers? And what happened to this theodolite? It's wrecked beyond all use! Is it the only one?"

"I'm very sorry," murmured the Intendente, military governor of the region. "One of the chronometers has apparently been stolen, and the other, see, there's a message here... is in Manaus for repair. I do not know what happened to that," he said mournfully, jabbing a finger at the damaged theodolite.

Fawcett ran his hand across his head in vexation. "I cannot believe this. The survey— of absolutely vital concern to Bolivia— will depend upon my own sextant and my chronometer watch. This does cap all, I must say." He turned and stomped off the Intendente's veranda, grinding his teeth and exercising all his self-restraint.

If the authorities are that uninterested in their own frontier, why should he continue with this? Why was he here, covered with insect bites, eating monkeys and snakes, listening to Dan and Chalmers whine, writing letters which would probably never reach his beloved little family? He kicked something white sticking out of the mud and realized it was a human skull. God in Heaven, what a place!

Nearby a little boy with a shriveled leg and a stick for a crutch smiled at him appealingly, a sort of resignation already visible in the thin, dark face. The child held out a banana to him. Fawcett, nonplussed, simply stared for a moment. Then he slowly took the banana.

Chalmers and Dan stood under a tree talking in low voices, not wanting to ruffle his feathers but both secretly hoping he would give up the expedition. In a few minutes, however, the Major returned with the crippled boy in tow, looking quite himself once more.

"Here, give this boy a few cubes of sugar, Dan, would you?" He turned to Chalmers. "We're going to complete this work despite the phenomenal inefficiency all around us. We are going to do it, and then we are going home." He quietly underscored the last word. He walked away to supervise some of the unloading, and Chalmers stifled a sigh.

Fawcett found plenty of helpers who had already begun unloading the mules. Residents of Cobija and soldiers from the garrison crowded around, trying to make themselves useful and, while they were at it, beg a bit of food and drink. While they languidly shifted crates here and there, Fawcett pulled Chalmers aside.

"Look, can we send out some of our Indians for game? We need to give these people a feast."

"A feast?" Perhaps the sun had gotten to him, Chalmers reckoned.

"Yes, it's obvious they're half starved, all of them! Even the soldiers; I heard from General Pando that the weekly ration of each man in the garrison consists of two pounds of rice, a couple of cans of sardines, and half a can of prawns! With all the physical labor they have to perform! Whatever they ask of you from our provisions, give it to them."

"But, Major— "

"Just give it to them; we can get more. And about this feast— "

"Well, our Indians just bagged a snake, which they're dragging in now; if it's big enough... "

It proved to be a twelve-foot anaconda, considered very good eating, so Fawcett had his Cobijan feast, including bananas, papaws, and sundry treats from his private supplies. It would be no exaggeration to say he was the most popular man in town.

Christmas Day, 1906 found Fawcett and Chalmers the hosts of another banquet, for the leading citizens of the town. This celebration included exorbitantly-priced eggs and fowl, as well as champagne, gin, brandy, rum, and coffee from Fawcett's stock. The liquor disappeared quickly, the Cobijans being as steeped in alcohol as their neighbors on the Beni. A phonograph played vigorously, occasionally drowned out by booming, expansive speeches which were cheered on by volleys of fire from the guests' rifles. Until Chalmers had had enough gin, he continually flinched from imagined ricochets.

"Drink up!" exhorted a Peruvian named Donayre, manager of a rubber barraca upriver. He had offered to take Fawcett and Chalmers as far as his barraca after he'd finished his business in Cobija. Donayre had downed a great deal of champagne but remained one of the few people whose conversation still made sense. He held a bottle of something over Fawcett's glass.

"No, thank you," replied the Major, covering his glass. "The liquor is for you, my guests. Now, Señor, earlier you mentioned something about 'white Indians'. I'd like to hear more, if you please."

"Well, there isn't much to tell. You have to differentiate, of course, between whites who have gone Indian— which is another subject entirely— and Indians who are white. They exist, I've seen them; they have red hair, at least the ones I've seen, and blue eyes. But they're Indians, make no mistake about it. Ask any of the Brazilian rubber men, they'll tell you."

"I've never heard of this before. Where did you come across them?"

"Oh, I lived with the Putumayo for two years; had a wife and the whole shot! Met up with some of these white Indians while I was out roaming the forests with some of the Putumayo."

"And what are they like, the Putumayos, I mean?"

"Generally good fellows, highly intelligent, well-ordered social and moral structure, and, of course, cannibals."

"Really! Did they eat their enemies, that sort of thing?"

"Hm, yes, men of other Indian tribes were the preferred dish; they don't like white people so much, ha! Seriously, they don't. And usually they ate their own dead, too."

"Did you, Señor, have to partake of flesh, also?"

"Of course; I had to 'go native' completely, you know, which meant eating what they ate. It tastes similar to monkey, actually. And you know, I personally feel there's little difference, if any, between eating a man's flesh and eating an animal's. Especially if they're going to have warfare, anyway, which so many of the tribes do— just like our 'civilized' nations, I might add— they may as well get some food out of it, rather than letting the corpses rot, all for nothing. Think about it."

Fawcett nodded. "I have thought about it, and I must say I tend to agree. Chalmers, you look shocked; or are you unconscious but forgot to close your eyes?"

Chalmers bristled somewhat, and blinked. "No, I'm still conscious, sir, but I don't think I'm quite ready to embrace cannibalism." He hiccupped, and Fawcett and Donayre laughed.

"Don't speak in haste," advised Señor Donayre. "One never knows what the forests will do to one's preconceived notions of propriety, or even to one's tastes in food! Ha!" He raised his glass for the hundredth toast of the evening.

"Well put," concurred Fawcett. "Merry Christmas, Chalmers!"

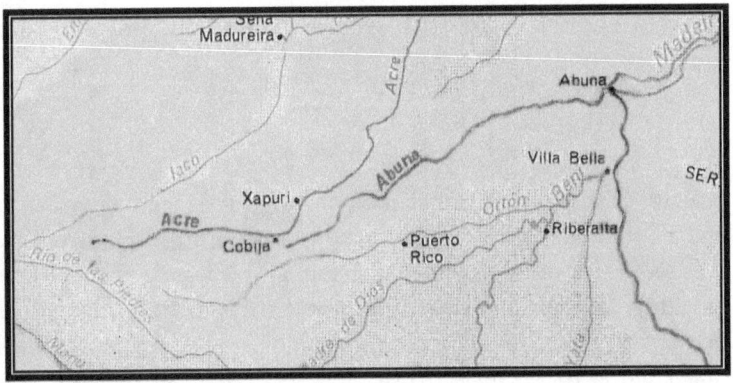

FAWCETT, CHAPTER 3
RIO ACRE

A barrage of rifle fire shattered the stillness of the river; birds took wing and complained volubly while echoes raced along the water. It was only a farewell salute to Fawcett and party, poling upriver in Señor Donayre's boat.

Almost immediately they crossed the frontier into Brazil, where the homes they passed were noticeably larger, better built, and better furnished, due to great quantities of rubber to be found in the area and the general navigability of rivers from that point on, allowing ease of transport to and from central markets. Bolivia, to its eventual regret, had sold this rich section of real estate to Brazil for two million pounds, and in three years' time Brazil had made that amount back, and more, in rubber.

They remembered their manners and stopped at most of the barracas to give their isolated residents news of the outside world and a half hour or so of conversation. Some outposts were found temporarily deserted, their inhabitants away working in the estradas. Valuable equipment, guns, and other belongings were left lying in the open, with little fear of theft, because although murder and rape carried small penalties, if any, stealing was not tolerated. A thief was the lowest of the low; consequently, few people would take a chance on incurring the wrath that would surely come their way if caught. Life and human dignity may be cheap in the forests, but goods were not, and they were scarce.

After a few days of camping by the river or at rubber-collecting stations along the way, they made Donayre's home, Rosario, where he and his family lived in relative luxury. Donayre, feeling increasingly ill for some time, was much relieved when they pulled up to the dock. "Welcome to my home," he said weakly. "I am going to rest, if you don't mind."

Rays of the setting sun slanted through trees and across the veranda and fell directly into the eyes of the most beautiful creature Fawcett had ever seen. He stood as one transfixed, and Miranda watched him with a mocking smile on her lips. She stood still on the garden path, having decided to treat him to a nice, long look. The large eyes held him; he marvelled at their ebony depths and their magnetism. She could have been a devil, a magnificent lure sent to tempt the purest, most stainless heart, but though quite mortal she succeeded in inflaming Fawcett. His gaze moved over all the exquisite features of her face, and then to her sumptuous figure, which caused her to entice him further by shifting her body slightly, alluringly, under the thin dress. Rattled, he tore his eyes from her torso and became lost in the long, lustrous jet hair which flowed beside the contrasting cream of her neck, down, down, to rest softly over one breast. There he was again, and with effort he looked upward once more at her face and managed a crooked smile and a nod. She continued to survey him evenly for a moment, and then she returned his nod, slowly lowering her head without removing her eyes from his, until snow white showed beneath her black irises.

Fawcett turned awkwardly and walked on rubbery legs back into the villa. Miranda disappeared silently into the trees.

"Lovely sunset, eh?" said Donayre, propped up on pillows in the parlor, a cup of coffee untouched on the table beside him.

"To be perfectly honest, I hardly saw it; I was distracted... In the name of heaven, who is that woman?"

Donayre only hesitated a moment. "Ah, so you've met the half-caste, Miranda..."

"Miranda..." echoed Fawcett, still a bit glassy-eyed. "Oh, well, we didn't exactly meet; one might say I just stood there like a schoolboy and gaped at her. I hope she wasn't offended."

"Miranda? Oh, no! In fact, you'd better watch out; if she likes you, you're in big trouble."

"Oh, not me, I'm a very happily married man—"

Donayre ignored him. "The ravishing Miranda is a true she-devil, the archetype of every fantasy of the jungle girl that ever was. At least eight men that I know of have met their Maker fighting over her; and any man so stupid as to try to force himself on her will find that she can wield a knife pretty well, herself; she's killed more than one. No, Miranda is a law unto herself, and she selects what *she* likes. But she's very dangerous, my friend, if for no other reason than the jealousy of other men whom she's driven nearly mad."

"Hm, yes, if she favors you, one of her other suitors might knife you in the back, I suppose." Fawcett laughed, a little nervously.

"Just so."

Donayre's wife, Francesca, had entered the room. "We must be speaking of Miranda," she said with a knowing smile. "Take care, Major Fawcett; you are likely to appeal greatly to her, married or not."

Fawcett wasn't sure if she was teasing him. "Oh, I'll steer quite clear of her, I assure you. But what a creation, is she not? I was very near hypnotized for a few moments."

" 'What a piece of work is woman', to paraphrase the playwright, eh? Is dinner ready, my dear? Can you find Chalmers and the other fellow?" Señor Donayre rose, with difficulty. "Let us go in for our meal, Major. I'm sure you must be starved, and we have a rather good cook."

It was late, but Fawcett wasn't sleepy. Señor Donayre had retired immediately after dinner, and his wife had gone to care for her ailing husband. Chalmers and Dan were sharing a bottle by the riverside; Fawcett could hear them laughing and cursing at insects. He found a comfortable chair on the veranda and settled down to listen to the night sounds, music of the Acre. The air had cooled and he inhaled deeply; his sense of smell had become noticeably more acute since his arrival in the wilderness, and he was beginning to take pleasure in separating various scents of the river and the jungle. He inhaled again and detected a familiar green plant whose name he couldn't recall, and cachaça, and the presence of goats somewhere to his right. He closed his eyes and leaned his head upon the high back of the chair, feeling his muscles gradually relax as he continued to breathe deeply. Maybe he would be able to sleep, after all...

He sniffed. A new odor had crept in to blend with the others, but it somehow stood away from the rest; it was like the subtle perfume of flowers released by the night, yet it was different. Still languorous both in body and mind, his senses were keenly attuned to the atmosphere. Without moving, he opened his eyes. Miranda stood not five feet away.

How on earth had she approached so silently, he wondered vaguely; had the chatterings and buzzing of the night creatures drowned her light step?

He raised his head lazily. She stepped toward him, her eyes on his, and when she was close he could clearly smell the fragrance he had detected, emanating from her body: a combination of perfume, sweat, and a musky female smell he had certainly never noticed on any English-woman. The tropical warmth releases new and unknown scents, he reckoned. She raised one hand and placed it on his forehead, gently but firmly pushing his head back to rest once more on the chair. She began to stroke his forehead as a mother strokes a restless child. Her hands were like silk on his skin, and despite himself he felt his eyes closing, like a man drugged. She caressed his face for several moments in which he felt himself unable to move, and then she knelt in front of his chair and rested her arms on his knees.

He lifted his head slowly and looked down into the dark pools of her eyes, gazing upward at him. He couldn't read her at all. In her face there was no apparent guile, yet he instinctively knew control was in her hands, not his; which for him was an utterly novel situation, and it surprised him to find he liked it. That he knew she was as dangerous as a bushmaster only added to her allure. All at once she smiled, revealing even white teeth, a rarity in the jungles; he realized then how spoiled she would've been if her teeth had been blackened or missing.

"You want to hear stories of the forest?" she asked in heavily accented English. The question disarmed him. Stories? She was going to tell him stories?

"Why, yes, I would. You must, uh, know many— "

"Miranda know all the wonderful stories. What you like? I can tell you of Las Amazonas, yes?"

"The area of the Amazon River?"

"No, no... the Amazons, the women who live without men, fight like men."

"Ah, yes; I've read the legends, of course."

"Well, I tell you *true* stories," she smiled teasingly. "My grandmother tell me many true things." She stood, took one of his hands, and gently tugged. "Come."

"Where?"

"To my house. I make you Guaraná tea, it make you strong. And we can be comfortable. Come."

It was almost a command. Fawcett found her self-assurance beguiling.

And even in the dizziness of the moment he felt curious about her "stories", her house, the way she lived, everything about her. Her smooth, long fingers held him firmly, as he hesitated. Then he squeezed her hand, but remained seated.

"Thank you, Miranda, but I can't. I'm sorry."

"Why you can't?" She was still smiling.

Fawcett sighed deeply. He realized he was not held back in the slightest bit by Donayre's warnings nor his own sure knowledge that she was trouble; he wouldn't be here in the bloody wilderness among snakes, disease, savages and murderers if he were one to shy away from jeopardy. No, the only fear that rooted him to the chair was the dread of abdicating his sworn principles. He had a certain instinct that these were what made him who and what he was, and to lose the backbone of himself, as it were, would be to lose faith in himself entirely.

To an outsider observing this scene of temptation, common as it is in the world, it would appear a simple matter for Fawcett to refuse Miranda's advances. He "did the right thing", and that was that. But the invisible struggle taking place within him was nothing short of heroic. To Fawcett Miranda represented something more that just an overwhelmingly desirable, exotic woman; she was the dark, magic, hidden side of him, the creature who does whatever pleases it from moment to moment, and to hell with civilization and its mores; to hell with ancestry and rules and duty and courtesies and integrity. Here was the animal who kills and mates and bellows with rage or triumph; with Miranda, he knew, he could unleash a part of him which had always been tightly reined. She was, perhaps, what he might be if he were a woman, because he could not imagine the body and soul of a true English lady containing all the roiling, restless aspects that comprised Percy Harrison Fawcett. But if the beast were freed, the fine and crucial counterbalance that carried him through his days with a sense of purpose, his spark of divinity, would be lost. He alone knew the latent power of that elemental facet of himself, and it was the only thing on earth he truly feared.

Miranda was still tugging on his hand like a gently nagging child, one who is accustomed to getting her way; his negative answer meant nothing to her.

"I simply can't. For one thing, I have a wife."

"Where? Far across the ocean?" She laughed, mocking him.

"Yes. Far away, that's true. But she means a great deal to me."

"She will not care if we talk. She will not know."

Fawcett stood up, freed his hand from her grasp and took Miranda firmly by the shoulders; he felt her hair sweep the back of his hand, soft as the night breeze, and sudden heat filled his body. He had to get away from her, now.

"Miranda, if I go with you we will not talk, and you know it." He was gripping her bruisingly hard, he realized. "You're a magnificent woman, but I must say goodnight." He nodded abruptly, and turned to make his escape.

"Coward!" she spat. He turned back and saw cold fury on her face; her eyes had instantly transformed from warm liquid to black ice, and she had bared her teeth in an expression of animosity which sent a cold chill down his spine. Shocked by the suddenness of the change, and knowing anything he said would only make it worse, he turned on his heel and walked into the house, her low, venomous curses following him.

In the dim lantern light, Fawcett unfolded his hammock from his backpack; he was beginning to feel very tired from the spent emotion of the evening. Although Donayre had offered him and Chalmers a bedroom in the house, since it was quite warm inside he decided to leave it to his now-drunken assistant and hang his hammock on a side porch of the house. Here there was at least a little breeze off the river. He hung the hammock on the ever-present hooks and arranged his mosquito netting. He was getting accustomed to sleeping in a hammock, finding it actually more comfortable than a bed; at any rate, he knew he would have no trouble sleeping, after all.

As he settled down his wife was much on his mind, however, and occasionally her image was brazenly interrupted by the last memory of Miranda, looking at him as if she would enjoy cutting his throat slowly.

In the middle of the night, insects singing in his ears and the lamp down to a mere flicker, Fawcett awoke suddenly with the sensation of something large and hairy scurrying up his left arm and over his neck. In a rush of adrenaline he instantly brushed it away, but the large apazauca spider landed on the back of his left hand, clinging stubbornly as he tried repeatedly to shake it off. At last the deadly spider dropped to the floor and raced through an opening in the mosquito netting, then over the edge of the porch, to freedom. Fawcett sank back, shuddering with both disgust and relief that he had not been bitten. *How is it the netting was open,* he wondered? He got out of his hammock and closed a large gap in the mosquito net, overlapping and tucking it the way he always did.

He crawled back into the hammock and tried to relax, taking a few deep breaths. It was then he noticed a familiar scent hanging in the air. It was— he was certain— the musky smell of Miranda. Small hairs rose on the back of his neck; he settled back into the hammock, but he did not sleep.

The following day, though Chalmers and Dan were dragging, Fawcett was up and about with first light, eager to push on and prodding the four Indians of his crew. Donayre seemed to feel a little better and arose to see them off in a driving rain. He had given them a large batelón, with a recommendation that they exchange it for smaller canoes as soon as possible, since it would soon be too big for the river. He was right; by the time they had reached the barraca at Tacna, the river was becoming increasingly shallow in places, and between snags and sand bars, the going was difficult.

"Damned shoals," grumbled Fawcett, as they all waded into the water to push the boat free for the tenth time.

"Damned rain. Damned mosquitoes, damned mariguis, damned snags, damned everything!" Chalmers erupted. He had been in a dark mood all day, scratching at insect bites and complaining that his head ached; Fawcett watched him closely, aware it was more than Chalmers' usual hangover slump.

"Damn yourself!" snapped Dan. "Just push the boat and shut up; you aren't doing your share."

"The hell you say!" Chalmers' eyes widened, showing bloodshot whites.

"Spend your energy working instead of whining," Dan shot back. "We all have our problems, you big baby; the Indians aren't griping."

"That's enough from both of you!" Fawcett thundered. "I'm not going to play headmaster to a couple of bickering boys. Let's get this great, clumsy boat free and get out of the water before we pick up parasites."

That was motivation enough for Chalmers; he pushed with renewed vigor, and he and Dan settled into an uneasy truce for the rest of the miserable day.

At Tacna they exchanged the batelón for two canoes, which would make navigating the upper reaches of the Acre possible. They slung their hammocks in the barraca and spent a restless night, exhausted from fighting the river, wet from the rain, raw from insect bites. Chalmers called out in his sleep several times, waking them all, followed up by Dan's dark curses.

The next day the going was easier due to the smaller boats and the unabated rain, which had raised the level of the river. They kept an eye out for Indians, having been told they could be troublesome; but Dan said the tribes lived well clear of the river in an effort to avoid enslavement in the rubber camps. Although Chalmers was clearly relieved, Fawcett felt somewhat disappointed; the few Indians they had glimpsed had vanished at sight of the rifles. "They can't know, of course, that the last thing I would do is shoot at them; I'd simply like to try and communicate."

"Ha! Good luck!" remarked Dan. "Sometimes they attack the centros, so the rubber men shoot them on sight."

"I thought the official policy of the Brazilian government was to protect indigenous peoples."

"That's true, Major; but what can the government do way out here?"

Fawcett's attention shifted from his curiosity about the Indians to the fossilized bones of some large animal of bygone years, which protruded from red sandstone bluffs above the river. The sandstone, gradually eaten away by rain-swollen currents, yielded its long-buried secrets from time to time; earlier in the day they had come across beautifully preserved petrified tortoises. Fawcett suspected some of the bones they passed, perhaps even these, could be the remains of monstrous, extinct beasts such as no human had ever seen.

Live animals were abundant, and so tame that Fawcett had to prevent his Indian crew from rampant slaughter. Tapir and capybara watched calmly as they passed. Dan, fishing off the stern of his canoe, leaned over the water and reached toward a capybara, sitting back on its haunches only a few feet away on the bank. The little creature didn't move or flinch, but stared back with curiosity. Just then a *lobo* otter shot up from the dark water and barked loudly in Dan's face. He promptly fell overboard, eliciting peals of laughter from the Indians, who of course poled faster to leave him behind, flailing in their wake. Dan, mortally terrified of crocodiles since a childhood experience, screamed as if he were already being attacked. The Indians laughed even louder and poled furiously. When he could make himself heard over the hilarity, Fawcett put a stop to it and Dan at last climbed shakily aboard.

Chalmers couldn't resist a cheap shot. "That was an otter, you fool; and even I know crocs are afraid of otters, so there are obviously none of those beasts around."

Dan made no reply. He had been noticeably leery of the water all day, having spotted an eleven-foot crocodile in the early morning. He couldn't put enough miles between him and that monster, otters or no.

They spotted, now and then, a type of delicate white monkey which Dan said existed nowhere but in the upper Acre region, to his knowledge. There were small grey monkeys called *leoncitos*, and at night the *nocturnos*— night monkeys— gleefully bombed them with buds, sticks, and other distractions while some of their compadres sneaked into camp to steal their stores.

Despite the smaller canoes, navigating the Acre grew increasingly difficult with every mile as the way became narrower and steeper. Frequently it was necessary to drag the canoes over rapids or fallen trees; they could sometimes chop through the trees, but this work was almost as exhausting as hauling the heavy canoes over them.

Signs of Indians were also increasingly evident: a footprint here, a glimpse of a face there, sometimes a carved, cone-shaped stump, apparently bearing religious significance; the men knew they were being watched continually, and it began to wear on their nerves. Chalmers was particularly jumpy.

"I hate this," he hissed. "Not seeing them, but knowing they're there. Waiting... If they're going to do something, why don't they go ahead?" Chalmers could not banish the image of a long arrow suddenly pinning him to the boat, his eyes staring in disbelief at the shaft in his chest. His imagination was just a little too good for the rainforest life.

Fawcett knew the importance of keeping everyone's trigger-fingers calm. "They're just keeping an eye on us, I think; we aren't large enough to be a slaving party or any other threat to them, yet we have rifles, so perhaps they think it's best not to bother with us."

"All the same, we'd better play it safe and put a guard out at night," advised Dan, watching the nearby bushes move out of the corner of his eye.

"I agree," replied Fawcett briskly. "We'll each take a three-hour shift, and we'll make camp at the next likely spot; it's getting late."

*

45

The sun rose on a peaceful, though tense, camp scene, and the men wasted no time in getting on their way. With every mile, however, Fawcett felt they were less and less likely to meet with trouble; after all, the hidden Indians had had more than enough opportunities, especially now that the river was only a few yards wide. In addition, they were constantly out of the canoes now, lugging them up rapids and over four-foot cascades—the men counted no fewer than one hundred and twenty of these obstacles—and were extremely vulnerable at those times.

Eventually they reached a much higher waterfall, and a short walk along the river bank convinced them the canoes, at least, had come to the end of the line. Beyond the cataract the river soon diminished to a creek barely a yard wide. A scant few miles distant was undoubtedly a spring: the source of the Acre.

"Well, we've made it, gentlemen; we've mapped the Acre to its source, for all intents and purposes. But what do you say we hike on up to the spring? I'd like to see it, since we've come this far." Fawcett looked around the group, his idea meeting only glowers. "Oh, come, come, it can't be much farther, and the Indians aren't going to bother us now."

Chalmers and Dan moaned, knowing they would cave in to the Major's will, but their Indian helpers stood fast. They were not going any farther, and that was final. No entreaties or bribes would budge them. Fawcett sagged with disappointment, and whispered to Chalmers:

"We don't dare leave the Indians here with the canoes; if they make off with them, we're stranded."

"Oh, God, then by all means, we must forget this idea, Sir!" Chalmers was instantly filled with all kinds of horrific visions at the mere thought of having to walk out of there.

Fawcett sighed deeply and walked to a large tree near the water, pulling out his knife as he went. He carved a few brief words to leave a record of the expedition, and then suggested that as soon as the men had eaten a bite, they should turn back.

The return journey was uneventful, except for a little side-trip which Fawcett insisted on making: He needed to map the Yaverija, a small tributary of the Acre, and there would be no arguing this time. All the men complied, but their sullenness wasn't lost on Fawcett, who found himself shouldering most of the burden of negotiating the numerous snags and fallen trees, since the others slacked off unless he watched, and nagged, constantly. But he felt somewhat rewarded when he spied a huge, petrified skull and several bones protruding from a clay deposit in the bank.

"A saurian!" he exclaimed, motioning for them to stop. He bounded from the boat, his fatigue forgotten. "Look at this! The skull alone is over five feet long! Hmm... Quite damaged, though, we'd never be able to remove it without breaking it to bits. Best leave it right here." Chalmers was now at his side, showing interest.

"We could possibly remove a few of these teeth, Major; look, they aren't difficult to dig out." The two men worked at it for a few minutes, and soon had several large, black teeth for their trouble. They walked around the area, and then Chalmers stopped in his tracks and caught his breath. At the bottom of a deep, clear pool lay the intact skeleton of another dinosaur, even larger than the first.

Fawcett rushed over. "Look at that! Positively beautiful! And no way whatsoever to reach it. I can try a few photos, but I think it's much too dark down there." He fetched his camera from the canoe and took several shots of both fossils. "Well, all we can do is make notes of the precise location, and a few sketches wouldn't hurt; then if any scientists want to drag themselves up here—" Chalmers couldn't help rolling his eyes, and Fawcett laughed. When he had completed his sketches, he reluctantly allowed the men to move on.

More crocodiles were spotted, some of great size. Twice, when his canoe struck a snag quite suddenly, Chalmers fell overboard; both times the Indians laughed, but even Dan joined Fawcett in hushing them and making them stop paddling immediately, and the two men rushed to haul Chalmers aboard.

"Damned river," Chalmers muttered, his teeth chattering despite the heat. His mood, elevated by the fossil find, had once more plummeted.

Rosario came slowly into view around a bend of the river, having the aspect of a heavenly home to the weary band. A servant called out, and in a moment Francesca came to stand on the veranda, welcoming them in. Dogs barked as they pulled Donayre's batelón, which they had retrieved at Tacna, carefully up to the dock.

"You look half-dead!" Francesca exclaimed sympathetically. "Well, you can have a good rest here."

Fawcett stepped on the planks and took her hand gratefully. "That sounds wonderful, indeed. And how is Señor Donayre?"

Her face fell. "He is very ill, Major. I'm worried about him, and my little son, too." Tears welled into her eyes.

Fawcett's brow furrowed. "Let me take a look at them. I can't promise, but maybe I can help."

"Oh, please, would you try? We have sent for the doctor, right after you left, in fact, but there's been no sign of him."

Fawcett insisted on seeing Donayre even before taking any refreshment or changing his filthy clothes. The other men went off for a wash in the bath house; in ten minutes or so, Fawcett had joined them.

"Looks bad, does he?" asked Chalmers.

"Yes, rather pale and seedy, very weak; but you know, I'm fairly certain it's simply worms— which, mind, can be serious if untreated, but at least it's something that I *can* treat. And I did."

"Did you see the boy?"

"Oh, yes, and I suspect it's the same thing; I'm giving him the same medications." He turned to the washtub and began to scrub at the grime which covered his body, humming as he did so. But he hoped he was right about the worms; a few days would tell, as improvement should commence very soon.

After a magnificent dinner, the stuffed little group sat on the veranda, all but Donayre, who rested in his bedroom; Fawcett wondered where Miranda was lurking but didn't want to ask, certain the question would be misinterpreted. But Francesca, with that way South American women have (and perhaps all women, he mused) read his mind.

"We haven't seen Miranda lately," she offered. "One of the servants told me she went off with a man down the river to Cobija. That was some time ago and she might be back by now, but I haven't seen any sign."

Good, thought Fawcett; he wanted to relax for a few days and was in no mood to watch his back continually. He'd been relentlessly observed by semi-invisible indigenes for weeks now, and he was weary of vigilance.

Fawcett slept, ate, and chatted with Donayre whenever the ailing man felt up to it; Dan and Chalmers slept, ate, drank, and fought, and the Indians seemed to be doing pretty much the same. In other words, each enjoyed the respite in his own way. In a few days Donayre showed definite signs of improvement, and there were now other indications that the problem had indeed been worms, as traces of them began to pass from his body. To everyone's added joy the little boy had also perked up considerably. Fawcett was now a hero at Rosario.

Very soon the evening came when Donayre joined them all at the dinner table, and ate heartily. As coffee was going round, he leaned across the plates and waggled a piece of paper at Fawcett.

He cleared his throat awkwardly. "My dear, dear friend," he began, shaking the paper again, "This is a document proving ownership of some rubber which I give to you, in deepest gratitude for healing my son and me; though I am ashamed at the paltriness of the gift."

Fawcett glanced at the paper. Paltry? The rubber was valued at six *contos*, or approximately £360, a healthy sum indeed!

"No, no, I can accept nothing for effecting a simple cure, and besides, I did it for a friend; no gifts are necessary."

"But you must— "

"No, thank you so very much, but absolutely not." Fawcett leaned back, waving away the paper, and smiled warmly at his new friend. To his surprise and discomfiture Donayre suddenly burst into tears. "Now, now, my man, really, I feel your gratitude and that is enough for me. Now, please— " He patted Donayre's hand awkwardly. Francesca rose and put her arm around his shoulders. Must be a residual from the illness, Fawcett was thinking, this emotionality...

Donayre wiped his eyes and smiled. "You are a true friend, Major, and one which I will never forget, I promise you."

"Likewise; your helpfulness has been boundless since the first day I met you, so I would consider us even. There are not many men like you, Señor."

"I would like to second that, Señor Donayre, and to include your wife; the past few days here have been a treasure." Chalmers raised his glass with a rather wobbly movement.

Wishing to avoid a descent into maudlinism, Fawcett cast about for a smooth change of subject but it proved unnecessary. There was a stir of servants at the front door, and then into the dining room stomped two men.

"Rinaldi!" exclaimed Donayre with evident delight. "What a pleasant surprise!"

The short, tanned man stepped forward to drop little bows to both the Donayres. "I see you are nowhere near death, Donayre, and here I went to all this trouble to bring you a doctor!" Smiling broadly, he motioned the other man forward. "This is Dr. Harry Kent."

Introductions went all around. "Señor Rinaldi is the administrator at Yorongas," Donayre explained.

"Ah, yes," said Fawcett, "We stopped at Yorongas on the way back, around February seventh, but were told you were in Cobija."

"I was; it was there I ran into Donayre's man, frantically searching for the doctor, who was dead drunk in Riberalta at the time; now, however, he is simply dead. Apparently, drink finally killed him. But Harry came into town, so I enticed him to come upriver with me... Now, here we are on our mission of mercy and you look as fat and sassy as a king!"

"I have Major Fawcett to thank for that; he cured both my son and me of worms, it seems."

"Good for you; nasty thing, worms." Dr. Kent put in, as he nodded to Fawcett and took a seat that was offered. Both men accepted a glass of wine. "We really should clean up before sitting at your lovely table, Señora."

"Please stay right where you are, and relax. You've had a long day, I'm sure. Do you live near Cobija, Dr. Kent?"

"No, Señora, currently I am living at Esperanza, on the Madeira near the conjoining of the Abuná, where I have a small plantation; I was only visiting a friend in Cobija."

"Really? My next assignment is to map the Abuná." Fawcett briefly explained his presence in South America.

"Well, you have your work cut out for you; I don't envy you, though I'm full of admiration."

"The Abuná is difficult?" asked Chalmers, at once perking up his ears.

The English doctor smiled dryly. "That is putting it mildly."

Fawcett wasn't sure he wanted Chalmers to hear any horror stories at the moment, and fortunately Rinaldi broke in. "Ah! I nearly forgot! We've brought mail for you, Major Fawcett; it's in my pack. When the Intendente in Cobija heard we were headed to Rosario he asked us to bring it up. Shall I get it now?"

"Mail! What a grand surprise! I must say, travellers in this wilderness are quite good about carrying mail, so I gather. But no, please sit, it will keep a while longer." He felt a rush of pleasure at the thought that surely there would be a letter from his Cheeky. He could hardly wait to be alone with her words.

Conversation moved to Rinaldi's plantation at Yorongas, where he grew bananas and mandioca, a staple food in Brazil. He was eager to get back. "The last time I was gone, I returned to find the Indians had burned down my house," he laughed.

"No!" exclaimed Chalmers, shocked that Rinaldi seemed so blasé.

"They did, but I can't say I feel any bitterness against them. I've seen the way some of these rubber expeditions treat the Indians, so I don't really blame them for tarring all of us whites with the same brush. I deal in rubber, too, so for all they know I could be as guilty as the others."

Fawcett looked at Rinaldi with new respect; he had never heard anyone in the rubber trade speak this way about Indians.

"Also," he continued, "It is almost the new moon, so I must get back and do my planting."

"Beg pardon. New moon?" Chalmers asked from his mental fog.

"Why, I suppose it might sound like superstition to some, but everyone here plants either four days before or after the full or new moon. It helps the plants resist pests."

Chalmers looked ready to burst into laughter, but he was immediately squelched by a meaningful look from Fawcett, who said politely: "I've heard of various customs in South America, connecting the moon with plant life; such as the proper time to cut palm fronds for thatching, et cetera. I'd be the last one to criticize it; people must have some evidence that it works, or they wouldn't bother. My intuition is that we have a great deal to learn about the influence of the moon."

"Well, after all, it certainly does affect our seas," added Dr. Kent diplomatically.

"By the way," interjected Fawcett. "Is this your normal rainy season? So far it hasn't lived up to its reputation."

"Oh, people do tend to exaggerate, no doubt," answered Donayre. "Though every seven years or so we get a very wet year, but in truth, the climate seems to be changing; the rains have been decreasing very gradually for many years."

"And the snows in the Andes," added Rinaldi. "They affect the river flooding, and one can clearly see by old high-water marks on the banks that floods used to be far more severe."

Fawcett looked thoughtful. "I wonder what effect it will all have, in the long run."

"What I wonder about is how different things might have been, a thousand, or several thousand, years ago." Rinaldi scratched his chin. "I've heard Indian stories of great, ancient cities in the forest, and vast plantations in places where there is now only impenetrable forest."

"Great cities!" This time Chalmers did let his mirth escape. "Really! I can't imagine any such thing in this vast swamp— "

"And who lived in these cities? Do the stories describe the inhabitants?" Fawcett had cut in, leaning forward, his interest piqued.

"White people, that's the intriguing thing," put in Donayre. "I've heard these legends, too. And what makes it almost believable is that there are white Indians, right here on the Acre; I've seen them myself."

Fawcett was remembering Donayre's mention of "white Indians" when they first met in Cobija.

"You mean the Inaparis?" queried Rinaldi.

"No, no; the Inapari are light-skinned, that's true, but these Indians are white, with reddish hair and blue eyes. They're big, handsome people, well-built, and they fight like demons. A Frenchman that I know killed one of them up the Tahuamanu tributary, after a group of them attacked his party, and the other Indians risked life and limb to get to that body and take it away with them."

"I've heard these rumors, myself, at Esperanza; even there they say that white Indians have been seen on the Acre," Dr. Kent said. "They must be half-breeds— Spanish and Indian— "

"No, no, no," Donayre shook his head most emphatically. "I've seen all types of half-breeds, and believe me, Doctor, they are not half-breeds."

It was hard to argue with Donayre's firm assertion, especially since no one else present had seen these elusive tribes. Fawcett found him convincing.

"Well, you should know, my friend," said Rinaldi. "After all, you lived with Indians for a time, and I'm sure you saw all sorts of things."

"I was disappointed to see so little of any Indians up the Acre, myself," admitted Fawcett. "Guess we were lucky, but I'm curious about them."

Dr. Kent laughed. "Hope you aren't too curious about the Indians of the Abuná."

All the local men laughed, and Chalmers woke up again. "What about them?"

"Oh, they're an evil lot, I guarantee."

"This is so, Major," agreed Rinaldi, his face serious. "The Pacaguaras, the Karapunas... they are not for idle study. They are to be avoided at all costs, and prepared for with plenty of rifles and ammunition."

The doctor was nodding in agreement. "The day before I left Esperanza, we heard of a German engineer and several of his men who had been killed by savages. And not long before that, forty-eight men went in search of rubber on a branch of the Abuná, but only eighteen returned; one of them had gone foaming mad from the whole experience."

Fawcett glanced at Chalmers, who had turned pale.

Donayre leaned toward Fawcett. "I dislike doomsaying, but all of this is worth listening to. The Abuná is a cursed river. It frequently overflows and forms enormous swamps, breeding-grounds for fever. To say nothing of the giant anaconda."

"Oh, yes, that's where the big ones are found," agreed Rinaldi. "I, myself, once killed one that was fifty-eight feet long. Think twice about this expedition, Major; if the anaconda and the Indians don't get you, the fever will."

Fawcett kept his expression appropriately serious, but inwardly he doubted the fifty-eight-foot anaconda, as well as most of the other tales. Ever since his arrival in South America he had heard hair-raising accounts of dread savages, but he had seen little of them so far. It also seemed to him that most of the Indians were simply defending themselves against enslavement by rubber barons. His expedition was obviously not a raiding party, and this was perhaps why they had left him alone. He was coming to the opinion that a great deal of what he heard, about everything, was exaggeration. Yet he knew "fools race in", and Donayre didn't strike him as one given to hyperbole; so he decided that although he would not let the warnings deter him, he would exercise due caution. After all, everyone, to a man, had said essentially the same thing about the Abuná.

The group now began to break up and go their separate ways for the night. Rinaldi and Kent went to fetch a few things from the boat, and soon the doctor found Fawcett, relaxing on the veranda in the same chair where he had had his brief interlude with Miranda.

"Rinaldi asked me to give you these." He handed Fawcett a small packet of letters. "He has some for your assistant, as well, and I believe he's trying to find the fellow, now."

"He's probably somewhere arguing with Dan, our interpreter, who didn't join us this evening. Dan's a good fellow, when he's sober, but he's a bit moody and often keeps to himself or drinks with the Indians." He glanced at the letters, thumbing through them in search of— yes, there it was, the return address in Nina's handwriting. He smiled.

"Well, I will leave you alone with your mail," said the doctor, bowing slightly as if to withdraw.

"No, please." Fawcett motioned to a chair beside him. "I'd enjoy your company. I can't read very well in this light, actually, but I wanted to take the air for a while before I retire to my room." On this visit to Rosario he'd decided it would be prudent to sleep indoors, heat or no.

Kent sat. "I'm afraid we spooked your assistant considerably; he was as white as a sheet when he left us."

"Frankly, Chalmers has been 'spooked' for some time; I fear he's about ready to pack it in."

"But you aren't."

"No. I contracted to map the Abuná, and map it I will. Besides," he smiled ruefully, "I have been cursed with this abiding– some might say fatal– curiosity."

"I share a bit of that same curse, so I can't lecture you. Brazil seems to have worked its way into me, like the flukes and the candiru, ha! But its fascinations are endless. Listen to those birds, for example... " Both men were silent, tuned to a hollow, echoing cry that rose and fell, floating on the evening air. It was twilight, Fawcett's favorite time of day, a time when he often liked to listen to the bell-like notes of a certain common bird or insect, he couldn't tell which.

Kent had tilted his head, listening intensely. "You know, that bird is quite far away, I think; sounds travel amazing distances along the river. Yet in the forest, it's the opposite... One can hear the loudest human shout only two hundred yards or so. Even gunshots are quickly lost, there."

"What creature is making this staccato, clucking sound I hear?" The clucking gradually rose to a crescendo and ended in a long, loud trumpet-call.

"That's the *trompetero*," Kent replied. "The birds here are so different from those of England, aren't they? And I say, the one that really interests me is a little bird that resembles the kingfisher. It lives in rocky cliffs above the river, building its nest in neat round holes in the rock."

"Oh, yes! I saw some of those. Usually very high up, right? What causes those perfectly round holes, in such hard rock? I mean, quite convenient for the birds, yes?"

"More than convenient. The holes are found only where the birds are present, and in fact they're made by the birds! One of these semi-hermits who lives back in the forest told me he has sat many a time and watched them do it. They fly in with leaves in their beaks, and hold onto the cliff face somehow with their feet while they rub the leaves over the rock, in little circles. They fly away after a while and return with fresh leaves, and keep rubbing away; after they've done this a few times, they peck at the spot with their beaks, and a hole begins to show. They repeat the process for several days until the hole is deep enough for a nest. And as perfect as if a human had drilled it!"

Fawcett had been listening with great interest. "But– do you mean to say that the leaves somehow enable them to peck through solid rock? Sounds impossible!" Another tall tale, perhaps?

"To be precise, these birds know exactly which leaf contains a juice which is capable of softening rock, or liquefying it to the consistency of wet clay."

Suddenly a memory of the gigantic, carved boulders of the Tiahuanaco ruins sprang to Fawcett's mind, and their perfect, mortarless joins; a light began to dawn, slowly. Could this be the Incas' secret? "Do you believe the man's story?"

"Oh, indeed I do, because I had an experience myself which confirmed it, in my mind. It was in Peru, but these birds are found there, too. I'd been riding, but had to leave my horse at a neighbor's ranch, since it had gone lame, and I walked home. I was wearing boots and spurs, the big Mexican kind about four inches long, brand-new ones at that. I had to walk through a great deal of thick brush. When I reached home, I found that my fine new spurs were eaten away; almost completely gone, I swear, only little spikes about an eighth of an inch were left! Later I told the neighbor about it, and he asked me if I remembered walking through a growth of plants about a foot high, with dark, reddish-colored leaves. I did indeed, I told him; there was a wide area, in fact, covered with these plants. He got excited and said the juice from the leaves will soften rock to paste, or even liquid, and that that was what had dissolved my spurs. He asked me to take him to the spot, and though we searched for hours, I couldn't find it. I had taken a short cut straight through the jungle, no trails, and it was impossible to recall exactly where I'd been. This neighbor said something about the Incas using these leaves to aid in their building— "

"Ah, ha!" burst Fawcett. "This is just what I was thinking; it could explain several mysteries, couldn't it?"

"Indeed. And as my hermit-friend says, these forests hold many, many secrets. He ought to know; he's lived back there for over twenty-five years, an Englishman, mind you, and very well-educated."

"How curious; and yet I've been hearing of several of his ilk... "

"Yes, it's an odd thing, but I've observed that the more educated the person is, the easier it seems to be for him to turn his back on the world and embrace a life of simplicity; he adapts more readily than others when he 'goes native.' "

Fawcett was thoughtful for a moment. "It makes sense, in a way. He'd probably have the mental resources it takes to live without the distractions and entertainment of so-called civilization. He'd be more able to appreciate, and learn from, all that is around him. I've heard that a man who has once experienced the simple life will rarely return to the artificiality of society; he doesn't realize what a burden it is until he's free of it... " He fell silent.

"I wonder if I shall one day wind up a crazy old hermit, myself," Kent said, stretching widely. He rose. "I must wish you goodnight, Major; I've enjoyed our conversation. Rinaldi and I will be off early in the morning, and if I don't see you then, I certainly hope you'll be my guest in Esperanza. I'll be back there within a few weeks. I shall be quite hurt if you don't stop." He smiled and shook Fawcett's hand.

"Thank you. I'll see you there, if I'm not devoured by an anaconda."

"Ha! See that you aren't. It's not easy to find good conversation, hereabouts."

Fawcett leaned back, enjoying the waning twilight and a playful little breeze off the Acre. The towering forest stood in silhouette against an indigo sky to the east, while the river reflected the remains of a pale gold sunset. Bats swooped in their crazed yet graceful manner, and the air was redolent with the scent of some night-blooming flower.

Then sweetly, teasingly, the strains of phonograph music began; not nearby, but travelling through the distance from a barraca three miles upriver, carried by the water like a man in a boat. Even the insects hushed their noisy performance. It was the *Estudiantina*, a popular piece, every note clear yet gently modulated by the miles. As he listened Fawcett deeply felt the perfection of the moment, the evening's innate beauty given even more poignancy by the unexpected, haunting quality of the music. When the last strains gradually died away, the sky was a deep black blanket studded with stars and the river had blended into the dark forest. Fawcett sat for a minute, and when the insect orchestra began tuning up, he went to his room to at last read his letters.

For the next couple of days Fawcett was busily developing the photos he had taken on the Acre. It was a frustrating task, as many photos were ruined by the warmth of the water he was using; but cooler water was impossible to find in the wilderness. The process couldn't wait until his return to a city, as the humidity would spoil all exposed film rapidly.

Chalmers helped as much as he could though he was still tired and lethargic. Dan, however, was utterly useless, having fallen into a pit of drunkenness from which he seemed unable to climb.

"He makes me look like a positive saint, sometimes," grumbled Chalmers. "Take my advice, Sir, and don't ever try to drink that man under the table; you won't live to tell about it."

"It's all ridiculous," Fawcett threw over his shoulder testily. "What is it about this place that sends men to drown in liquor? Harry Kent echoes General Pando's opinion: There's nothing inherently unhealthy about the forests. It's the habits of the outsiders, which many Indians adopt— like alcohol— that weakens people and makes them prey to illness."

Chalmers realized too late he had opened himself to a lecture, so he adroitly changed the subject. "Why didn't Kent stick around a bit? To monitor Donayre's and the boy's progress?"

"He's just upriver at Yorongas if he's needed. He had to attend to someone on Rinaldi's plantation. Besides, he told me the two patients look well on their way to full recovery." Fawcett had awakened in time to see Kent off, and the two had spoken over breakfast; the doctor gave Fawcett some more remedies which he thought might come in handy. "He's a good chap and will offer us hospitality on the Madeira, I'm sure."

Again Chalmers felt inclined to change the subject. "How do you like the Stereoscopic?" he asked, picking up Fawcett's camera.

"It's a fine camera, but I wish it were lighter."

Chalmers looked at the pictures lying in the lukewarm fluid. "Well, if you want to save on weight, why do you use such large film? These exposures are, what, four by six?"

"Four by six and a half inches, to be exact."

"Well, if you switch to a smaller picture, you can get more exposures for less weight."

Fawcett regarded his assistant. "You know, that's not a bad idea; even the slightest extra weight will be important when we get to the places where we must pack all our gear on our backs. I think I'll take your suggestion the next time I buy film. Thanks."

But Chalmers had fallen into a funk again at the thought of trekking through the jungle with a ton of goods on his back. He sighed deeply, but Fawcett didn't notice; the photo of the fossil skull had come out nicely, and he was grinning with delight.

As the Indians loaded the canoes, Señor Donayre handed Fawcett a small parcel. "This is a little farewell gift, nothing important, but it may be helpful."

Inside, Fawcett found two very odd objects: an item which looked like the leather sole of a shoe, but which was rougher than sandpaper;

and a solid, hard brown cylinder with a musky odor. He looked at Donayre quizzically.

"Give up? This," he explained, picking up the cylinder, "Is *guaraná*. You make tea from it by rubbing it against the catfish tongue." He took the other object and rasped it along the chunk of guaraná, releasing a powder. "Now, this tea is very hard to come by; the plant from which it's made is found only in the lower Amazon, and is highly desired. It is quite an invigorating tonic with no ill effects that I've ever noticed. For strength and energy, nothing can top it. And my determined friend, I've a feeling you might need it." He clapped Fawcett on the back.

"Hmm... catfish tongue?"

"Ha! Yes. A good rasp, useful for many things besides guaraná."

Fawcett decided not to mention he had turned down an offer of guaraná from Miranda, an offer which sounded even more interesting now that he understood the properties of this tea.

He shook hands with Donayre, thanking him and Francesca profusely.

"It is we who are in your debt," said Donayre. "And don't worry about Dan, we'll eventually succeed in sobering him up, then we'll send him straight to you in Cobija." Dan, in an uncomprehending stupor, was utterly unable to travel, and by this time Fawcett was inclined not to care.

"Give him a big kick in the pants for me before you do." Fawcett waved as the batelón pushed off and floated slowly away. The little boy clung to his mother's hand, waving back shyly.

The trip downriver was easy and unexciting, and on February 23 they pulled up at the docks of Cobija. It was the height of rubber season, and things were booming; everyone felt rich, everyone had food.

More mail awaited them, and they fell upon it eagerly.

"But where are the newspapers?" asked Fawcett. "There should be bundles and bundles of them."

The postmaster looked regretful. "I'm so sorry. A note says the mules that carried the mail were starving, and had to eat the papers."

"What? Mules eating paper? I know goats do, but mules?" The man just shrugged.

"Damn," said Fawcett, as they walked away with their letters. "Guess there's not a thing we can do about it. Mules, indeed... " He heaved a sigh, a thoroughly disappointed man; at that moment, he would rather have had those newspapers than a good meal and clean sheets.

SYLVIA: DREAM LOG

Dream: August 3, 1994

A tall man with whom I've been corresponding returns from explorations in the wilds of a continent such as Africa or South America. He brought back a fabulous costume and a large mask, that of a tribal chieftain or shaman, which he displays for me. He shows me a map to King Solomon's Mines, saying we can find them together if I'll come with him. I see on the map an area of water I'd need to cross.

He begins his trek, walking down a trail. I hesitate, filled with doubts; my sandals are inadequate for such a hike. But suddenly I call to him, "Wait, wait for me!" I've decided to risk it. He hears me, and whoops for joy that I'm coming with him. I join him on the long trail.

Dream: November 30, 1994

Walking down a road, which ended at an immense mountain of bare rock in the middle of nowhere. As I stood looking at it, the sheer rock face slowly opened to reveal a passageway. I went through to the other side of the mountain, and found myself looking down on a green valley and a town, hidden away from the world.

Dream: Feb. 9, 1995

There wasn't much to this dream, but I'm jotting it down because it was so vivid and real. I'm coming out of an apartment building where I live (though I've never actually seen it before), passing through grand doors of some ornate, exotic design in black. I'm looking out on a large courtyard, and there are plants and trees, very lush and tropical.

A misty rain is falling, but the morning sun shines through. I look around, breathing the mild, moist air, thinking how pretty it all is.

Dream: Dec. 18, 1996

...Driving through a wilderness area, unique and hard to reach, negotiating a road with many switchbacks and hairpin curves. On a high, long ridgetop I see a strange tree which at first sight appears to be in flames, but it isn't consumed; rather, an intensely bright light blazes around it. Its distinctive branches, silhouetted against the golden light, are like arms stretching straight out and turning slightly upward to the sky. I'm transfixed by the spiritual beauty of it. Then the light, which seems to come from above, moves to the next tree on the ridge, setting it temporarily afire, and then so on along the line of trees on the ridge. They are all of the same odd species, which I've never seen before.

Dream: Jan. 9, 1997

The hotel was nice; in bygone years it may have been one of the best. I've arrived in a Latin American country. The taxi driver takes me through glass doors and sets my suitcase near the counter. I look around at sage green and gray marble walls, until a boy comes to the desk and motions to a large register. I sign my name, using the title, "Doctor", and replace the book on its stand. The boy's mother takes me up a wide flight of marble stairs to my room; she's speaking to me in what I think is Spanish, but although I speak that language I'm having trouble understanding her.

A few people are waiting in my room, and they greet me with courtesy and respect, as if I'm to be the main speaker at a conference, maybe. They help me settle in, and then leave. At first it seems there are no windows, but I realize they're hidden behind tapestries. I push one aside and look out at the sea, but dominating and almost blocking the view is an enormous, spreading tree, with large leaves.

"Oh! The Tree," I say.

The woman, who's still with me, says, "Yes, the Tree."

SYLVIA, CHAPTER 1
CALIFORNIA
Los Angeles, 1998

Sylvia took a deep, slow breath, and held it. With a slender twig firmly in her fingers she started the video camera, mounted on a tripod, with her other hand and took a few seconds of test footage, holding the twig as still as possible in front of the lens. Then she reviewed the tape.

Dang; the macro lens reveals the slightest tremor. I'll have to be steadier than that.

She tried again, this time slowly bringing the tip of the twig to a small, orangish-colored flower positioned in front of the camera. The results were better. *Movement is the key; I can hold the twig steadier, actually, when I'm moving my hand.*

She tried a take. Holding her breath again, but in a more relaxed manner, Sylvia moved the twig into the soft depths of the inch-wide monkey flower, closer, closer, entering the throat of the blossom until she touched the delicate stigma with the twig. Immediately the stigma began to close, until it was tightly shut. She stopped the camera. Now, if she wanted to try a second take she'd have to get another flower from the refrigerator, or wait a little while for this one to reopen. As far as the flower knew, it had been fertilized and was no longer open for business; that is, until it recognized the deception.

She reviewed the footage. Not bad for a first try. There were sounds at the studio door.

"Knock, knock," a voice said. "Sylvia? Oh, sorry, didn't know you were taping; the door was ajar and the warning light was off— "

"It's okay, B.D., come on in. I just finished a take. I forgot about the light and all that... "

The museum's Exhibits Director sat on the corner of a table. "Listen, Sylvia, we know you're almost finished with the chaparral exhibit, but Connie and I had a brainstorm for one additional display."

"One more! Where are we going to put it?"

"Don't worry about that. We worked it out. And you'll like this. "

"All right. I'm listening." Sylvia plopped down in a chair, suddenly weary.

"Okay. Since the chaparral room is across the corridor from Greg's rainforest exhibit, and visitor-flow should go from one exhibit right into the other, we need a display that compares the two types of forest, since they're so very different. Yes?" He held out his hands questioningly.

"Mm... You're right, I like it. In fact, wasn't that my idea, originally? Remember the first planning meeting, over a year ago? B.D.?"

"Uh– you could be right. I wasn't there. Was I?"

Sylvia laughed. "Yes! You were! Sheesh–"

"The main thing is, it's a great idea you had, Sylvia, so let's do it."

"Yes, 'let's'!"

"I ran it past Greg; he's ready to help you with any resource material you want, but he's swamped with the rainforest right now, so this is your baby."

"Okay. I'll talk to him. Now, scram! I want to get home at a decent hour today, and I'm not quite finished here."

B.D. beat a hasty retreat, his mission accomplished.

Sylvia took a long breath. She wanted the display; she had always thought something of the kind should be included; she hoped they were planning to place it in the wide corridor between the two exhibits. But Greg might not be easy to deal with; he was even more of an eccentric loner than she was. Being more or less an outsider at the museum, an independent contractor, she tried to avoid stepping on staffers' toes.

She shut down the camera. This was a good time to take a break. Might as well go grab the bull by its horns.

"I'm happy to help, Dr. Garth– "

"Sylvia, please."

" --Sylvia, then... " Greg always felt awkward around her. Brainy women were fine, he wouldn't want any other kind, but beauties made him nervous. Thought petite and slender, she stood very straight and was somehow imposing. He'd heard she was one-quarter Shoshone, which he could see in the high cheekbones and faintly olive skin; but her startling blue-green eyes and dark auburn hair also reflected Scot ancestry, he guessed.

"I'm behind schedule on my exhibit so I don't have much face-time to give you. But look— come with me— "

Sylvia followed her greying, disheveled colleague down the dim hallway. 'Face-time'? She was smirking a bit, clearing her expression as he looked back at her.

"Now, try not to move things around too much, but here's my resource room, I call it. In the blue folder are sketches for my displays, the labels are at the back, flow charts for interactive exhibits are in this pocket, see? Oh, here's the copier, and here—" he spun around to face a long table— "Are the resource books, articles, what-have-you, just be sure to leave everything where you found it. "

After a few more warnings and directions he vacated the room like a whirlwind, leaving Sylvia standing amid dust-motes in a shaft of late afternoon light streaming through the tall windows of the old Natural History Museum. She gazed around her at total chaos, it seemed to her. Books and papers and sticky-notes were everywhere; the walls were covered at random with photos of bright red frogs, tree sloths, bromeliads. Where to begin?

She picked up the blue folder, which was somewhat organized, at least. She sat on a dusty chair near the windows and began to make a few notes. After a while she closed the folder and tried to recall exactly where it had been lying so she could replace it. She knew how it felt to have someone come into her workspace and shift things around; she had a "piling system" of her own.

Her eye fell on an open volume, secured by a large clip that held the place at pages 24 and 25. The right-hand page contained a sidebar article entitled, "Searching for City X," which consisted of a few short columns of text under a large photo. It was the photo that arrested her attention, though years later, in retrospect, she was never able to say why. It depicted a confusing jumble of dense forest and a group of eight men at rest, their faces small in the wide shot. A couple of the men appeared to be Indians. In the center sat a bearded man, holding a small dog on his lap. The brief columns of text summarized this man's story.

marized this man's story.

He was Percy Harrison Fawcett, an explorer who spent his life on the quest for an ancient city hidden in the vast rainforests of Brazil, a pre-Columbian colony formed by a group who had, he believed, escaped the destruction of Atlantis. Also mentioned in the article were a stone idol in Fawcett's possession, an old map, and a psychic who claimed to receive telepathic messages from Fawcett after he disappeared into the wilderness forever, in 1925. She glanced at the book's cover: *Mystic Places,* one of the Time-Life series on unexplained phenomena.

Entertaining gabble, she thought, wondering why Greg had the book among his resources. But she supposed that from his viewpoint anything pertaining to the rainforest and its famous explorers would be worth looking at; she knew he had one display that traced the routes of bandeirantes and others who braved the wilds of South America many years ago.

She turned back to the photograph. It was dated 1908. Though it had nothing to do with her task, she used Greg's copier to reproduce the page for herself. Then she carefully replaced the book, and left the room.

Sylvia stood at a computer in the cavernous Main Library of downtown Los Angeles, researching obscure botanical details for the rainforest/chaparral display, when she found herself typing "Percy Harrison Fawcett" into the search engine. Just to see what comes up, she told herself; take a little break from plant life.

Fawcett's story intrigued her. It had several elements, it seemed to her, the public currently craved: wilderness adventure, the South American rainforest, ancient civilizations— and the paranormal. So why hadn't there been a blockbuster novel, a best-selling biography, or a movie about this explorer? When she'd taken a second look at the article she photocopied, she could see all sorts of possibilities. The writer in her wished she had time to pursue it further. The idea nagged at her, and she filed it in the back of her mind among a growing list of things to consider when the exhibit was finished.

But it wouldn't stay put.

The computer gave her a short list of references, including a few magazine articles: one from Newsweek and another from Time, both from 1953 and both of which turned out to be reviews of Fawcett's posthumously published memoirs. She also found and photocopied a longer article from Life Magazine, 1951, about the continuing mystery of Fawcett's disappearance. Human bones had been discovered and an Indian chief had "confessed" to his slaying, but there was reason to doubt the authenticity of both the bones and the chief's story. She discovered from the article that Fawcett had called his phantom city "Z", not "X" as the Time-Life book had written.

There were a couple of other references to Fawcett in books about Brazil's explorers, and a few books briefly mentioning his quest and subsequent disappearance. She found a book about a 1932 expedition that set out to find him, though it appeared to be more about the expedition and its leader than Fawcett. But she took it.

She started reading, sifting through the information, making photocopies. Was this all there was on the man?

Rush hour traffic had thinned, and Sylvia wound her way up Laurel Canyon Boulevard's curves without any stops until she reached the light at Lookout Mountain Avenue. She turned left and accelerated up Lookout Mountain, realizing she had been so lost in thought that she didn't recall any of the drive after she exited the freeway. And now she was almost home. At the elementary school, she took a right fork onto Wonderland and climbed the hill in second gear, slowing as she reached her driveway. The summer solstice was drawing close and there was still plenty of golden light; bougainvillea vines smothering the porch roof greeted her with their shocking fuchsia. She grabbed her mail from the box and gave the wind chimes a smack as she crossed the porch.

No messages on the machine. Good. No calls to return. She plopped all the books and papers down in a heap on the counter, then thought better of it. She took a few minutes to sort through the botanical research materials and the items that had resulted from the Fawcett search. The latter pile was pretty skimpy.

What am I doing, she wondered, as she peeled a banana and diced it into the blender along with a soy smoothie mix. *I have plenty to do without getting involved in some way-out-there project which has no connection to my field or to anything I've ever done. I should be advancing my career by writing about instructional design or learner control or online courses...*

She took her smoothie to the bedroom, brooding. *Why can't I be like my grad-school peers, who've singlemindedly written textbooks and started businesses and made mucho dinero; but the very idea of writing about this stuff puts me to sleep... I'm not exactly bored with my field, not at all; so why the restlessness? I sometimes feel there's something more, something I'm missing, out there. Somewhere.*

She was more conscious than ever of having no attachments; one brief marriage when she was very young, no children, and now, no pets. She missed her old cat, who had finally died. He had always met her at the door, and was usually more interested in smelling her shoes than in eating his dinner. *It's a good time to make the best of my freedom, maybe follow up some tentative offers for work in Rome, or London. Shake myself up a little.*

She pulled her straight, shining hair back and wound it into a thick French braid. A few grays were appearing at her temples, just as they had in her dad's hair when he passed forty. Donning shorts and running shoes, she swallowed the rest of the drink and went outside to take advantage of the long day. She warmed up her legs by walking uphill, until she reached a side road that ran along a ridge where she began to jog.

What is this Fawcett fellow to me? Maybe I can relate to him. According to one of the magazine articles, he was a man who couldn't make himself follow the pre-ordained career track. He needed challenge, like some people need money. Or love.

It intrigues me that no one seems to have written very much about him, but I'm not sure I'm the one who should be trying to change that. In that entire, data base there was very little to be found about him. So what is there to write?

By the time she returned from her run, she'd decided she'd make another attempt at finding more information on Fawcett, and if that went nowhere, she would give it up.

The next day was a Saturday. Sylvia dialed the number of a Burbank bookstore that dealt in used, rare, and old volumes. Two of the magazine articles she'd photocopied had reviewed Fawcett's memoir, published at last in 1953 by his son, Brian, and titled *Lost Trails, Lost Cities*. It wasn't to be found in the Los Angeles library system, but a librarian suggested she try the bookstore.

She got the owner on the line, and gave him the title and other details about the book.

"Well, it's kind of a long shot, of course, but give me your phone number and I'll keep an eye out for it."

She gave her number, thanked him, and figured that was that. Small chance. Time to put her energies back into the museum display, and think about some professional writing projects she'd been mulling.

About an hour later the telephone rang.

"Hey, it's Jay, from Burbank Books. Guess what? I'm holding that book you wanted, in my hand right now. "

"Huh?"

"It was the strangest thing. After we hung up I went upstairs where I have hundreds of books I haven't had a chance to organize yet, to get another book somebody wanted and that I'd seen up there. I found that one, and was dusting off some of the others when a book literally fell out. It was yours!"

"I'm leaving right now for your store. *Thanks!*"

The little ant struggled along with its burden, a piece of green leaf several times larger than the ant; encountering a twig, which to the ant was a great log, it gamely climbed over, wobbling a bit.

A cry of dismay from Greg pulled Sylvia's attention from the film; but he was all right, just frustrated. She looked back at the screen and saw that the film of real ants had now gone into an animated segment: Ants were chewing the leaf pieces to remove surface waxes, then infecting them with a fungus which produced little fruiting bodies the ants would later eat. It was a symbiotic relationship, the narrator explained: The ants used the food, and the fungi used the ants as dispersal agents.

She left the ant display and crossed the echoing space to Greg, teetering high on a scaffolding beside an extensive mural reaching to the ceiling, depicting the layers of the rainforest from ground to emergent trees soaring above the canopy.

"More problems?"

"It's the same ding-blasted sloth," he complained, removing a small panel camouflaged in the trunk of a tree.

"Your language shocks me! Can I help in any way?"

"Yes. When I give the go-ahead, select the sloth on the Where to Find Me panel."

"The sloth..." Sylvia looked among the photographs of various creatures on a long, child-friendly panel just a little above knee-high for her. She walked along the bright display: emerald boa, red-eyed frog, jaguar, howler monkey, ah— here. Tree sloth.

"Okay, now." Greg removed his hands from the electric panel.

Sylvia laid her fingers firmly on the touch-screen.

"Bingo!" cried Greg. A brightly-lit tree sloth appeared like magic, holding onto the tree trunk. "Try each one while I'm up here, if you don't mind."

Methodically Sylvia began at her far right and touched each photo, watching for the corresponding creature to show up in the area of the rainforest that it normally frequented. A few were revealed in two places, such as the jaguar, seen crouching on a lower tree branch and peering around a tree trunk on the ground.

"They all work, Greg."

"Finally," he muttered, sticking a few tools in his waistband and climbing carefully down. "I know I'm not supposed to be tinkering with the mechanisms, it's someone else's job and all that, but if I know what to do I just want to get it done!"

"My lips are sealed."

"Hey, I have coffee here... Want some? You can unseal them for that." He made a beeline to a large thermos on a worktable.

"If you have an extra cup I could use."

"Mm— I'm sure there's something... here!" He unscrewed a bulb cover from a nearby display and wiped it out. "It's thick glass, should be fine." Sylvia laughed as he poured steaming coffee for both of them.

"Thanks. Cheers."

After a few swallows, Greg said: "So. You spent the weekend delving into Fawcett's memoirs, huh? A good read?"

"Surprisingly so. Exciting, witty, fascinating stuff. I also looked around on the Internet and found out Fawcett was the prototype for the Indiana Jones character." Her companion raised his eyebrows, impressed. "Greg, how did you happen to have the book that I saw in your room? My new obsession is all your fault, by the way."

"Ha! I just requested info on any and all rainforest explorers, and the grad student who helps with research gave me everything she came up with, including that book with the blurb on Fawcett. I thought it was interesting, too, but I wound up not using any of it."

"I might not do anything with it, either, but I played around with an outline for a book... Not that it's in my line, at all."

"Well, I don't know about that, Sylvia; from what I've seen, your career interests always seem to gravitate to nature topics. You could be getting much richer doing what you do in the business world, you know."

"So true. Designing training programs for investment bankers never hit my hot-buttons, though."

"Have you ever been to Brazil? South America?" Greg abruptly asked.

"No. I've seen rainforests in other areas, on tropical islands... but I've always intended to see the Amazon forests, one day."

"If you're researching a book, it's a tax write-off." He winked, pouring more coffee for both of them.

Dream: June 15, 1998

A large, colorful rooster somehow enters my home. I'm afraid, but he urges me to trust him. I surrender, and feel at one with the animal. We leave our physical bodies and rise upward, through the ceiling and roof, into the sky. Where should we go? the rooster asks.

Somewhere exciting, I tell him, like the Brazilian rainforest... I've had my mind on that area lately. We don't need to fly, I say, we can "think" ourselves there instantly.

Well, my thought-travel skills need work. Suddenly, the rooster is nowhere in sight and I seem to be in a crowded city, with a view of people's legs walking all around me as if seen from the ground. Apparently I'm sitting on the sidewalk; when I look at myself, I see that I'm in the body of a dwarf with no legs. An angry man is bending over me, yelling because I won't sell him a ticket of some kind— a sort of lottery ticket. At last I sell him the ticket, and he leaves.

I feel I'm somewhere in Brazil; the language the angry man spoke sounded like Portuguese. Suddenly I float away from the dwarf's body and the next thing I know, I'm in a lovely forest which seems to be near the city. I'm sitting in a stream below a waterfall. Ah, this is more like it...

All at once I became lucid, fully aware I was dreaming, and I looked all around my dream world, noting how perfectly real and detailed the surroundings were. Then a rooster crowed, and I awoke.

"Excellent work, excellent, both of you!" The president of the museum board pumped Sylvia's hand, and then Greg's. She stole a longing glance at a nearby table laden with canapes; she was hungry, but she hadn't been able to manage a plate of food or even a glass of wine, with all the hand-shaking. Board members and other museum mucky-mucks had been invited to review the new exhibits before they opened to the public. After the museum closed for the day, the guests had streamed in to explore the Rainforest Room, and the Elfin Forest Chaparral exhibit.

B.D. approached them bearing two glasses of champagne.

"Here! You two look dry. Why aren't you drinking? You deserve it!"

Greg hesitated. "I'm crossing my fingers so hard that all the displays function correctly, I don't think I could hold a glass."

Sylvia smiled in sympathy. "I know what you mean. I actually had a nightmare last night about one of the interactive kiosks going berserk..." She reached for a flute. "Gimme that, I do need it."

"Ah, the good old days," B.D. said, "When exhibits were just a bunch of stuff in glass cases. Yawn! It's all stunning, you two, public education at its best, and everything's working perfectly."

"So far, so good." Sylvia handed a glass to Greg, tapped his glass with hers, and they each took a long swig.

"Ah! Dr. Pereira!" B.D. waved over a stooped, gray-haired man wearing a gentle expression. "Sylvia, Greg, this is Dr. Edivam Pereira, from the Museum of Natural History in São Paulo, Brazil. He's touring natural history museums in the U.S. " He turned to Dr. Pereira. "These two designed the exhibits you've just seen."

"Yes, of course; I read about you both in the pamphlet. I'm so pleased to meet you." His English was perfect.

"Likewise, Dr. Pereira, " Greg replied. "Your colleague, Senhor Morel, gave me invaluable advice when I was designing my exhibit. We never met face to face, only by email and telephone, but he was very generous with his time and resources."

"I'm glad he was able to assist you. The end results are fabulous!"

"Thank you." Greg smiled broadly.

"And Dr. Garth, I have learned a great deal about the chaparral ecology from your displays; it's unique, but it reminds me of our scrublands in some parts of Brazil."

"I'd like to see those areas someday."

B.D. spoke up. "Dr. Garth has far-flung interests, actually; she's designed exhibits on subjects ranging from marine biology to plate tectonics; and she's our local expert on distance learning."

"Really? Such broad experience you must have..."

Sylvia explained, "Well, I work with subject-matter experts on the content, though I do a little of my own research, too. Often my job is just presenting information to a wide audience, and making it seem more entertaining than educational, if possible."

"You succeeded. I learned quite painlessly," Dr. Pereira said amiably, reaching into his coat pocket. "May I give each of you my card? If either of you is ever in São Paulo, you must come see me at the museum. And perhaps we can all work together on a travelling exhibit, someday."

"That sounds like a great idea," put in B.D., taking Dr. Pereira's arm to steer him elsewhere. "See you, gotta schmooze everybody, introduce him to a few others. Again, congrats!" He wandered off with the Brazilian in tow, smiling happily.

Greg released a tired sigh. "I start on the whale exhibit in a few days. I envy you free-lancers at times like this; you can take a break between projects. What's next for you, Sylvia?"

"Well, B.D. contracted with me to make two interactive CDs, one on the rainforest and the other on chaparral fire ecology... for sale to schools, primarily. Anyway, before I start on the CDs, I need a vacation, so you might not see me for a while. And I'm already knee-deep in Fawcett's story, so I want to work on that a little."

"You're really hooked, aren't you?"

"I guess. The man creeps into any little crevice of my mind that isn't busy at the time. It's like escaping into another world... But as we were saying the other day, I need to go to South America. I can't write about a place I've never seen. I just don't think I'll see anything authentic, though, on some Amazon cruise boat full of tourists. Every trip I've looked into really turned me off. Air conditioning, cocktails, you know— "

Greg nodded. "I was thinking about you the other day when I got this invitation— wait— it's here somewhere, I brought it to show you— " Greg fished in his pockets with his free hand; even his lumpy suit looked somehow disorganized, and several small slips of paper fluttered out. Sylvia picked them up as they fell, hiding a grin.

"Here!" He unfolded a letter which had been creased about eight times.

As Sylvia read, her heart started to thump a little harder. The

Smithsonian Institute was sponsoring two-week camping expeditions into the Igapo Flooded Forest, for an overview of that ecosystem and adjacent areas. It was by invitation only and the guest list consistently primarily of scientists, graduate students in earth sciences, natural history museum personnel, and science writers. The expedition, conducted by an outfit based in Manaus, would be offered three times during the June-through-September dry season, and each party would consist of only seven or eight guests. Conditions would be very primitive and good health was a must; there would be no cell or satellite phone service available, no quick rescues possible. The group would journey by small boat into uninhabited wilderness, beyond the most remote Indian settlements.

"Does that fit your needs, you think?"

"This sounds more like it. But the invitation is for *you*– "

He waved his hand. "Not a problem. I got it because I'm active in the Institute; but I called the guy in charge and asked if a colleague of mine might go instead... "

"Greg, you're tops! I do appreciate this."

"You'd better call him in the morning and secure a place on one of those trips; he said he wouldn't be able to hold any openings, it's first come, first served."

Sylvia looked at the name and telephone number on the letter. "I'll leave a message tonight, as soon as we can get out of here, then I'll call again in the morning."

Greg smiled at her excitement. "Wish I could go, too, but I hear the song of the whales, calling me... "

And I, thought Sylvia, *hear the ghost of Percy Harrison Fawcett, calling to me.* Suddenly, she thought of the dream. "Come with me, and I'll show you King Solomon's Mines... "

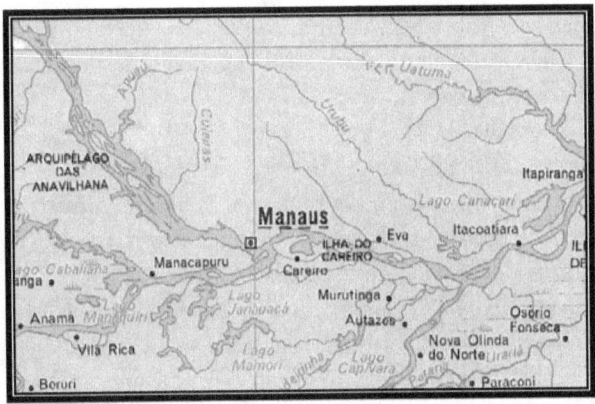

SYLVIA, CHAPTER 2
AMAZONAS: FOUR FORESTS

The tea-colored waters of the Rio Negro slid smoothly beneath the boat and felt silken to Sylvia's fingers, dangling limply over the side. The craft sat low in the water, an intimate nearness that invited contact; now and then someone swung bare feet over the side, toes dipping in and out of the cool wake, or dragged a washcloth in the water to mop a sweaty brow. But the breeze off the river was refreshing after the crowded, stifling streets of Manaus.

It was early in July. The little group had assembled at their hotel at noon the previous day for lunch and an orientation meeting. Sylvia and six other paying guests from diverse parts of the U.S. had convened in Brazil for what was described as "two weeks of remote field study." Will Greene, a lean, tanned naturalist—their fearless leader— a boatman, and a cook brought the total to ten. Educated in Great Britain, Will was of mixed parentage. "My late father was European, my mother is Brazilian," he explained during the introductions. "I've lived in Amazonas for twelve years, and I've been taking out groups for at least eight of those."

He looked around the group and continued: "Now, some details of our trip: We'll be in the boat all day tomorrow, and the next day as well; there are many miles to cover if we want to get beyond the frontier; that is, the last settlement. Our goal is to visit an area where it's likely few non-indigenous people, if any, have been. We'll explore a pristine biome, study its known species, and perhaps even turn up something new."

"Find a new species in only two weeks?" asked a man named Sam.

"Happens all the time in Amazonas. Ah, here comes our lunch. I'll try to answer your questions while we eat. Oh, don't eat the salad; don't eat anything raw in Manaus."

"But we were told vaccinations weren't necessary, so— " began a young woman named Katie, with a worried look.

"They aren't, not where we're going. Diseases flourish where humans live, all crowded together. We'll be out in the wilds where there's none of that. Just take care while we're in town."

The guests had had the rest of the day to themselves; a few wandered, bleary-eyed and jet-lagged, to take a look at the opera house built by rubber barons in 1856, Teatro Amazonas, and have an early dinner. Sylvia went to an Italian restaurant with Sam, a large, balding man, and his wife, Betsy. The two were from Chicago, retired science professors; Betsy was also a widely published nature photographer. Sylvia liked them right away, especially gray-haired Betsy with her mild ways and perceptive comments.

The next morning after a dawn breakfast, the group found themselves on a dock looking down at the boat that would be their transportation for two weeks: Condor, it was grandly named, was thirty feet long and not quite six feet at its greatest width. There were four bench rows that were visible; the rear two were hidden under stacks of supplies: toilet paper, dry goods, coolers. Just enough room remained in the very back for the cook, Federico, and the boatman, Berto, who had to lean out and peer around all the boxes to see the river ahead. Stalks of bananas were tied to every post supporting the wooden roof, which sheltered all but the first bench, a short one in the tapering bow. The wooden benches had no cushions, but there were slatted backrests which folded down to allow access to the back rows.

Sylvia's attention was drawn to the boat's name, lettered with a flourish on both sides. She was remembering one of Fawcett's more bizarre tales concerning an Andean condor and shaking her head at the coincidence, a bemused smile playing at the corners of her mouth. Her expression was misinterpreted.

"Whoa! Simple, isn't it?" observed Pauline, a biologist from a Boston museum, plump, fortyish. "It's like a big, white canoe with a roof."

"And a motor," Sylvia added.

"Only one? What if it breaks down?" asked Katie, a Florida State student of earth sciences, at twenty-one the youngest in the group.

Will heard. "I know my boat doesn't look like much, but it's a rugged thing, you know, and if we want to get up these small, lesser-known rivers we need a craft this size and one that only draws a couple of feet beneath. It's called an *igarité*. Not to be confused with *igarapé*, which is a small stream. And as for the motor," he added, looking at Katie, "We'll be headed upstream all the way, so if it conks out we can drift back down to civilization. Besides, Berto is an expert mechanic and he brings extra parts."

He looked around at everyone. "Okay, now?"

The gear, mostly duffel bags and backpacks, was securely (they hoped) lashed to the roof as they watched, and a couple of tarps were tied over it all.

Will and Federico helped everyone climb down into the boat. As Sylvia settled onto a bench and stowed her day-pack beneath it, she felt a quick thrill down her back. The craft was perfect in its simplicity. This was what she had wanted, to travel as close as possible to the old style. She blessed Greg, toiling back at the museum, for sparing her from the tourists in their big, air-conditioned cruise boats.

Berto freed the Condor from its moorings, and they were off.

"Hope everyone likes bananas," said Sam dubiously.

The igarité moved away from Manaus' busy docks and settled into the sedate pace of twelve miles per hour. The first order of business was to cross to the other side of the Rio Negro, second largest river in the world, so broad the other side couldn't yet be seen.

"Here, it's almost half a mile wide," Will explained. "For purposes of river conditions and navigation, we need to ascend the river along its south bank for a while; when we reach a place called the Narrows, we'll cross back to the north side."

It was a bumpy, windy, wet ride as the tail end of a storm passed through. When they reached the opposite side they followed the shoreline northwestward, as the sky gradually cleared.

Sylvia frequently referred to a map Will had drawn for her at the hotel, in reply to her questions about the route. "We'll go up the Rio Negro into this region," he had said as his finger circled around a tributary he labelled *Apuaú*, "And after a week or so up there we'll come back down Rio Negro to the Varzea— see, this area here— on the Amazon River... so you can see how different the two rivers and their biomes are."

The group ate lunch in the boat, without pausing. Cruising along to the hum of the outboard motor, they passed around various containers of food that issued from Federico's station at the rear: bread, tomatoes, onions, tuna or egg salad, mayo and mustard. They put together their sandwiches, sharing ingredients with courtesy, pouring lime or orange drink for each other, gradually getting acquainted.

Sylvia watched the group, a little amused, wondering just how long everyone's beautiful manners would hold. At present, there was a touch of gingerliness, even awkwardness in everyone's behavior. The women from New York City, Fran and Dale, museum researchers, patiently passed all the containers from their position at the rear. Pauline and Katie declined the tuna but tried not to make a big deal out of their vegan vegetarianism. Everyone took pains to be sure their gear wasn't in anyone's way. They could sit two to a bench, with plenty of room, if two people were willing to sit on the unsheltered first row. Otherwise, some rows would have to accommodate three.

Inwardly Sylvia, self-described "loner and privacy freak", wondered, too, how she would handle being in intimate proximity with strangers for a couple of weeks. But she was beginning to feel a lightness of being that increased with every mile the boat chugged into the wilds. *I can tolerate them all*, she thought, *no matter what they're like, as long as no one gets hurt or sick and makes us come back.*

She ate her tomato and onion sandwich quietly, listening to her companions make superficial conversation.

"I think Will said you're a vegetarian, too?" Katie asked Sylvia.

"Yes. For many years." Sylvia smiled at the younger woman, so artlessly lovely, her face as clean and fine as a child's; the blue eyes were clear and healthy, the corn-silk hair in short, pixie wisps around her face.

"Well, it's not exactly a subject for mealtime, I guess!" Fran, a tall, rangy woman with an assertively jutting chin and close-cropped brown hair, was showing an object to the group, a gray plastic funnel of some sort. "It's called a female funnel; Dale and I found them in a travel store. They're great for a trip like this." She demonstrated in a vague way how the funnel was held next to a woman's body as she urinated, so the stream could be directed wherever desired: "In a bottle, like the guys do, ha! Or over the side of a boat– "

"Do feel free to show us," Will interrupted with a snicker.

Dale broke in. "It's just so much easier to stand and use this, than to squat in the weeds." She adjusted her glasses self-consciously.

The men on board were smirking, but most of the women could see some distinct advantages to the gizmos.

In fact, the only shore stops they made all day were a couple of "bathroom" breaks. Having been roundly warned by Will that "The greatest danger in Amazonas is dehydration," they drank water all day long from the tin cups Federico gave everyone.

"We brought water for today," Will told them, "But when we make camp we'll filter river water, from now on."

All the drinking made pit stops highly desirable, though no one, it seemed, wanted to be the first to ask for one. The Battle of the Bladders.

"Don't be shy, people; speak up, no need to suffer." Eventually Will would call back to Berto, and Berto would look for a good place to step ashore; sometimes this took a little while to find. Then, the rule was: women wander off to the right, men to the left.

By lunchtime they were in the Igapo, or Blackwater Flooded Forest. Between bites of food Will described the trees and plants that spend most of the year with their feet in the water, and how the Rio Negro is stained dark as root beer by the tannin leached from leaves; how the water's high level of acidity explains the scarcity of mosquitoes and various other insects. "In this biome," he said in teacherly fashion, "There's relatively low species diversity but high species endomism— that is, when a species evolves or adapts particularly for its environment."

Sylvia put the sandwich down and grabbed her journal, scribbling his exact words; this was one of the reasons she'd come, after all: to learn. But as he rambled on, her pen lay still. It was delicious to skim over glassy water and lose oneself in the mirror-perfect reflection of trees and shrubs, and strange to move among trees that stood in several feet of water. Behind the Flooded Forest, Will was saying, is Terrafirme Forest, another biome they'd explore, where trees were larger and never flooded. They could see this forest from the boat, and it became more beautiful the farther upriver they went. Tremendous philodendron— not one's little office plants— climbed up giant tree trunks; a wealth of epiphytes nestled and bloomed in the crotches, splashes of contrasting color amid the greens.

Late in the day the Condor wove its way through the flooded trees to firm, relatively dry land near the site of an abandoned forest lodge, where they disembarked; a dim trail leading from the riverbank was the only indication there had been a lodge in the vicinity.

"The site is a good, flat spot," Will told them, "to pitch the tents. It's just a ten-minute walk. But before we go, perhaps everyone might like a little swim?" He glanced around at the group. "Don't know about you folks, but I need a wash, myself," he said cheerily, getting towel and soap from his bag. The group looked at him, and each other, with uncertain little smiles.

He removed his T-shirt and waded in, shorts and all. "Mmm... It feels great! Nice and cool, ahhh... " He sank into the dark water, until he disappeared under its surface.

They fidgeted, fussing with their stuff.

"Oh, I'm not very dirty, really," said Fran, rummaging in her bag. "I'll just wet a washcloth— here it is— and sponge off a little."

Will resurfaced. "Come on, everyone! The water is perfectly clean, and there's nothing to harm you. Besides, this is it, as far as bathing goes; may as well get used to it. Hand me the soap, would you?" He gestured to a nearby shrub, where he'd hung a pouch bulging with several bars of soap.

Clever, Sylvia thought. Someone will have to go into the water to hand it to him. While he was demonstrating how safe and delightful the Rio Negro was, she had slipped behind a bush to exchange her shorts for swimsuit bottoms, leaving her T-shirt in place.

"I'll get it." She fetched the pouch and headed for the water.

"What's that you're wearing?" asked Betsy, pointing to Sylvia's feet.

"Speedos. Reef shoes. Thought they might come in handy in this soggy 'biome'." She spoke casually but she was glad to have them. Wading in, she could feel rotten leaves and what-all swirling around her ankles; the bottom was lumpy and mushy under the rubber soles. She could imagine what it must be like to bare feet.

But the tepid water, now at her waist, was silky and soothing. She handed the pouch to Will, who met her eyes briefly. "Good girl," he muttered. "Here, have a bar of Amazon soap!" he added more loudly.

"I brought biodegrable soap, thanks, I can go get it."

"No, use this; it's for acid waters. The other soaps seem to never rinse away." He soaped his thick, brown hair, which had grown a bit long and shaggy from general neglect.

Katie was wading tentatively in and Sylvia tossed her the pouch. "I'm going to have a swim, first," she told Katie. "He's right; the water feels good." Sam suddenly did a belly-flop to the left of them. Soon the others were in, albeit reluctantly.

It was the first of many river baths, and the last time they had to be coaxed. Before long the group would look forward to this part of the day, when they rinsed away the heat and sweat, never giving much thought to critters— with one exception— since Will didn't seem to worry. They would become utterly dependent on him to tell them how to live in their new environment, what to fear and what to forget.

"Oh, wait, there's one thing, " Will announced, as people waded in, "Don't urinate, anyone. "

"How's that?" Sam asked quickly, as if he'd been caught mid-stream.

"It's advisable not to do it in the water. There's a type of tiny liver fluke, you see, that's drawn to the urine stream and follows it into the urethra; it can lodge itself inside there with a barb, and it's bloody painful to remove. But it's the only thing you need to worry about, around here."

Individuals went off to themselves a short distance, turning their backs, soaping their bodies beneath their clothing. Some of them swam around cautiously, beginning to relax.

After they changed into fresh clothing the group hiked back to the erstwhile lodge, now only a collection of crumbling huts which the jungle was rapidly absorbing. Quickly Berto and Will put up tents, while Federico started dinner; darkness falls rapidly near the equator, and the dense terrafirme forest was dimming. To add urgency, thunder rumbled nearby.

"Do you have a rain fly for my hammock?" Sylvia asked Will. Fawcett's comments in his memoirs on the superiority of hammocks over beds had inspired her to request one for the trip.

"I guess we could rig something," Will told her. "But I think you should spend the first night, at least, in the tent."

She looked doubtful. "My back doesn't like flat, hard surfaces..."

"It's going to *pour*," he urged, "Plus it's getting late."

There were tents for Sam and Betsy and for Fran and Dale; one for Will, one for Federico and Berto, although they usually slept in hammocks, and a very large one intended for Pauline, Katie, and Sylvia, if she chose to use it. The large tent doubled as a dining room for everyone in wet weather. Despite generous-sized windows, given the climate all tents were stuffy. But raindrops fell as they began dinner inside the large tent, and Sylvia gave in.

After the meal Will talked about the forests and the rivers, until he was interrupted by a distant roar that perked everyone's ears up. "Listen!" he said, unnecessarily. The dull roar grew steadily louder, and nearer.

"Good Lord!" exclaimed Betsy, the woman from Chicago, "It sounds like a tornado coming!"

"Or a hurricane... " This from Florida-born Katie.

"No, you're not even warm." Their guide sat tranquilly, as the sound grew into an insane clamor all around them like a screeching witches' wind that made one's hair stand on end. Fran was near panic when Will, enjoying himself greatly, yelled over the din, "Howler monkeys!"

Instantly their expressions changed into delight as the forest continued to reverberate with the uncanny howls. Too soon the troop moved on, taking their racket with them, until the forest once again belonged to the insects— which did a nice job of entertaining the humans, as it was.

"What is *that*, now?" Sylvia asked, as a high-pitched whistle, similar to that of a train, pierced the night, gaining volume until it almost pierced the eardrum.

"It's a cicada," replied Will. "*One* cicada."

"The size of a bus," Betsy guessed.

Then there was "Whip! Whip!", the loud call of a frog, a bufo-something-or-other, which Will said was a celebration of the rain.

Federico stuck his head through the tent flap and said something to Will in rapid Portuguese. "He wants to know how dinner was."

Everyone broke into applause. They had been promised good food, including plenty of vegetarian fare, and Federico delivered. Rice and beans, Brazilian style, cucumber-tomato-onion salad, a little plain pasta, and some sort of meat dish, all seasoned expertly, with fruit for dessert.

Neither Federico nor Berto spoke more than a few words of English. Sylvia haltingly explained to their cook she was trying to learn Portuguese, and added a compliment:

"Er— *Eu gostei tudo. Foi ótimo.*" I liked everything. It was excellent.

Will regarded her curiously. "That's commendable. Not many people work on a language just for a short trip."

Sylvia settled into the tent with Katie and Pauline, after the others had cleared out. They were seventy miles from Manaus, so they were told, and that made her very happy.

*

"The Brazilian coffee we get at home is super; this tastes like shit."

"I heard that, Sam," Sylvia laughed as he and Betsy whirled around.

"The chocolate's better." Betsy sipped tentatively, then yawned at the rising sun.

"Let's try mixing it." Sylvia took a fresh, re-issued tin cup and poured a 50-50 blend. "Not bad! That's the solution." They quietly passed the word around.

"How was your night, everyone?" Will asked, as he headed to the boat with yet another armful of gear. He received varying replies.

"Mine was hell," Sylvia offered pleasantly. "Tonight, even if it's raining bufos, I want my hammock. The ground got harder by the hour."

"How can anyone sleep in all the commotion?" asked Dale, laughing. "It's noisier than Manhattan. Where was that buzz-saw coming from?" Yes, what *was* that, they all wanted to know.

"Ha! That's an amazing little katydid! Just one!" answered Will. "You'll get accustomed." And to Sylvia, a trifle snappishly, she thought: "And you'll get your hammock. Rain or starshine."

No one was truly complaining, not yet; they found it all great adventure, and pushed off in high spirits for another day of cruising.

Recrossing the Rio Negro at the Narrows, they continued north; before lunch they had reached the confluence of the Apuaú and the Rio Negro. The Condor slid across the tranquil surface of the water, skirting islands here and there, a virtual maze of them. Without knowing exactly when they left the Negro behind, the party moved into the wide mouth of the Apuaú, itself island-strewn; they were still threading their way through flooded forest.

Throughout the dream-like day, Will educated and entertained the group whenever he came across anything of interest, and in the interim he let them float in peace, absorbing their impressions; the world they'd left behind fell away bit by bit, the tight coil inside each of them gradually relaxed.

As for him, Sylvia noticed that when he was quiet a certain cast of melancholy dropped over his handsome features until he appeared to shake it off. Aside from that he was hard to read; he was evidently well-travelled, thirty-five years old, knowledgeable, high-strung. And for some reason, he didn't seem to like Sylvia very much.

She couldn't fathom why. She had kept a low profile the first couple of days, talking little, primarily listening and observing the others and their surroundings; she didn't see how she could've gotten on his nerves with her rare comments, though when she did venture a remark he tended to contradict her somewhat brusquely. Otherwise, except for the moment in the river he avoided eye contact, and sneered rather than smiled in her direction. Maybe it was her imagination.

It didn't matter. She found it more important that he had the sharpest eyes and ears any of them had ever encountered in a human. He spotted creatures that were camouflaged in the trees or on the far side of the river; he identified a species of bird or butterfly that was a mere fluttering speck or distant silhouette. He heard birds that weren't yet audible to the others and then "called them in" with a mating cry or a male-challenge call, which the bird would come to investigate. He could identify hundreds of birds of the Amazon and mimic their calls, when humanly possible. He could call other species, as well: insects, mammals, amphibians. That day he called in a pink river dolphin he had spotted.

The air was rich with a delicate fragrance of flowers and vegetation, bringing wistful smiles, as they inhaled deeply, to the faces of people whose daily lives were filled with rank odors they'd long ago accepted.

"Water time, everyone." Will passed the pitcher around, and everyone dutifully held out their tin cups. They began to see how easily dehydration could occur. Though it wasn't excessively hot— rarely over 90 degrees— it was consistently near 90% relative humidity. The least bit of exertion brought streams of sweat.

"I've noticed I don't feel very thirsty in this humid climate," Betsy observed.

Will heard her. "That's right; combine lack of thirst with all the perspiring we do, and you've a recipe for serious dehydration."

That night the group made camp at the site of an Indian home that had burned down. There was a clearing and several large, flat areas for the tents. Everyone had their river bath, this time with less squeamishness, and some washed shirts and underwear while they were at it. Sam hung his white jockey shorts on the tent line, strung from a tree.

"It'll help us find our tent after dark," he joked.

They ate under a starry sky this time, a tasty meal rather similar to the first. Sylvia yawned sleepily and looked forward to a little privacy, one of the other reasons she had wanted a hammock; it could be hung some distance from the tents.

But Katie had other ideas.

"I asked Will for a hammock, too," she told Sylvia after dinner.

"Oh?"

"Yes— but he gave me sort of a vague answer... "

Sylvia hoped that was because he sensed she wanted a shred of solitude; and his keen eyes that missed nothing had no doubt seen how Katie was attaching herself to Sylvia. The two women had chatted on the boat, and found themselves in agreement on many issues. Katie was surprisingly knowledgeable and well-travelled, Sylvia thought, for a young woman of twenty-one. Later she noticed that wherever she sat on the boat, Katie maneuvered for a position beside her.

Just before nightfall Sylvia saw two hammocks, side by side, suspended from the main posts of the burned-out house. *One for me, one for Katie*, she sighed.

But Katie approached her, saying, "Guess I won't be getting a hammock. Will said he's putting his there, and there's only room for two."

Sylvia's eyebrows rose. She hadn't known he liked a hammock. If he thought she'd be nervous sleeping out alone, she'd have to correct that notion right away. As she gathered her gear for bedtime, suddenly an idea struck her. Of course; that would explain why he didn't seem to like her. An old story: sexual tension, a little sparring... *Only two days in the wilds of Amazonia, and I have Katie on me like a Band-aid and a soap opera cranking up with the guide! How far do I have to go to leave the human drama behind?*

She walked down to the burned house, Will not far behind her. He cleared his throat awkwardly.

"I hope you don't mind a little company; it's such a nice night, I wanted to sleep under the stars, myself."

"It's okay, Will. The sky is a beautiful sight, isn't it?"

Before the two crawled into their hammocks, they juggled flashlights and shook the hammocks free of any interlopers, such as scorpions, at his insistence. "Do this each night, see?"

Then he demonstrated how one properly sleeps in a hammock.

"On the diagonal, see, so the hammock spreads out rather than curling around you like a corn husk."

Sylvia tried it, and he was right; it worked much better that way.

"You know," he began after they had settled in. "I've been trying to clarify everyone's personal goals for this trip, so I can keep my eyes open for anything that might be of interest. Yours were rather general on the application you filled out... Would you like to be more specific, or add anything?"

Sylvia hesitated. She might as well spill it.

"I was deliberately vague. I need to experience the rainforest because I'm writing a book, but it isn't scientific. The topic is a man who explored South American wilderness: Percy Harrison Fawcett, if you've ever heard of him."

"I have, in fact. He's quite well known in England, and actually, there's a sort of cult built up around him in Brazil."

"A cult?"

"Well, down in, let's see— somewhere south, maybe Mato Grosso, or Goiás?— there's a group of people living out in the wilds who believe he was really onto something with this search of his, for an unknown ruin or whatever it was... "

"I'd like to learn more about that group."

"I can't recall the details now... Let me think about it. When you get back, maybe you can get information from the Internet."

"Okay. I'm aware we're not in the area he explored, but I couldn't figure a practical way to retrace his trips, so I thought the Rio Negro would at least give me a sense of the forests."

"This group claims they *have* retraced his steps, now that you mention it. And I think I heard he kept some of his routes secret, and deliberately misled people; so he might've been in this region, or near it, at some time."

Lying a few feet apart, looking up at the Milky Way, they talked comfortably for almost an hour. He's all right, she thought sleepily.

"Good morning! Rise and shine!"

Six a.m., and the start of a daily routine. Will arose by his watch alarm, dressed, and walked among the tents calling reveille in English-prep-school tones.

"How was the hammock?" Katie asked Sylvia over cocoa-coffee and pancakes.

"Hey, that's the ticket for me. Slept like a corpse."

Sam walked toward the group, holding something on the end of a stick. It was his jockey shorts, or what was left of them. They were so full of gaping holes they were unrecognizable.

"Good Lord!" laughed Will. "The rodents must've enjoyed a cotton snack, or maybe they needed nest lining... Okay, all, let's pack up our gear, time to get going."

Farther up the Apuaú, Berto cut the motor and the Condor drifted to a narrow dock floating in a quiet backwater of the river. In the green depths of the forest a small hut could barely be seen; a young Indian man, wearing T-shirt and shorts, walked toward them. He had been listening as the boat approached, an uncommon event this far upriver; when he heard the motor slowing he came to see who his visitors might be. He smiled upon recognizing the Condor, and Will.

"Oi, Armando!" Will called. The Indian nodded shyly as Will quickly introduced him to the group.

After a brief conversation standing on the dock, Armando nodded decisively and hopped into the boat. It was as simple as that; he didn't take any belongings or secure anything at home, he just left.

"Armando is an old friend of mine," explained Will, "And he's going to take us to a river only Indians visit, called the Bariaú. He told me about it once and I've always wanted to go up there."

"He's never been there," Fran whispered to Dale. "We're relying on this Armando now?"

The Condor slid smoothly upriver, passing a little hut not far from Armando's home. This is the last one, Sylvia heard him say in Portuguese. Will turned to face the others.

"That's it for so-called civilization, folks; we've passed the frontier. No more settlers."

Sylvia's spirits soared higher. They were in true wilderness, something most modern-day people never experienced in their lifetimes.

Armando positioned himself at the point of the bow, watching the river. By late morning he'd spotted the Bariaú to the left, and called back to Berto. The Condor turned north into this flow which only the Indians had named, one that didn't appear on any of their maps. Will carefully drew it into his own, estimating the distances. No one but Armando had any idea what lay ahead, and he had told Will there was a series of cataracts and beautiful, untouched terrafirme forest to explore. Infrequently an Indian or two might make their way there, he said, to look for gems, but they stayed close to the river.

The Bariaú quickly narrowed to a width of fifty feet or less. The water, which at first had looked like clear root beer, then Cherry Coke, soon became the color of garnets, or blood.

"Cranberry juice!" Fran insisted. "'Blood' sounds, well, too gory..." she laughed uneasily.

Armando spoke, and Will translated: "He says the water's pure and good to drink. He thinks the odd stain comes from these shrubs, which are common all along the banks." Campina, another type of forest for their notebooks, lined the river on both sides, its low, wiry trees and shrubs flourishing in sandy, acid soil.

They weren't the only life-forms that liked it, the visitors discovered when they tried to make a pit stop.

"EEEEEE— Ants!!" squealed Pauline, dancing around in a panic, her ample breasts bouncing up and down.

"Be calm, be calm— " said Will, brushing at dozens of healthy-sized ants swarming Pauline's pant legs. She released another earsplitting scream.

"Gees, you'd think she was covered in vipers," Sylvia mumbled to Betsy. "Yow! I'm in 'em, too! We're on an ant megalopolis! Ow!" She was laughing and cursing at the same time as everyone yelled, stamped, brushed, and then ran headlong for the water, nursing painful bites.

"Oh, well, I didn't really need to pee anyway!" Katie panted. Pauline's reaction amused them, but privately Sylvia was a little alarmed as she watched Will try to calm the woman. *If she reacts this way to ants, what if something truly awful happened?*

They continued upstream at minimum speed. The bottom was rocky, the crimson water clear as crystal. Armando was alert, directing Berto around snags and rocks. Now and then the bottom of the wooden boat scraped ominously on stone, and finally became caught, dragging to a halt. Everyone had to disembark and, standing in thigh-deep water with uncertain footing, help heave the boat free.

"*De lados,*" Berto shouted. "*É perigoso detrás.*" Stay on the sides, he told them. It was too dangerous to be at the stern; the tempo of the Bariaú's flow had quickened, and the Condor could jump backward at any time.

Katie gave Sylvia an evil grin and a wink as they gripped the boat, waiting for Berto's signal to heave. "Leeches!" she yelled gleefully.

"Yike!" Sylvia screeched. "Leeches!"

"Be calm— there are no leeches— " Will began, then he saw their smiles. "Stop that!" he said, laughing, "You'll start a panic. There *are no leeches*, people— "

He was too late. Pauline was already scrambling over the side of the boat, prompting Berto to curse her for all he was worth. But her violent rocking of the Condor caused it to suddenly release itself and surge downstream. "Heave!" Berto yelled, *"Empuja!"*

Everyone heaved, Berto gunned the motor, and the boat sprang free into deeper water. They had a fast swim and an awkward struggle to catch up and get back aboard, where Katie and Sylvia collapsed on a bench, dripping wet and laughing uncontrollably.

"Not cute! I saw 'The African Queen', too!" stormed Pauline.

"You're very bad girls," Will shook his finger at the two. "No dessert tonight for you!" But he looked cheerier than they had yet seen him. The others were in high spirits, feeling proud of themselves, with the exception of the steaming Pauline and a sheepish-looking Fran, who had been right behind her over the side.

Their real-life adventure had begun.

"Looks as if this is as far as we go, folks." The group stood in the shallows as Will and Berto surveyed the river. After a couple of hours they had reached a place where the Bariaú widened considerably and another stream joined it from the west. At this junction there was a series of rapids and small cascades; here and there in the churning reddish water were calm pools. On the west bank, some yards below the stream, was a large area of flat, smooth rock. Scrubby campina growth formed a narrow buffer zone between the river and the towering terrafirme forest.

While Berto and Federico found a safe place to anchor the boat, Will offered a proposal.

"Let's unload our stuff here, where it's shallow, and organize it all on those flat rocks. We can hike into the terrafirme about one-quarter mile and set up camp, then later we'll make trails and explore deeper into the forest. Sound good?"

Everyone nodded.

"But we'll take all our meals at the riverside," he added. "It's much easier for Federico to cook on the boat, and besides, you'll want frequent dips in the river, I'm sure.'"

That was their cue; while Will and the Brazilians fussed with the boat, the others quickly unloaded their gear, trudging through the rocky shallows. As soon as they'd dumped their belongings on the warm, dry rock, everyone headed back into the inviting waters of the Bariaú. No leafy, squishy bottom here, nor tepid, opaque water; they walked on coarse sand and gravel and refreshed their bodies in a cool, transparent flow.

"About 74 degrees, I'd say," Sam estimated as he leaned back into a foaming cascade.

Soon, Will, sweating heavily, joined the rest in the water, dunking his head in a pool of bubbles. "The Indians sometimes come here for amethysts, Armando says. They use them to barter with river traders, though truly high-quality stones are scarce." He scooped up a handful of gravel from the water churning beneath him, and examined it. Several pretty pieces of quartz lay in his palm, but no amethyst. "Reach into the pockets between rocks, at the base of little cascades; they tend to settle there."

Some of the party caught the amethyst bug and dipped into the rapids with gusto, Armando, Federico, and Berto in particular. But Sylvia quickly lost interest in it.

Berto and Federico led the way, blazing a trail with gleaming machetes. It was hard going through underbrush that was thick and tangled. The least exertion in mid-afternoon warmth and humidity brought streams of perspiration. The group followed, laden with gear and unaccustomed to the climate, panting.

The ground was covered with layers of leaves that occasionally concealed a treacherous hole, some of them soon discovered. They needed to watch their step, but the grandeur of their surroundings lured the eye upward. The larger trees towered to 150 feet or more; smaller trees grew close together, generally straight and skinny. The canopy of leaves was far above their heads, and that was where the action was: birds, monkeys and other creatures were noisy but difficult to see.

On the ground, the world was damp, shaded, and redolent with earth-must. Daily forays to the bright riverside, with its fresh breezes, would indeed be welcome. Dark clouds were moving in with a rumble of thunder, and before long rain pattered on the canopy above, which functioned, for a while, as an umbrella.

"Takes a few minutes for the rain to work its way through all those branches," said Will, glancing upward.

They came to a small area where there were mostly shrubs but few trees.

"This is probably as close to a clearing as we'll find," Will said, turning to speak to Federico and Berto. They set about hacking at the smaller bushes, trying to make room for four tents which would have to be fairly close together. Berto and Federico would swing hammocks in the boat for themselves.

Will looked at Sylvia. "A hammock for you? Are you sure?"

She nodded firmly. The brief shower had passed and the sun was back. If it rained again, she would deal with it somehow. "And please, ask them not to put it too close to the tents; I'm a light sleeper. Okay?"

While the Brazilians made camp, Will whacked the trail a bit farther, leading them through the virgin forest where they would spend the next few days.

"Later the fellows can cut the trail another quarter-mile or so," he said over his shoulder.

The party hadn't gone too many steps when Will paused beside a large tree.

"Aha! I thought I smelled cat. And it's a big one." He pointed at long, vertical shreds of bark, starting about seven feet up the trunk and dangling downward a few feet. "See? The jaguar stretched itself up high and sharpened its claws."

"Jaguar?" repeated Fran, dully.

"Yes, of course, though I doubt we'll be lucky enough to see one. They're terribly shy of people or anything out of the ordinary."

She looked doubtful, and a little pale.

When they returned to the base camp, it seemed small and fragile amidst the vast, dense jungle.

"*Onde está o meu hede?*" Sylvia asked Berto, Where's my hammock?

He gestured for her to follow. He'd made a narrow trail that wound into the trees and ended some distance from the tents, far enough so that she could indeed neither hear nor see the others, and there hung her hammock. It looked quite lonely and vulnerable, but she said nothing, thinking it may have been a little joke to test her courage, since she *had* asked not to be close to the group.

Some of the others joined them.

"Good grief!" exclaimed Sam. "Will, you're going to let her sleep here? Are you sure she'll be all right?"

"Yes," added Dale, the quietest member of the group, "After all, we know there's a jaguar in the vicinity."

"Not necessarily," Will replied. "It most likely moved on. They roam over a large territory, and usually, as I said, avoid people. Jags

89

don't creep up on camps and snatch people from hammocks. They prefer to stick to their usual prey. She'll be fine."

Though this was no doubt normally the case, Sylvia knew anything was possible. They had invaded the big cat's territory. And she had read Fawcett's skin-tingling accounts of jaguars prowling their camps, so she wasn't so sanguine.

Still, she reasoned, one had to look at the overall odds of a problem, which were small. And a point no one had brought up was the false security of tents, which were no real protection against a determined animal. Besides the fact that she didn't want to feel like a coward, she truly did want a little privacy, so that settled it.

Before the light was utterly gone from the forest, they hiked back to the riverside for dinner beneath the Milky Way; beans and rice and the same old stuff with it, they were realizing, but they were hungry and it was good. Some of the group carried cups of wine into the river for a starlight bath. Their laughter rang out in the night, hushing the crickets and nightbirds who paused to listen to these strange creatures, splashing in the falls.

Eventually they headed wearily back through the woods by flashlight, single file on the narrow trail.

"Ah, look!" Will bent and shined his light on a column of leafcutter ants, carrying their burden of green leaf sections. The ants continued about their business, weaving under and over debris of the forest floor, as if unaware of the humans or the bright light. How many times had Sylvia seen such ants in nature films? Now she wondered how many tiny treasures they had trampled in the dark.

"We can locate creatures by their eyeshine," he said quietly as they walked. "Everyone, hold your flashlights at eye level, like so, and v-e-r-y slowly scan the woods, and— oh, there! See them? Two tiny, tiny lights beaming back at us?"

Walking carefully through the underbrush, the group approached the glowing eyes, hoping their source would remain where it was. As it happened, they belonged to a wolf spider, which was about four inches across.

"These fellows can jump," Will mentioned.

Fran showed them she could jump, too, bounding backwards a few spaces. "How f-far?"

"Ha! I don't know, a yard or so, but you're a bit large to be their prey. Relax. In future, folks, notice the eyeshine color. Spiders tend to reflect green or blue, vertebrates are red or orange."

They reached their little camp, pausing to admire the elegant—there was no other word for it— latrine which Berto had constructed at the end of a short path. First he had dug a hole two feet deep. Next, he cut a small tree into lengths which he nailed together to form a sturdy stand, on which he lashed a toilet seat they'd brought along; then he placed his makeshift toilet over the hole. Every day he would shovel a little dirt into the hole, to discourage flies and odor. He had even made a bent stick into a holder for toilet paper, covered with plastic in case of rain. Last, he hung a tarp from the trees, for privacy.

Will announced to the group, as they said their goodnights, that since there had been some concern about "a certain someone" he would hang his own hammock nearby, even though he had pitched his tent, "Which I still may need if it rains."

"Well, I'm glad to hear it," remarked Fran. "I mean, now that it's dark even the latrine looks awfully far from my tent, and I'm hoping I don't have to get up in the night... I don't see," she addressed Sylvia, "How on earth you could have the nerve to sleep outside."

Though Sylvia was proud of her "nerve", she was secretly relieved Will would be nearby. Even by day the forest was intimidating; by night it was suddenly filled with unknowns.

Will and Sylvia held the light for each other as they shook out their hammocks, only a few feet apart, then each of them crawled in. They looked upward at the canopy so far above them. Scraps of sky and a few stars were visible through the leaves; but the meager starlight could not penetrate to the floor of the forest. When Sylvia brought her gaze downward, the blackness was profound. She literally could not see her hand before her face. But a few friendly fireflies glowed and winked at them.

"Fireflies," she breathed softly. "It's been years since I've seen them. Look: There are two types."

"Yes, that little, greenish one, and the big, bright, golden fellow! I must learn more about these varieties..."

"Hey! Foxfire!" Sylvia exclaimed.

"Huh?"

"Will, look down, at the ground!" There were dimly glowing patches here and there.

"I saw that, but I assumed it was moonlight breaking through the trees."

"There's no moon tonight, remember?"

"Quite right! It's phosphorescence, then; what did you call it—'foxfire'?"

They discovered, after switching on the light a couple of times to examine various leaves, it was only certain ones, at just the right stage of decay, that glowed.

"Even rot is beautiful out here," Sylvia sighed.

"'Girl of the forest', you were named appropriately. Or prophetically."

"That's me, sylvan Sylvia." She yawned broadly. "You're one of the few people I've met who're aware what 'Sylvia' means; even my parents weren't. Do you know what Garth means?"

"No... "

"Protector of the Garden. How's *that* for coincidence?"

The great forest was full of magic, so deep and dark yet sprinkled with its own sources of illumination. Having a companion helped to chase away the shadows. But she was getting terribly sleepy, and Will didn't seem to want to say goodnight. He was keyed up, reluctant to settle down, chattering on.

"Will," she finally said, "Please, let's sleep now."

Sylvia fell right away into a deep sleep and was far, far away when a voice abruptly woke her.

"It's raining; wake up!"

"Damn," she said groggily, not wanting to move. But Will had his flashlight on and was hastily gathering his bedding. Only a few drops had made their way through the thick canopy so far, but Sylvia, too sleepy to think, followed suit. As she gathered her bedding, it suddenly began to rain harder.

"Quick! My tent is closest!" They raced down the path, and as they plunged through the flap he said, "You can go to the big tent if you want, or stay here. It's up to you."

In the uneven light, she couldn't see his face clearly. But even as addled with drowsiness as she was, she knew the implications of her decision.

"I'll stay."

They sorted out their tangled bedding, and Will insisted she use his sleeping pad. She settled in at one side of the roomy tent, and for a while they lay listening to rain pelting the canvas. They were in total darkness.

Sylvia wondered how he would make his move.

Soon she heard rustling sounds and felt him pull his bedding close to hers.

"Nothing but roots over there," he mumbled. "Hope you don't mind."

She smiled in silence. He was so close she could feel his breath and body heat. The rain drummed, tension and expectancy buzzing like an electric barrier between them for a few still moments.

Then he chuckled ironically. "Funny how things turn out, isn't it?"

Abruptly the wall was down. "Yes, it is," she chuckled back.

He snuggled closer and quickly found her hand without a shred of light to guide him. With his other hand he stroked her face. She raised her head and kissed him lightly. Odd, how they could instantly locate body parts in pitch blackness.

Sylvia hadn't met anyone she wanted in a couple of years; she'd lost interest in the concept of romance, and wondered at the years she'd spent in its pursuit. She wasn't sure why she was doing this now, except, perhaps, to find out if she were alive or dead to such feelings.

Now, in the dark, wet, Amazon night, creeping through summertime toward her forty-fifth birthday, she thought she felt a spark of life; but it may have only been a spell cast by exotic surroundings, the rich earth smells, the blackness, the pounding rain.

At 5:45 Sylvia heard Will's watch alarm. He dressed, and soon he was calling his lilting "Good morning!" to the others. She heard someone asking, What on earth had Sylvia done in all that rain? and his explanation that she had dashed into his tent, which was closer, and she didn't want to awaken Katie and Pauline in the big tent.

She was sure this raised a few eyebrows; at breakfast Katie and Pauline eyed her curiously. Will and Sylvia were careful to behave no differently, though he seemed lighter of heart that day. He found a rare flower and casually handed it to Sylvia, as if showing her a lovely species to share with the others... But it was a gift.

The group explored the side creek, and found a calm pool where they floated around like fallen leaves. Sylvia noticed a unique spider on a rock; so hair-fine and utterly flat that it looked as though someone had drawn it with a sharp pencil— until she touched it with a stick and it sprang to life and scurried away.

Unfortunately, the horseflies found them.

"Damn," complained Betsy, "There always has to be some blasted pest in Paradise, doesn't there? These things *hurt*."

The flies' modus operandi was to swarm around, buzzing madly, until one of the bolder ones dashed in for a taste of human flesh; then one by one the others joined in. They had a diabolical way of biting the same spot repeatedly, until it was tender and juicy. They were particularly numerous up the little stream, which Sylvia named Horsefly Creek in their honor.

"It's too bad," said Dale. "I like that shady little pool. I get burned in this powerful sun."

Katie had been careful of her skin, too, but now she had a new worry. She approached Will, lifting her shirt to reveal a creamy mid-section. "What do you think this is?" she asked worriedly.

Will examined the angry red welts as she added, "They itch like hell."

"Chiggers," he pronounced. "Very common here. I told everyone you shouldn't be sitting on logs and the like, remember?"

"Oh, yeah... Will they get worse? Will they leave scars?" Will tried to soothe her fears, but she didn't seem to be listening. Frequently during the day she peered at the bumps, and talked of nothing else.

"I have some of them, too, Katie." Sylvia showed Katie her waist, where the little parasites had embedded themselves in the skin, merrily sucking away her blood. "They're pregnant females, Will said. On my ankles, too, see? It's my small way of contributing to the ecosystem."

Katie smiled in wan appreciation of Sylvia's efforts to cheer her; but she was becoming obsessed, alarmingly, some of them thought. Will offered her a salve to ease the tormenting itch, but she refused, saying she preferred to suffer. Most of the others began to avoid her.

"All she can say is 'chigger-chigger-chigger', like some kind of locust," Fran griped in a nasty whisper, when dusk and dinnertime brought them all back to the vicinity of the flat rock.

"Cut her some slack," Sylvia retorted. She was rapidly deciding the only person in the group she didn't like was Fran, who talked constantly about herself and her professional feats, unless she was saying something hateful about someone else.

"What is that, a bird?" someone asked, as they hushed their chatter to listen to four clear, rather sad notes, falling down the musical scale. Will told them the proper Latin name, which Sylvia immediately forgot, remembering only his whimsical rendition of the sound, put into these words: "Poor me, all alone..."

"Speaking of being alone, Will," Sam asked, "Have you ever spent any time in the forest by yourself? It seems to me it could be intimidating."

Will paused for a moment. "Well, no. But a naturalist friend of mine once set off for a week on his own. After a couple of days he couldn't take it, he got a bad case of the creeps and returned."

"I don't blame him," Fran stated firmly. "I think it would be terrifying to be out here alone."

"Listen," Sylvia began, as she and Will lay once again in their hammocks— she refused to sleep on the lumpy ground, man or no man— "I'd like to skip the morning cruise, if you don't mind; I'd love some of that terrifying alone-time, for a change."

Will laughed ruefully. "*That* I well understand. What do you want to do with your solitude?"

"I don't know... walk in the forest, relax at the river?" She shrugged.

"Okay. Just do me a favor and take a snakebite kit along; I'll put it in your backpack in the morning. Remember how to use it?"

"Yes." Will gave the group a lesson in emergency procedures the first day.

"Another thing. If you go in the forest, keep to the trail. You have no idea, Sylvia, how easy it is— and how terrible— to get lost once you're away from the river. There are no landmarks; everything looks the same. You lose all sense of direction. And if you shout, no one hears you, because the forest absorbs sound."

"I promise I'll be careful. I need to be alone, that's all; I'm tired of always walking in a line of people."

"I understand. Especially *these* people, eh?"

"Oh, it's not them, so much; Fran's the only one who gets my goat sometimes."

"Really? I'm taking a dislike to everyone, except you and maybe Sam and Betsy. You're the only normal ones. The others are crackers."

"They're an odd bunch, I'll admit. They have so many fears, even about little things... "

" --Like Pauline nearly passing out when she sees a bloody column of ants— "

"Yeah. Makes you wonder why they wanted to camp in the Amazon at all." She picked up a glowing leaf. "Look at this. Wonder why human decay, feces and all, is so ugly? Why can't a dead body phosphoresce like those leaves, or release a delicious scent?"

"Good question... But to a maggot, a dead body's a thing of beauty; and to a fly, a dung pile, is, well— "

"A fragrant feast! So, it's a matter of perspective. Guess these things weren't meant to attract *us*. The bacteria could make us sick."

"Speaking of attraction, won't you come join me in my hammock? We can muss up my bed, not yours."

"Will this work?"

"Let's find out. Climb in."

Soon the leafy tops of two skinny trees began swaying and shaking. It flicked through Sylvia's mind that the others might wonder what was making the clamor in the trees, on a still, windless night. Mating sloths! she'd claim. The hammock bounced energetically, then all at once there was a loud CRACK! and Sylvia's bottom hit the cushioning leaves.

She erupted into laughter, and Will clapped his hand over her mouth.

"Don't laugh! Or they'll know for sure we broke the bloody tree!"

He groped for his light and beamed it upward. "Look at that! Were we lucky!" The broken tree had caught against the side of another tree. Lucky, indeed. "This tree is hardwood; it might've done real damage to our heads," he whispered.

Quietly they tied the loose end of Will's hammock to the nearby tree that held an end of Sylvia's hammock. "This is the strongest tree around, and the only one I trust right now," he said.

But when it was time for sleep and Sylvia returned to her hammock, being fastened to the same tree caused a problem. Whenever Will stirred, the tree jerked, and his movement was telegraphed to Sylvia's hammock.

"We'll have to tie your hammock to another tree," Sylvia said wearily.

"I don't know if there's a nearby tree strong enough... And I don't feel like searching. I'll just go sleep in my tent. Do you mind? You can come, too."

"Uh— no, thanks, no more hard ground for me."

"You'll be all right here, and I'm nearby. Feel free to sneak in with me if you get nervous, or if it rains."

"Okay. Good night."

"Here, keep my torch; it's quite powerful; I'll take your silly light." Sylvia had brought only the smallest Maglite on the trip, a mistake she regretted. He switched it on and disappeared down the path.

Well, she told herself, *I'm not really all alone; Will's tent is only a short walk down the path. Of course, this is the natural haunt of jaguars, and we smelled cat again on our evening hike— I smelled it this time, too, a musky scent— and jaguars do hunt at night...*

I wonder if things ever fall out of trees here, like scorpions or spiders? And Fawcett often had rats in his hammock, so I suppose they can crawl down the ropes...

Since childhood Sylvia had not slept in a totally dark room; now she was in the deepest black night imaginable, listening to all manner of mysterious movements around her. Leaves suddenly rustled in the trees; there were odd little "plops' here and there on the ground, even small footsteps. Just opossums, maybe, she thought, switching on Will's light to check out every sound. She held the light at eye level, hoping she wouldn't see large, red-orange eyeshine. There was nothing. At last she grew tired of it.

I can't keep flashing the light around at every sound; he'll see it and think something's wrong, and besides, I must sleep...

She focussed on a sharp, twinkling star peeping at her through the sheltering canopy, and told herself she had protection of the highest kind, and nothing would happen to her that wasn't meant to be. Fatalistic, maybe, but it was comforting to give up the need for control, along with its wellspring, fear. Out of this poisoned source flowed so much that was unhealthy and confining. She yawned, following the lazy flight of a golden firefly that came to hover near her like a warm little guardian. *I choose to believe even the tiny things will watch over me. And, hey, if I'm devoured by a jaguar in the Amazon, it'll make a sensational end; people will speak of it for years.*

She slept like a baby in the soft arms of her hammock, and, strangely, with a deeper sense of security than she ever found with a telephone beside her, in a dead-bolted house surrounded by neighbors.

*

Dawn's gentle arrival brought Sylvia many rewards. She opened her eyes to see, in the canopy high above, dozens of birds flitting through leafy branches, their song as fresh as the morning air. Her bedsheet was covered in a blanket of leaves and small, orchid-like flowers, and while she watched, another large leaf drifted slowly down and landed on the ground beside her with a soft little sound. So that was the "plop" she kept hearing the night before. How threatening.

She felt sorry for the others who slept in their close, muggy tents, missing the foxfire and the chance to challenge both forest and fear, missing the glorious awakening to a great green arch of trees overhead. A cathedral ceiling, but one alive with movement.

She heard Will waking the others for a morning cruise. It was 6:00.

Someone crept near and called her name softly.

"It's me, Betsy. Don't get up, I'm just taking your picture." The camera flashed, and then Sylvia heard receding footsteps. She drifted deliciously back to sleep.

When she finally arose, it was a small luxury to get dressed in an unhurried fashion, without worrying about keeping the others waiting, to collect her things and walk slowly through the woods to the river, alone on the narrow trail with no one's back in front of her, stopping when she wanted without holding anyone up.

She ambled downstream to the boat, where Federico was washing dishes. He had saved her some pancakes and toast and she ate them cold.

"Olhe," he said, nodding toward the flat rocks.

She turned to see Katie, spreading her laundry in the sun. She had stayed behind, too! Federico laughed when he saw Sylvia's expression.

He told her, as best she could understand, that Will had been annoyed with Katie and advised her firmly to leave Sylvia in peace.

To her credit, she did. Sylvia walked over to exchange a few friendly words with her before going off on her own; Katie mumbled something about wanting to do a little data-collection, but Sylvia never heard the word "chiggers" even once.

After a quick dip in Horsefly Pool, Sylvia plunged back into terrafirme.

When she'd passed their camp and started down the continuing trail, she began watching for cuts on trees, remembering Will's warning. "Everything looks the same. You lose all sense of direction..." As she walked, she made sure there was an obvious cut both ahead of and behind her.

It was, at first, eerie to be alone in an endless forest, so far from any form of civilization. Jaguars came to mind again, but she convinced herself they primarily hunt at night. On the whole it was better to hike alone; all around her there was only the forest, and she paused and listened to birds without human sound or distraction. At one point a flock of noisy parrots landed in a tall tree above her.

The trail eventually reached a dip where a small stream bubbled, and there it ended. She wanted to sit for a while, but where? Logs harbor chiggers, they had learned, and swarm with ants. (Ants: the most ubiquitous rainforest inhabitant, and probably the most troublesome. Amazon ants also bear the distinction of stinging like hell, she now knew.) A huge bee took an interest in her, and then a horsefly. Ignoring all these, she spread her rain poncho on a log and sat. It was hard to truly lose herself in meditation; the log was uncomfortable, the horsefly aggravating, and she knew she had to stay alert and wary.

But I'm alone! she thought triumphantly. *Unless, of course, you count the hundreds of life forms surrounding me, the ones that fly, crawl, burrow, slither, and, um, photosynthesize.*

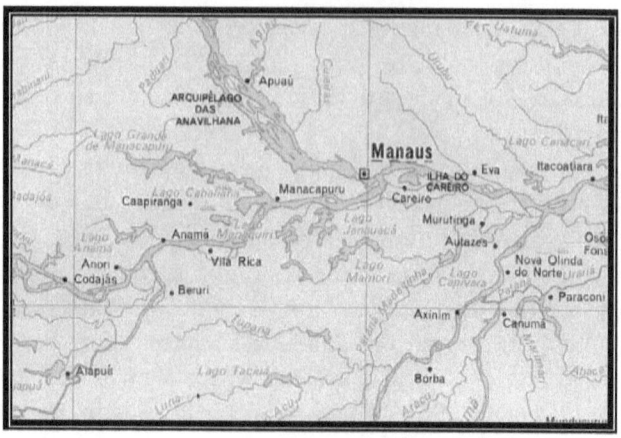

SYLVIA, CHAPTER 3
AMAZONAS: BLACKWATER, WHITEWATER

"Look, people; Federico has a little treat for you." Will and Federico approached the group, carrying open boxes. Those who had gone cruising were comparing notes on the morning's adventures with the two women who had stayed behind. Everyone lounged on the rocks where Horsefly Creek met the Bariaú; a gigantic, overhanging tree shaded them, and they dipped their feet and splashed their faces in the water, trying to cool off.

"What do you have there?" Fran peered into the boxes. "Oh! Coconuts!"

Federico was rewarded with grateful smiles and a heartfelt "Obrigado" from each as he handed out drinking coconuts; he had lopped off their tops and inserted colorful straws.

"They're cold!" exclaimed Sam, helping to pass them around. "How'd you manage that?"

"They've been down at the bottom of the ice chest," Will explained.

"Mmm, so perfect... " Katie's eyes rolled back with pleasure. "Just what we all needed."

They drank the sweet, refreshing coconut water, the music of two streams mingling as one soothing song. Sylvia looked around the group. All of them were so vulnerable, barely capable of surviving in the wild. Fawcett abruptly came to mind, and she wondered how he would've fared in the modern concrete jungles of New York City or Chicago, intricate and brutal in their own way. He'd find them hard to fathom, just as she had no inkling what the Amazon had been like for the early explorers who blazed paths others would follow; others who'd sip from coconuts cooled by ice, in the middle of the rainforest, and play at exploring. If they had not been born too late, were there any in the group who would've followed Fawcett?

Katie stood knee-deep in the stream beside Sylvia. Suddenly a snake about two feet long drifted around her ankles and then, as Katie felt it and moved, fearfully darted away to hide under the rocks. Katie merely laughed with mild surprise. The others who had seen laughed, too, but nervously. They hadn't thought much about water snakes.

Dale slipped down the rocks behind Sylvia and tapped her shoulder. "Did you hear? Sam found a fungus this morning before our cruise, and he and Will think it could be a discovery."

" 'Previously undescribed' is the jargon," put in Betsy.

"Yeah, I'm naming it 'Jock Itch'," Sam called.

"Fungi *are* his specialty, all kinds," Betsy said wryly. "Anyway, he didn't want to take the specimen, since there was only one, so I got micro-lens photos and he's making spore prints."

Sylvia's thoughts were once again brought to Fawcett and the painstaking drawings he had made of plants, animals, terrain. It thrilled her that all these years later, people were still uncovering the rainforest's secrets.

"That's the way it is here," Will added, joining them on the largest rock. "You find one individual sample of a species, and you can look for miles or for years before you find another. As they say, 'Common species are rare and rare species are common.' So only a mere fraction of all the life forms here have been described and named, including insects and vertebrates."

"Well, I have a name for the ant that was in my shoe this morning," Pauline interjected, "But Fran can't print it." She was soaking her red, swollen toe as they spoke.

"Funny how people attract what they hate and fear, isn't it?" Katie whispered to Sylvia.

Everyone bathed after lunch. Some slipped their clothes off once safely in the water. Modesty was fast disappearing. They squatted in the skimpy bushes whenever necessary, without a thought for anyone who might see; Fran and Dale merely turned their backs like the men and used their funnels. When anyone needed to change clothes, he or she walked off a few paces, turned away, and stripped off. The unwritten rule was that no one should pay any attention.

Late that night, after an hour-long evening cruise, Will found Sylvia sitting alone by the Bariaú and gave her his flashlight. "You can use this," he said in a low tone. "I prefer to sleep in my tent and I won't need it. Are you sleepy?"

"Very."

"So am I. And exhausted, in general. Did you enjoy the night cruise?"

"Yes! I wasn't aware baby emerald boas were pink."

"The term is 'juvenile', dear girl."

"Will, you don't like sleeping in your hammock?"

"No, I can feel no-see-ums biting my face out there."

She hesitated. "I don't feel any, and my skin's super-sensitive to them."

"You might feel them later. Come sleep in my tent; just be sure to slip out at dawn, back to your hammock."

"Hmm... I don't think so. I slept so well out there last night. But thanks."

He said nothing for a moment. Then, "Have it your way. See you in the morning." He gave her hand a squeeze, and called to the others. "Time to hike back to camp, folks."

This time, though she kept the big light in her hammock, she didn't need it. She lay in pitch darkness, listening to all the mysterious movements of flora and fauna, imagining what they were: a large rodent climbing down a tree and jumping with a soft ker-plop to the ground; little creatures scurrying though the leaves; the plip-plop of dewdrops. Very comfortable and tired, she soon drifted off.

There had been a brief shower during the night, but Sylvia hadn't moved. She was always a little damp anyway, she thought groggily; what was the difference?

At breakfast, things were tense. Fran was mad at Dale for not arranging the tent underliner correctly, she said, so they'd gotten wet. Pauline was furious with Will because she found a small puddle in the big tent, which was somehow all his fault. Will blew up at Katie, who had imperiously contradicted him for the umpteenth time on a botanical detail. He grabbed some rags and stormed off to dry Pauline's damned puddle.

"But he's *wrong*," Katie whispered to Sylvia as they ate.

"I believe you, though I think that isn't the point. When he's obviously mistaken, he admits it, you know. I think it's the *way* you correct him that's irksome, Katie; your manner."

They had only two more days to explore the Bariaú terrafirme, to bathe in the garnet stream and dip their hands in search of gems. They had dubbed the area Amethyst Falls; and since an unmotivated Sylvia hadn't found anything more exciting than quartz, Will gave her a couple of small amethysts he dredged up. During the long, lazy day, he calmed down and was mollified by the sighting of an undescribed bird, which he was able to photograph with a zoom lens.

"Well, if anyone should know birds, it's you," said Katie, trying to placate him. She was rewarded with a slight smile and a nod.

On the last day, another early morning cruise was planned, but Sylvia again remained behind, telling Will she needed more time alone in the forest. He understood.

"But we have other interesting areas to see, Sylvia; it's time to break camp and move on."

After camp was empty she arose from her swinging bed and struck out on the path. Everything, save the birds, was very quiet and peaceful. She made her way carefully, having learned to be careful of touching things. Several of the party had grasped little trees, a type of palm, whose trunks bristled with needle-sharp spikes containing a toxin that stung their hands for hours.

At the end of the trail she settled herself on the log. She was beginning to grasp the real meaning of *saudade*, the Portuguese word describing painful longing and sweet nostalgia merged into one emotion. This place was as far from the man-made world as she might ever get in her life, and the hours were passing faster than she could savor them. She loved being far, far away in the vastness, a little speck of human life under the towering trees; lost from the world. Why was that so compelling?

After a couple of hours, her watch— damned watch!— told her it was time to go, and she started back down the path to camp.

There was a loud shriek behind Sylvia.

"Spider!!" Fran and Dale sat paralyzed, eyes bulging.

Sylvia was by herself on the front row of the boat, the unsheltered bench. No one else wanted it, and she was now so deeply brown that the mid-morning sun wouldn't burn her. She wanted an unobstructed view of the Bariaú as they floated downstream.

"Be calm!" Will yelled back at the two, who looked ready to abandon ship.

"It's right above your head!" Dale shouted to Sylvia. There was nothing directly above her head but sky; she leaned back, and on the inside edge of the overhead shelter was a large brown spider, some three inches across, perhaps one of the smaller wolf spiders. She shrugged and relaxed back in her seat, amused by their overreaction. The trip was revealing how much fear and loathing of nature some people feel, even those who journey afar to experience it. She glanced back and saw the spider crawl around to the roof, where their gear was strapped. Ironic if it found its way into Fran's duffel, she thought wickedly.

Katie looked at her appealingly. "Don't you want to sit back here?" she asked, patting the bench between her and Pauline. Katie avoided the sun like poison.

"Not now, maybe later." Sylvia smiled at her. In a while, she would sit by Katie and teasingly ask, "How are your chiggers? Are they getting fat and healthy on your blood?" But right now, Will was climbing up to join her at the bow and she was fine just where she was. Fran and Dale sat behind them, still nervous, Katie and Pauline in the next row— Sylvia had begun to notice that Pauline was constantly staring at her; it was unnerving— and Betsy and Sam behind them. Federico and stacks of supplies took the next row, and Berto was almost completely hidden at the back, with the motor, leaning to his left to see ahead. When Berto helped her stow her gear on board, Sylvia had smelled alcohol on his breath— not for the first time. And it wasn't even noon.

The water level had dropped, and a couple of times they had to "get out and push," as Will put it; which had its exciting moments, as once the boat was free, it surged ahead with the strong current and they had to climb aboard quickly.

They reached the Apuaú and continued to the burned-out Indian home where they had camped. The owners were busily rebuilding, but they paused for a visit; not to do so would be rude, Will explained. The group had a swim while he chatted with the Indians. After a few minutes he walked down to the river's edge, looking pale and shaken.

"What is it?" Sylvia asked, alarmed.

He swallowed a couple of times. "Well... " Everyone had gathered to listen, and he looked around hesitantly. "It seems that four hunters— they were poaching jaguars, actually— were in terrafirme forest recently... Their habit was for two to hunt at night while the other two slept in camp, then vice versa during the day— " He stopped.

"Go on," urged Sam.

"When the daytime hunters returned to camp, they found the two hammocks soaking in blood, the bodies of their comrades still lying there. A jaguar had killed both of them."

Every eye turned to look at Sylvia.

Will sputtered, "I've never heard of such a thing! And in the daytime! I'd never have been so quick to let you sleep out there; I— "

Sylvia stopped him. "It's okay. I'm not so shocked; I felt all along it was possible. But the risk was, and is, very small."

Katie stepped forward, putting her hand on Sylvia's shoulder. "These guys, remember, were hunting jaguars, kind of asking for it. You're in harmony with nature, maybe they'd never bother you."

It would be nice to think so, anyway, Sylvia mused.

Beans and rice, cucumber-onion-tomato salad, "naked" pasta, as they had dubbed it, occasionally mashed potatoes or fish... by now they were tired of the diet. They ate and talked under the stars beside the Apuaú. They had continued downriver to a beach that made a suitable campsite; by 8:30 p.m., as usual, everyone was yawning.

In a low voice beside her, Katie asked Sylvia, "Will you be sleeping in the big tent with us tonight?"

Conversation halted; her voice hadn't been low enough. Sylvia felt Will's eyes on her.

"No, I asked Berto to hang my hammock up the slope, there."

"You are kidding!" Pauline burst out.

"You're nuts," said Fran with her usual diplomacy.

"Maybe so," Sylvia retorted. "Let's just say I'm more afraid of that hard ground than of all the jaguars in the Amazon, ha!"

No one laughed.

"Listen, what's changed, really?" Sylvia asked reasonably. "We heard a horrible story, that's all." She stood up. "Matter of fact, I hear my hammock calling me now. Good night, everyone."

"Good for you," called Betsy approvingly.

"Yeah!" agreed Sam, adding with a devilish grin, "And sweet dreams..."

"Wait up." Will had jumped to his feet. "I've a lantern I want to give you." He fetched something from a pile of supplies. It was a large kerosene lantern, the one Federico usually used when he cleaned up after dark.

"I don't need that."

"Maybe not, and I know I can't change your mind, but this should help repel any intruders. Use it for me, all right? I'll feel better." He lit the lantern and walked up the slope with her; they wound through lush shrubbery to the little trees which supported her hammock. He set the lantern down a few feet away.

"If you insist."

He lowered his voice. "My tent is just there." He pointed. When I flash my light twice, use your little torch to come over. That is, if you'd like."

"I'd like."

"See you later, then."

When they were alone in Will's tent, Sylvia listened to him vent his frustration.

"The others are driving me round the bend," he said. "Thank God you came along on this trip."

He didn't see how she could abide Katie; and he, too, had noticed how Pauline constantly watched Sylvia. "How do you stand it?" he asked.

"Well, I *did* need those mornings alone... If I can get off to myself, for a while, it helps me put up with people's b.s."

" 'Antes só que mal acompanhado', as the Brazilians say. 'Better alone than in bad company.' "

"I couldn't agree more! Oh, poor Will, you can barely get a moment of solitude, and you have to be polite to everyone no matter how you feel about them... "

"Yes. And now Sam, whom I liked, sometimes seems— disapproving, as if I'm not managing the group well, or something." He ran his hand through his shaggy mane. "How do you manage a bunch like this??" he whispered frantically.

Sylvia realized it was easy for her to ignore them and laugh about it; but Will was solely responsible for everyone. Even more than showing them an interesting expedition, he needed to get the party back to

Manaus without mishap.

"Everything will work out all right," she said softly. "We're nearer to civilization now."

"That's true. Soon this loony trek will be over."

Yes, all too soon.

Alone, back at her hammock, Sylvia thought of Will's attitude toward the quirky, irksome little group. They weren't really so bad; but he thought so, and that was worrisome in itself.

She tried to go to sleep, but the lantern, though turned to its dimmest, bothered her. She had grown accustomed to the deep black of a rainforest night. She got up and extinguished it.

In the comforting darkness, she fell quickly asleep.

"Hey, good morning, you survived," Sam boomed.

Sylvia looked up from her pancake. "Yeah, but I was tempted to let loose with a throat-shredding scream, just to fake everybody out."

"Huh! You would've had to bury Fran," Betsy whispered.

They pushed on, headed for the Varzea forest on the great Amazon River. Before the sun sank into the forest yet again, they were back on the Rio Negro. At the farthest point of their journey, up the Bariaú, Will said they had been at least 120 miles from Manaus.

"Considering that a person could *walk*– not boat– for one hour in any direction from the center of Manaus and find himself in virgin rainforest," Will told them, "You can see how far into wilderness 120 miles puts you, in this part of the world."

They had a good deal of travelling ahead of them. They wanted to reach the point where they would cross the Rio Negro early enough to allow them time to get to a campsite in the Varzea. They were beginning to see more people now, settlers' isolated homes and a boat on the river now and then. When they came to a small village, Nova Airão, Will suggested they stop and look around.

"There's a general store up here," said Will as everyone disembarked. "Let's see if they have anything you might want."

The muddy riverfront, they saw with dismay, was covered with all manner of unspeakable refuse. The group walked up the gravel road, dodging from one shady patch to another; the sun felt merciless.

Panting under a small tree, Sylvia grabbed Katie's arm. "Look."

They stared at a weathered, wooden hut, bearing over its doorway a familiar factory-printed logo: Avon.

"You know, I remember reading somewhere about canoe-paddling Avon reps in the Amazon," Sylvia said, "And now I believe it."

The general store was dark and airless. As their eyes adapted from glaring sunlight, something caught Sylvia's attention, and she gravitated toward it like one in a trance. She stood over the Coca Cola cooler for a moment. "Oh, Lord," she prayed earnestly, "Please let them be cold. *Really cold.*"

She opened the cooler, grabbed a Coke bottle from the ice, quickly paid for it, and flipped off its cap using a hickey screwed to the side of the counter. She chug-a-lugged a Coke so cold it hurt. And in a bottle! One little perverted bit of civilization that truly hit the spot, at times... The only thing to compare had been the coconut water they sipped beside Horsefly Creek. When the soda was gone, she bought another, for the road.

It was time to attempt a crossing of the river. Since the wind was up, there was some question about it.

"The width of the river allows big waves to develop," Will told them. "All the baggage on the roof has to be moved to bow storage, to make the Condor less top-heavy and prevent us capsizing. And, people, it's going to be wet, so you might want to use your rain gear."

Sylvia sat on the front bench again, with Sam, who besides Will was the only other person tanned enough to take the sun. As they started across, the water became rough, and the boat bounced and plunged. Sam and Sylvia were first splashed, then as the waves grew, drenched. Great sheets of water washed over them, and the people behind them began to get soaked as well. Even Fran and Dale, who were now on the back row where it was dryer, had covered themselves with one large rain poncho.

At last they were forced to turn back. The waves were growing and Berto feared they'd be swamped. Will's face was drawn and anxious.

The Condor cruised around until Berto found a pleasant beach to stop for lunch and a couple of hours' wait, in hopes the wind would diminish. While Federico got their lunch together they inspected a dead yellow anaconda, about nine feet long, floating nearby.

"Probably killed by fishermen," Will said. "A pity. It wouldn't hurt anyone; it isn't large enough to swallow a person."

They believed him, but still felt creepy, since they bathed in the river every day. They hadn't worried about anything such as anacondas, because Will didn't seem to.

The group took the opportunity to hang their wet clothing out to dry in the warm sun. Will served everyone limeade, and went to help Federico with lunch.

All at once he broke away from the meal preparations and dashed over to the group, where they sat relaxing on the beach, sipping their limeades.

"Wait! Stop! Don't drink! Pour it out!" He snatched the tin cup Betsy was putting to her lips, splashing its contents on the beach sand. "Give me your cups!"

He refused to explain himself, shaking his head as he ran around like a mad thing, grabbing their cups and pouring out the juice.

"It must've been contaminated, somehow," Pauline said.

Sylvia watched Will, worried. Has he snapped?

He fetched paper cups and passed them out silently, then poured more juice from the same pitcher.

"Nope, not the juice," whispered Sam, "Must be the cups."

Fran and Dale sat silently. Everyone watched Will gradually calm down, but Sylvia thought he looked more infuriated than worried.

No one had a chance to collar him for an explanation, because almost immediately after eating they tried the crossing again. But although it was barely breezy on the shore, when they neared the center of the river the wind became high. It was evident they wouldn't be able to make it, as the boat pitched wildly and volumes of water poured over them once again.

"Let's not take any risks!" shouted Sam to Will, clearly alarmed. "There's no one to help us out here if we capsize!"

"Don't worry; we're turning back."

They would have to find a place to camp for the night. Berto weaved the Condor among a multitude of islands of the Archipélago Anavilhanas, until they found the most beautiful beach they'd yet seen, with crescent curves, white sand, and shallow, clear water.

Darkness was descending quickly. The soaked, bedraggled group changed quickly to dry clothes and gathered on the beach, while Will and the Brazilians made camp.

In the midst of the great, dark expanse of forest and water, a distant cluster of bright lights held them transfixed: Manaus, city of a million and a half souls, dwarfed by Amazonia. Its low, pulsating hum dominated the peaceful evening, an eerie combination of all the sounds, machine and human, emanating from the man-made habitat. Rarely does one encounter such a discrete pocket of humanity completely surrounded by the wilds, so that its collective voice is perceived as one entity, distinct as the cry of a bird at sunset. Sylvia was spellbound by the ominous, unceasing murmur of mankind.

During the days on the Bariaú, they had become attuned to the sounds of the natural world: crickets, frogs, birds, rustling leaves, flowing water, rain, dewdrops falling... and stranger sounds, such as the sawing-wood racket that Will said was two sloths mating. All their senses quickly grew keener; they could now smell rain on the way, the musk of cat, and formic acid from ants.

The sparkling electric lights of the faraway city vied with a spectacular array of stars that were appearing and which would be drowned by the glare of the city once you were a part of it. *When we're again in the middle of that place,* Sylvia thought, *the glorious stars, the voices of the creatures and the water, the scents of the earth, will all be submerged in the light and clamor and artificial stink that overwhelms everything. How have we come to create such disharmony with the very whole that sustains us?*

But tonight, right now, she was still Out Here. It was (as they'd been told earlier) Berto's fortieth birthday, and he'd already begun celebrating. Federico had a special dinner planned, including some fish he'd caught; Sam and Betsy produced a bottle of wine they bought in the village as a little surprise for Berto. *Just what he needed,* thought Sylvia. Will had a small gift for him. The strange incident on the beach, still unexplained, had been set aside and the group made merry.

The party petered out early, after the long, eventful day. Everyone but Will and Sylvia drifted away to their tents. The couple watched them all, their tents lit from inside, revealing their silhouettes in golden cocoons: those fragile, canvas homes that magically protected them from wild animals.

Berto and Federico produced a potent bottle of *cachaça,* which they offered to Will and Sylvia.

"Huh! Now the real party begins," Will said in Portuguese, as he drank. Berto poured some for Sylvia in a paper cup.

"Careful," warned Will, and Berto laughed, understanding the English word.

As Sylvia raised the cup to her mouth the vapor seemed to wrap itself around her head and twist it. "Wow!" she exclaimed. "The fumes alone will kill you!" She took a cautious sip— it was good!— and two more, and the wide beach rocked like a boat. Federico turned on a radio he hadn't been allowed to use, previously; the group had complained, including Sylvia— and as it softly played, Will and Sylvia danced on the beach to a samba while Berto and Federico clowned around. From the corner of her eye Sylvia saw Pauline farther down the beach in semi-darkness, wading in the water, watching them. She elbowed Will.

"Yeah, I saw her." He took another sip and swung Sylvia lightly around.

"Okay, Will, now tell me what the hell happened today."

"Oh, Godfrey! 'Rico, she wants to know what happened," he called in Portuguese. Federico spat on the ground and said some words Sylvia hadn't learned yet.

"Syl, see if this doesn't top everything. Remember the first rough crossing we tried, how the water blew into the boat and all? Well, Fran and Dale— silly bitches!— were on the row just in front of 'Rico today, with a big rain poncho over them... and he saw them, get this, use those funnels to *piss in their tin cups*, then toss the urine overboard!"

"What?!"

"'Rico was just livid. I mean, he washes the cups each evening, and then wipes them out with alcohol, but he has to handle them every day! And we realized they have been doing this ever since the Bariaú camp! After the rainstorm there, when we were drying their tent underliner, we wondered why we smelled urine. We figured out today that they were too afraid to go to the latrine at night so they used the cups, which got kicked over, no doubt."

"Hmm... Maybe *that's* what Fran was mad at Dale about."

"Oh, yes. Perhaps. Well, I took them aside before dinner and read them a lecture about the whole thing. They didn't dare to deny it. You may have noticed they were a little subdued tonight."

"I did notice Fran didn't shoot her mouth off, as usual."

"Sam's been after me to explain what happened, so I'll probably tell him tomorrow. And I don't care if he tells everyone else."

"Oh, good; then I can tell!"

He pinched her bottom. "Let's go swimming."

Slightly drunk, they wobbled along a graceful arc of the beach, following its curve to a point of white sand that projected into the slow, tepid river; above them, the Milky Way was a swath of glory that dazzled their eyes. Federico's radio crooned softly, down at the boat, where he and Berto washed dishes and laughed. Will launched into his usual rant about the eccentric group, but Sylvia interrupted.

"You're stuck in a groove, Will; hop out of it. Forget them for now."

He exhaled forcefully, as if blowing all the irritating people away. "Quite right. Let's just admire that sky!" The opposite riverbank was far away and the arching dome of the heavens appeared grand after the closeness of the Bariaú. They waded out chest-deep, feeling it was safe to cuddle together in the relative darkness of the river. The water was silky and sensuous. Will stroked Sylvia's back under her shirt.

She jumped. "Ooh! Something nipped at me."

"Just small fish, you know how they nibble with their little mouths." He kissed her neck to demonstrate.

"Ouch! That was a *bite*!" She jerked around.

"Now, be— "

"Don't you tell me to 'be calm', Will Greene— the man who swore I was safe in a hammock!"

"Ow!" he yelled. "Get out! Out of the water!"

They hurried to shore. "Be calm, Will! It's only piranha, nibbling with their little mouths," Sylvia giggled, as they fell onto the sand.

Before daybreak the travellers packed up, determined to make the crossing in the early-morning calm. As soon as Sylvia's gear was stowed aboard the Condor, she sat on the beach, watching the sky slowly brighten and listening to the birds begin their ruckus. Nearby, a very hungover Berto was readying the boat, standing thigh-deep in the river.

Suddenly a loud argument broke out.

"Leave me alone!" screeched Pauline.

"You must get your stuff out so we can take down the tent!" Will yelled back.

"Stop rushing me! You're driving me crazy! I can't take it anymore, you treat me horribly!" Pauline ran from the tent, racing around the sand hysterically, flapping her arms like a chicken.

Will shouted after her, "I've had enough of you!"

The little scene was over as quickly as it had begun.

Sylvia turned from watching them, and once more faced east.

Normally, altercations upset her, but for the past week nothing had disturbed the core of peace inside her. The others were a distant human hum, like Manaus.

Her serenity was the magnet that drew Katie. The younger woman's unvoiced fears seemed picayune when she was with Sylvia. Sylvia had perspective and aplomb, and Katie wanted some of it, too.

The sun slowly rose behind tall trees on the far bank, a great red orb so softened by the humid atmosphere that she could look directly at it. It left a molten, glowing path across the water. As the others stowed their gear and boarded, speaking little, she continued to gaze at the lavender sky around the sun and dancing, golden sparks on the water. Will quietly pushed the Condor offshore and into the current, as Berto started the motor.

With a pale sun rising higher and fresh morning air on their faces, they traversed the Rio Negro. It wasn't a bumpy ride this time, but it nevertheless took an hour to cross. They turned south toward the confluence of the Negro and Amazon rivers, where there was a large peninsula cut through with river channels. The Condor moved slowly through the region, known as the Varzea, on its way to the mighty Amazon.

By late morning they had threaded their way to the heart of the Varzea on one of its myriad channels. The Whitewater Flooded Forest stood in contrast to the Igapo, collecting a vast amount of sediment from the Andes which enriched the soil with nutrients; hence, everything was more numerous, and larger: plants, insects, animals.

"Diversity of species," Will reminded them, "is lower than in terrafirme, but species density is greatest of all in Whitewater Forest. Including insects, so be prepared."

The channel was narrow and exquisitely beautiful, the water glassy, reflecting the towering forest like a mirror. Everywhere, tree roots snaked their way down green banks to sip from the stream. Now and then they passed an Indian sitting silently in a canoe, holding a bow and arrow over the water, hoping for a fish. There were giant kapok trees, their folded buttresses soaring far above the ground. January Lake, in the middle of the peninsula, was sprinkled with large, flat lily pads, up to four feet in diameter and perfectly round. Small Indian children played on the floating pads, some with captive three-toed sloths, creatures with beautiful, expressive faces that appeared almost human.

They moved on until they reached a wide dock where Berto tied up the Condor. Federico readied lunch while the group stretched their legs. The dock was a shred of civilization, Amazon style; it had a crude refreshment stand, a few tables, a couple of hammocks. They bought Antartica beer and a cola called Guaraná from the cooler, while three local men barbecued fish on a grill. With typical Brazilian hospitality they offered to share their fish, but seeing how little they had, everyone declined with many thanks. Will bought them each a beer.

Another quarrel broke out over lunch.

"Hey!" Fran exclaimed hotly. "As always, Katie, you and Pauline took every last slice of tomato! This has gone on long enough!"

"But we don't eat tuna or egg," Katie tried to explain. "We have to eat something..."

Pauline stood nodding her head, her face set defensively, but said nothing; she didn't relish a second fight in the same day.

"Some of us might like a slice or two, at least," Betsy said coldly.

Sylvia agreed, yanking a few slices from Katie's sandwich with her fingers, tossing a couple to Betsy and Sam, and plopping the last one on her own plate. She grinned defiantly at Katie's surprised look.

"Thanks for the tomatoes, Katie," Sam called.

Katie then laughed. "You're welcome."

But Pauline glared. "You leave *my* sandwich alone," she warned Sylvia.

Federico rolled his eyes, and went to cut another tomato.

Sylvia took her food and sat on the end of the dock, her feet dangling just above the water's surface. Immediately one of the local men approached and told her, in Portuguese, she shouldn't sit there. She looked at his friendly, smiling face in puzzlement; she had understood his words, but not his purpose. Motioning her to lift her feet onto the dock, he pulled hard on a thick rope tied to a post beside her. To her shock, he raised the two-foot-long head of a truly huge caiman, and then let it sink back into the murky water. The other men laughed and motioned toward her feet, signing that they could be bitten off tidily. She thanked them and moved to another area to eat. But she felt sick to think of the creature, tied to the dock. Will had been watching, and he crouched beside her.

"Such a magnificent caiman, it's a pity," Will said to her in a low tone. "They'll either sell it to someone who'll show it off to tourists, or maybe kill it for food. Wish I could sneak back later and set it free. " He paused for a moment. "By the way, you won't be using your damned fool hammock in the Varzea, will you?"

"And why not?"

"You'll be eaten alive by insects, of course," he snarled at her.

She was taken aback by his tone. "Federico says there's a half-net; I'll be okay," she hissed back at him. "What's with you, Will? If I don't use my hammock, I'll have to sleep in the big tent, and I don't think I want to deal with Pauline."

"I don't care anymore what anyone thinks; you can sleep in my tent." And he stormed off to join the others, leaving Sylvia staring.

"Yikes, where's that DEET?" Dale fished around in Fran's pack. There were definitely mosquitoes in the Varzea. Sylvia slapped at them as she wrote:

We're presently camped for a couple of days on a pretty little lake, and we just returned from a hike. The Whitewater Forest is easy walking– little underbrush, big trees growing far apart. The strangler figs fascinate me. Each begins as a harmless-looking liana, climbing up a big tree; the vine grows wider and wider with age, branching out, until it wraps itself around the victim tree, encasing and eventually smothering it. Finally the dead tree will rot away inside the fig, which by then is a tree itself, usurper of the dead tree's spot in the sun. We found many figs in various stages of this slow, patient takeover.

Everyone appears to be getting tired and testy, and Berto is drunk now from morning to night. But the one I worry about is Will, who's unravelling fast. He's even turned on me, his only friend in the group of guests, ragging me about the hammock and everything else I say or do... Though at times he acts as if he's ashamed of himself. (Maybe I'm stubborn, but I've slept in my hammock, still, though the sound of mosquitoes buzzing just outside the net drives me mad, I admit.)

At first I didn't understand his attitude; but hiking along behind him today, the truth gradually sank in. Back in terrafirme, there had been no "no-see-ums"; and getting rained on in a hammock isn't such a problem, since tarps are available for the purpose. He had given up at the very first drop that fell. And I now understand why he wouldn't stop talking the first night we were out in the forest.

He was afraid.

Sleeping out in a hammock spooks him. He can't admit it, of course, partly because he has continually reassured us we're safe out here. I under-

stand a guide has to instill confidence and help the group hold down their fears, trusting him in case anything does go wrong... And intellectually he probably believed the chances of harm sleeping outside the tent were almost nil; but in his gut he was scared, he couldn't handle the feeling of vulnerability. He began to resent me because I wouldn't cave in even after hearing about the poachers.

I also realize now that the naturalist who came back after only two days alone in the forest was none other than Will, himself.

I don't despise him for it. And it isn't absence of fear on my part, it's just that I want so badly to overcome it.

"I'm going to miss my plane, Will!" wailed Katie, wringing her hands.

"So you've said about a hundred times! Can't you see I'm doing everything I can?" Will and Federico stood knee-deep in mud, trying to untangle the boat's propeller from a slimy mass of roots; they'd been struggling for over an hour. Berto, currently persona non grata for having maneuvered the Condor into the midst of the lakeside trees, stood aside, red-eyed and silent.

Katie would have been cutting it close under the best of circumstances; though the others were heading back to the U.S. via a midnight flight to Miami, she had a tour group to meet in Brasilia and her plane left in late afternoon. All the gear was stowed aboard and everyone stood around helplessly, except Sylvia, who had stolen away for a few more minutes in the woods.

At last: "Let's go! Aboard, everyone... Sylvia! Where the hell are you?" Will yelled. He wheeled on Berto. "Do you think you can get us to Manaus, now?"

As the boat slowly moved out of the Varzea, pointing once again toward Manaus, Will gradually relaxed, and his shifting mood had a positive effect on the others. He slipped back into his role of guide and naturalist, answering their questions, scanning the wide skies for birds, trying to end the trip as normally as possible.

On the way down the Amazon the party took a different route, skirting the peninsula in order to experience the Meeting of the Waters, where the Amazon and the Rio Negro converge. These, the two mightiest rivers on earth, do not mix easily; at first, not at all. The dark water of the Rio Negro flows beside the café-au-lait Amazon, and the line of distinction is surprisingly clear.

"This is the point where the Solimões officially becomes the Amazon," Will told the group. "Takes them quite a while to truly merge, since their waters are a different density and they move at different speeds; the Amazon's faster. Temperatures are another factor. See here, when we cross the 'line', put your hands in the water and you'll feel it."

Everyone obeyed and dangled their hands over the side, their faces lighting up as they crossed into the Rio Negro waters and felt the drop. "It's about ten degrees cooler," he said. He had Berto cross and recross several times, while the group dipped their hands and took photos.

"There's a metaphor here somewhere, " Betsy said. "I just have to think about it."

Sylvia nodded absently. The mention of Solimões, Portuguese for Solomon, had reminded her of the dream about a man who wanted to show her King Solomon's Mines.

It was still a long way to Manaus; the group had their last lunch in the boat. Will sat next to Sylvia. There was no opportunity to talk, but he put extra tomatoes on Sylvia's sandwich with a lopsided grin and quickly whispered, "Sorry if I've been an ass... " Her eyes answered, *You have, but never mind.*

"Oh!" Will suddenly said, looking across the river. He whistled, stood, and waved his arms. A long, narrow speedboat slowed and began to turn toward them. "Katie, gather your things; you're in luck." Everyone looked at him in puzzlement.

"A water-taxi. Much faster than the ol' Condor, here... *Venha cá!*" He waved the boat in.

Katie was thrown into a dither. As Sylvia helped collect her gear, she said, "I have your address; I'll send copies of my pictures. Have fun in Brasilia, dear."

Will spoke to the boat's driver and passed Katie's duffel bag and other belongings over. Katie muttered something to Sylvia in a choked voice. The two hastily hugged, and the girl was whisked away with a roar of the big outboard. Sylvia's last sight of her was Katie waving back as the sleek boat sped down the Rio Negro.

While Will was dealing with Katie's belongings, Pauline had moved into his spot beside Sylvia. *Damned woman, with her staring eyes,* Sylvia thought. She tried to engage Sylvia in small talk, but Sylvia pointedly turned her head to watch the passing riverbank.

She needed to be alone with her thoughts, and with her last minutes on the river. She wanted to absorb all of it, to peacefully make the transition from wild places back to the city, swarming with people and their ugly constructions and sicknesses. She was coming down hard. Her mind was left behind in the forests, and ahead lay a sort of soullessness. She was leaving a place where she'd felt whole.

She was grieving.

They neared Manaus, encountering more and more boats and houses. They pulled up to their mooring, the same place, greeted by the smell of leaking gasoline. They disembarked. Their gear was loaded into a van, and they walked to their hotel. Sylvia felt like an automaton.

It was three p.m.; they had several hours before leaving for the airport. They checked into rooms, most of them wanting a shower and a nap. Pauline suggested she and Sylvia share a room, for such a brief time.

"No, thanks!" Sylvia said, too abruptly. "We may as well have our own."

Will and Sylvia had to shake hands and say good-bye in front of the others. Behind their backs he pantomimed, "I'll write you." But she knew he wouldn't.

She had a shower and washed her hair. It felt good, but she hadn't missed those things the way the others did. The river waters had cleaned her just as well. *I didn't miss anything at all while we were gone; I felt perfectly at home there, outdoors continually. Isn't that strange?*

She sat down on the bed with a towel over her face and sobbed for several minutes. It was all over, and now back amidst the world of people, she felt a terrible loneliness; she who was seldom, if ever, lonely.

Enough! Finally she hopped up and re-packed her jumbled, damp belongings, hoping nothing too weird crawled out of the bag.

They looked so nice they shocked each other. Fran, Dale, Pauline and Sylvia, after a good nap, had decided to go out for dinner. Sam and Betsy begged off, saying Sam had a slight case of the runs and they'd rather sleep. The others hoped the couple wasn't simply tired of their company. After all, they, too, were sick of each other, they admitted, laughing, but they could still share one last meal.

But they were barely recognizable, with their hair neatly styled and a touch of makeup, wearing the "good" clothes they'd left behind at the hotel.

They'd decided to spring for a fine meal, after two weeks of a limited diet. They took a taxi to the elegant Tropicão Hotel on the outskirts of town, where there was a lavish buffet; for about $27 they could turn into pigs. They treated themselves to a magnum of champagne, as well. A little tipsy and holding large plates, they attacked the buffet, rubbing shoulders with German, French, Dutch, and Brazilian guests of the hotel; scarcely an American in sight.

While Pauline's head was turned, gaping at someone, Dale and Sylvia dumped a large pile of tomato slices on her plate. She turned back and grimaced. "Ugh!"

"Oh, look, girls!" Sylvia cried. "Beans and rice!"

More "ughs".

As they ate, Fran pattered on in her usual obnoxious style; her target tonight was Katie. "Can you believe how afraid of *chiggers* she was?"

Since Katie wasn't there to defend herself, Sylvia spoke up.

"Wait a sec, Fran. As I recall, you were afraid of many things, yourself. You wouldn't even leave your tent to take a piss!"

Dale saw the glint in Sylvia's eye and hastily tried to change the subject, but Fran stammered, "Well, that was different... " And she wasn't finished with Katie. "She really admired you, Syl. I think you could be some kind of mentor for her, or mother figure. Do you plan to keep in touch?"

As Sylvia skewered Fran with a frosty glare, Pauline added slyly, "It seems to me there was more than one person who admired Sylvia..."

All during dinner the three other women danced around the issue of Sylvia and Will; but Sylvia never gave them an opening to pursue it, and not even big-mouthed Fran dared barge into the subject cold. Somehow, without loss of amiability, Sylvia had maintained a shield of privacy about her during their days together. There was something about her that didn't invite familiarity.

Back at the hotel, the desk clerk handed Sylvia a folded note along with her key. It was unsigned, but she recognized the neat handwriting from the map he had drawn and labelled— was it only two weeks ago?

"Bless you," it read. "Without you, I would've gone mad."

Whattaya know, he wrote to me, after all.

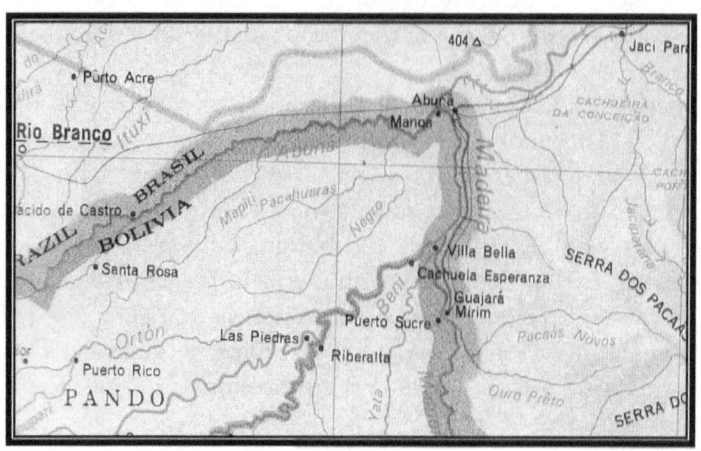

FAWCETT, CHAPTER 4
RIO ABUNA

High-heeled yellow boots clattered on the plank sidewalk, then paused as their owner took a long look into a window which made an excellent mirror. Hoots of laughter broke out from a group of rowdies standing nearby with bottles in their hands.

"Look, ain't he quite the dude!" shouted one weaving fellow in a Cockney accent. There were other rude comments, some in Portuguese, as the knot of men turned their attention to the young dandy who was admiring his canary-bright new suit and hat, fingering his gilt watch-chain and ignoring their jeers. He wished he could see his feet in the glass.

"Now, t'would be a shame if that spanky new suit got all messed with mud, wouldn't it, hee, hee... " The Cockney took a couple of lurching steps toward the dude, his buddies murmuring behind him, chuckling dryly.

Across the muddy road, Fawcett and Chalmers came out of a shop in time to catch the little scene.

"Lord! Will you look at that!" Chalmers exclaimed, his eyes bulging. "Those ungodly hideous boots! With elastic sides, no less!" He burst out laughing. "The whole get-up is just too much! Where's the camera?"

"We have to step in, before this gets out of hand... "

"No, no, let them have at him! It'll be the best show— "

Fawcett threw his assistant a look of disdain. "Come on, Chalmers." He started across the street, bellowing: "Dan! What in God's name is this?"

"Do you like it?" Dan asked innocently, turning from his makeshift mirror to display himself proudly to Fawcett. "It took damned near all the pay you gave me in Cobija." The threatening group of toughs grew quiet as Fawcett and Chalmers joined Dan. They would've robbed Dan and cut his throat just for the fun of it but they weren't quite sober enough to take on three of them; and there was something about the tall one which made them doubly uncertain. They hesitated, giving the three dark looks.

"Oh, charming, Dan; you're just the fashion plate, really." Chalmers was smirking.

"Oh, shut up! You're jealous!"

"Let's go, both of you," commanded Fawcett in a low voice. "Whether you know it or not, my good man, you are about to have your new clothes and a good portion of your skin ripped from your body. Follow me, and do it *now*."

Dan offered no argument. Ever since he had caught up with Fawcett in Cobija, penitent and full of promises to forswear drink forever, he'd tried hard not to raise the Major's ire. So far he had avoided Demon Rum everywhere they'd stopped.

They checked out of the ramshackle hotel and walked to the docks. "I've hired a boat," Fawcett told Dan. "We've been looking everywhere for you. I want to get out of Xapuri; it's full of disease and liquor and the very worst type of human beings. I've been told the mortality rate at the barracas around here is fully twenty-five percent per year! The greater part of the sickness, by far, can be traced to alcohol." Chalmers and Dan exchanged glances, sure another sermon was coming; but Dan knew Fawcett was right. Xapuri was a haven for thieves armed to the teeth and soaked with liquor, and no one ever seemed to die of natural causes.

"I've arranged to have mules waiting for us in Capatara, so we don't want to waste time. Ah, here's the boat; let's take an inventory and make sure all our belongings are aboard. And Dan, as soon as we've pushed off, I want you to get changed into more suitable clothes, got it?"

As they floated away from Xapuri, they were stunned to see an ocean-going steamer making its way up the river: the *Antonina*, Hamburg, it read. Fawcett and Chalmers gaped, incredulous. It seemed strange and unbelievable to see a steamer from so many miles away, here in the heart of the continent and surrounded by jungle. In that unlikely setting she seemed a giant.

"My stars," declared Fawcett. "She's made her way up sixteen hundred miles of river; proving, of course, that the Acre is navigable at least to this point! Hmm... displaces about a thousand tons, I'd say, not huge, but big enough!"

"She's here for rubber," Dan said, "And probably bringing up heavy machinery and the like. But you don't see this every day, that's for sure."

At Capatara, Colonel Placido de Castro, Governor of the Acre, had the mules ready, and offered them the hospitality of his barraca before they left on the overland trip to the River Abuná. Fawcett was now down to three Indians, Dan, and Chalmers, so the Colonel also lent him a couple of his Indian employees as guides and mule drovers.

On the morning of their departure, Chalmers complained of fever, and clawed restlessly at his insect bites. Dan took delight in tormenting him further by telling him grisly tales of local wasps which go straight for the eyes, and the needle-sharp stings of *katuki* flies. "And there's a snake here, very dangerous, with the head and first third of its body completely flat, and the rest is round. Then there's the red one, with a white cross on its head— "

"That's enough, Dan," Fawcett admonished the grinning young fellow. They followed a trail through dense jungle, frequently crossing yawning ravines on crude log bridges. This was nerve-wracking enough, without snake stories.

"Bloody mules," grumbled Chalmers. "They must enjoy scaring the wits out of you. On mountain trails they walk as close to the outside as they can get, and here on these blasted slippery bridges they do the same!" It was true; a light rain fell, and the center of the bridges appeared to be slimier than the edges, so the mules invariably chose the outer log. Thus these logs were much more worn.

"They must know what they're doing; we have to trust their instincts," Fawcett replied mildly, hiding his own apprehension.

A short while after this exchange, they were faced by another deep channel with a large stream at the bottom. Fawcett's mule started across a worn-looking log. Midway on the bridge, there was a chilling crack and the log suddenly gave way, plunging man and mule into the stream before anyone had a moment to react. Fawcett felt himself slip under the animal as they hit the water, and its weight pushed him deep into the mud of the stream bed. The frantic gyrations of the mule pressed all the air from Fawcett's lungs, and he felt his head spin. Hovering near unconsciousness, he at last felt the terrible weight remove itself and he struggled out of the mud and toward the water's surface, not a second too soon. As his head broke free, he saw a terrified face above him and a hand reaching out.

"Major!" screamed Chalmers. "Grab my hand!" The young man was waist-deep in the stream; Fawcett took his hand and let Chalmers pull him to the side. "Are you all right?" Chalmers was ashen and trembling.

Fawcett sat at the edge of the stream and checked himself for broken bones, fearing he might have a few cracked ribs, but he had been lucky. "I seem fine; no harm done, thank you, Chalmers."

Dan was busy retrieving the mule and its saddlebags. "I have to say, I've never seen anyone move like ol' Chalmers, here; he was down that sheer bank like a lizard! How'd you get down there so fast?" It was a good question, because even with the Indians' help the three men had a difficult time getting themselves and the mule back up. Fawcett made light of the incident, but he knew he'd had a close shave. If the stream bottom had been hard he would have suffered many broken bones, and he could easily have drowned.

They rode on, Chalmers in a high state of nerves; a grateful Fawcett took pains to be kind to him. At length they reached Santa Rosa, on the Abuná. All were wet and dispirited, and it didn't help to discover Santa Rosa was considered such a dismal place that the barraca there was used as a penal settlement. In the middle of an enormous swamp, it was fit only for snakes, especially anacondas, which were apparently the terror of the area. The manager, a Frenchman who kept a small harem of Indian women, told them the rubber pickers there usually work in pairs because men who go out alone disappear at an alarming rate.

"It has to be the anacondas, who crush and swallow their prey, of course. Though even some of the snakes that bite are so venomous they can kill a man before he could get back to the barraca. Three of our pickers died of snakebite this very day."

The men sat at table, served by the pretty harem, and their host added to the many warnings they had already received about hostile Indians on the Abuná. "Believe what you've heard," he said simply.

Fawcett regarded Chalmers, who was staring at his plate. "You've hardly eaten anything, Chalmers; are you feeling ill?"

"I'm the same, you know. Bloody fever. I'm just tired." Then he raised bloodshot eyes to gaze miserably at Fawcett. "I'll die back here, I imagine, of one thing or another... " He laughed mirthlessly, scratching at festering bites on his forearms, and began to shake, slightly.

"Here, have some brandy." The Frenchman poured a glass and Chalmers gulped some of it thankfully.

Fawcett looked thoughtful, watching his assistant hold the glass with both hands to keep from spilling. "Didn't you say you had a boat going down to Riberalta in a day or two?" The host nodded. "Well, I say, Chalmers, your condition is not good; it may be difficult for you to go on, and now's your chance to go back, if you like. I can release you from duty. It's quite all right, if you want to."

The young man brightened visibly. "Oh... if you're sure it's all right with you, Sir, I think I'll accept, and thank you." Fawcett was taken a bit aback, not having expected him to agree so readily; it was almost embarrassing. He realized then just how near a complete breakdown his assistant truly was, physically and mentally. Chalmers may have been right, and if he stayed, he would not live much longer.

The small boat and its five passengers slid easily along the glassy surface of the water; the river here was deep and quiet, its currents mild. On each side the forest loomed, with height so great and mass so thick that the men felt dwarfed between impenetrable, unscalable walls. Here and there a bird called, but the atmosphere was one of silence and expectancy. The very calm of the river seemed deceptive. Overhead, the sky grew darker, heavier, bearing ever downward upon the spirit, yet no rain fell. A sense of gloom and foreboding had turned all the men inward; they spoke little, and when they did it was in low voices, as if to avoid disturbing the Amazonian demons.

"The air is oppressive, isn't it?" murmured Fawcett. "If it's going to rain, I wish it would get it over with."

"*Whatever's* going to happen, I wish it would be over with," said Dan darkly, and Fawcett shot a quick look at him. He didn't want to give in to this mood of dread, but he couldn't blame Dan; he was echoing everyone's feelings.

"It's a rather grim place, I admit, though nothing one can put a finger on. Just a pervading quality of— I don't know— "

"Doom!" finished Dan, suddenly laughing. "There are dark spirits here, plain and simple."

"Don't start that," Fawcett warned, glancing around at the Indians, who poled the igarité upstream with somber expressions.

But they continued without incident to map the source of the Abuná, a large spring which was not far from Santa Rosa. This, Fawcett knew, was the easy part of his assignment; what lay ahead may be more troublesome, but it was necessary to survey the rest of the river. Though previously explored, and sprinkled with barracas here and there, the Abuná and its tributaries had not been accurately surveyed and mapped.

Now and then the dense clouds broke up and a few bright shafts of sunshine streamed down into the spring. After a brief rest, they started back down the Abuná, and this time they stopped at a barraca which they had passed on the way upriver; its owner, a Tumupasa Indian, was waving them in, and it would be rude to pass again without a visit. The barraca was dingy, but the Indian, named Medina, was extraordinarily wealthy from the rubber trade and he offered them a generous repast. As they sat down to table, Fawcett's mouth dropped open; he found himself gazing at a beautiful blonde Indian girl.

Medina chuckled. "Major Fawcett, I'd like you to meet my daughter, Vitoria."

Fawcett nodded, entranced by the tall, slender young woman who looked like a princess in a fairy tale, with her fine cloud of golden hair falling about white shoulders. Medina was dark, so she must be a half-breed, he reasoned, though her mother was nowhere to be seen. He couldn't help but watch her as she ate, her dainty hands and fine manners seeming almost bizarre in the crude, dirty barraca. After the meal he asked if he might take a few photographs of her, and permission was granted.

As he focused on her delicate features, a sunbeam igniting the mass of hair like a halo around a saint, he could visualize her waltzing in the most elegant ballrooms of Europe, on the arm of a gentleman. Medina watched the photo-taking with amusement.

"Everyone who sees Vitoria wants her," he stated proudly, as Fawcett packed up the camera and Vitoria wandered shyly away.

"I can easily believe that; and I hope she does well for herself. What are her plans, if I may ask?"

"Oh, she is spoken for, of course. She is going to the Manager at Santa Rosa." He seemed pleased.

Fawcett stared at him in dismay, but wisely decided to say nothing.

An exquisite, virginal creature like this, he thought, part of the Frenchman's harem! In a cesspool like Santa Rosa! What a tragic waste of a human who seemed to have natural gentility. He wished he could rescue her, send her to a life of grace and refinement; she didn't appear to belong here at all. Now, she seemed innocent and gay, but he wondered what life would do to her in the coming years.

The clouds began to build once more, darker than before, and as they left the barraca a light rain finally started to fall. Medina and Vitoria stood on the bank, waving, and the girl took on an ethereal aspect as she stood in the misting rain, her hair sparkling with droplets, the dark forest her background. *What a strange world, this wilderness,* Fawcett was thinking, almost overwhelmed by a sense of unreality. The boat floated silently around a bend of the river, tiny raindrops pocking the surface of the water, and he could see her no more.

Melancholy had taken him over once again. The rain increased, hissing across the water; but as soon as it had them all throughly wet, it stopped. Fawcett made an effort to shake himself out of his mood, taking in the details of the forest and drying himself as well as possible so he could make a few sketches.

Dan was a bit more chipper after the meal at Medina's. He looked over Fawcett's shoulder as he drew trees and flowers, and when he put the sketches aside and began work on his maps, Dan sat down beside him.

"You know, Major," he began, poking a finger at the map, "These rivers all have Indian names, but some day all those old names will be lost and forgotten."

"Hm, yes, the Acre was *Macarinarra,* wasn't it?"

"Right. Means 'River of Arrows', because along its bank is where they find the bamboo they use to make their arrows."

Fawcett's interest was piqued. "What other names do you know?"

"Well, let's see. The Rapirrar, which we're coming up to any minute now, was the 'River of Sipos', and that's a vine they use in building their houses. And there's the Caipera, or 'River of Cotton'—"

"So, in other words, the names were descriptive of the area or its resources."

"That's right. The names might tell you what minerals were plentiful there, such as silver or gold, or they told you something about the river itself, such as, 'River of Rapids', or 'River of Snakes', and on like that."

Fawcett was writing it all down. He looked up. "It would, indeed, be a shame if these names are lost. They're not only interesting and colorful, but they could be of help in the search for minerals or herbs... "

Dan's expression became wry. "I don't know the Indian name for the Abuná, but my guess is it's something like, 'River of Evil'."

Fawcett smiled.

"Díos!!" Dan screamed as the boat's bow suddenly reared into the air and the coils of a giant snake stirred the water beneath them. Fawcett barely had time to grab his maps and notebook to keep them from flying overboard. The men held to the sides of the igarité as a triangular head thrust itself from the water. "Anaconda!" Dan yelled, reaching for his rifle. The reptile had started for the shore, but Dan fired at its head; all three Indians tried to grab his gun as he fired again, begging him to stop, telling him a wounded anaconda would attack the boat and destroy it, and then its passengers. They looked around, terrified that the snake's mate was nearby, as they knew an anaconda will defend its partner to the death.

But it was too late; the snake had been struck with the bullets, and was pulling itself ashore, slowly. "Pull over," Fawcett ordered. The Indians complied, cautiously, their wide eyes still searching the forest and river for another monstrous snake. Fawcett approached the dying snake, taking Dan's rifle. "We'll have to finish it." An ungodly odor rose from the creature, and one of the Indians said it was its breath; local lore said that the anaconda's breath was one of its weapons, stupefying and even paralyzing its prey. "I believe it," Fawcett replied, feeling his head spin from the penetrating stink. Before he could fire, the snake shuddered and then lay still.

"It's dead," said Dan, obviously relieved. "Look at the size of the thing!"

Fawcett and Dan measured a length of forty-five feet lying out of the water, and approximately seventeen still in the river.

"Sixty-two feet!" exclaimed Fawcett, now repenting of his former disbelief; the stories had been no exaggeration. "Though not so thick as you might imagine, for the length; about twelve inches in diameter."

"That's probably because it hasn't eaten in a while," Dan suggested. "I've seen snake trails in the swamps that were six feet wide."

One of the Indians, who understood a little of what they were saying, spoke to Dan and he translated for Fawcett:

"He says this is by no means the biggest snake around; he's heard of some that were eighty feet long!" The Indian spoke again. "He said there is one type called a *dormidera*, which means 'sleeper', because it makes a loud snoring sound; it's black, and positively gigantic."

This time Fawcett didn't scoff, outwardly *or* inwardly. Everyone felt uneasy, casting frequent glances over their shoulders lest the snake's mate should give them a nasty surprise. Fawcett took hasty photos while the other men cut a few large chunks of the edible flesh, and they left, the Indians paddling vigorously.

Fawcett had promised to stop at Santa Rosa on their way down-river. He found the Frenchman, of course, and Placido de Castro waiting for him there; the Colonel had come over from Capatara to wish him well on his mapping of the various affluents of the Abuná.

"And how is the igarité working out for you?" he asked Fawcett over lunch.

"Quite well; it's a nice little boat, much superior to a batelón, in my opinion. Though I imagine an anaconda might find it easier to crush." He relayed the tale of their adventure, and neither of his listeners seemed surprised. Both the Colonel and the Frenchman pleaded with him to stay over for a night, but he was eager to push on; there were many hours of light left in the day, and privately he didn't want to stay in Santa Rosa a moment longer than necessary.

"Take care!" Placido de Castro called as they cast off, words which applied to the Colonel, as well. Fawcett had no way of knowing it was the last time he would see him; on the trail back the good man would be murdered, and no one would ever discover why, or by whom.

As they drifted along, the oppressed feeling began to return to Fawcett; again, there was no particular reason for it, but all about him seemed dark and gloomy and forbidding. The water, though calm, was murky, the sky above was darkening, threatening rain, and the dense mass of rainforest gave one the feeling it was closing in, though the river didn't appear to be narrowing. As the quiet minutes passed, the forest increasingly took on the aspect of a conscious presence. Fawcett had the distinct sensation it was watching them. Dan had grown silent, as well, looking over his shoulder uneasily from time to time, and the Indians murmured darkly in their language, also casting glances about them.

After half an hour the current picked up speed abruptly, and about that time a light shower began. One of the Indians turned and spoke to Dan.

"He says we're approaching the Tambaqui Rapid. It shouldn't be too difficult to handle."

Before Fawcett could answer, Dan suddenly pointed toward the forest and shrieked, "Savages!" Fawcett looked up to see a group of Karapuna Indians on the bank, their bodies painted red with the juice of a jungle bean, feather quills through their nostrils; they held enormous bows and wore quivers of arrows.

"Wait; be calm— we can stop and make friends— " But Fawcett's words were ignored, or not even heard, in the Indians' panic to paddle away. Dan was scrambling for his rifle. "No, don't, Dan!" Fawcett tried to reach the rifle before Dan; as soon as the Karapunas on the bank saw the strangers' reactions, they raised their bows and loosed several arrows. The arrows came so swiftly as to be invisible in flight, and one hit the side of the boat with a loud thunk, tearing straight through the inch-and-a-half-thick wood to protrude from the other side. Fawcett could barely believe his eyes, that a bow and arrow could exert about as much force as one of their rifles.

More Karapunas shouted from the other side of the river. The igarité, in mid-river, could be reached by arrows from both sides. Dan had raised his rifle but Fawcett pushed it aside and forbade him to fire; most of the arrows were passing them widely, and maybe, just maybe, it was only a warning. If they saw that no one meant them any harm... At any rate, as dozens more reddened bodies began to appear, running along the banks on both sides, he knew there was no escape if the Indians were determined to kill them. The Karapunas were numerous and had ample forest cover, whereas Fawcett's little party was completely exposed in their boat.

They'd scarcely noticed the current had increased and they were entering whitewater; the igarité sped along, helped by the frantic paddling of the Indians. Another arrow pierced the boat's side, and then the Indians stopped running, firing off a few more for good measure. They were in the rapids now, bouncing crazily, sliding down chutes of foaming water which splashed over the bow, drenching them and their goods. Before long they appeared to be through it.

"All right; that wasn't so bad," said Fawcett, loosening his grip on the side of the boat. "And our friends on the bank seem to have given up on us."

The water beneath them was rippled and they moved along quickly, but the Tambaqui Rapid was behind them. One of the Indians was saying something to Dan, pointing ahead and gesturing wildly. "Fortaleza", Fawcett heard.

"Major," Dan's voice was urgent, "We're coming to a dangerous rapid, we can't run this one, they say, we have to get out. Wait." He held up a hand, listening. Ahead of them there was a deep roar. "It's a cataract!"

The Indians were already paddling furiously toward shore, not waiting for Fawcett's order. Dan and the Major grabbed paddles and helped, but the quickening current kept sweeping them toward the center of the river. They were entering whitewater now, and soon it would be impossible to get to the bank; they would be swept over the falls. Just ahead, the river curved to the left.

"This is our chance," shouted Fawcett over the intensifying roar of the waterfall. "Paddle like hell!"

They beat the water like madmen, and the bend in the river helped propel them toward the bank on the right. Finally, fully spent, they leaped from the boat at the river's shallow edge and pulled it onto land. Looking around for Karapunas, they sank thankfully to the ground to catch a breath.

Their rest was brief; none of them wanted to linger in the area. Ever watchful for Karapunas and carrying rifles, they walked downriver to see what lay ahead and how they might get around it. Before them was an awesome stretch of river; the cataract they had managed to avoid consisted of, first, a straight ten-foot drop, then another, and then another. After that there were other perilous-looking chutes and holes and long drops, squeezed between a tumble of huge granite boulders.

"We would have dashed out our brains," remarked Fawcett cheerily. "Well, my good men, we shall have to portage the boat past all this; there's no other way."

Dan sighed, turned to the Indians and gave a few orders. Ahead of them was a back-breaking task, especially for so few hands, and it needed to be completed as soon as possible. They didn't want to be caught so near the Karapunas after dark. They first set about to round up a few tree trunks of the same size, which, fortunately, were not hard to find; there were many fallen trees in the thick forest, saving them the chore of cutting live ones. These served as rollers upon which they placed the boat, hauling it along the uneven, rocky ground along the bank. By the time they had dragged it beyond the Fortaleza Rapid, they were too exhausted to put up a fight if they'd been attacked by Indians. Their labor had taken hours.

"Come on," urged Fawcett. "We can rest in the boat. Let's get going."

No one argued. They pulled the igarité into the now-benign Abuná and were on their way.

A couple of hours below Fortaleza, as the sun was dropping, they reached the confluence of the Rio Negro, a small stream compared to the Brazilian river of the same name. Though all were tired and grumpy, Fawcett urged them onward, wishing to see at least a portion of the tributary; so they turned upriver on the Negro, the Indians once more poling their way against the slight current. Fawcett and Dan pitched in with the poles and they made as much progress as they could, Fawcett occasionally taking readings with his inadequate instruments until dusk finally gave them all an excuse to quit.

Dan walked a short way into the jungle and shot a few monkeys for their dinner. Silently they ate, then Dan rose and said: "I'm dead on my feet. I'll be asleep in half a minute." It was now deep twilight, but he fumbled around and found a clear space to sling his hammock, between two sturdy trees some distance from the campfire. Fawcett sat smoking his pipe for a short while, then he carefully hung the leftover meat from the branches of a nearby tree and crawled into his own hammock.

Sometime in the night, Fawcett was dragged from sleep by a bump on his backside; something large had walked under his hammock. The bright moonlight revealed a jaguar standing a few feet away, facing him, and for a moment Fawcett wondered if he might truly be dreaming, this time. The silvery light cast odd shadows over the surrounding foliage and over the beast itself. It stood still for a few seconds, looking back at the man, and Fawcett's sleepy head spun with a sense of the unreal, a strange, beautiful dream world where the jaguar would at any moment turn into Miranda, or would disappear before his eyes.

When the animal moved the spell was broken, and Fawcett jerked fully awake, his heart beginning to thump heavily. The jaguar glided gracefully away, its muscles rippling sinuously beneath the rich, velvety fur; its scent wafted along the night breeze to Fawcett's nose, and he remembered it. The big cat was interested in the monkey meat, not Fawcett, and it stood on powerful hind legs, clawing at the bloody carcass above. It was a sight to behold, and it both thrilled and terrified Fawcett. For the same reasons as before he wouldn't attempt to shoot it at such close range; and there was another reason... The animal's elegant beauty as it had stood in the silver light, meeting his stare directly with an intelligence of its own, was something he knew he didn't want to destroy. *But don't be a romantic fool*, he thought, *admire it all you want, but just to be on the safe side...* He decided he should at least have his gun in hand in case the beast attacked without provocation.

He reached slowly for his handgun, but as he slid it from the holster the leather creaked slightly. The jaguar, having just hooked its claws into the meat, let go of the prize and whirled toward Fawcett, snarling and showing the man its long white teeth, glistening with saliva in the moonlight. Then it bounded into the forest and was gone with scarcely a rustle. Beads broke out on Fawcett's forehead. He hadn't even had time to get a grip on the gun. *It could've killed me then. Guess neither of us wanted to destroy the other, for different reasons, no doubt. I'm sure it didn't think me beautiful. Two close shaves with jaguars; do I lead a charmed life, indeed, or is it a warning?*

Fawcett laughed softly with relief. If he had nine lives like a cat, he was rapidly spending them in these forests.

In a surprisingly short time, perhaps because he was still bone-tired from the exertions of the day, he began to drift off. Suddenly he was jolted upright; a horrible scream rent the still night, coming from Dan's direction. *The jaguar: It was tearing Dan to shreds. No! It's the Karapuna!* He leaped from his hammock, gun in hand, fighting his way through the mosquito net. All was confusion, the Indians grabbing their weapons, dodging unseen arrows that would at any second pierce their innards; running toward Dan's agonized cries, seeing vague forms flit through the shadows around them. When they reached his hammock they saw Dan running at full tilt to the river, shrieking madly, plunging into the water. And silence.

Fawcett whirled around to scan the forest, peaceful and innocent with its moonbeams and shadows moving in the little breeze. The Indians were looking about them in mystification, still befuddled with sleep. No arrows tore into their flesh.

"Dan! Are you all right? What the hell is going on?!" No response. A few splashes. "Dan! Answer me!"

The young man's head broke the surface, and he groaned. "Ants."

"What? *Ants?*"

Dan crawled to the bank, rubbing himself, shivering, and moaning. "Help me get them off, some of them are still alive... Fire ants." The Indians shuddered and began helping to pick the insects off.

"How on earth did you get into those?" Fawcett asked, brushing at Dan's red, raw skin.

One of the Indians began to laugh, and Dan glared at him murderously.

"Palo Santo," the giggling man said, and one of the other Indians ran over to look at Dan's hammock. He called out something, and all three Indians began to laugh uproariously. "Palo Santo!" they gasped, between guffaws.

"What the devil is that?" asked Fawcett, not in the mood for humor. He had had enough for one day.

"It's a damnable tree," Dan moaned, standing in the moonlight, dripping wet, picking at the ants. "Some of them are still biting; Díos!" Cursing and shuddering, he told Fawcett about the unique Sacred Tree. "It grows near rivers and streams. These blasted fire ants like to live in it. They're aggressive little demons, and if you so much as touch the tree, they come crawling from their holes and swarm over you or they jump onto you from the branches. Their bite is excruciating."

Fawcett helped him pick off the insects as he raved on about the exquisite torture of engulfment by the venomous ants.

"Sometimes, if a tribe's having bad luck in hunting, they blame a devil-spirit called Kurampura, and they try to gain his favor by tying a man— an enemy or sometimes one of their own— to a Palo Santo tree, as a sacrifice, you might say." He sighed. "I'd rather be crushed by an anaconda, truly."

"Well, how the dickens did you get into them, Dan?"

The young man looked sheepish. "It was late, and dark; I was tired... I guess I tied my hammock to those trees... "

Fawcett took a lantern to cautiously examine the trees supporting Dan's hammock. One of the Indians accompanied him, using signs and a limited vocabulary of English to show Fawcett that the trees should be easy to spot, for absolutely nothing, not even a blade of grass, grows within several yards of them. They stand alone on bare ground, every other living plant avoiding their vicinity no matter how thick and lush the nearby forest growth. The wood is soft and light, and there are no branches on the lower portion of the trunk.

"I don't know how he could've overlooked them," muttered Fawcett. Ants were still crawling along the hammock ropes and all over the hammock itself.

Dan was busy plucking ants for the rest of the night, and in the morning all the tired men had a lengthy process before them: figuring a way to untie the hammock and brush away the ants without being themselves attacked.

"Had enough of the Rio Negro?" Dan had asked in a surly tone as they were packing up. Fawcett had told him of his second encounter with a jaguar. The Indians found fresh-looking human footprints near their camp, and they, too, were beginning to wear rebellious expressions. If ever the Abuná had been shrouded in gloom, this branch of her was worse, so he reluctantly agreed they had gone far enough.

By the time they pushed off the sun was high and Dan, covered with angry red welts, was grumbling something to the effect that he would sell his soul for a bottle of liquor.

As they drifted downriver Fawcett worked on his maps, pausing only to make a sketch of a *bufeo*, a mammal of the manatee family, which followed their boat for some time.

"Looks amazingly human, doesn't it?" he remarked.

"Yes, especially with those breasts!" cackled Dan. "They're feisty animals, though; they'll kill a crocodile if they've a mind to. *And* they're good eating." Dan deeply admired a creation that bore the triple assets of large breasts, good flavor, and the ability to destroy his nemesis.

A couple of hours of drifting and desultory paddling brought them to the confluence with the Madeira River. Fawcett realized he had discovered yet a new level of depravity when they landed at the Bolivian Customs post at the mouth of the Abuná. Literally everyone was sick, due to alcohol and a limited diet of charque and rice. It was the old story: other food was available in the forests, but no one bothered to seek it out. All miseries were drowned in more alcohol and pathetic revelry. Fawcett and his men were stranded for eight interminable days amidst the filthy and rag-tag bunch, trying to arrange passage to Riberalta aboard a freight batelón. Two of his Indian crew showed signs of illness, and needed rest; suddenly a big, awkward batelón, with others to do the work, seemed the ultimate in comfort. The Madeira was known for perilous stretches of rapids which would have to be laboriously skirted.

At last they found a boat which was bound for Villa Bella, halfway to Riberalta. Its crew of twenty Indians didn't look any too hale, but Fawcett was desperate to get away.

The same dark feeling of the Abuná hung over this stretch of the Madeira. At times Fawcett felt it keenly, and he re-read his wife's letters many times, hoping to dispel the heaviness with her cheery news and descriptions of the children. He could visualize his boys rolling and tumbling amidst the tame, neat little garden trees; he could see himself playing with them and puttering with herbs and shrubs, then settling by the fireside at night with Nina, bent over her sewing. He would read a fresh newspaper every morning over a pot of tea, and listen to local gossip as interpreted by the housemaid or the village parson. He would forget all about slavery, sickness, and brutality as he enjoyed mild weather and the hum of honey bees, and the touch of his wife's soft hand. If he closed his eyes he could almost smell her sweetness and feel her long hair brush his bare chest in the night.

Before long the crew had battled its way to Esperanza, location of a large rubber centro as well as the home of Dr. Kent; Fawcett looked forward to paying a visit to Kent, and hoped he had returned. As they approached the villa, he was relieved to see the doctor's smiling face at the door; here was a touch of civilization to lift his spirits. He was greeted warmly.

"I wasn't sure if you were back yet," he said as they shook hands.

"I arrived home last week. Come in! I'm so glad I didn't miss you. You can stay the night? Good!"

Kent pulled out all the stops in offering the most lavish hospitality that he could. The meal was the best that Dan and Fawcett had had since Rosario. Unfortunately, Dan freely availed himself of the wine and brandy, feeling he had well earned it, and was soon on his way to blissful oblivion. All meaningful looks from the Major were either unnoticed or deliberately ignored.

Fawcett leaned back in his chair, savoring a cup of rich, dark coffee, and shook his head. Dr. Kent watched Dan stumble out to the veranda. "This place does things to people, good people. I don't know how long I can stay here, frankly, though there is no other doctor in the area and I know I'm needed. I came with such idealistic notions... Anyway, the rubber barons hereabouts see to it that I'm well taken care of." He ran a hand through his hair and took a generous sip of brandy. "But! Enough of the dismal rot. I'd like to hear all about your adventures on the Abuná. Did it live up to its miserable reputation?"

The men talked until the wee hours and played a game of chess, while Dan wandered out in search of an amenable Indian woman. That night Fawcett slept between clean sheets for the first time in weeks, and Kent had handed him a stack of periodicals to read, so he was a happy man.

Dan, however, was not so lucky. He managed to find an extremely friendly woman, but before his yellow boots— donned in honor of the lavish dinner— were off, she had slipped some sort of forest herb in his cachaça which knocked him out cold; whereupon she found his cache of money, his watch, and a silver flask. And as if that weren't insult enough, he awoke with a near-terminal hangover to find that she had also absconded with his boots.

From the veranda the Madeira looked deceptively peaceful and inviting, sparkling in the morning sun. Fawcett and Kent sat with their feet stretched to the railing, cups of coffee in hand, talking idly and watching the birds busily starting their day. Dan, curled in a nearby divan, nursed his head with a wet rag and glared darkly at the world, now and then hurling himself from the veranda and into the bushes where he retched mightily.

A tall, stout man walked down to the river, stretching, and waved toward the villa. Kent waved back.

"That's my manager. He's a Bolivian. Pretty much of a rotter, but he's an efficient manager and that's about all you can hope for."

The man was carrying a rifle which he proceeded to polish, sitting on a stump in the sunshine. In a few minutes a small group of Indians emerged from a pathway leading beside the river, and approached the Bolivian.

The doctor sat up and lowered his feet to the floor. "I wonder what these fellows want."

"Who are they?"

"Araras. They barter with settlers sometimes, but this bears watching."

"They look friendly enough; casual."

"Yes, they do," Kent admitted. "But in light of what happened...
See, the manager's brother was killed not long ago, by Araras, apparently. So he decided to get revenge by leaving poisoned cachaça at the pescana— that's a campsite the Indians often use— and it worked; no fewer than eighty Indians died there."

Fawcett emitted a low whistle. "Quite the shotgun approach, wasn't it? If you can't figure out who, exactly, did it, just kill them all?"

"Precisely. And knowing the Araras I can't imagine them letting him get away with it, if, that is, they know he's the one who did it. And that's not hard to figure out, I suppose."

Both men watched warily as the Indians laughed and talked with the Bolivian, who, though on his guard at first, now appeared relaxed. They were pointing at his rifle and expressing evident admiration for the handsome firearm. They seemed to be pleading with him to fire it. As this was his pride and joy, the man was glad to oblige, raising it to the trees and shooting at nothing. He would show these damned savages the power of a white man's gun. The Indians made a show of their delight at the big boom, jumping and cheering, and asked for an encore. Another loud crack, more laughter and hand-clapping; this was repeated again and again until the magazine was empty and the Bolivian shrugged his shoulders.

One of the Indians, who appeared to be the chief, then smiled and held up his bow and arrow, stepping forward and facing the trees far across the river. It seems it was now his turn to demonstrate his prowess, Indian style. With his powerful muscles, he drew the bow to its full extent. Poised like a bronze statue in the sun, he hesitated a moment... then turned smoothly toward the Bolivian and released the arrow into his chest.

Kent gasped; Fawcett was stunned. The manager, transfixed by the arrow, stood perfectly still for a heartbeat or two, then dropped to his knees and fell forward, propped a foot or so from the ground by the protruding end of the arrow. Dan, standing on the veranda, made an incoherent sound, a shriek beginning to bloom in his throat.

"Quiet!" commanded Kent, not sure whether to try for his gun, a few yards away inside the house, or remain still. The Araras looked toward the villa and then ran for the path, disappearing into the jungle. Fawcett and Kent moved quickly inside, gesturing to Dan. All three men got their guns at the ready and Kent rang an alarm bell on a back porch, an emergency signal summoning all hands. A few men showed up with their weapons; the rest apparently decided it was safer to hide out in the forest. At any rate there was no need to fight, as the Araras were gone. A couple of men ran down to the riverbank, cautiously, to verify the manager was dead.

"I guess they have no beef with me, only with that poor devil out-side. I have treated a few of them for snakebite and fever; so either they're capable of gratitude, or they fear our rifles." He called to his men to help him retrieve the corpse and dig a grave.

Fawcett would have stayed another night if he had had his say; he wanted to assure himself his newfound friend would be safe, and Dan was in terrible condition for river travel. But the crew of the batelón was eager to continue. They had loaded all the rubber in the Es-peranza centro, and had no further reason to linger but every reason to get out of there. He bade Kent good-bye with his thanks and with the hope they would meet again. In this wilderness, who could know?

As they slowly made their way to Riberalta, the Madeira did not get any kinder. The boat was now heavily laden and even more difficult to manage in the rapids; there was a bare three inches of freeboard. The crew worked themselves to exhaustion, and when they stopped for the night they collapsed on the solar-heated rocks, falling asleep in seconds. Kent had warned Fawcett that this was the cause of rampant pneumonia among the rivermen, but the crew would not listen to the Major.

Dan wouldn't, either. At one point Fawcett caught him surrepti-tiously sipping from a bottle of whiskey, snatched it away, and threw it overboard angrily. To his surprise the crocodile-shy man immedi-ately leaped into the river and retrieved the half-full bottle before it sank, quickly scrambling back aboard the batelón with the help of the Indians. He confronted Fawcett.

"Anyway, I have other bottles; and they're mine. Call it insubordi-nation if you wish," he said, his eyes red and rebellious. "But you don't need me right now, not nearly as much as I need this."

Fawcett saw there was little he could do; Dan had gone off the wagon, but good, and he was weary of struggling with the headstrong young fellow. In a couple of days he'd snap out of it, penitent as ever.

They successfully, though tensely, negotiated the whitewater of Ara-ras and Periquitos, but when they reached the Chocolatal Rapid it was necessary to pause and reconnoiter. One of the crew told Fawcett it usually took up to three days to bypass the Chocolatal. There was a road which was used to portage the batelón, but it was sometimes blocked by fallen trees which had to be laboriously removed.

While the pilot went to inspect the road Fawcett took his rifle and set out in search of a turkey for the evening meal. Hours later he returned, bird in hand, to find the crew abuzz: the pilot should've been back some time ago.

"All right, let's not just stand around," Fawcett said. "Get your weapons and let's go look for him." Dan, having difficulty standing but afraid to remain alone with the boat, stumbled along behind the group. They had walked for half a mile when they found him, lying in the road. Fawcett counted forty-two arrows in the man's body. *It could just as easily have been me,* he thought, looking down on the bloody pilot. *I was alone in the area, yet I saw no one.* He had the uncomfortable feeling he had just spent another of his nine lives.

Things were much more difficult without the pilot, whom they buried beside the Madeira. The custom was to tie the corpse to a pole, lay it in a shallow trench, and place upon the grave a cross made of sticks tied with grass. The man had been highly skilled in river navigation, but they made do as best they could without him. Adding to their troubles was the illness of several crew members, two of whom had pneumonia. One by one, four of them died. For each there was the usual burial accompanied by a drink of cachaça for everyone and much laughter. Whenever anyone fell ill the Indians went into fits of laughter which greatly disturbed Fawcett, who found it incomprehensible. The sick man would be teased and bullied mercilessly, and when he finally expired the others would nearly die laughing themselves. Four deaths in as many days was simply hilarious.

Some distance below the Chocolatal there was a large waterfall, a drop of at least twenty-five feet into a deep, green pool. Well in advance, the crew began to maneuver the boat toward the bank.

"Sit down, would you, Dan?" begged Fawcett. The drunken man had been weaving from one end of the batelón to the other, bottle in hand, talking in a loud voice to anyone who would listen. "You're making me nervous."

No sooner had he gotten the words from his mouth than the boat struck a hidden snag; the abrupt halt threw Dan overboard in an instant. When his head emerged from the water, Fawcett was already at the side of the boat, throwing him a rope. But Dan was caught in the quickening current and was rapidly pulled out of reach of the line. Fawcett's pleas to the crew to try and save him were wasted; they were now close to the bank and would take no chances in being drawn over the falls themselves. To hell with Dan!

Helplessly, as the crew dragged the heavy boat onto land, Fawcett watched Dan drift toward the falls. He could be heard shouting and cursing, and Fawcett suspected he had no idea what was ahead. Laughing hysterically, the Indians motioned to Fawcett to follow them quickly. All the men ran at breakneck speed to a spit of rock from which they could witness Dan's literal downfall; from this point they could see the cataract spill into the green pool.

"Oh, my Lord, it's a long drop," moaned Fawcett; but at least, he noticed, there appeared to be no rocks directly beneath the falls. He had a chance...

Soon Dan's bobbing head came into view and then he was swiftly swept over the edge, his arms and legs flailing. The Indians cheered raucously and a few of them fell onto the ground, holding their sides from the ache of laughter. For a breathless few moments Dan was not visible, and Fawcett feared he was being held down by the water-fall; then all at once his head appeared, together with his right hand, still holding onto his bottle. The Indians screeched deafeningly with delight and raced down to the river bank. Before they could get there Dan had managed to haul himself out of the pool, and when they reached him he was tipping back the bottle for a long drink.

Fawcett stood over him, dumbfounded. "Are you all right?" The Indians were pointing to the bottle and clapping him on the back in obvious admiration. Dan just grinned and serenely took another swig.

After that the Indians treated Dan with the respect of a national hero, offering him cachaça and refusing to let him help with any of the work, which galled Fawcett considerably.

"What? In jail again? But I just bailed him out, and it cost a pretty bribe, too!" Fawcett stared at the new Governor of the Beni in cha-grin. The foppish Governor gingerly let himself down into a chair next to Fawcett's on the veranda of Riberalta's so-called hotel.

"Sorry to bear bad tidings, Major," he said. "But apparently Dan could not pay for some debts he's managed to run up— for liquor which he has already consumed— so the merchant ordered his arrest."

Fawcett set his jaw firmly. "Well, I'll not be rushing to his aid again. I've better uses for my money, and besides, it's time he paid the consequences."

"I don't blame you at all, my dear fellow. I'm sure you've been very patient."

You don't know the half of it, Fawcett thought. And his patience was being sorely tried in ways that had nothing to do with Dan. "Tell me, is there any word on my passage to Rurrenabaque?"

"I'm terribly sorry," replied the Governor, adjusting the tassels on his ridiculous jacket. "The government launch, alas, cannot be repaired. I hope to find a boat for you soon."

Fawcett sighed heavily. The batelón which brought him to Riberalta had gone up the Madre de Dios for rubber with a new crew, and there seemed to be no other craft available. For three weeks he had not complained about being trapped in Riberalta. There had been various duties and distractions to keep him busy: reports to be written, maps to complete, and mail. Lots of lovely letters from family, newspapers, and official correspondence. Included in the latter were instructions to postpone future expeditions until some financial matters were resolved. Fawcett, far from being disappointed, was positively gleeful at this news, wanting time to relax and complete his maps before plunging once again into the unknown.

But now he was getting restless. He had caught up with his desk-work, he was rested and well-fed, and he was thoroughly sick of Riberalta. There might be many things that galled Fawcett in a minor way, but there was one thing which he absolutely could not abide: inactivity. Several schemes to obtain a boat had fallen through, and he was beginning to feel like a prisoner; Riberalta was laughing at him, teasing him with the possibility of release but never letting him quite carry it out.

"Riberalta is a miserable place, isn't it, Major?" the Governor was saying.

Fawcett woke from his glum reverie. The man must have read his mind.

"Well, it's shocking in many ways, I must say. The last of my Indian crew died today. All gone! All of them!"

"Ah, yes, the Indians do die so easily... "

"With the help of a little alcohol and a few of the white man's diseases," Fawcett couldn't help adding. "Not to mention brutal treatment by slavers."

"Yes, one of my purposes here is to deal with these beasts— "

"Governor, to refer to those sub-humans as 'beasts' is to insult all creatures that were not endowed with human barbarity."

The Governor laughed, then saw Fawcett was serious. "I suppose so. The government is taking steps to protect the indigenous peoples. We would like to understand them better. But there are many different tribes, some of which we've barely contacted. Perhaps it's better that way."

"Perhaps."

At length, Fawcett resorted to vague threats to use his influence with governmental officials against the Governor if a suitable boat was not hastily procured. He realized with chagrin that he should've done so weeks ago, when a batelón almost immediately appeared out of thin air and was put at his disposal.

"Now the only thing," simpered the Governor, still worried by Fawcett's threats, "You must share it with a Customs official and the Army Colonel, who are also bound for La Paz, eventually; you don't mind, do you?"

"No, no, that's fine." Fawcett would've shared Charon's ferry with Lucifer himself if it meant he was quitting Riberalta.

But of course, merrily re-packing his crates of Quaker Oats, sardines, and hard bread, he was unaware of what he had let himself in for. They had a grand send-off. The garrison turned out for the Colonel and the English population was there for Fawcett; amid shouts of farewell and rifles firing their smoky salutes, the Governor brought a chill to Fawcett's soul with his parting words: "I'm sorry to see you go, Major. Your work here has been most useful; too bad you are not our permanent prisoner!"

Instead he became a prisoner of the batelón. Three-quarters of the way through the journey he wrote a letter to his wife.

Dearest Cheeky,

Finally I am free of Riberalta; I hope you will receive the letters I wrote you while stranded there. Now, however, I find myself trapped in another miserable prison, in the form of a batelón making its tortuously slow way to Rurrenabaque. Will we ever arrive??

My travel companions are far from the most charming. (Dan was left behind in Riberalta, I am sad to say... in jail again.) The Colonel, an obese fellow who has yet to bathe in all the thirty-three days we have passed together in this boat, has broken out in stinking boils over his entire body; as we are forced to share very close quarters in the shelter, I am nauseated by his person. He brought along his prize possession: a chamber pot, which, in addition to its customary uses, serves as his dinnerware.

The Customs official who accompanies us is a nice enough fellow, but both he and the Colonel help themselves to my store of food (having brought none of their own), and complain that it lacks variety! He seems as allergic to bathing as the Colonel, and both men expectorate continually and let it fall where it will. When it rains and we are cooped up in the shelter, I feel I will go mad with disgust.

There is a mestiza aboard as well, and like most Indians in this area she enjoys catching sandflies and other flying insects to supplement her diet. I thought she would choke to death on a mouthful of flies the other day when the batelón struck a sudden snag. This snag, by the way, pierced the rotten hull and we had to use all the crew's clothing to plug it, until we made the next barraca where it fell to me to repair the damage.

This is quite the most ignorant and inadequate crew I have ever seen. They are fueled by alcohol and when the alcohol runs out, they stop. They seldom pay attention to what they are doing, and consequently there are constant mishaps... Just this week, one of them gashed his foot badly on a stingray in the shallow water, and another lost two fingers to a piranha while washing his hands in the river. Neither will do anything at all now but moan and groan and drink, joining those crew members who have been laid low by fever and influenza.

I tried my best to arrange overland passage to Rurrenabaque when we reached the mouth of the Madidi– there is a mission there– but the Padres had no mules available. I am trapped, and I feel much the same as I did in Riberalta. Will I ever be free from this voyage through Hell? I would rather, a thousand times over, face arrows and rapids and jaguars.

In re-reading what I've written, dear wife, it's clear I rely upon my sense of humor (what's left of it) to help me through this. But there is nothing like watching a smelly man picking his boils to kill all mirth in one's soul. . .

Kiss the boys for me– Your long-suffering, loving husband,
P.

Forty-five interminable, indescribable days later, Fawcett was released from his torture; on September 24 the rotten batelón docked at Rurrenabaque, and the Major had to restrain himself to keep from kissing the beach. The hotel was like a palace to him.

Even better, a mule train arrived from Sorata, and Fawcett rushed to book it for his overland trip to La Paz.

"I would like to rent you the mules, Señor," said the arriero. "But I have heard that the Colonel is going to requisition them."

Fawcett nearly jumped out of his skin. The Colonel! He began thinking desperately, his fighting spirit roused: *There is no way on earth that I am going to let that bag-of-boils take this mule train from me, nor am I going to spend another few weeks with him and his chamber pot! I must 'shoot a line' to the arriero, and it had better be a good one.*

"Listen, my good man, if you let him requisition your mules, you will wind up being paid nothing. I, on the other hand, will give you half your fee in advance." Fawcett jingled the gold coins in his pouch. The man looked at the pouch hungrily.

"But how can I stop him from commandeering my animals?"

"Easy. We leave tonight. Quietly." Fawcett winked.

As the mules made their slow and laborious way along the steep trails, Fawcett frequently sighed with pleasure; he had burst free of yet another potential trap. Bundling up against the freezing surusus wailing through the forests, he recalled how difficult this same trip had seemed fifteen months ago. Now, the homes in which he stopped for food and accommodations seemed the height of luxury, with proper meals and plates and forks, and freshly-baked bread! The houses of Sorata were so stable-looking and grand, and when they at last arrived in La Paz, on October 17, the city almost overwhelmed Fawcett. So many people, so many houses and buildings, so many conveniences!

He checked into a wonderful hotel and went to his room, throwing his dilapidated baggage on the floor. Suddenly he received a bad fright. He had caught a glimpse of himself in the large mirror, and now he understood why he had gotten so many stares as he rode into La Paz on his mule. His beard was scraggly and long, his skin burned dark by the sun, and his clothes— well, disreputable. Even in this city on the fringe of the wilderness, he looked like a wild man. He burst into laughter, which made him appear even more savage.

As he sank between the clean, crisp sheets, he looked forward to a shave the next morning and some new clothing. And there was something he looked forward to even more. All night long he dreamed of dreamed of the tender hills of England, of the silky arms of his wife, of four-year-old Jack and the baby, Brian; he was fed up with the piti-less wilderness, with swarming insects, isolation, and death. He wanted to go home.

Before he could leave it was necessary to take care of official busi-ness. When he turned in his reports and maps to the President, Gen-eral Montes, he was offered the opportunity of further boundary delimitation with Brazil, along the Rio Paraguay.

He thought for a moment. Tired of it all as he was, the offer was tempting, as it would take him into unexplored territory; this ap-pealed to the adventurer in him and he couldn't deny it.

"Well– I am interested, I must say; but I would first have to obtain permission from London... Could I contact you with my answer after I've spoken with them?"

"Of course, Major Fawcett."

He made his farewells, pushing all thought of wilderness explora-tion from his mind. All he could see was England ahead of him, like firelight deep in the forest: Home. . .

Carols of Christmastime played softly on the gramophone of a nearby house, a gentle, atmospheric background. The sweet fragance of his youngest son's skin filled his senses as he held the boy on his lap, the little head close against his chest. He looked across at Nina, mending a shirt by the fireside, just as he had pictured her so many, many times. She looked up at him and smiled, her eyes alight with contentment. He had presented the Bolivian government's request for his further services, and was awaiting a reply from British authori-ties. If they declined, so be it; he halfway wished they would.

Little Jack approached, clamoring to join Brian in his father's lap. Fawcett laughed. "Of course! Climb aboard; room for all! Would Mother like to climb in, too?" The boys squealed with delight, plead-ing with their Mummy to crowd in with them.

"I have a pot on the stove, my loves," she said, rising and putting her sewing on a table. She kissed each of the three faces, lingering on her husband's forehead for an extra touch of her lips. "But I'll be back!" she warned.

The days passed happily at Dawlish Warren, and Fawcett satisfied every ordinary little daydream he had had while lying in his creaking hammock in the wet forests, which seemed now like some shadowy, unfathomable world that only existed as a dim memory. Even when he regaled his family with tales of his adventures, to his own ears his stories had a sense of unreality about them. It was all so very far away, and so strange. He sat by his wife in church and sang the familiar hymns, and tucked the boys in their cozy beds at night, finding it hard to believe there was any other life but this.

It was late in January when the quiet, tenacious voice of his Mistress reminded him once more of her presence deep in his soul. He was puttering in the garden with Nina and had paused to listen to the distant sea. At that moment, their neighbor put a record on the gramophone, and the strains of the music pierced Fawcett's heart like a tiny, painless, but deadly dart. It was the *Estudiantina*.

All at once the garden, the sea, even Nina, all disappeared. He was standing beside the Acre, flowing like a river of gold before the setting sun. The trees stood in silhouette above him, bars of a prison cell so high that he could never climb out nor did he want to try; elegant music wove incongruously through the chatter of monkeys and shrieks of unseen birds. *I've heard the voice of the wild places, now part of me forever.* Tendrils of the bewitching forest had twined themselves around him like the arms of a dangerous lover, drawing him closer; he knew she would kill him on a whim if she wished, yet he couldn't stay away. Her ungodly bed was where he belonged.

Yearning and regret simultaneously coursed through his body as he looked at his wife, innocently digging in the English earth, unaware she had lost him.

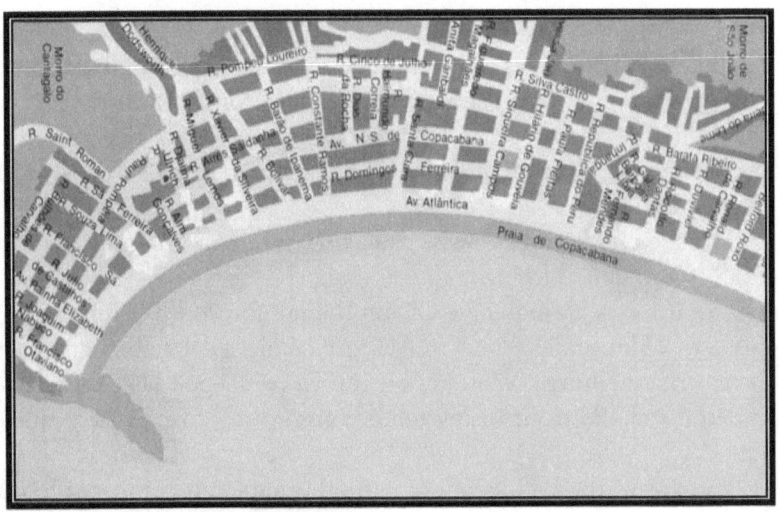

SYLVIA, CHAPTER 4
RIO de JANEIRO

The spotted jaguar moved indolently through dappled sunlight, pausing beside a large tree. For a few moments it rubbed its hind-quarters against the rough bark, enjoying a good scratch. Then it wheeled around almost playfully to grasp the tree with its forepaws, digging curved white claws into the bark; slowly the beast walked its forelegs up the trunk, arching its back until its rump protruded, stretching up, up, as far as it could go and still keep its hind feet on the ground. Then the jaguar dug deeply into the bark, powerful muscles in the forelegs and haunches rippling, drawing its claws downward one paw at a time, over and over, sharpening its lethal weapons until the tree bark hung in long shreds.

Sylvia hit the Pause button and slumped back in her chair, checked by an almost physical pang of longing. *Saudade.*

Greg looked at her with concern. "Is something wrong?"

"No, nothing... Just indigestion, probably. Well, actually, I was remembering something—" She rubbed an area near her solar plexus, as if in so doing she could make the yearning go away.

"Look, it's none of my business, but you haven't seemed like yourself, lately. I mean," Greg looked flustered, "Not that I know you all that well, but... " He trailed off.

Sylvia restarted the video and watched the big cat as it gracefully returned all four feet to the ground and sauntered away from the torn tree.

"I know," she said, as she continued to watch her computer screen. The photographer had captured rare footage of the notoriously shy animal before it disappeared into the foliage. "Doing this project is tearing me up, like that bark!" She gestured at the screen, and laughed hollowly.

"Maybe you should've worked on the Antartica program, instead, huh?" Greg smiled feebly.

"Oh, if I weren't making a CD on the rainforest, I'd still be feeling this way. Unusually bored. Like part of me got left behind down there, or something. Working on the Fawcett book also keeps that wilderness at the front of my mind constantly." She paused, thinking.

"You know, the U.S. is full of natural beauty, but compared to the Amazon, even our wilderness areas seem sort of— circumscribed, and controlled. Did I tell you there's still a 'frontier' in Brazil? I did? And it's still possible to homestead there! It's kind of like the old days in our country... Is this what it means to hear the 'call of the wild'?"

Sylvia had shared her vivid impressions of Amazonas with Greg when she returned to the museum, talking with him for hours over coffee, trying to express what it was like to sleep in the dark forest and awaken under a blanket of leaves.

The after-effects were peculiar, she reflected. It was simply an exotic jaunt, like many she had taken before; it was always a little hard to come back down to earth after a Magical Mystery Tour somewhere radically different from home, but it wasn't normally like this. At first she thought she had changed in some fundamental way, on a level her rational mind hadn't been able to analyze. Then she began to suspect the trip only crystallized impulses that had been boiling around in her psyche for quite some time.

She turned to Greg. "I feel different now, about the city. In fact, this whole artificial world of ours seems sort of pointless... Though I'm aware our little adventure in the Amazon wasn't all that genuine, either. I'm sorry to be such a bore; maybe it's a midlife thing. Perimenopause!"

"Look, I have a sense of what you mean, I think. In our society, we're all just playing games, in a way. Going around and around the Monopoly board. You got a little taste of a particular reality few people nowadays can imagine. Maybe there's a primitive core inside us

all, that thrives on that type of challenge, but few of us ever access it."
He was thoughtful for a moment. Then, "Sylvia, go with your instincts. You're completely free, single— Why don't you go back down
there? Spend some more time exploring whatever's eating at you... ?"

"I've been thinking about that. After I wrap up work on this program, I have no commitments. So why not? But I have to earn a living, I'm not rich enough to dally around in the woods for long."

"Maybe you could find work there. You have many talents to offer.
The Brazilians are real technophiles, I've heard."

The wheels of her mind began turning, turning.

"Now boarding rows K through R... "

Sylvia stood. "Thanks so much, Greg, for the lift and for waiting
with me..."

"My pleasure. Knock 'em dead on the interview! I'm living vicari-
ously through you, so don't let me down."

Once aloft, lulled by the drone of the engines, from her window
seat she watched the crimson sun slowly setting and hoped she could
sleep. She had a few melatonin capsules handy for the red-eye flight.
Right after the meal service she would down one or two and say
nighty-night. She half-listened to the flight attendant's directions in
the use of life jackets; they would be flying over a portion of the Pacific.

Her flight to Manaus weeks earlier had taken place during daylight
hours. After they had descended below cloud cover on the approach,
she'd been able to see the endless green blanket of forest, with a
quick glimpse of Manaus, before the plane banked steeply and
cruised in for a landing. And on the return midnight flight, she had
conked out immediately; the two weeks of camping finally caught up
with her, and even violent air turbulence hadn't awakened her. The
passenger beside her decided she'd fainted from fright.

During the present flight she didn't expect to see anything until
they neared Rio, after sunrise.

Rio de Janeiro! A far, far cry from the Amazon. One half of her
said, "Might as well be in L.A." But the other half argued that at least
she'd be in Brazil, and in a better position to research the areas where
Fawcett went.

She opened her Portuguese grammar and tried to concentrate on a list of idioms. She flashed back to the moment she and Greg had simultaneously thought of Dr. Pereira, in São Paulo.

"Call him!" Greg urged.

After that, it seemed as if a force took hold, moving things along at a breath-taking pace: A job for you in Brazil? Why, quite possible, the courteous Dr. Pereira had told Sylvia, giving her the name, telephone number, and email address of an acquaintance of his in Rio.

"Send her your C.V. by email," he recommended. "She speaks and reads English. She's looking for someone, and you might fit her requirements. Or perhaps she can refer you elsewhere."

Sylvia's message to Senhora Julia Carreca of Instituto Duas Americas, in Copacabana, resulted in an immediate, somewhat astounded, reply.

"Your qualifications sound ideal for our needs," Sra. Carreca wrote. "We could scarcely believe it when we read your vitae."

After a rapid exchange of messages and telephone calls, an interview was arranged. Sylvia would fly to Rio at her own expense, and the Institute would cover her hotel bill, including meals.

As the airliner levelled off and flight attendants began serving drinks, Sylvia gave up on the grammar and looked over the information she'd received from Julia. Instituto Duas Americas— Two Americas Institute, or IDA as it was familiarly known throughout Brazil— was a non-profit organization founded in 1962. Over the years its mandate had shifted focus, but its central aim had always been to provide a non-governmental link between North and South America.

Currently, IDA's primary function was the operation of cultural and educational exchange programs, chiefly connecting Brazil and the United States. Their programs were immensely popular with Brazilians eager to take advantage of the freedoms of democracy, after having rid themselves of many years of military rule. Artists, poets, and musicians vied for opportunities to expand their horizons with a stint of training and performance in the U.S. Their counterparts in the North crossed the equator to expand their craft in the colorful environs of Bahia, Rio, São Paulo, and elsewhere.

But by far the greatest number of participants in IDA's programs were students: Brazilian high school students aged sixteen or older applied for placement with families in the United States, while U.S. juniors and seniors came to live and study for a year at a stretch in Brazil.

Before sending teenagers abroad to live and study, IDA required thorough orientation in national culture, as well as a strong running start in the language. Most Brazilian students had been taking English courses for several years, but that was no guarantee they could speak the language even at a beginning level. IDA required prospective exchange students to either pass rigorous English exams or enroll in courses designed by Institute staff. For their part, students coming from the U.S. were expected to take courses in Brazilian history, culture, and geography, and instruction in Portuguese, at IDA facilities.

IDA needed a tech-savvy individual to update all courses from the current one-size-fits-all classroom presentations, which the teens found sometimes irrelevant, to a more efficient, interactive, individually-paced curriculum, with portions delivered via video and computer. In addition, many applicants hailed from far-flung corners of Brazil's twenty-six states; travel to Rio for orientation and coursework was complex and costly for both student and the necessary chaperone. Television and the Internet could be immensely useful in supplying online courses and minimizing the time spent at IDA headquarters— if only someone could be found who was well-versed in their usage and in all aspects of distance education.

Sylvia shook her head in wonder. She could see why the people at IDA were surprised when they saw her résumé; she was a remarkable fit for the job, having had experience in most of the areas of need, including curriculum design.

But she wasn't sure about Rio. She'd pictured herself living closer to the forests; in Manaus, for example. However, she had to get her foot in the door. Maybe she'd make valuable contacts while she was in Rio; and she was looking forward to seeing that renowned city.

Flight attendants pushed the meal cart down the aisle. Sylvia conversed with her seatmate, a Brazilian gentleman, trying her Portuguese with him.

"You speak the language so well!" he told her.

You sweet liar, she thought. *My mouth feels full of marbles.* Sylvia spoke Spanish and Italian fluently, but she was finding Portuguese difficult by comparison.

When the trays were removed, the gentleman settled himself for a nap. Sylvia turned to the window; the sun's light was long gone, the evening hastened by their flight into eastern time zones. She took the little bottle of melatonin from her bag, but before she could open it the pilot came on the P.A. system.

"We'll be flying over Bogotá soon," he said chattily. "You folks on the left of the aircraft will have a view of its lights... "

Sylvia, on the left side, began watching. In a few minutes, from the midst of utter blackness came the dramatic sight of a big spatter of sparkling lights. The air was so clear Sylvia could trace roads and highways lined with streetlights.

Just as abruptly as it had appeared, the brightness that was Bogotá ended at the city limits and a deep, velvety black background took its place. Passengers who had roused themselves long enough to behold the view now settled back, reclined their seats, and pulled blankets to their chins. Rio was still a long way off.

Sylvia remained at the window, the pill bottle lying forgotten in her lap, held by the sight of the inky earth beneath. As the minutes ticked by and the jet covered more and more miles, it dawned on her what a truly vast area of complete darkness they were passing over. The Amazon Basin.

A full moon was rising in the east. *What luck,* Sylvia thought, *that I was seated on this side of the aircraft.* She gazed dreamily out, imagining pale moonlight shining on the Blackwater Flooded Forest. Somewhere down there were the garnet waters of the Bariaú, and jaguars prowled the dim forest for prey, padding silently through glowing leaves.

When the moon had risen near its apex, its light began to reflect in each body of water below, from small lakes and streams to large rivers. Winding through the profound darkness of the forests were luminous silver ribbons whose paths Sylvia could discern until they dwindled and vanished in the blackness where their sources hid.

Now and then a large, placid lake reflected the orb of the moon itself for a few seconds as the jet passed over.

Sylvia was riveted by the scene and forgot all about sleep, awed by the sheer size of the wilderness. For at least an hour the great darkness and gleaming threads of water continued to pass beneath. Then another glittering splash of electricity appeared in the distance: Manaus. Soon she looked down on the Rio Negro, and then the great Amazon River itself, its shimmering, serpentine course seeming without beginning or end.

After the gentle radiance of the moon, Manaus was too bright for Sylvia's eyes. But soon the glare was behind her, and for another hour the plane hurtled through a night sky, far above the immense basin, moonlight shining down upon the craft and reflecting from its wings.

Sylvia yawned. *Only a few weeks ago I saw the black night of Amazonas from a different perspective: a hammock swinging between two trees, somewhere in the forests that crowd the Rio Negro...*

Some time after they had flown over the Araguaia River, a sliver of light gradually grew on the eastern horizon. They passed into the air space over Goiás State and neared Brasilia, the nation's capital. More lights appeared. Sleepiness finally overcame Sylvia; she dozed for an hour or so until the craft began its slow descent over Rio de Janeiro State, and landed at Galeáo, Rio's international airport.

"*Está perto daqui,*" the driver said as he slowed the vehicle. "*Ah, aqui está!*" He stopped the taxi in front of the Copacabana Sol Hotel. Senhora Carreca had praised it as a pleasant hotel within easy walking distance to IDA.

"It's where the IDA staff sends most of our out-of-town visitors. I'll make reservations for you, but if you don't like the hotel please let us know."

It looked just fine to Sylvia, lightheaded from sleepiness and the confusion of a foreign airport. Julia had sent a special taxi and a reliable driver to take her directly to the hotel. The interview was scheduled for the following afternoon.

Now, Sylvia followed the driver as he took her through wide glass doors and deposited her suitcase on the gleaming marble floor. He told her he had been paid, and refused a gratuity. She approached the counter, with no employees in sight, and suddenly an intense sensation of *déjà vu* swept over her. *Must be jet lag; I really am feeling the lack of sleep...*

A youth perhaps twelve years old appeared at the door of an office behind the counter. "*Bom dia,*" he said shyly, gesturing toward a large register and handing Sylvia a pen. She was aware social manners were more formal than she was accustomed to in California, so she signed her name and title, in Portuguese: Doutora Sylvia L. Garth. The eerie sense that she had done all of this before continued.

She looked around her at the lobby. Her gaze rested on marble walls, their green and gray patterns merging elegantly; each panel of marble was joined by a narrow strip of gold-colored metal. And there at the back of the lobby, as she knew it would be, was a wide flight of shallow, marble steps leading up to the next floor. Sylvia's head reeled. *My dream. That's where I saw this place.*

Something stirred behind her. She spun around and faced a smiling woman who was now coming from behind the desk. The boy was picking up her suitcase.

"*Bem-vindo,*" the woman said, Welcome, as she led Sylvia up the staircase. "*Voce fala português?*"

"*Só um pouco,*" Sylvia answered. I only speak it a little. The woman went on talking in a friendly way, but Sylvia couldn't understand most of her remarks.

As they entered the room, the experience of *déjà vu* ended. The room was as Sra. Carreca had said, pleasant and well-furnished. There were no tapestries on the wall. No magnificent tree. Years ago there would have been a view of the sea, but it had been long blocked by newer, higher buildings. Sylvia washed her face and fell into bed, too tired to puzzle it over. This time she dreamed only of the bright face of the moon, shining back at her from blood-red waters of the Bariaú.

"French or Italian. It's your choice, Sylvia," said Paulo Oliveira, IDA's Operations Manager.

"Both restaurants we have in mind are by the sea, and very lovely," Julia added.

"Mm... Italian."

"Then the Internacional it is! Don't forget, we take two hours off for lunch in Rio, so we'll make it a true celebration!" Julia beamed. Formalities had been dropped, and everyone was on a first-name basis. Before long they'd be co-workers.

Sylvia thought she'd like working with Julia, a thin woman in her early fifties with sandy hair and sallow skin, an admitted chain smoker, with slight pouches under her tired brown eyes; she was fashionably but casually dressed in a pantsuit and high heels.

The week was passing quickly. After the formal interview Monday afternoon, attended by Julia, Paulo, and two Board members who sat in but asked few questions, and a lengthy tour of IDA headquarters, Julia and her assistant, Carlina, took Sylvia out for a typical Brazilian *churrascaria* dinner and an introduction to *caipirinha* cocktails, consisting of *cachaça* with lime juice and sugar.

"Whoa! It tastes like limeade but packs a punch, doesn't it? I learned in the Amazon I can only handle a little bit of *cachaça*." The Brazilian women laughed knowingly.

The following day there was a luncheon in her honor at a nearby restaurant, attended by most of IDA's management-level employees, a bright, forward-thinking group of friendly and enthusiastic Brazilians. All of the managers and directors, more or less evenly balanced between men and women, spoke English; most of the other employees did not, although some were in various stages of learning. Courses in U.S. English were offered free to all IDA employees.

Aside from the mid-day meal, she was on her own on Tuesday. The first place she went was Copacabana Beach, for a run and a swim.

It was August, still wintertime in the southern hemisphere; the weather was sunny but mild, and the ocean felt temperate to Sylvia, accustomed to the bracing Pacific. Julia had told her about the Humboldt Current which swept up South America from Antarctica in Brazil's steamy summer, cooling Rio's surf to a refreshing 76 degrees, on average. By contrast, in winter the current was absent and the sea temperature dropped only a few degrees, but due to the cooler air it felt relatively warm.

"That's unusual, but perfect! So you can swim comfortably, year-round?"

"Oh, yes," Julia answered.

"Then I already like it here."

As she jogged down the long, curving beach, she noted that she hadn't seen a single piece of trash. That did not match her impression of most third-world countries she had visited. And the beach, on a weekday, was almost deserted.

She took buses to see the sights of the city, and gradually she became enthralled with Rio de Janeiro. Yes, it was crowded and noisy, yes, there were problems, poverty, crime, as in any large city. She was accustomed to all these. And Rio was many miles away from the Amazon. But it was still gloriously beautiful, tropical, and vastly different from any place where she had lived before; there would be much to experience and learn.

In sum, she was in Brazil.

Wednesday morning she had another appointment at IDA, where the position of Curriculum Director was offered, accepted, and now, about to be celebrated.

In less than half an hour after selecting the restaurant, Sylvia found herself clinking champagne glasses with her two hosts in the Hotel Rio Internacional's elegant restaurant. The grand old hotel faced the sea on Avenida Atlântica, an elegant concourse which followed the long sweep of Copacabana Beach. Julia and Paulo intended to show off the beauty and charm of Rio's seaside, while honoring a valued new employee; the four-star restaurant was also meant as a subtle assurance for Sylvia that IDA, though a non-profit organization, was generously endowed and could support the plans they had laid for her department.

Sylvia was duly impressed.

"This is magnificent," she said, as they stood with their wine on the second-floor promenade overlooking the beach. "I can't believe I'm going to be living in Rio."

"This has all happened very fast, hasn't it? You can think it over, if you want, after you return to Los Angeles... " Julia thought she should give Sylvia a chance to back out gracefully, in case she had been swept up in the heady excitement of an exotic city.

"No, no, Julia, thank you; but I've made up my mind. Everything feels right."

She couldn't tell them about the dream of the hotel: a glimpse into her future. Perhaps it wasn't logical, but the dream seemed to point to the choice she would— and should— make. And there were other, more practical factors that influenced her decision, number one being the position itself. She'd be creating an entirely new curriculum, from video to online courses; she would establish distance learning outposts in several of Brazil's states, and the lure of travel had been one of the most attractive features of the offer. Sylvia, who thrived on the challenge of building "from scratch", would in fact be forming a brand-new department within the organization.

Good restaurants could be added to the list of Rio's assets, she decided.

"How is your meal?" asked Paulo. An Italian-Brazilian, he was secretly happy she had chosen Italian food. He himself was a superb cook.

"Delicious. I've eaten well all week, though sometimes I wasn't sure what I was ordering; my food vocabulary needs work. And speaking of language, Julia, you mentioned something about Portuguese courses being a perquisite of my job?"

"Yes, we want you to gain language skill as fast as you can; you'll need Portuguese when you travel, especially. Very few people in Brazil speak English."

Sylvia was realizing what a steep learning curve she would face; everything, not simply the language, was very different from the U.S. or Europe. She hadn't been able to so much as buy a cup of coffee or use a public telephone without learning a new procedure. Fortunately, the Cariocas, as the people of Rio were called, were extraordinarily patient and helpful.

"You must return on Saturday?" Paulo asked.

"That's right. Two more full days to enjoy Rio." Now that business was taken care of, Sylvia was thinking, she could relax.

"Oh, but we're going to need you for a couple of hours at the office," Julia said apologetically, "to fill out paperwork, I'm sorry to say. We have to apply for your work permit, and the bureaucracy in Brazil is terrible."

"That's okay. It can't be avoided."

Paulo spoke up. "I'd like to compensate for that inconvenience. If you have no other plans, I can show you some of Rio's nightlife on Friday."

"I'd love it! Thanks, Paulo."

"Julia, you, too?"

"Thank you, Paulo, but I have an engagement. Is Isabel in town?"

"No, she gets back from São Paulo late Saturday."

He explained to Sylvia, "Isabel is my girlfriend, she travels on business sometimes; you'll meet her eventually." He had an idea. "You know, if you could be available Friday when I leave work at six-thirty, before dinner I'll show you a place that's difficult to visit without a car."

"Sounds wonderful; where is this?"

He paused. "It's a surprise."

The car purred smoothly up Estrada Dona Castarinha, through lush foliage which became more beautiful with every kilometer. Paulo had driven Sylvia first to Ipanema Beach, and then circled Rodrigo de Freitas Lake, before turning onto the green byway which climbed gradually into the hills.

Sylvia glanced at her companion. Her first sight of Paulo Oliveira had made her flash back to Milan; he reminded her of the tall, fair-skinned northern Italians, so she wasn't surprised to learn his great-grandparents had emigrated from that area to Brazil's Minas Gerais State, where they purchased a large *fazenda*, meaning ranch or plantation. Paulo, at six feet four inches, towered over her and seemed almost too big for his Volkswagen Golf; his brown hair was greying at the temples but his body was that of an avid cyclist and ocean swimmer. Not over fifty and very active, Sylvia had assumed.

"It's amazing to me how quickly we went from the crowded beach communities to this," Sylvia said, gesturing toward the tropical forest where she suddenly found herself. "I guess, when I looked at the view from the monument yesterday, I was more focussed on the shoreline and didn't realize what was behind me!"

"Ah, yes; how did you like Corcovado? Was there a clear view?"

"It was fabulous! I was lucky, there were no clouds." Sylvia had found the vista, and the famous Christ the Redeemer statue, more imposing than they appeared in photos and films. "It was a good way to get oriented to the layout of Rio, actually. That lake we went around— I've forgotten the name already— was lovely from up there."

Sylvia had gazed for a long time at her future home and its landmarks: Sugar Loaf Mountain and all the other granite "bread loaves" protruding dramatically from the earth; Guanabara Bay, the white sand of many beaches, the bridge to Niteroi. Her overall impression was of an unexpected quantity of deep green foliage and trees throughout the city and covering the hills, and the azure blue of the bay and ocean. She thought of Fawcett, who had also fallen in love with Rio, and what he wrote about it:

Nobody who has not seen Rio can realize what a paradise it is... The Brazilian has reason to be proud of it. He has the finest of all harbours, landlocked by picturesque and lofty mountains, and in this perfect setting has built himself a jewel of a city, abounding in wealth, in luxurious hotels, magnificent shops, wide avenues and superb boulevards.

What Rio must have been like in 1920 she couldn't imagine. It truly must've seemed like Paradise then...

"I can see why you wouldn't have a true idea of Tijuca Forest from that viewpoint," Paolo was commenting. "You literally would not see the forest for the trees; they block the view on that side."

Sylvia laughed. Paulo was proud of himself for pulling that English expression out of a hat. "So this is the surprise? Floresta da Tijuca?"

Sylvia asked with a delighted smile.

"You've heard of it?"

"I have, indeed. The largest urban national park in the world! I read about it in National Geographic, and I've been wanting to see it. How big is it?"

"It's thirty-two square kilometers; every Carioca knows that, so you may as well learn it now." He swung the car along the increasingly curvy road.

"What a wonderful idea to bring me here; you're right, I wouldn't have done this jaunt on my own, not on this short trip."

"I wanted you to know before you go back home, that Rio is not all pavement and buildings, like Copacabana."

Paulo's instincts were keen. When Sylvia had told everyone at Tuesday's luncheon a little about her Amazon experience, Paulo sensed her love of the natural world. Whenever she had been asked—by nearly everyone—why she was motivated to live in Brazil, her stock reply was, "While I was in Amazonas I became fascinated with Brazil and everything in it." He could see this was a true statement; but when she mentioned her research for the book on Fawcett, he knew she had more than a passing interest in the wilderness.

Now, he added, casting a glance her way, "In fact, Brazil is still mostly undeveloped; ninety per cent of its people live on ten per cent of the land—mostly on a narrow strip along the coast. If you go inland a hundred miles or so you begin to leave all the crowds behind."

Sylvia's mind buzzed with questions regarding the interior near Rio, but there would be plenty of time to ask, later. She was overwhelmed by the beauty of the forest around her. They stopped at a vista point, and walked down a path where masses of impatiens in all colors grew wild; her eyes were dazzled by the blossoms.

"Well, this is their natural habitat, I suppose!" she observed.

"I think they were brought in from Africa, but they've found themselves a home here. This type of forest is called *mata Atlântica*, and it used to extend for many miles all along the Atlantic coast of Brazil. Most of it's been destroyed now, unfortunately. Do you know the story of this particular area of the *mata*? Of Dom Pedro?"

"Um—no... "

"It was all planted by him."

"What?" Surely she had misunderstood.

"Not by his own two hands, of course; but it's an inspiring example of reforestation. The early colonialists cleared all the native *mata*, or forest, and put in its place vast coffee plantations, which flourished for many years, until the early 19th century, in fact. But a disease of some kind attacked the coffee trees, and the growers abandoned the area. Erosion set in. Emperor Dom Pedro the Second, who had a love of nature, decided to replace the forest. With legions of workers he began a monumental project of restoration, planting all the native species he could find, like *ipé, pau-ferro, jaqueira, peroba...* many others, including tiny plants. And this is the result."

Sylvia was speechless. The forest looked primeval, as if it had always been there. It gave her a sense of hope; if something like this could be done by humans... She shook her head in wonder. Finally she said, "I'd like to learn more about this Dom Pedro."

"Yes, you would identify with him, I think... "

"Thank you, Paulo, for showing me a nearby place I can go to be alone, and get away from the crowds sometimes."

"Uh— you shouldn't go alone... "

"No?" She felt let down.

"Please don't; it could be dangerous, you never know. I'm sure you've noticed Rio's slums, the *favelas.*"

"Yes. On hilltops, with great views, I imagine. In California that's where the high-priced real estate would be."

"Well, here, people who can afford it like to live near the beach. The poor built their shacks where there were no roads or services, just forest. Now, they're everywhere, huge favelas above Copacabana, Ipanema, all over. Rocinha, the favela south of Ipanema, has over 300,000 inhabitants."

Sylvia whistled.

"Let's continue, shall we? There's more to see before dinner."

In a few minutes, Sylvia was standing in the cool spray of an impressive waterfall. It looked familiar to her, somehow.

"They're called Taunay Falls," Paulo shouted over the roar.

"Well, Paulo, you've accomplished your mission: I'm surprised!"

He looked pleased. "The question now is, are you hungry yet?"

"I'm getting there."

Paulo laughed. Another American expression.

"Then here's a choice for you: Would you prefer to return to the beaches, and dine in a restaurant by the ocean? Or would you like to eat here, in the forest?"

"Oh, here! Definitely."

"I thought you might like that idea."

*

La Maison Forêt would've been described as home-like, but for its august air of decay, its phantoms of former grandeur lurking in the fine tiling of the patio wall and two giant, mossy urns standing guard over the diners. In fact, it had been the manor house of a pre-Dom Pedro II coffee plantation.

Sylvia and Paulo settled themselves at a spacious table beneath a blooming jacaranda tree. The waiter came to light their candles; he swept aside a number of lavender-blue flowers with his arm and spread a clean white cloth, saying something to Paulo that brought a little laugh. He left menus as he departed.

"What did he say? I didn't catch that."

"He said we would have to fight off macacos, the little monkeys, if we sat out here. I think he felt we should eat inside."

"Oh! I saw them in the Botanical Gardens; at first I thought they were squirrels... Maybe they're the reason there's only one other couple out here."

Paulo looked at his watch. "It's barely seven-thirty; it's early for a weekend dinner, in Rio. Also, not everyone here is as enchanted with the outdoors, and the selva, as you are... " A tiny red spider suddenly dropped onto the tablecloth. "Ah! You see what I mean?" He moved to brush it away.

"Wait." Sylvia picked up a leaf from the patio floor, and put it close beside the spider. Warily the creature crept aboard. She picked up the leaf by its petiole, her hand steady; the spider froze until she placed it gently on the low stone wall behind her. Paulo watched silently.

Without further ado she turned back and picked up her menu. Paulo was smiling at her. Self-consciously she said, "Well, that was a tiny mite compared to the Amazon's wolf spiders."

"Do you need any translation of the menu?"

"Mm... a bit, maybe... " Sylvia asked a few questions; Paulo patiently answered.

"You should practice your Portuguese with me; would you like to?"

"Good idea. I'll say what I can in Portuguese, and fall back on English when I need to. Please correct my mistakes."

As they dined the jacaranda blossoms fell on the cloth, which annoyed the waiter no end. But Sylvia was reminded of something

161

pleasant.

"When I awoke in Amazonas," she said carefully in Portuguese, "my sheet was covered with leaves and tiny orchids from the canopy."

"You slept outside?" Paulo raised his eyebrows.

"Mm-hm. In a hammock." She took a bite, and Paulo regarded her keenly. He had many questions, but now was not the time; they needed to keep the conversation simple.

As it was, by the end of dinner they had dropped back into English; there were too many things that Sylvia found difficult to express, or follow, in the new language. Paulo, on his part, began to feel the strain of speaking English for several hours. Sylvia was aware of the exhausting effort it took; she recognized its effect on Paulo, and became quieter, asking fewer questions.

When the waiter brought their *cafezinhos*, they sat back in their chairs and listened to the chorus of crickets hiding in the darkness of Tijuca Forest.

"No macacos joined us," she said a little regretfully.

Their next stop would be Vinicius, a nightclub in Ipanema where Sylvia could hear Brazilian performers. It would give both of them a rest. Paulo was looking forward to a break from conversation, and Sylvia could let go of her frustration, as she sensed they had much to talk about, but many nuances would be lost behind language barriers.

Sylvia rolled over and looked at the clock. Oh, heck, overslept again. Her brain immediately began racing. There was so much to do. She threw back the covers.

Where are my lists? Sylvia's To Do lists now occupied an entire notebook, and every day she added more tasks than she checked off. Visa paperwork, people to notify, utilities to shut off, insurance issues, storing the car... it was overwhelming.

She stared at her packing lists, befuddled. How does a person pack for two years? She had signed a one-year contract, which was renewable at the end of that period. After a year she would have a month's vacation; she could return to the States then if she wanted, but she suspected she'd prefer to spend that time travelling in Brazil. Deciding what to take along was an interesting exercise, as it forced her to focus on the essentials of a stripped-down existence, plus a few sentimental items to help her feel at home.

"Hope I'll be ready when my work permit come through," she told Greg when he dropped by to pick up some of her plants.

He lifted a heavy plant into his station wagon. "I'll take good care of your babies. You can also have them back, when—if—you return." Sylvia had been surprised how hard it was to give away her plants.

"Thanks, Greg."

"Any word on your living arrangements?"

"No, and that's the weirdest thing about this crazy, rash decision I've made. I don't even know where I'll be living! Julia's still looking for a room; but I'll be moving in with a complete stranger, Greg. This whole thing is a huge leap of faith, you know?" Half of IDA's staff was on the lookout for a comfortable apartment not too far from the office, where Sylvia might rent a room with someone they knew and trusted.

"I think it'll be good for you, and you know, I admire the hell out of you for doing this. We should all be so adventurous and— flexible."

"Easy for you to say." She smiled at his kind words. "I haven't had a *roommate* in twenty years," she muttered, putting a beloved old Swedish ivy in his car.

Sylvia handed the Varig agent her one-way ticket to Rio, and he gave her a boarding pass with a friendly nod.

This time, there was no moonlight, no magic, silvery rivers; it was early morning, she was finally off, and she was exhausted. She had been awake all night, frantically packing last-minute items right down to the minute that a friend arrived to take her to the airport. Though the day was just beginning, she fell asleep as soon as the breakfast tray was removed and didn't awaken until they were nearing Rio, twelve hours later.

Paulo was at Galeão to meet her, and introduce her new roommate: Isabel.

"I am so happy to meet you," Isabel said in English, grinning from ear to ear. She kissed Sylvia on both cheeks, a custom Brazilians had long ago borrowed from the French. Sylvia stammered something polite, distracted by the stunning beauty of the tall blonde who was relieving her of the heavy shoulder bag that contained Sylvia's most vital possessions.

"I have your room ready; yesterday I bought a new— *como se diz?*— cover?"

"Bedspread," Paulo supplied. "Isabel's very excited to have you stay with her. By the way, I ordered the largest radiotaxi they have. From your description of your baggage, I think— I hope— it will all fit. I'll accompany your things to Isabel's apartment, and she'll drive you in her car. That way you two can get acquainted."

Sylvia had been increasingly concerned about where she would live, when Julia telephoned, two days before she was to leave Los Angeles, to tell her Paulo's girlfriend had volunteered her apartment. Ipanema, where she lived, was adjacent to Copacabana, and her guest suite was empty.

"My parents left their city apartment to me," she explained to Sylvia. "It is too big for one person, but I can't convince Paulo to move in," she winked at him, "so I often have exchange students with me, temporarily. It's fun and I can practice my English."

Paulo added, "Whenever we have any problem with the placement of a U.S. student— sometimes there's a delay, or some part of the arrangement isn't working out— Isabel helps us until we solve the problem."

"But since I've been travelling now and then with my new job, I haven't been able to take in a young person. I've missed them, actually."

She flashed a radiant smile, her hazel-green eyes dancing. Sylvia began to warm to the graceful woman who, at five feet eleven inches, towered over her. Isabel's long hair swung to and fro as she helped Paulo lift Sylvia's trunks from the conveyor belt.

"No, please, rest," she said to Sylvia. "Point to your things, we get them."

With difficulty Sylvia had boiled her necessary belongings down to fit two trunks, three medium-sized boxes, and a large suitcase. She was pleased with herself.

The two women chatted on the long, congested drive to Ipanema. The sun was low in the sky. Sylvia learned Isabel was thirty-six years old and was a marketing representative for Apple Computers.

"Macs are now beginning to be popular in Brazil," she said. "Before, the duty was too high, and only a few people could afford them. Now we build them here, everything is different." She waved a hand jauntily.

"Good! Because I want a Mac for my office."

"All right! I give IDA a good price."

Sipping IDA's sweetened coffee, Sylvia read her email. She arrived at the office early each morning in order to deal with personal messages from the States. To Greg's message, she replied:

Yes, once again I've been lucky. Things are great at Isabel's; we get along as if we've known each other for years, though sometimes the language is a problem. I'm trying as hard as I can to improve my Portuguese, which is a devilishly hard language! I have it all mixed up with Spanish.

The apartment is beautiful and enormous. Everything is outsized in Brazil; I've never seen such gigantic apartments! I have a large room, my own bath, and a little balcony. But the bed is killing me... Seems as though a popular type of bed here is basically a board with some foam padding over it, and not much of that. Someone must've sold people a bill of goods about hard beds being beneficial for the back. The bed motivates me to find my own apartment, though Isabel says not to hurry.

There are many adjustments to make; I'm like a child, learning to do the simplest things. It's humbling and energy-consuming. I make many cultural gaffes, such as eating french fries and pizza with my fingers; the only food Brazilians touch with their hands is bread. They have beautiful table manners. I turn up a soda can or bottle to drink; everyone here uses straws. And I'm doing many things I was told not to do, for safety reasons: I walk alone on the beach and everywhere at night, I've hiked in Tijuca Forest alone. Isabel believes I come and go in safety because I've learned to blend in. I try to look like a local, and not a very rich one at that.

Actually, I'm disturbed by all the cautions I receive. I appreciate the intent; no one wants me to have a bad experience in their country. But I also think they might be overly fearful... Everything is "dangerous". The word's overused. I picked up some trash in a park the other day; my companions refused to touch any of it and hustled me immediately to a faucet so I could wash my hands.

Which reminds me, I was dead wrong about the clean beaches. On the weekend I was horrified to see beach-goers walk away from all their rubbish; glass bottles, cans, paper...Plastic bags and straws blow into the surf where they swirl around your ankles when you wade in. By Sunday evening the beach is covered with garbage; on Monday, legions of low-paid workers trudge the beaches and pick it all up! (I first saw the beach on a Tuesday, you see.)

But there are many joys. Kiosks at the beach sell cold drinking coconuts (with straws) every day of the year, for about a buck. Finally, my fill of coconut water!

"What did you buy? Let me see." Isabel helped Sylvia through the door with her parcels, including one very large one. Sylvia had been to a Friday afternoon artisans' street fair in a nearby plaza.

"I bought some candles, and marmalades for breakfast," Sylvia answered in Portuguese. "Then I saw this." She pulled something cream-colored out of the big sack.

"A hammock! Beautiful. You can hang it on your balcony; the hooks are already there."

"I saw them." The hooks had given Sylvia the idea. She could escape the board-bed by once again taking to a hammock.

"Come, have some burgundy." Isabel was making soup in a blender.

Sylvia poured herself some wine and began washing salad vegetables. "Paulo said to tell you he might be a little late; he's in a meeting with Julia and the Board."

" *'Ta bom.'* " Isabel turned off the blender and peered closely at the soup. "Tell me, Sylvia, how is it to work with him?"

"Beg pardon?" Sylvia often doubted her comprehension of Portuguese. She attended classes faithfully every day, but she needed more study time.

"Is he easy to work with? Is he flexible, or demanding?"

"Oh... He's actually very, um—" she switched back to English. "In the U.S. we say 'easy-going'; he's relaxed, *not* demanding. Why?"

"Well... Paulo is not an easy person to know. I feel there are many sides to him that I don't see. Sometimes people are different at work."

"That's true." To Sylvia, Paulo was most relaxed at the office, though often he seemed a trifle bored; he held one of IDA's top-echelon positions, but she sensed he had talents that were wasted there. When she saw him after-hours at Isabel's home, he was sometimes constrained, even guarded. Perhaps it was simply because she was present, an outsider.

"We've been seeing each other for almost two years, and I still feel he's sort of a stranger."

"Oh, surely that's an overstatement, Isabel."

"Maybe. But he holds back... And he's not ready to live together. But I guess it's good to be cautious."

Sylvia wasn't sure how to respond. Paulo was a fool if he didn't see what a treasure he had; Isabel was childlike and sophisticated at the same time, intelligent yet modest, hardworking, but fun. They appeared to have much in common. What more could he want?

Finally she said, "Anything worthwhile takes time..."

After a while Isabel said, "Did you know Paulo was married, years ago?"

"No, I didn't."

"He worked for FUNAI, the Indian agency, out in the west. His wife was pregnant. She and the baby were killed in an accident."

Sylvia was silent.

"Perhaps he has fears about love," Isabel added. "Perhaps—" The doorbell rang. "That's him. He's not very late, after all!"

The hammock barely fit on the small balcony, with a little room left for the potted fern. It was made of canvas, with long fringes of macramé. Sylvia tied it securely in the metal rings, and then fetched a sheet, pillow, and blanket.

She had excused herself soon after dinner, leaving Paulo and Isabel in privacy in the living room, watching television. She looked over a list of irregular verbs while her bathtub filled. This was a convenient arrangement, here with Isabel, she reflected; she had everything she needed, and a wonderful, English-speaking friend, to boot. Isabel was helping her learn colloquial Portuguese, showing her around Rio, and introducing her to people who didn't work at IDA. And now that she had a hammock she might actually get some sleep.

But she shouldn't get *too* comfortable. True, Isabel had been out of town on business for almost a third of the month Sylvia had lived there. But it was intended to be a temporary tenancy, and she thought it best to leave before she wore out her welcome. Having a roommate could surely not help Isabel's relationship with Paulo.

As she soaked she reluctantly made her resolve: She'd begin looking for her own place next week. Maybe she could find a furnished apartment, though Julia said they were rare in Rio. Setting up a household from scratch would be daunting... lists of needs ran through her mind: furniture, an iron, brooms and mops, pots and pans, linens—Lord, everything...

Later she slipped into her hammock, glad that the Avenida Henrique Dumont was lined with trees shielding Isabel's second-story apartment from most of the neighbors' lights. Some of the people in higher floors across the street could look down into her balcony, but with her lights off they wouldn't notice Sylvia, ensconced in her yielding, gently swaying bed. *Ah, Fawcett, you were so right. A hammock beats a bed; especially one with a board in it!*

For the first time in four long weeks, Sylvia slept without painfully tossing and turning. She dreamed she was in terrafirme forest by the Bariaú, where winking stars floated down through the canopy and became fireflies.

"Good morning! Rise and sparkle!" It was Will, moving among the tents, calling reveille...

No. Sylvia looked up to see a white building across the street looming over her. The melodious voice belonged to Isabel. She heard male laughter.

"É 'rise and shine', *cara*," Paulo was saying.

Isabel tapped on the door, opened it and stuck in her head. "Are you awake?"

"Yes, good morning!"

"Where are you...? Oh! You slept out there! You poor thing!" Isabel came to the balcony doors.

"Knock, knock," said Paulo. "May I come in, too?"

"Sure, come in." Sylvia rubbed the sleep from her eyes.

Isabel shook her head. "I feel very bad about that bed. You know, I don't like mine, either, though it's softer than this one. I think that's why I fall asleep on the sofa."

Paulo, carrying a cup of coffee, stopped and looked at Sylvia. "I wish I had a handful of orchids to throw over you... "

"Ah! So do I," she replied, remembering.

"O que é que é isto? Orchidea?" Isabel asked.

"I'll tell you about it in the car," Sylvia said. "Thanks for waking me up. I'll be ready in a jiffy. Er, soon."

"Take your time," said Paulo. "You're in Brazil. Here, this is for you. Instead of orchids." He handed Sylvia the coffee.

While she sipped, gradually waking up, Paulo and Isabel plopped down on the bed. "Ow!" exclaimed Paulo. "*Deus*, this bed *is* horrible... "

They were taking Sylvia on an overnight trip to "a very special place," as Isabel had said. As she drank her coffee they discussed the route and the long, torturous road, pocked with potholes. They gave Sylvia several suggestions for packing.

"Whenever we Cariocas want to be cold, we go to the mountains," said Isabel with obvious delight. "Prepare for a change in weather."

"Well, it's cool up at Mauá, not really cold," Paulo amended. "But do bring something warm for evening. And a swimsuit for daytime."

"Yikes, I see what you mean!" Sylvia braced herself as Paulo swung the car abruptly around a gaping pothole. "Are you all right back there?" she asked Isabel.

"I'm fine. I never get carsick." Isabel had insisted Sylvia sit in the front, for a better view and to avoid nausea on the relentlessly twisting road. After heading out of the city on highway 116 toward the westernmost corner of Rio de Janeiro State, at Penedo they left any semblance of a paved road and headed up into the mountains. The scenery quickly became breathtaking. Sylvia was amazed to see forests and vistas rivalling the wild beauty of Amazonas.

Visconde de Mauá was only 200 kilometers from Rio, not quite 125 miles, but it took them almost four hours to reach it. Higher into the mountains they rose, riding quietly, letting Paulo concentrate on the challenging hairpin curves. Slowly they wound their way upward through a great canyon.

"Wait! Stop! Please stop the car!" Sylvia shouted, staring out the window.

Paulo immediately swerved onto the narrow shoulder and stopped, setting the emergency brake as Sylvia opened her door and jumped out.

"I knew it," said Isabel. "Sick! *É pena—* "

But Sylvia wasn't retching; she was looking at the long ridge on the other side of the wide canyon, shaking her head in disbelief.

"This is too weird," she mumbled, as Paulo arrived at her side.

"What is the matter?" He followed her gaze, but saw only the ridge and some trees.

"Those trees; what are they?"

"The trees? Why, they're araucária," Paulo answered, as Isabel joined them.

Sylvia felt lightheaded, the peculiar dazed sensation she'd had when the other dream had been realized. The trees weren't burning, but the late morning sun lit the ridge with gold.

"I'm sorry; I didn't mean to be so dramatic." She hesitated. Couldn't seem any crazier than she already did, may as well spill it. "I saw this ridge, and these strange trees, in a dream. Exactly like this, except they were burning, one at a time... I've never seen trees like this before, I'm sure of it."

"Oh, I believe that," responded Isabel. "These trees are special; they only grow in certain places, usually in the south of Brazil. They have huge, heavy cones, with delicious seeds."

Paulo regarded Sylvia closely. "There are other kinds of araucária; some are from Australia. But this is the only type that looks like this; they *are* odd, aren't they? The Indians say the araucária is sacred." She looked at him quickly. Burning trees and plants were also sacred symbols in many cultures.

"Let's drive on," she finally said. "I'll tell you about my dream as we go. The road is becoming familiar to me, too, the switchbacks, everything."

That evening, over dinner beside a crackling fire in the lodge dining room, Sylvia wound up telling them about the other dream which had come true. The two had been so interested in her story of the araucária that she knew they weren't laughing at her. They had arrived by noon and had a wonderful afternoon swimming at the waterfall called Maromba, and exploring crafts shops in the village; Sylvia felt relaxed and trusting. It was as Fawcett had written: Brazilians tend to open their minds to the unfathomable, the impossible.

"Do you write down all of your dreams?" asked Paulo.

"Only the ones that seem worthwhile, or particularly vivid; and sometimes, just on a whim. "

Isabel spoke thoughtfully. "In Brazil, some say people who dream the future are chosen by God. They have a—*destino*—"

"Destiny."

" ...a destiny to be a spiritual leader or complete a mission of some kind. You've dreamed about Brazil; maybe your destiny is here."

Sylvia watched the flames and cradled a cup of herb tea. "Well," she said at last. "It's something to think about."

170

*

Julia had been right. Furnished apartments were rarities in Rio, quite expensive and normally used by business people on a short-term basis. Worse still, she discovered, unfurnished apartments in Brazil did not include appliances such as refrigerators or stoves. She was facing considerable expense, on top of the mortgage and other payments she had to send every month to the U.S.

Maybe, she thought, she should look for a room to rent on a permanent basis; another "roommate" arrangement. But she was beginning to feel a need for her own place. After work and on weekends, she looked at apartments in Copacabana and Ipanema. Nothing was right; they were too large or too expensive, too dark and gloomy, or on a "bad" street. She was discouraged.

"But there is no hurry to leave," protested Isabel. "Don't worry if you don't find anything."

"Isabel, you've been wonderful, and I'm very happy here. But it's time I return your guest room to you, *before* you get tired of me."

At least things at work were humming along smoothly. Sylvia had learned to do as the Cariocas at IDA did: work hard, enjoy your job, and go home when it's quitting-time; no one worked overtime hours unless something unusual occurred. But she looked forward to every Monday morning.

One Monday she was talking with Leonor Sousa, one of the vendors of language videos and workbooks, agreeing to use one of the new products on a trial basis. As Leonor, an amiable woman whom Sylvia had liked right away, wrote up the paperwork Sylvia had a sudden, odd urge to tell her about the apartment search.

That's not appropriate, she thought. *We're doing business. She isn't interested in my personal problems.*

The urge grew stronger, more insistent. *Well, what harm—*

"You know, if you hear of any apartments for rent in Copacabana I'd be grateful; I'm having a hard time finding a suitable place."

Leonor handed over the forms for her signature. "It's not easy, I know." She looked thoughtful for a moment as Sylvia went through the papers. "A one-bedroom apartment is big enough for you?" Sylvia nodded. "You'd probably like my place; I have something rather special... " As she described her Copacabana apartment and its unusual setting, Sylvia wondered why she was telling her all about something that was not available.

"Well, Leonor," she said politely, "your home sounds lovely, and if you decide to move, I'd certainly be interested."

"Well, you see, I sometimes think about moving in with my boy-friend. We could save money, and buy a place later. But it's just an idea, I can never decide if I want to give the place up. The rent is only 450 reais, which is quite a bargain." She closed her briefcase. "It's only a few blocks from here. Would you like to see it?"

Leonor drove her little car along Rua Barata Ribeiro; before she reached the tunnel which pierces Morro do Cantogalo— Cock's-Crow Hill— and leads to Arpoador and Ipanema, she made a couple of twists and turns.

"One of the best things about this building," she was saying, "is that it's at the base of the hill, so it's at the end of a little driveway. Very quiet, very green."

It was hard for Sylvia to imagine anything "very quiet" in Copaca-bana. Abruptly Leonor turned down a narrow drive. At its end were very big, old-fashioned iron gates and the green dimness of dense shade. She paused for a moment in front of the gates with the motor idling, and soon they began to swing open slowly, into a big, cobble-stoned courtyard. "The guard sees us, he opens it," she explained, driving through.

Sylvia gasped.

"Pretty, yes?" asked Leonor. With a multitude of flowers and ferns and trees, and a graceful Art Deco building at the back of the circular courtyard, yes, it was extremely pretty; but Sylvia hadn't been startled by the beauty.

It was the place in her dream, where she lived.

Leonor parked her car, while Sylvia gaped at the imposing entrance to the building: giant doors with black, Oriental patterns. The area around the courtyard was lush with tropical growth, so thick she couldn't at first see a path leading up the hillside. There were a few old, circular picnic and game tables, made of stone. As they walked across the cobbles, Sylvia's knees shook.

"This is truly special," she said to Leonor, who hadn't noticed her pallor.

Leonor greeted the guard positioned at a window in the spacious lobby, where he could see the entrance. They took a little elevator up to the fourth floor, and entered Leonor's apartment. It was filled with quaint Art Deco details which Leonor proudly pointed out, such as a radio built into the wall, dark, gleaming, wood parquet floors, and old marble countertops in the kitchen. But the loveliest thing, Leonor was saying, is the *varanda*. She flung open louvered doors to reveal a long, tiled balcony; Sylvia followed her out, and gasped again. Before them was a huge, spreading tree, with leaves the size of small platters; its branches were close enough that Sylvia could reach out and touch a leaf. She knew the tree; it was the one she had seen in the hotel dream. It completely blocked the sight of any other buildings, giving the apartment the feel of someplace far from the city. Below, the courtyard was paved in the wavy design so typical of Rio's tiled sidewalks.

"This apartment is on the corner against the hillside, so there's a nice view from the bedroom, too, and you don't hear anyone." She paused, looking out at the tree. "I have loved living here. It's hard to know what I should do... I'll think about it for a week, okay? Then I'll let you know."

Sylvia agreed, sure beyond doubt that her search had ended.

After five days, Leonor telephoned Sylvia at the office. The apartment was hers. Leonor had discussed it with the landlord, who was happy to have an American for a tenant; he could raise the rent to $550. Sylvia was ecstatic.

"That's still much less than it's worth, isn't it?" Leonor said. "And by the way, I don't have any place to store all of my furniture and large items... Could you use them? And the stove and refrigerator? My boyfriend has everything we need in his place. I can leave some of my dishes and pans, too, if you need them... "

Just like that, Sylvia had a home.

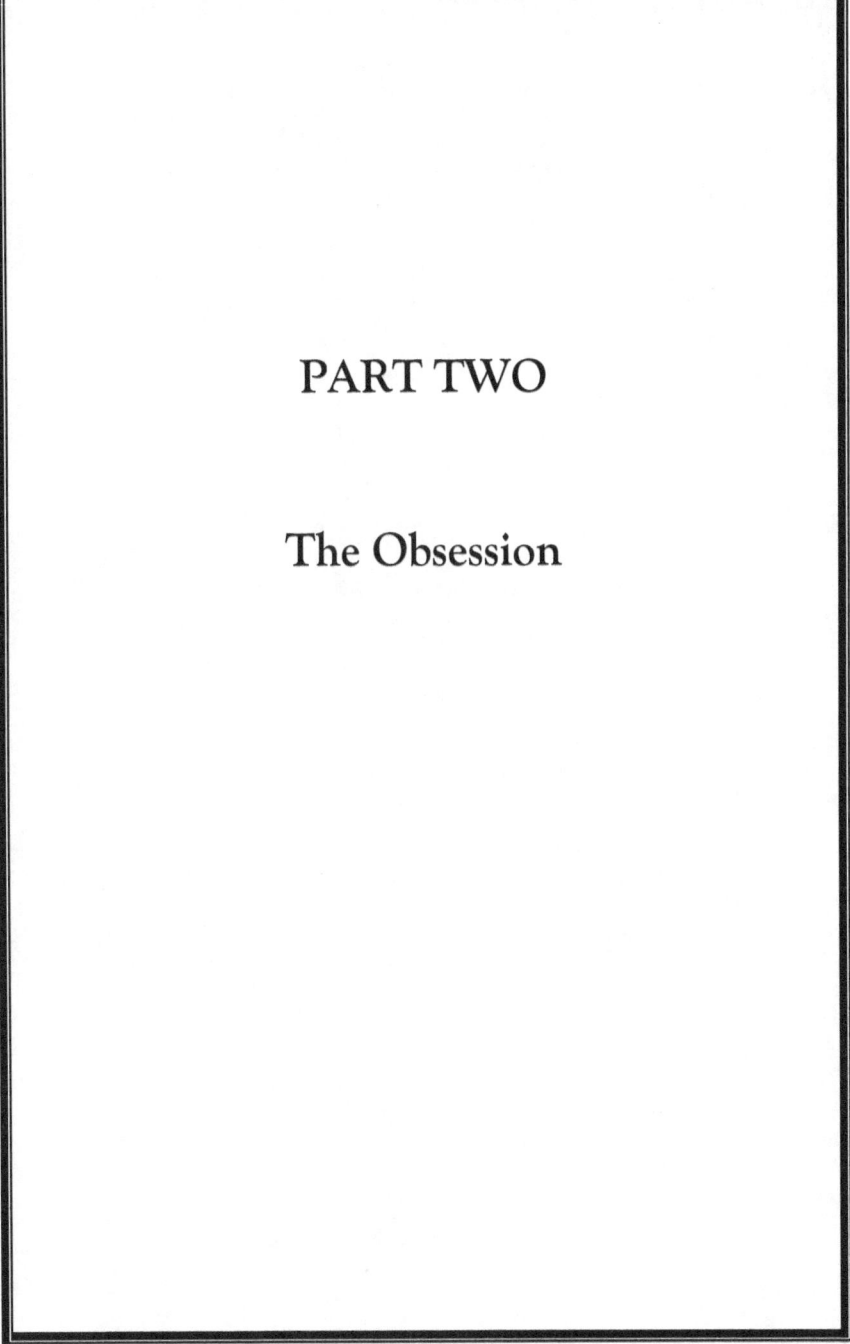

PART TWO

The Obsession

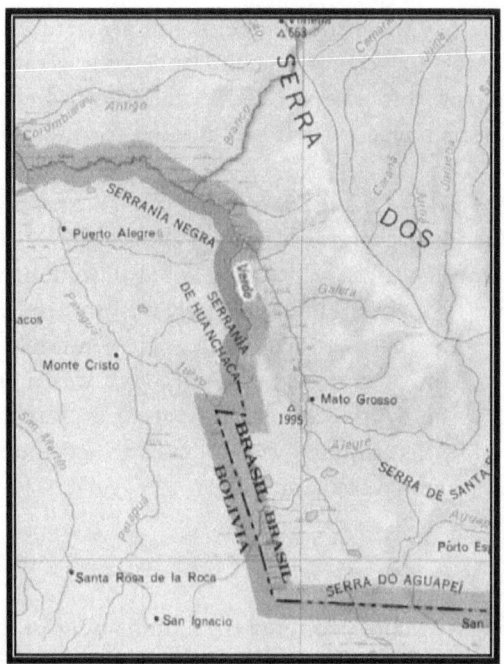

FAWCETT, CHAPTER 5
RIO VERDE

On March 6, 1908, Fawcett stood once more on the deck of a ship, the *Avon*, at Southampton and waved farewell to his wife. This time an enormous lump blocked his throat and his heart was a stone, cold and heavy, in his chest. He felt as if two discordant beings inhabited his body: One of them wanted to cling to his family as if for dear life, but the other, mad with restlessness and unnamed hungers, tore him away with a sure grasp. That this turbulent being was the stronger was no longer in doubt. So Percy Fawcett, husband and father, stood helpless on a ship bound for Buenos Aires. Nina sensed that some threshold had been crossed and she had a rival who would always win; her husband would be hers only now and then, a charitable relief, before being reclaimed by his rightful owner. Her life would be letters and loneliness, and fleeting desires to be a man and walk the forests with him.

Little did Fawcett know he was about to enter a refiner's fire. The forces governing his destiny had a few fine touches to add to his preparation. The forest shares her mysteries only with worthy suitors; the half-hearted need not apply.

Fawcett had always been aware of sudden death trailing them all like a scavenger as they wove their hopeful and arrogant way through the wilderness. It was not so hard for him to be courageous in the face of momentary horror; this was part of his training, and ego, as an Army officer. A different type of hell was needed to discover the limits of his commitment.

The Rio Verde— Green River— a pretty name for a watercourse which no white man had ever ascended, which fact alone was enough to make Fawcett's mouth water. He itched for exploration, for risk; this he'd freely admit. (To covet glory, however, was unseemly, and these desires had to be hidden even from himself.) He genuinely craved knowledge and the satiation of curiosity, and this, too, was morally acceptable to him. And so he would eventually agree to explore and survey an area not required by his contract, without the vaguest notion he was fulfilling an altogether higher covenant.

"Champagne, Major?" offered the Commander of the garrison.

"No, thank you," answered Fawcett, somewhat stiffly. He was inwardly cursing the Bolivian secretary who had made Corumbá sound undeveloped and crude, like Riberalta, perhaps from the Bolivian sense of rivalry toward Brazil; but a sartorially unprepared Fawcett had instead found a civilized town inhabited by a well-dressed populace. He was extremely uncomfortable sitting at table in his work clothes, but he had brought no other, and the Brazilian Boundary Commission had insisted on welcoming him with a grand dinner aboard the steamer that had brought him up the Paraguay River.

"I feel a fool," hissed his new assistant, Fisher, reading Fawcett's own mind. "Sitting here in my forest kit! To think that we left every proper suit we own in Buenos Aires... "

"I know. At least these dear people are so polite they pretend not to even notice."

"How was your journey, Major?" one of the Brazilian naval officers was asking.

"Oh, our crossing was uneventful, thank you. Then Mr. Fisher and I spent a couple of weeks in Buenos Aires before boarding this steamer."

"And how did you like Buenos Aires?"

"Well, the women are quite stunningly beautiful." The men laughed appreciatively, and Fawcett diplomatically refrained from mentioning that that was all he found to admire in the Argentine capital, which to him had seemed disappointingly crass and corrupt. "We have found the trip up the Paraguay very interesting, as well." He also avoided mention of Asunción, where they had paused on their trip upriver, as the wounds of Paraguay's war with Brazil were still quite tender among the citizens of that city.

"We were just remarking what a pleasant surprise Corumbá was," said Fisher. "Quite lovely and sophisticated."

"Thank you, yes, indeed, it is," agreed the Commander. "Its only drawback is the swamp— such low land, you know— a haven for snakes of all kinds, especially anacondas."

"Yes," one of the naval officers put in, "You must always carry a little bag of bichloride of mercury; it's a repellant, it will keep all snakes far away from you."

"Indeed?" responded Fawcett politely. He was later to learn that defying logic, everyone in the area swore by the folk wisdom; and who was he to question it?

"You will be surveying as far as Casal Vasco, Major?" someone else was asking.

As he nodded his head and wiped his mouth before answering, the Commander added: "And farther than that, if we can persuade him to trace the River Verde."

Fawcett smiled. "That's not in my contract, I must remind you."

"Yes, yes, I know, but it's problematic for both Brazil and Bolivia. Since no one has ever ascended the Verde, our maps are useless, sheer estimations of its course. That could cause difficulties."

Fawcett knew that "difficulties" could be, in South America, a euphemism for bloody battle. He also found the idea of exploring unknown territory extremely intriguing. But it could be risky, and he had Fisher to think of. "We'll see," was his only reply, and the Commander wisely dropped the matter for the time being, having detected the hungry spark in Fawcett's eye.

"Well, if you do," remarked a member of the Commission, "You will need more than bichloride of mercury to keep away the ghosts." He laughed, but not everyone at the table found his comment so humorous, and a couple of the guests surreptitiously crossed themselves.

"No," put in a naval officer, "Other than this lake we're sitting on, the primary haunt of the spirits is the Mato Grosso, not the Verde."

A lively little argument broke out concerning the habitat of non-corporeal beings; in the end all present agreed, many of them quite seriously, that Lake Cáceres was haunt-ed by the dead, and Mato Grosso, the vast, unknown region to the north, provided refuge for the "Bats", who could be either phantom or physical.

"I beg your pardon— " Fawcett was confused. "What kind of bats are we discussing?"

"Oh, sorry, Major," explained the Commander. "White Indians are rumored to live in Mato Grosso, and they're called "Bats" because it is said they come out only at night."

"I see. And can you be more specific about where they live? Mato Grosso is an enormous area."

"Well, no one really knows... somewhere north of Diamantino, where the lost Martirios gold mines are supposed to be. Quite a few expeditions over the years have headed off in that direction, toward those hills, but none have ever returned. So it is impossible to say what lies there. If you ask me, I'd say we should wait until one of these flying machines can do the job; that's the only way."

Fawcett's eyes took on a faraway look, and although for the remainder of the evening of dining, drinking, and speechmaking he smiled at the right times and murmured the correct phrases, his mind was elsewhere. He was remembering a conversation he'd had with Cecil Gosling, British Consul in Asunción, when the steamer had stopped there a few days earlier. Mr. Gosling had told him the Indians of Paraguay, as well as all tribes of Tupi origin, believed they had descended from a great and highly civilized people who had come in ancient times to colonize the country.

"There is a cave near Villa Rica which contains very unusual drawings, as well as some writing in an unfamiliar language," Gosling had added.

Now, as Fawcett smiled absently at the long-winded Commission speaker, scarcely noticing the other diners were raising their glasses in yet another toast, the pieces of a large puzzle were beginning to tantalize him with hints of a complex picture yet to be revealed. Fragments of knowledge and evidence he had gleaned over many months in South America, a trace here, a particle there, were taking on some kind of shape. The Incas had a tradition, accepted by experts, that they were the descendants of a great and wide-spread race. Places such as Tiahuanaco and Sacsahuaman had not been constructed by the Incas; archaeologists agreed the Incas had merely inherited these cities. Why should it not be possible, Fawcett was now wondering, letting his imagination roam, for remnants of these ancient peoples to live even now, in the uncharted wilds? And ruins; there had to be other cities...

Fawcett was jolted by a discreet elbow, belonging to Mr. Fisher, whereupon he automatically raised his glass and adjusted his facial expression to accommodate a larger, happier grin. But his mind was still buzzing with electric possibilities, racing across synapses and blazing new pathways to the inner dark places. He would never let go of it now. It was all part of the maddening game She would play with him for the rest of his life.

By early July, Fawcett and Fisher had completed their survey of the territory lying near Corumbá. The work had gone easily, aided by a full set of instruments and more than adequate supplies. In fact, it was a bit too routine to suit Fawcett; 'dull' was the word that came to mind.

Once again in Corumbá, ensconced in a comfortable hotel, Fawcett broached the subject of the Rio Verde with Fisher.

"The Commission knows they can't demand it; but we all realize that if this is left undone there will be continual quarreling over that region, perhaps ending in more bloodshed. The Verde is the boundary agreed upon by both Bolivia and Brazil, and it must eventually be mapped. I feel as if the job really isn't finished, contract or no."

"I suppose you're right, Major... But out-and-out exploration is not the usual thing, in this line of work."

"Quite so. But then I've never done the 'usual thing', I suppose. At least, I've never found any great satisfaction in it. And what will we do with our time otherwise, sitting around this town with little to occupy us while we await further orders? Tedium is a fate worse than death, my man." He didn't want to apply too much pressure to his assistant, but by this time Fawcett was itching to be the first to enter the private parts of the Verde. "Well? Game?"

Fisher sighed. "All right. I'm a bit bored, too. I'm game, Sir."

"Good fellow!"

The Commission was thrilled. As soon as possible they provided a launch and six native soldiers, or peons, and the little party set off up the Paraguay River on a blazingly beautiful August day. Unlike the dank gloom of the Abuná, there was nothing to foreshadow their journey, no warning at all. Fawcett, his spirits high, patted the two hunting dogs he had acquired for the trip, pulled his hat into place, and stepped aboard the craft. This was the sort of thing he was born to do.

A few weeks and one hundred and eighty miles later, they reached the cattle ranch of Descalvados, where they hired carts and proceeded overland to San Matías, a small village on the Bolivian side of the frontier. Instructions by no less a personage than the President himself had filtered down to this miserable settlement, to render all possible aid to Fawcett as a representative of the Boundary Commission; so the procurement of fresh animals was expedited, much to the relief of the two Englishmen.

"I've said this several times since I first arrived in South America, but I do think that this village is the worst place I have ever seen." The citizens of San Matías had only two discernible pastimes: drinking and killing. The gauchos and the Indians had a pointless war going on, year after year, and regularly slaughtered each other for pure entertainment. The inebriated residents respected only ghosts— of which there were plenty by now— and representatives of the Boundary Commission. They were unanimously friendly and helpful to Fawcett and his party.

"This place is so awful," Fawcett went on as they rode away, "If I had to live here even I would stay drunk night and day."

As they rode out of the settlement they passed a hill which they decided to climb, to better see the lay of the land. From its summit they had a view of the faraway palisades of the Ricardo Franco Hills, a line of sheer, high rock walls, heavily forested at their feet and along their flat crowns. Even from that distance, some seventy miles or more, they appeared secretive and enigmatic.

The group pushed on to Puerto Bastos, and as the glorious springtime of the Southern Hemisphere was beginning, Fawcett filled his journal with rapturous descriptions of the abundant flowers of the campos. Here and there all over the plains were islands of forest covered in blooms of all colors. Butterflies of various hues also abounded, like blossoms detaching themselves and flying away to the blue heavens. Fawcett and Fisher had never seen so much vivid color in one spot.

"It's like a painter gone mad!" exclaimed Fisher.

This is going to be a journey of discovery, I feel it in my bones, thought Fawcett, staring in awe around him. *I feel something waiting for me.*

At Puerto Bastos the carts and animals returned to San Matías, and the group pushed off down the Barbados River in a montería, a small boat having a deck. Soon they had reached Villa Bella de Mato Grosso, at the conjunction with the Guaporé River. Villa Bella had once been a city of some substance, boasting fine houses and churches, but the nearby gold mines had been worked to death; and shortly after, a dread disease known *ascorupçao* worked the people over pretty thoroughly, until all had either died or fled.

182

As they entered the ghost town, Fawcett fancied he could feel spirits of its former residents in the deserted streets and chapels. He grew pensive and heavy-hearted, and he noticed the normally rowdy peons had become quiet, even morose. It seemed to him that structures retain echoes of the beings who had inhabited them, and Villa Bella lay forlorn in the silent wilderness, forgotten by all but the dead. Perhaps on account of superstition, no one had touched the churches' treasures, chests full of silver candlesticks, statues, and other objets d'art.

"I say! Look at this, Fisher." Fawcett was admiring a magnificent bishop's ceremonial chair, canopy and all, in one of the churches. "It's fallen apart, but all the pieces appear to be here."

"It's quite something, Major. Amazing what fine things were left here to rot."

"Indeed. If the seat and back were repaired, it would be perfect. You don't think there's anything wrong with taking it, do you? As you say, it's simply lying here, rotting. I wouldn't touch the silver; but the Church should have no use for this, since soon it will be nothing more than debris if it's left."

"I see nothing wrong; you'd be rescuing a work of art."

"Well, then, help me, if you will; let's gather all the parts and wrap them in a canvas. I would like very much for my wife to have this. How grand she'll look sitting in a bishop's chair at the head of our dining room table! Of course, I'll have it thoroughly disinfected before I present it to her; I shan't take a chance on any infection remaining."

They cached the chair, along with some of their stores, until their return from the Verde. Fawcett was eager to push on and shake off the oppression that appeared to have settled over the group since they had entered Villa Bella.

Moving downstream on the Guaporé, they soon found the mouth of the Verde.

"Ah ha!" exclaimed Fawcett, striding along the bank to inspect an inscribed wooden marker. "Here is the frontier post which was placed by the 1873 expedition. Beyond this point, Fisher, no white man has ever gone."

"Hm, yes, very exciting, Sir."

"Now: From here on, guards must be posted at night; it's said the region is rife with dangerous savages, and though I doubt it, we won't take any chances."

"Yes, sir. That sounds wise."

The flora and fauna of the area were of constant fascination to Fawcett, and he continually asked the peons for names of things, which he carefully wrote in his journal. He thought he spotted a plant he had seen on the Brazil-Paraguay border, which had leaves that were sweeter than sugar and was known as *Caa-he-eh*. Another pointed out to him was *Ibira-gjukych*. One of the peons tore a leaf from the small plant and put it in his mouth, offering one to Fawcett. Fawcett chewed, and immediately a surprised expression lighted his features.

"It's salty! Why, it's as salty as Caa-he-eh is sweet. What a useful plant!"

The river abounded with otters, bufeos, and stingrays; and nocturno monkeys, with their enormous, soulful eyes shared the trees with rare birds none of the men had ever seen before. Great turtles sunned themselves on the riverbanks, looking wisely at the men as they poled upstream on the crystal-clear water.

As long as the land was flat they continued on without difficulty, but when the hills began, so did the rapids, and soon they were stymied.

"It's getting steeper and steeper," said Fawcett. "We'll have to hoof it."

"Continue on foot? You can't mean it!"

"Mr. Fisher, do you have any other ideas? It won't be easy, but the only thing to do is follow the river's course by land. We'll have to sink the boat in a pool so any local Indians won't be alerted to our presence by it, or worse yet, destroy it. That would leave us quite stranded up here."

Fisher looked dubious, even frightened. "But what about food? We can't carry enough on our backs to last us."

"No, of course not. We'll have to live off the land. There seems to be plenty of game hereabouts. We can't take much food at all, actually; we'll be burdened with the instruments, but they absolutely must go with us."

The men found a likely pool and sank the montería. Then they buried their supplies in a spot on the bank which looked high and dry.

"Here," Fawcett said, holding a bag of gold. "This is £60, and is much too heavy to carry. Not much to spend it on around here, anyway." He tossed it to Fisher, who placed it in the metal case with the stores. The hole was covered and carefully hidden with rocks and branches.

"Come on, fellows," Fawcett called to the dogs, to whom he was becoming attached. "Ready, everyone? Let's go find the source."

*

"Yow!" Fisher was slapping his own face and ripping at his shirt, in a dance of pain that made the peons guffaw until they, too, were slapping at themselves and cursing. It was the red bees again, tiny things no bigger than a gnat with hugely murderous dispositions. They bit rather than stung, attacking every portion of skin they could reach, including the insides of ears, nostrils, and eyes. They crawled under clothing and into the hair, relentlessly.

It was September 17, and the men were starting their third day on foot. The first day had not been too difficult, but after that the undergrowth became increasingly dense, until they had to hack their way a foot at a time with machetes. This upset local insects considerably, and the Fawcett party found themselves fighting off frequent assaults by wasps and red bees.

"Cut your way to the water!" Fawcett shouted, and the men slapped with one hand and hacked with the other.

"Oh, merciful Lord," moaned Fisher as he sank into the river and the drowned bees floated away. "Major, can't we skirt this underbrush somehow? This is slow and agonizing progress."

"I know. But as I explained before, our job is to survey the river, since it is the boundary; if that isn't done very precisely, this entire expedition was a waste. How can I map it if we don't stick close to it?"

Fisher sighed. "You're right, sir. I'm sorry to be such a complainer." He took a sip of the water, which was now not as clear as before. "Have you noticed the bitter taste?"

"Yes. I've also noticed there aren't anymore fish these last couple of days. Even they don't like whatever is in it."

"Well, let's hope it doesn't make us sick."

"We may have an even greater problem than that. We haven't seen the first sign of game since we left the boat. That may have something to do with the water, also."

"All the racket we make, chopping our way inch by inch through that mess, would scare away all the animals for miles around, I'd think."

"True. Well, Fisher, since we've seen no trace of Indians, either, I think we can dispense with guard duty at night. The dogs will be adequate sentry, do you agree?"

Fisher did. They hauled themselves onto the bank and had a brief meal. The Englishmen ate lightly, carefully rationing their portion of the food, which had been divided evenly among all in the party, but the peons ate as if food were not a problem.

"Shouldn't we do something about that, sir? If they continue that gluttonous eating, they'll go through their share in a few days."

"I tried talking to them about it; it did no good whatsoever, as you can see. I told them that with restraint, our rations could last us three weeks, perhaps, but their appetites seem uncontrollable. I don't know what else to do. We don't want to get into a fight over food."

The group marched on. By September 21, as Fisher had predicted, the peons had exhausted their food supply. There was nothing for Fawcett and Fisher to do but share their own portion with the six soldiers. In a couple more days, this, too, was gone. Still they had seen no game. On the 25th they came across some palmetto cabbages, and ate those.

"Are you all right, Fisher?" Fawcett inquired later in the day.

"Yes, I think so, sir... My stomach is just a bit upset. Those palmettos didn't agree with me at all."

"I know what you mean. I feel weaker than I did before we ate them, actually. Look!" He grabbed his assistant's arm with a bruising, though shaky, grip.

The dogs were standing like statues. A turkey was just ahead of them. All froze, but alas, the turkey had seen them, too, and before they could raise their guns it had disappeared in the thick brush.

"Damn!" Fisher sounded as if he would weep.

Fawcett clapped him on the shoulder. "Come on, my man; if there's one, there are others. This should encourage us. Let's continue."

They trudged on. Five empty days later, they were still walking, though more slowly every day. The odd-tasting water added to their misery by keeping them all slightly ill.

They came to a stop, facing a tacuara forest. Fisher stared dully ahead.

"We can't get through this," he said simply.

The peons also stood still, hungry and exhausted, machetes hanging limply at their sides.

"We have to." Fawcett lifted his machete, which seemed now to weigh a ton, and began to hack at the pitiless bamboo, whose tough stalks send out shoots of thick and tangled branches bearing malicious, stinging thorns. For a minute or so he worked alone, little droplets of blood forming here and there on his forearms where the thorns made contact. Then the others, waking from their hopeless daze, slowly raised their machetes and joined him. It took most of the day to get through the stand.

The following day there was great excitement when they came upon a honeybees' hive, and fought the bees for it, hardly feeling the stings by this time. They fell upon the honey, though it had a strange, fermented flavor.

An hour later, all the men lay on the ground, violently ill, clutching their painful abdomens. "Remind me never to touch fermented honey again," moaned Fisher. "Or any kind of honey!"

They recovered, and moved on. They had seen no more turkeys, no game at all. On October 2 the dogs, forever rummaging hither and yon in the underbrush, desperate for food themselves, set up a cry. The men rushed to the spot; one of the dogs had found a bird's nest containing four large, blue eggs. The dogs sat looking at the eggs, saliva dripping from their mouths and their legs shaking, but they had not touched them. Fawcett divided one of the eggs and gave it to the dogs. Then the men divided the rest. Shared by eight men, the little meal only served to make them feel their hunger more keenly.

October 3 found the debilitated band of men standing at a spring in the rocks, under several chonta palms.

"Well, we did it!" Fisher exclaimed. "This is the source, is it not?"

"Yes. The source of the Verde. It was thought to be a lake, but now we can report otherwise. We did it, Fisher." Fawcett's tone was flat, but inwardly he felt a great deal of satisfaction. Shakily, he set up the camera and took a few photos of the group. In one, he held a dog on his lap and squeezed the bulb with his other hand.

The peons were uninterested in the historical moment, having retrieved several nuts from the palms. Unfortunately, they proved iron-hard and inedible.

Fisher and Fawcett erected a crude post, carved a message, and Fawcett completed his survey, having one more thing to do: make a triangulation connecting the Verde's source with Villa Bella. He had some difficulty with this, as his hands trembled almost too much to take observations and perform the calculations, but he knew it must be done. As he packed the instruments carefully away, Fisher asked:

"What now? Do we retrace our steps, or just leave our bones here?"

Fawcett glanced up and was unnerved to see that Fisher didn't appear to be joking. He closed up his pack, thinking. There had to be a better way than that hell. The dense undergrowth, the bees, the absence of game, the near-poisonous water...

"All my mapping is completed; there's no need to follow the river now. If we strike out over those hills, we're bound to find a better route."

"I should hope so, Sir! What could be worse than the way we came?"

Fawcett slipped into his thirty-pound pack and led the way. The Indian peons were beginning to mutter darkly among themselves. Their voices drifted up to Fawcett's ears as if from very, very far away, as he put one foot before the other like an automaton. Beside him, Fisher stumbled and fell for the tenth time in as many minutes. Fawcett knew that the frequent falls that all of them were taking, the loss of hearing, the hollow-headed feeling, were signs of true starvation. He gave Fisher his hand and pulled him to his feet. Fisher tried to sit down, but Fawcett held him firmly upright.

"Don't you dare!" he hissed severely. "If we show weakness the peons will utterly give in. Control yourself and put a good face on it if it takes every ounce of will power you possess." He shook Fisher's arm. "Do you hear me?"

"Y-yes, Sir."

"Good man. Now let's go. Wipe that expression off your face. Look cheery."

Fawcett had begun to notice the peons, and even Fisher, looking at the dogs ravenously. Fawcett knew he'd have to settle that matter, and the sooner the better. Besides the fact that he was probably the world's biggest dog-lover, there were other reasons.

"Look," he told them, pulling both dogs to his side challengingly. "Forget about eating the dogs. Forget it entirely. They are only skin and bones and would provide little nourishment, yet they could be of the greatest value to us in finding food. They can smell game when we are completely oblivious to it." The peons stared at the Englishman resentfully. "This is an order, men. If any of you touch them, you'll have me to deal with."

At night, though some of them may still have dreamed of the dogs, all of them also reported dreams of sugar. To a man, they had nightly gluttonies of sweets, and they got some perverse pleasure from reporting and comparing their dreams in the morning: what they had eaten, how much of it, how good it had been. They laid plans for the desserts they would gorge themselves on when they returned.

"I think I will simply eat myself sick on pure sugar," announced Fisher, eliciting a feeble laugh from the others.

The Ricardo Franco Hills loomed above them, a forest-covered plateau whose heights had never been challenged; its sides were too sheer, too deeply cleft. Anything could be there, even creatures unaltered by time, Fawcett imagined, hypnotized by the mystery of those virgin summits. In his light-headed haze it seemed unassailable, protecting its secrets forever. A lost world...

The hills at the feet of those mighty cliffs proved just as impregnable for Fawcett and his desperate little band. The clefts in the sheer rock above widened into great canyons down below, and repeatedly, the group found themselves staring into a yawning, impassable chasm. They would drag themselves back the way they had come, and try again in a slightly different direction— only to come upon a similar impasse. They grew weaker with each attempt, and Fawcett felt a dim sense of anger that they should wind up as just another expedition that never returned. Perhaps it was this anger that kept him going, and gave him the will to prod the others.

"Where is the *capataz*?" He asked Fisher as they lay resting, once more blocked by a sheer-sided canyon. He hadn't seen the peons' captain, Chaco, for a good while, and he had been watching the gradual break-up of the man. He was afraid the Indian had gone off somewhere to die, as was their custom in a hopeless situation. Fisher, beyond caring, didn't respond. Fawcett pulled himself to his feet and searched the area until he saw the man's tracks. He followed them through the scrub forest for a short distance, and then heard the sound of deep, wrenching sobs.

He found the capataz leaning against a tree, crying his heart out.

"Get up!" He commanded, shaking the man hard. "Stop that crying!"

The Indian pushed his hand away. "Leave me to die! I can't take it anymore... I want to die, don't you understand? We're all going to die soon, anyway. Go away!"

Fawcett looked at him for a moment. Feeling like a demon but knowing it was the only way, he drew his hunting knife and put it to the man's throat. "Get up," he ordered, his voice cold and hard. The Indian stared at him, his eyes growing wide.

Fawcett pushed the knife into his throat until it drew a trickle of blood. "I said, get up! You have only two choices, Chaco: You can die on your feet, walking like a man, or you can die wallowing and weeping like a baby; but you'll die by my knife if you sit here any longer, so help me God!"

The peon looked at Fawcett with hatred, but he stumbled to his feet and made his way back to the group, his commander close behind him with the knife.

"It's getting dark. Let's make camp here." Fawcett walked over to the other peons, who were standing in a huddle and looking over the tops of the distant trees at drifting smoke.

"Savages are all around us now. Last night we saw their fires, also," one of them said, looking balefully at Fawcett.

"I know. I saw them. I wish to Heaven they would show themselves."

The peons looked shocked and terrified at the very thought.

"Well, if they would approach, they just might give us some food. Did you ever think about that?"

No, they had not.

Taking Fisher aside as they cleared away spaces for sleep, Fawcett spoke in a low voice.

"Listen. We cannot escape by way of these hills; the canyons prevent that. And it's out of the question to go back the way we came. I'm getting a strong feeling that we must follow the watershed."

"Major— that is the greatest gamble... If you're wrong— "

"I know it's a risk, but I have an instinct about this. I've had some dreams... Now, the peons are going to feel that it's the wrong direction entirely, and they may desert. The only way to prevent that is to get their guns away from them; without firearms, their fear of the 'savages' will keep them with us."

"I see. So we should stay awake until they're sleeping."

"Right."

When the six soldiers were fast asleep, Fawcett and Fisher crept stealthily among them and gathered all their weapons, putting them in their packs. It would be extra weight to carry, but so be it.

The next morning, Fawcett explained the new plan, truthful about his reasons for confiscating the guns, in his firmest and most authoritative voice. When he had finished, to his surprise the dejected men hardly protested, and he realized they expected to die anyway; what did it matter now, where they went?

Onward they plodded in the new direction. Now their falls were dangerously frequent, because it was becoming harder and harder to get up again. All the men experienced a great desire to simply lie there where they had fallen, resting, giving in to the need to be very, very still; even Fawcett had to exert all his will to force himself to his feet one more time, then once more, and once more.

The peons began to refuse to get up, turning Fawcett into a beast he thought he'd never become. It was against all of his ethics to strike anyone under his authority, and he despised men who did. Yet he found it was the only way to keep them moving, the only chance to save their lives; the terrible weight of responsibility for bringing all of them into this situation was bearing him down more with each day, and proved to be one important factor which kept his energy elevated to an extraordinary degree. He had a duty to get them out of there alive.

And so he beat them and kicked them and prodded them with his machete, and they came to fear him almost more than they feared savage Indians. To say it hurt Fawcett more than it hurt them was not an empty cliché; every blow, every threat cut him to the quick and he would remember his own apparent cruelty far longer than they would. But if he made them hate him enough to put a bit of fight into them, it was worth it.

Somehow they kept moving. The dogs had kept alive, too, by hunting, apparently. They were horrendously thin, but they did not act as if they were starving to death. No one saw them catch anything, but they must have occasionally found lizards and insects and other small prey. Then one day, they curled up together in the soft grass, drifted off to sleep, and never awakened.

Fawcett stood looking down at the two; companions, as they had always been, looking as if they might bound into wakefulness at any moment. "A peaceful death; even beautiful, in its way. It appears they didn't suffer, and I'm grateful for that. We should all be so lucky when our time comes."

The peons had come to stand beside him, gazing at the dogs. One of them lay down beside them; evidently he, too, felt it was an appealing way to ease out of this vale of tears.

Fawcett delivered a vicious kick to his backside. "I said, 'when our time comes!' And it isn't now!"

By the next day, the 13th of October, Fawcett could feel they were coming to the end of their strength and will. They could barely move, and when they stopped to rest, they found that none of them seemed able to get up again. He turned to Fisher.

"My dear man, there is one thing left to do, and we must believe it will work. It has never, so far, failed me when my need is dire and I've exhausted my own resources. I don't call upon this aid lightly. Help me to know we will be answered."

He stood shakily and turned to the east. He raised his voice in a prayer for God's help. Then he turned to the west and called out to Deity again, begging that their lives be spared. Fisher and the peons watched him in wonder, a faint glimmer of hope in their eyes. After several more minutes of supplication, he sat on the ground and bowed his

his head, striving to replace all doubt with certainty that his prayer would earn a response.

Fifteen minutes later, as they sat together in a strangely peaceful silence, a lone deer appeared about 300 yards away.

All the men held their breath. Fawcett reached quietly, so quietly, for his rifle, aware that the distance was almost impossible for the Winchester. With violently trembling hands, he raised the gun to his shoulder and tried to aim.

"Oh, please, please don't miss, Major!" Fisher whispered breathlessly.

Out of deepest humility came a sudden calm. Fawcett's hands steadied, and he knew beyond any question that he would not miss, even with the distance, even with the wild kick of a Winchester. The prayer had been answered, and that was that. Thank you, Lord.

He fired. The deer, its spine perfectly severed, dropped instantly.

The group rested, satiated, around the bloody remains of their meal. The peons had eaten skin, fur, and all, Fawcett noticed with a faint smile. Then a thought struck him, and his smile faded; he suddenly looked ineffably sad, and Fisher put a hand gently on his arm.

"Major: What is it? Is something the matter?"

Fawcett shook himself and took a deep breath. "No, no, Fisher, it's nothing... I was just thinking— it's a shame the dogs could not have lived just a little while longer... "

The party's "luck" seemed to have turned. The following day, they found another beehive, and this time the honey was fresh. Fisher quite forgot his vow of abstinence and wolfed down his share along with the other men. Then on October 15 they struggled down the cliffs and found themselves in the forests of the Guaporé. They had come the right way.

On the 18th, the bedraggled band of explorers found that dreams do sometimes come true.

"Look ahead, Major! A settlement!"

"Ah, yes, so it is! I believe I see Negroes!"

They straggled into the village of blacks, who were busily grinding cane into juice, which was then boiled down into head-sugar. They welcomed the wayfarers generously, immediately sharing their scanty food supply. But what Fawcett's group wanted more than anything was the sugar. They stuffed themselves with it voraciously, without restraint, laughing and reminiscing about their dreams.

"Fisher, this fills the bill perfectly for you, doesn't it, my man? Pure sugar!"

His assistant nodded happily, trying to grin around an obscene mouthful of cane sugar.

But later that night, they dearly paid the price.

"Oh, Lord," groaned Fisher, doubled up with pain. "Are you as sick as I?"

Fawcett couldn't answer. He was in the nearby bushes, vomiting as if he would eject his very stomach itself. In between gasps, he could hear the peons retching, too.

"Just what we deserve," he finally called to Fisher, chuckling a little despite his misery. "But you know, it was fun, wasn't it?"

"I say, Fisher, Villa Bella doesn't seem so depressing this time around, does it?"

"No, Sir!" replied Fisher cheerily, munching on a bowl of Quaker Oats with condensed milk. It was October 19, and the group had arrived back at the ghost town and gratefully retrieved the supplies that were left there. They had had enough sugar to last them for a while, and were enjoying the oats.

"We can pick up the bishop's chair, too; I can hardly wait to see it fully restored. And my report will be a source— pardon the play on words— of great delight for Bolivia, since the new and correct map will give about 1,200 square miles of potentially valuable land to them. There were countless untapped rubber trees up there, and who knows what other natural resources." He put a long, strong hand on his loyal assistant's shoulder. "It was not in vain, my friend."

Postscripts:

Five of the six peons never completely recovered from the stresses of the journey, and died soon after their return. The capataz, Chaco, was the sole Indian survivor. Rather than hating Fawcett, he had come to respect and even revere him, telling everyone who would listen of the Englishman's unbelievable moral fortitude and physical endurance. He begged to become Fawcett's "Man Friday", wherever future expeditions may lead them.

Arriving in Corumbá by launch, the group was greeted as heroes, with great fanfare— to Fawcett's considerable discomfort.

In 1909, both the Brazilian and the Bolivian Boundary Commissions accompanied Fawcett back to the source— as did Chaco. The accuracy of all his maps was confirmed to their satisfaction by another survey. The frontier post was replaced by a larger and more permanent one. Fawcett and the men dug up the buried supplies and the gold, and raised the launch. And oddly enough, deer abounded in the area, this time.

A funny thing about the buried £60: Somehow a rumor had spread, no doubt instigated by one of the peons before he died (or even Chaco), that gold had been buried near the source of the Verde. Over the years the stories grew until the "buried treasure" had reached the princely sum of £60,000! Fawcett heard the tales in various places in Brazil, over and over, highly amused at the thought that someday treasure-seeking syndicates may spend thousands on a search for £60, which had been reclaimed in 1909. As he told Nina, no doubt this was the way many reports of buried treasure had begun.

Speaking of Nina, in due time and at great expense the bishop's chair was beautifully restored, complete with Morocco leather covering the seat and back. Eventually he could gaze at his lovely wife sitting at the head of table in a chair fit for a queen, just as he had imagined her. But soon after he had presented her with the reconditioned, fumigated throne, she began to fall ill with one strange set of symptoms after another; nothing life-threatening, but simply miserable and baffling ailments.

At last, one day, she and her husband looked at each other, then at the chair.

"I don't want to say it," Nina demurred, putting up her hands. "You'll think I'm superstitious, and that's not exactly right— "

"Then I'll say it. You can call me superstitious, I don't care. I've seen many things in my life that can't be explained by normal means. So... shall we get rid of it? Is it cursed, or something, do you think?"

Nina laughed. "Perhaps someone or something doesn't care to have a Protestant sitting in the chair of a Catholic bishop!"

"Possibly! Enough said. It should return to its own religion. I'll send it to Brompton Oratory tomorrow!"

He did just that, and to his knowledge the chair never caused anymore problems.

A year and half after the expedition, in London, Fawcett sat chatting with Arthur Conan Doyle, showing him photographs of the Ricardo Franco Hills, describing them and the feeling of mystery they had given him. Conan Doyle asked for more information on Central South America, as he had a germ of an idea for a novel. Fawcett was very willing to oblige, supplying the writer with many of his notes and answering countless questions. In 1912 *Lost World* was published, first as a serial in Strand Magazine, then as a highly successful book.

Fawcett lived the rest of his life believing he had discovered the River Verde source. At the time, all believed it. But it wasn't until 1946 that Colonel Bandeira Coelho found the true source, southwest of Fawcett's spring. Fawcett thought he'd been following the main stream, but in actuality he had gone up one of the many wide branches of the Verde.

When his younger son, Brian, heard this news he was glad his father hadn't lived to know that all his trials had been for naught. But had they? Perhaps the source of the Verde, and even the boundary itself, was not really so important in the overall scheme of things. Eventually, rubber trees didn't matter. The squabble between Brazil and Bolivia, and all the other nations fighting over this and that, fade into memory along with other petty desires and fears of tribes. The blood would be shed one way or another, whether over gold mines or rubber acreage, or a cow rustled by an Indian from a gaucho.

What did matter was the gold refined in Fawcett during his hellish days beneath the Ricardo Franco Hills, in Fawcett's own Lost World. He had indeed found the Source: something invaluable within him that he'd draw upon in times to come. Stripped of human strength, he had gone past despair and into a fountainhead of faith. This he took with him forever, and was above earthly price.

SYLVIA, CHAPTER 5
MATO GROSSO

A light rain fell, but only the cobblestones beyond shelter of the great old tree shone with wetness. The tree's thickly-massed leaves provided an umbrella over a tremendous circle of the courtyard. This reminded Sylvia, who had walked to the veranda as she brushed her teeth, that she'd better take something along; her raincoat, perhaps. The umbrella was an annoyance on Copa's crowded sidewalks.

The rain stirred up scents of foliage and earth from the jungle on the hillside above her. Sylvia inhaled deeply, grateful for any bit of the natural world, still amazed she'd found such a green pocket in the city. Though she now had a comfortable bed (it *was* possible to find soft mattresses in Rio) she often slept in her hammock on the veranda, especially in wet weather. She loved the smell of rain, and when a sudden gust blew showers her way, the mist on her skin in her drowsy state brought dreams of sleeping in the forest.

As she left the building, beams of morning sunshine broke through the continuing rain. "The Devil is beating his wife," she thought, wondering if Brazilians knew the old saying. She'd have to ask Paulo when she got to work. Ferns and other plants glistened wetly in the sunlight. All at once she stopped and looked around the courtyard. And laughed out loud.

This is it. This is the moment from my dream! Years later, I'm living it. How very, very bizarre...

But she had no time to ponder. There was a busy day ahead. She walked briskly across slick stones to the pedestrian gate. She turned left onto Rua Leopoldo Miguez, a quiet residential street which she preferred to the parallel Avenida Nuestra Senhora de Copacabana. Soon she reached a newsstand where each morning she bought a paper, either O *Globo* or O *Jornal*. Newspapers, in particular the comics, with their many colloquialisms, were helping improve her Portuguese. But sometimes she was lucky enough to find a copy of Time magazine, in English.

At the next intersection she skirted a dinner platter containing a dead, bloody rooster, some fruit, and flowers, eyeing the gore with distaste. A *candomblé* offering, she figured, or that of another Afro-Brazilian cult or religion. Isabel had told her there were reasons such offerings were often placed at street corners.

Sylvia tried to put the dead rooster out of her mind as she walked the rest of the way, cutting over at Constante Ramos to the Avenida. Seven blocks' walk to work was just perfect, long enough to get a little exercise and observe the local scene, but not far enough to get sore feet from the ubiquitous cobbles. She enjoyed it rain or shine, but if she had anything heavy to carry home, such as produce on Farmer's Market days, she hailed a taxi.

She had been impressed by the friendliness and good manners of Rio's cab drivers, who sometimes engaged her in lively, often profound conversation. Isabel was able to shed a little light on their unusual erudition.

"I read somewhere that some professionals," she told Sylvia, "maybe teachers and even physicians, have to take a second job as taxi drivers to, how do you say, 'make ends meet'. Maybe this is why they seem different. They probably appreciate a little stimulating conversation to brighten their day, and with an American, too! That doesn't happen often."

"Yeah, they're always very curious as to what brought me to Rio, how I learned Portuguese, all of that. And they give me such good service, and extra favors sometimes, that I frequently offer them a tip— though I know it isn't required for Brazilian cabbies— and guess what? None of them will accept it! They wave it away and say they enjoyed talking to me."

Isabel laughed. "You see, good conversation will take you far in Brazil; it's worth more than money to us. We learned that during the days of runaway inflation."

"The doctors and dentists here also impress me, Isabel. They give me their home telephone numbers, and I can promise you, that doesn't usually happen in the U.S."

During the first few months Sylvia was sometimes overwhelmed by culture shock. On the negative side of the ledger, pervasive distrust caused unending inconvenience. As she vented to her journal:

There's an assumption that no one can be trusted. So, public telephones can only be operated by paper cards that you have to buy at newsstands, and soda machines require a token; if there were coins in the machines, people might break them open. In shops and pharmacies you're assisted by a clerk, but then to pay for the item you have to get in a cashier's line; the cashier is the only person who can accept money. Utility bills have to be paid in person at the utility or at a bank; Isabel told me they tried taking checks by mail, but there was thievery and they gave it up. All of these procedures waste time.

Oh, well. There is definitely another side to the coin. Brazilians seem so willing to share. The other day when I was closing up my office to go home, I peeled a tiny tangerine I'd been saving all day. One of our secretaries, Zezé, walked by with another employee just then, so I offered them each a slice; not to do so would be considered rude, here. But I must confess, I was begrudging it... Then Zezé held out a bag of cheese balls, and I took one. When I was getting off the elevator, I ran into one of our teachers, who spontaneously handed me the rest of her little bag of cookies. I gave her the last slice of tangerine, and ate a couple of cookies as I walked down the sidewalk, getting thirsty. Passing a juice bar I saw another employee, Bianca, having a soda, and like a mind-reader she said: "Here, let me get a cup and pour you some of this..." I continued on, and when one of our office-boys passed me, I offered him the cooky bag. He looked inside. "It's your last one."

I said, "Take it!" I wound up having a much more interesting, soul-satisfying snack than the one little fruit I'd planned for myself, and it seemed like an object lesson in the way human society should function. I feel something beginning to breathe within me, some natural part of all of us, maybe, that can be slowly strangled by years of self-interest.

I also have to admit I enjoy the benefits of the hierchical structure at work. Since my position is at some height up the ladder, there are people who handle all the routine tasks, such as copying, typing, filing. Someone brings me coffee or tea, and go-fers will run personal errands, such as that obnoxious bill-paying or a trip to the post office. The attitude at IDA is that those employees with higher education or specialized skills shouldn't be doing tasks someone else can do; their time and energy is best spent on work only they can perform. It makes a great deal of sense; it also provides work for the less skilled, which are

198

great in number in any nation.

On the subject of work, I have another business trip coming up. After two trips to São Paulo, I'm finished with that area for a while, thankfully. Though I worked with terrific people, that sprawling city is twice as big, polluted, and crowded as L.A. This time I'm going to Cuiabá, in Mato Grosso State. I'll be setting up a distance learning station, as in S.P., only smaller. We're hoping to get our online English writing courses operating soon, which should help students qualify for our program.

The hope, of course, is that the exchange program will lead to opportunities in U.S. universities. Brazil needs many well-educated leaders with a command of English and extensive knowledge of the outside world; the nation as a whole can't afford to remain relatively isolated. The people here tend to be innovative, eager workers, adopting new technology and ideas rapidly; if they can overcome some of the political, social, and even geographical issues, nothing will stop them.

Clickety-click, clickety-click. Almost two a.m. Sylvia lay awake, listening to the ceiling fan for a few minutes. It was a warm, midsummer night, but when she used the fan she tended to wake up chilled. She sighed. The ceiling fan in the living room had adjustable speed, by means of a little dial, but this one was either on at helicopter velocity, or off.

She got up. She was thirsty, anyway. She switched the fan off and went to the kitchen without turning on any lights. The small night light plugged into a socket was adequate, and easy on the eyes. She took a tall glass of water through the open french doors to the veranda, where the air was fresh and sweet.

All was quiet, and she went to lean over the wide wall. She could smell the tree, which she'd discovered was a tropical almond. Its large leaves were medicinal, and it bore an edible fruit, so she had heard. She looked down into the dimly-lit courtyard, and froze.

Was she dreaming? Several men in uniforms, holding rifles at the ready, were creeping silently across the cobblestones toward the trail leading up Cantagalo Hill, their bodies tense. One of them, a leader, suddenly motioned everyone down, and the men crouched behind nearby cars. Sylvia watched, aghast, wondering if she should crouch, too, but she couldn't tear her eyes from the bizarre scene. All at once the leader signalled, and the group fled toward the building's entrance drive, scaling the high, locked gates rapidly. Other men began to pour into the courtyard from the trail, dressed roughly but carrying sophisticated arms, in hot pursuit of the uniformed party. Sylvia heard sounds from the other side of the building and realized more men were descending from the hilltop slums via the steep granite face, into which, she had noticed earlier, shallow footholds had been cut. All the men swarmed over the gates as quickly as the uniforms had and, like them, disappeared down the driveway into the night.

The courtyard lay empty, still, but for a black cat which slinked quietly across the cobbles to hide beneath an auto.

Sylvia stood amazed. She thought she might've been the only one in the building who saw what had happened; the apartments above and below her were dark, silent. It had been surreal. Maybe it didn't happen. She turned and went back to her bedroom, still holding the glass. She drank, realizing her mouth was very dry, and crawled into bed, thinking.

The men in uniforms were police, obviously; they had the inferior weapons. She laughed aloud, her voice sounding hollow. She glanced at the clock; it was 2:16.

Paulo was upset. "Sylvia, if something like that happens again, stay inside! Do not stand on the veranda, watching! People have been hurt, getting in the way of stray bullets; it's very dangerous."

"You're right. I promise to remember. I was— mesmerized, you know? It was all so quiet, it didn't seem real... "

Paulo wore a worried frown throughout the day. Sylvia decided not to mention the incident to anyone else.

It was Wednesday. Sylvia finished the week at work, and on Friday evening she had a drink with Julia and then went home to relax.

At 12:30 a.m. Sylvia was deep in sleep when a sudden eruption of racket sent her bolt upright in bed. It sounded like the Fourth of July right in her bedroom, firecrackers and roman candles and even cannons! As her head cleared she knew it was gunfire, and more: deafening explosions and deep booms, and it went on and on. Was she safe? She remembered Paulo's warning and resisted the impulse to dash to the window. But she knew that this time, the activity was taking place on the hill. Loud as it was, it was not near; there was no light, no flashes to be seen, no cries and no sound from any of her neighbors.

Everyone was doing as Sylvia did. She stayed right where she was, in her bed, listening to the uncanny clamor pounding her eardrums. It seemed to go on for a long time, but was probably over in fifteen minutes. Then all fell quiet, but for a few scattered pops and bangs. Then nothing.

Her heart thumping, she pulled the sheet up to her chin, and lay still.

The following day Sylvia stuffed a few bills in her pocket and went out. (She sometimes reverted to the habits she'd learned in Rome and Manhattan: You can't have your purse snatched if you don't carry one.) In the lobby, she spotted the moço, Rogerio, at his post by the window and started to walk over and ask about the little war of the previous night; but she remembered he didn't work the late shift, and who knew where he lived? Perhaps some distance from Copacabana, which was one of the more expensive Zona Sul, or south zone, areas. She'd have to talk to Edwin when he came on duty tonight.

Meanwhile, she crossed Rua Djalma Ulrich and got a newspaper before continuing to the beach. At a seaside kiosk she bought a drinking coconut, and stopped to admire a fantastic sand castle a family was sculpting just a few feet from the sidewalk. The father was the designer and detailer, while his children followed directions; little ones brought buckets of sand and sea water, and the older kids formed basic shapes using buckets, boxes, and cylinders such as toilet paper tubes and Quaker Oats containers. Mom walked around applying seawater here and there to keep the structure moist and intact. Sylvia estimated it to reach six feet at the highest turret, and to cover sixty or seventy square feet. It had arches and courtyards, and a moat surrounding everything; scallops, curlicues and other designs adorned every section to which Dad had applied his artistic hand. It was astonishing. One of the boys had made tiny flags from toothpicks piercing red and yellow leaves, and he was carefully placing them atop every turret.

A small crowd had gathered. Sylvia temporarily forgot all about the disturbance of the night, watching the family work together on their creation. A basket containing a few coins had been placed on the sidewalk next to a little sign bearing the family's surname. Before she left, Sylvia tossed in a couple of bills, and looked up to catch a smile and dignified nod of thanks from the man. *Creative way to make a living,* Sylvia thought, feeling a tad better about the world.

She wandered along the wide sidewalk, tiled in the characteristic wavy design. On the beach nearby, a volleyball game was in progress, but she'd never seen a game like this. The players were all well-conditioned young men, their muscular, bare bodies gleaming with sweat. They sent the ball expertly across the high net without use of their hands. They employed their heads most commonly, and sometimes knees, feet, and even shoulders; the game went so smoothly it was obvious they always played this way. Soccer players, Sylvia assumed.

She plopped down on a bench and scanned the newspaper. Though she looked carefully, there was not a word about the brouhaha. And it seemed a typical Saturday at Copacabana Beach; all was peaceful and pleasant.

Around sunset Sylvia was relaxing in the hammock with a cold glass of *caju* juice when she heard a vehicle enter the courtyard and stop. There was a bustle and purposeful-sounding voices of men. She peered over the railing to see a police van. Just then two men were coming down the hillside path that led to the favela, carrying a stretcher with a body in a black plastic bag. Another couple of men, with another body, followed close behind. Casualties of the war, she assumed, shuddering. The bodies were put inside the van, and everyone left.

That evening, Edwin wasn't on duty; he'd taken the night off. Sylvia remained in the dark about the incident until the following day, when she encountered one of her acquaintances in the building, Almerita, feeding stray cats in the courtyard.

"Wasn't that a racket!" Almerita shook her head disgustedly. "It was a gang war. Big guns, hand grenades, the whole thing! And the police can do nothing."

"Does this happen often?" Sylvia asked dubiously.

"No. Well, now and then. Don't worry, our building is safe. Just stay inside. And be glad we don't live on the *other* side of Morro Cantagalo."

"Why?"

"There are a couple of high apartment buildings over there, you know, in Ipanema, where the favela is low on the hillside and you can see it from the upper floors of the buildings. A friend of mine lives in one of these, on the ninth floor. Thursday evening, some young men from the favela— gang members, I'm sure— went around to all the residents who live on the favela side of the building, telling them there would be some fighting on the weekend and they should go somewhere else... Go stay with relatives, or with the people who are on the opposite side of the building. They didn't want anyone to be hurt; the building might be in the line of fire!"

Sylvia's laughter bore an hysterical note. "How thoughtful of them!"

"Yes, isn't it. We live in an insane world." She shook her head. "Don't you have gangs in Los Angeles, Sylvia? Don't they fight each other?"

"Oh, yes! All the time. The difference is, and it's a big difference, their neighborhoods are usually far away from places, well, like Copacabana. It isn't like it is here, with favelas just above the better neighborhoods."

"I see. Yes, here, they are right on top of us. God help us if they ever decide to make war on *us*."

When the junction came up, Sylvia was ready. She turned from Interstate Highway 40 onto a state road that led to Teresopolis. But she wasn't going quite that far. She had visited Teresopolis before, on a previous weekend jaunt; this time she wanted to check out a national park she had zoomed past along the way. She had the rental car for a three-day weekend, and if the park didn't suit her fancy she'd wander elsewhere. The main thing was to be out of the city for a while.

It felt good to be driving an automobile again, even if rentals did cost an arm and a leg in Brazil. But she really had to stay awake. She had already plowed into the queen of all speed-bumps with no warning, and it sent her head smashing against the ceiling of the car. She suspected the locals removed the "Quebra Mola" signs for the entertainment of watching unsuspecting drivers hit the hard-to-spot bumps. She told herself the signs must mean, "break molar", as she gingerly checked her teeth, but she found out later the translation was "spring-breaker".

The getaway trip was welcome. Soon she'd be gearing up for another business trip. She needed to forget about work for a few days.

The park's sign came up: *Parque Nacional da Serra dos Órgãos*, National Park of the Organ Mountains; so named because of the unusual pipe-organ-like spires of rock, such as the peak called the Finger of God, that soared into the sky. Sylvia turned right and drove down a narrow road through dense woods until she reached a modest kiosk.

"*Bom dia*," said a smiling ranger.

"*Bom dia! Quanto é a entrada?*"

The ranger replied that the day-use fee was six reais. But, he noted, it was three o'clock; it didn't seem fair to charge her all that... His sharp eyes had seen the rental sticker on the car's front plates, and his ear caught an accent.

"*Americaine?*"

"Yes! Good guess," she replied, in Portuguese.

"No fee for you today," he told her, beaming. It wasn't often a pretty American came, all alone, no less, to visit the park.

"*Muito obrigada*," she thanked him, and asked what he recommended she see in the park during her short visit.

Immediately he told her his own favorite spot was called *Poço Verde*, or Green Pool. He told her where to find the trail head, and added,

"Keep going until the trail appears to end at a cave. Then keep on going! Down into the cave... You'll see."

She gave him her best smile, and drove on until she arrived at an unpaved parking area. There was one other car. She made sure her swimsuit was in her daypack and took off down the trail.

For about twenty minutes Sylvia meandered through strikingly beautiful *mata Atlântica*, stopping frequently to admire a fantastic flower or bizarre fungus. After a while she could hear the Rio Soberbo rushing vigorously on her right. Up ahead, though the view was partially blocked by foliage, the path appeared to end at a towering mass of stone and jungle. As she approached she saw that the wall of earth opened into a cave at its base. The cave sloped downward, and its floor was covered with large rocks; Sylvia couldn't see very far inside, but there seemed to be a little light ahead.

Carefully she made her descent through the damp boulders, reminding herself the ranger had said, "Keep on going"; so this had to be the right way. After she had climbed over a number of rocks, she paused to look ahead— and saw green, shimmering light below: water!

As she neared the jade sparkles, the roof of the gloomy cave rose and was replaced by a verdant tangle of lianas, roots, bromeliads, and masses of plants, shot through with sunlight. The dull roar of water she had been hearing suddenly seemed to crescendo, just as a fresh breeze touched her face. Sylvia squinted in blazing sunlight as the full view of Poço Verde came into sight.

Before her was a scene from a secret Utopia. A powerful cataract, perhaps fifteen feet high, thundered out of lush forest and into a crystalline green pool a hundred feet wide. Where Sylvia stood there was nowhere to sit but the rocks. On the opposite side there was a flat, mossy area, shaded by a gnarled and aged tree that leaned far over the pool, trailing aerial roots from its great branches; a magic tree that belonged in an old fairy tale. Sylvia almost expected it to speak.

There was not a human soul in sight; the occupants of the other car must've taken a different trail. Sylvia slipped out of her shorts and into her swimsuit; then she waded into the cool, clear water and carefully skirted the pool along its shallow edges, bound for the moss-beach. When she reached the point where the river exited the pool, squeezing itself between large, flat rocks to spill exuberantly down the ravine, she held to the rocks to avoid being swept off her feet.

She deposited her daypack in the area sheltered beneath the tree, where she found sand and spongy moss as green as emeralds. She waded into the deep pool and began to swim, the cool water pumping endorphins to her brain with every stroke of her arms. Superwoman in Paradise! She swam to the pounding cataract, which pushed her away with great power, and saw there was a small cave behind it. She was able to slip around the edge of the cascade and crawl onto a flat, sloping rock where she sat, grinning like a kid, looking out through the white curtain of water at a blurry, green world beyond.

Sylvia felt hidden. No one would be able to see her behind the falls. *What thin layers of protection we have between security and mayhem, like the frail tents separating predator from prey. Safety is an illusion. If we didn't convince ourselves we had it, the strain would be unbearable...*

Sitting there, water seeping through the hard rock behind her, Sylvia realized one of the reasons she needed regular breaks of solitude, away from any city, was a subliminal unease in the midsts of humanity. The ordinary thousands could shapeshift into an extraordinary mob under the right set of circumstances. There was nothing new about it, only more humans massed together, with more powerful weapons.

Awareness was both her blessing and her curse. At times she wished she could believe in tents. And police.

She was getting cold. She swam to a big, flat rock and lay face down on its warmth, the sun toasting her back. For now, there was only bliss.

As the sun dipped below the treetops, Sylvia made her way back down the path. She looked up and saw the ranger approaching. At first she thought he was coming to tell her it was time to leave the park; then she saw he was carrying swim trunks. He smiled shyly.

"*Gostou?*" he asked. "Did you like it?"

Sylvia's face lit up, supplying his answer. "Thank you so much for telling me!"

He gestured to his trunks. "I go there every day when my work is over, to cool off. Come back soon, *senhora.*"

She hummed softly, happily, as she walked to the car. She could take the crowds, violence, and mystifying paradoxes of Rio life in stride, as long as places like this were close by.

"All ready for your trip?"

"Paulo, I'm really looking forward to it."

"The hotel room is reserved, airlines, everything is ready for *you.* And have you made your plans for the Pantanal?"

"Yes! I do appreciate the free days. Since I'll be in Mato Grosso anyway, it's a perfect time to see the surroundings."

"Well, you deserve it. You've worked hard, and put in many extra hours; and IDA policy is, if you work overtime, you get time off. We like that better than paying you."

"Ha! It's fine with me." She looked at her watch. "Want to get some lunch?"

"Thank you, no, I'm meeting Isabel… " He looked at the Persian-style rug Sylvia had bought to make her office homier. She'd filled the corners with plants and the walls with artwork, and added plush, upholstered chairs. "It looks nice in here. It helps to balance the cold look of all the electronic equipment, doesn't it? Well, see you later; have a good lunch."

Sylvia knew Paulo and Isabel had had words the previous weekend. She'd planned to meet them for Sunday brunch, but Isabel called in the morning and begged off, mentioning the argument briefly and saying Paulo had gone home early Saturday evening.

"I think I'd like to spend today with my aunt in Niteroi. Would you forgive me, dear?"

"Sure, Isabel. We can do brunch any time." Sylvia had no idea what the problem was and now, she noticed, Paulo was adroitly avoiding the subject. But she was glad the two of them were having lunch; they could talk things out, surely.

It was a street-market day. After eating at one of her favorite *comida-a-kilo* places, where the buffet-style selections were weighed and paid for by the gram, Sylvia decided to spend the remainder of her two-hour break at the market.

Carrying a shopping bag, she wove her way through the midday crowds on Avenida Copacabana, made even more congested by street vendors selling their wares on the sidewalk. She knew the shop owners resented these *camelôs*, who took business from them but paid no overhead nor taxes.

The sea of lunchtime bodies parted for a moment and Sylvia saw, seated on a blanket, a dwarf with no legs. Someone was bending over him, shouting and shaking a bill in his face, and the dwarf had a *bicho* ticket in his hand. He was obviously one of the sellers in the illegal animal lottery similar to a numbers racket, and immensely popular in Brazil.

Sylvia suddenly halted, causing the woman following close behind to fall against her. Rear-end collision. The woman swore.

"*Desculpe*," Sylvia said. "I'm sorry." The moving mass of citizens closed like a curtain and the lotto vendor disappeared from sight as she was swept along with the human current. She wanted to go back for another look, but what would she do: stand there awkwardly staring at a crippled man? Confused, the patterned tiles rushing by beneath her shoes, the air around her close with people, she kept going.

When she reached the market lane and freed herself of the mainstreet throng, she could breathe again. *Another dream come to pass...*

As she absentmindedly fingered the produce and sniffed melons, she decided she'd watch for the lotto vendor on her way back, and buy a ticket from him if he was still there. The tickets bore the pictures of Brazilian animals: sloths, jaguars, monkeys, the like, and sometimes the payout was pretty good, Paulo had told her; it varied. She bought some fruit, and glanced at her watch. Time to get back to work.

When she reached the place where she'd seen the dwarf, he was nowhere around. Lotto vendors usually kept moving, to avoid tempting the lenient police too greatly.

Who is calling me? Sylvia sat upright in bed. *Why can't I see anything? Who awoke me, and where am I? I'm not at home...* The darkness was profound, and she had no idea where to find a light. Someone was calling her name, several voices.

She arose and moved blindly toward the sound. Somehow she found a door, opened it, and stepped outside where there was enough faint starlight to discern a line of Indians, maybe seven, or seventy; she couldn't see the beginning or end of the line. They wore feathered finery, like chieftains might, and they were facing her, looking at her hopefully.

"We are Shivante," she thought one of them said.

"We need you! Please help us." Sylvia stared at them uncomprehendingly. "Will you? Will you help us?" Some of them held out their hands in appeal.

Abruptly she found herself lying in bed, her mind foggy. As she awoke, her heart began to race. *Was* someone calling her? She listened; all was still but the noisy frogs, and it was very, very dark. *Oh, it was only a dream. I am— I am in the Pantanal, at a ranch... Where's the light? I need some light...*

She remembered a kerosene lamp, on the night table. She remembered the generator was turned off at nine p.m. Fumbling for matches, her hand made contact with her flashlight, the same little light that went to Amazonas with her, and she thought it might be a better idea. The bright flame of the lamp would drown her night vision, and she wanted to take a look outside.

She briefly shined the light around the room to make sure she was alone and all was well, and then used its focussed beam to see her way to the window, where she switched it off.

Everything appeared peaceful. It was very warm, and she opened the door. The night air was heavy with unknown scents, of plant life and earth must, and something familiar— cows. *Damned cows,* she thought, *taking over the planet.* Grumbling, she walked outside in her bare feet, wondering how many acres of forest had been sacrificed so people could eat hamburgers, which (poetic justice?) were adding plaque to their arteries.

Oh, don't go there, not now. Just appreciate the moment... Look at those stars!

How grand it was to stand in the middle of the flat basin of one of South America's great watersheds; 139,000 square miles of flood plain.

Driving south from Cuiabá two days earlier with her guide, Elisabeth, she had been thinking about Fawcett. She wished she'd brought along her notes, or his memoirs; all of it had come with her to Brazil, but she hadn't given it a thought when she was packing for her trip to Mato Grosso.

I should be researching his route through here, trying to retrace come of his movements; do something more than just fart around the Pantanal with the cows. I've been so caught up in my job, in learning the language and how to live in this country, that I've all but forgotten what brought me here in the first place.

As the Jeep bounced its way around deep potholes, Sylvia tried to remember where Fawcett had been when he came to the immense region known as Mato Grosso, now a Brazilian state. It was no use. Much time had passed since she'd read Fawcett's story. The weeks of preparing to leave for Brazil, then adjusting to her new life in Rio, further blurred the memory of details.

I recall he was in Cuiabá a couple of times– though he spelled it "Cuyabá"– but it seems most of his trek was west of here; he used the word bañados, the Bolivian Spanish term for a marsh, instead of Pantanal. He wrote about following many miles of ancient raised causeways, and seeing extensive ramparts; this very road we're taking now could be one that was built on the packed earth of the old ones.

It began to sink in what an unusual civilization must've inhabited the area, raising countless miles of causeway above the bogs without bulldozers or trucks.

Elisabeth broke into her reverie.

"The bump-bump is almost over! The pousada is near. Are you tired?"

"A little." Sylvia shrugged. She'd be glad to see the bump-bump come to an end for the day, but it was invigorating to be out in the wilds again. Four days of Cuiabá had been enough, though IDA had put her up in a comfortable hotel near the university, and her work had gone smoothly. The people she'd dealt with welcomed her warmly; she couldn't have asked for greater friendliness.

The university would work in partnership with IDA to let high-school upperclassmen use a campus distance-education center. It was evident to Sylvia the university personnel wanted to learn from the ambitious project. They had designs, they told her, for satellite campuses in Campo Grande and Corumbá; distance learning via television and computer would be a critical part of the plan.

Sylvia had been wined and dined and shown around Cuiabá, which was a nice enough town, just hot, crowded, and noisy, like Manaus. Only one of her university hosts spoke passable English, so Sylvia had had to rely on her Portuguese most of the time. Though improving rapidly, it still wasn't automatic and she felt the strain.

She experienced the same reaction she'd had when she lived in Europe: Each day she reached a certain point, usually sometime after dinner, when the language department of her brain simply shut down for the night. It wouldn't process incoming Portuguese— not very well, anyway— and it refused to assist her efforts at speech. It had been so in São Paulo, and often occurred during social evenings in Rio. When it happened, she was cast adrift in a sea of chattering humans, feeling alien and alone, and tired. Only those who had been in her shoes could understand.

Her sweet guide, Elisabeth, was one of those, and the two women had quickly reached a comfortable rhythm involving some English, which Elisabeth spoke fairly well, some Portuguese, and long, restful silences. The two were about the same age, but had little else in common. Elisabeth had spent her entire life in Mato Grosso; she was educated and bright, but shy. Her wardrobe consisted mostly of shorts and T-shirts, and her salt-and-pepper hair was always pulled back in a bushy ponytail.

On the paved road from Cuiabá to Poconé, Sylvia asked questions, and Elisabeth pointed out various sights as they rolled along. After Poconé the road was primitive and sometimes awful, and Elisabeth had needed to focus her energy on driving. Occasionally they stopped to look at animals, such as a big family of capybara crossing the road.

"Here we are!" Rather suddenly, they rounded a curve and arrived at a short, muddy drive leading to a modest *fazenda*, or ranch. The guide set the brake, and stretched.

"You must be tired, Elisabeth; you did the hard work."

"*Sim*, I'm sore here— " she touched her shoulders— "But it's good we get so far south of Poconé today; tomorrow we have more travel to make."

And indeed they did. After a good sleep and a tremendous Pantanal breakfast at dawn, the women continued down the excruciating road toward Porto Jofre.

The view from the window was becoming more and more interesting with every mile that fell away. The Pantanal was well into its wet season, and normally, Elisabeth had said, the road they were on was becoming flooded by this time. This year, for some reason, things were drier; but only for now. Next month this trek wouldn't be possible. As it was, Sylvia could see *baias*, areas of standing water formed by the rain, like small lakes that would grow, and grow, until their borders blended.

"Everybody here has boats," Elisabeth said. "They take a boat where they need to go during the wettest time, or they just stay home until the waters are gone. Ow! Sorry, that was a big one, yes? I thought the whole Jeep disappear in there, maybe!"

Sylvia snickered. It made the road to Mauá look like a turnpike. "Oh, look! Stop, can we?"

Elisabeth pulled over. They were passing by a stream which curved into a mar-shy area, where two big caimans were sunning on a dry island, their mouths open to cool themselves. The two women got out of the vehicle.

"Eh, we're getting close to Rio Cuiabá; lots of water here, streams... I hope we can get to Porto Jofre with no floods. Wait, I get drinks." Elisabeth went to the cooler where she'd stashed plenty of ice, Guaraná, and beer. "*Chopp?*" She held out an Antartica.

"No, thanks, I'll just have a cola."

Elisabeth gave her a Guaraná and they walked as close as they dared to ogle the beasts. "Always leave the doors open, eh? We may need to jump in, caimans can move fast."

Sylvia tipped the cold drink back— Elisabeth wasn't one for straws— and let the beauty around her sink in. There was water, water everywhere, its sun-spangled expanse broken by islands of tall trees. The air moving over the marsh had a smell she couldn't describe, it was so full of earth and moisture and life.

They went on, now reaching gullies where the vehicle had to ford shallow waters. It began to happen more often and the water got deeper.

"Say, Elisabeth, is it possible there could be a lot of rain, and we could get stuck down there, where we're going? The road flooded too much for the Jeep?"

"It's possible." There was a silence.

That was all there was to say. Abruptly Sylvia laughed. Elisabeth glanced her way and smiled, and they drove on.

"We made it! 'Now the fun begins', as you say in English!"

Sylvia didn't care what, exactly, that meant; the main thing was, they were through driving for a while. She wondered if Elisabeth's butt felt as sore as hers.

Porto Jofre was a small settlement on the Cuiabá River, which showed signs of having once been a bustling river port. Now it was quiet, and the people seemed taciturn after the amiability of Cuiabá. But the women weren't there very long. They ate sandwiches, and engaged a boat to take them downriver to a remote ranch which Elisabeth had recommended, saying, "It is so peaceful. You're surrounded by silence." Sylvia thought she would travel to the ends of the earth for silence.

Well, to the end of the Transpantanal Highway, anyway. Now, the only practical means of continuing was by boat. The women embarked, the boatman started an outboard motor, and the Rio Cuiabá carried them swiftly to the Fazenda Jabiru.

The spine-jarring drive had been worth it, Sylvia decided now as she stood outside listening to bufos croaking, clearing her head from sleep. She had escaped the world. If she made a full 360-degree turn, there wasn't a single electric light to be seen, or even another dwelling. The fazenda was thousands of acres in size and very isolated; it had taken at least a half-hour's boat travel down the Cuiabá, and then more miles up a tributary to reach the fazenda's dock.

Humans had created a little pocket of comfort in the vast flooded land. Built on an area of higher terrain called a *cordilheira*, which was covered with forest and *cerrado* scrub and never flooded, the ranch home was dry and snug. Most of the time snakes couldn't get into the house, and ranch dogs helped discourage other creatures from an excess of curiosity. There was food for the taking all around, but the people had also planted a small fenced garden, and stored quantities of beans and rice and other goods. There was a fireplace for times when the temperature fell into the 50s.

The same family had owned the ranch for over a hundred years, and it hadn't changed very much in that time. There were solar panels for warm water now, and a generator for electricity, but it was operated only for part of the day; then the washing machine hummed and beer got cold. The owner was planning to put in a satellite dish. The kids wanted a television, though their mom had resisted for years. Her instincts told her to protect them from the ugliness of the "outside".

One wing of the rambling wooden house had a couple of extra rooms, and in these, Sylvia and Elisabeth stayed. Nowadays, quite a few Pantaneiros opened their homes to paying guests.

Sylvia padded over to a nearby fence and sat on the low rail. The dream had seemed so real that she could still visualize several of the Indian faces. They appeared to have been standing along this fence. She had never, to conscious recollection, heard of any tribe called Shi-VAHN-tee, or so it sounded. Where in her mind did such a dream arise?

A small movement to her right, caught by her peripheral vision, startled her and she whirled around. There was something, someone very tall, in the shadows.

"Who's there?" she asked.

She was answered by a movement and an odd sound. As she fumbled for her flashlight which she'd laid on the fence she realized she was looking at a jabiru stork, sitting farther down the rail. It moved its big, folded wings, making the flapping sound she'd heard.

Though jabirus, the fazenda's namesake, can be six feet tall, this one was not quite so big but it was perched on a two-foot high fence. Sylvia stood up, and backed slowly toward her door. The bird was awake; she saw its eyes, gleaming, watching her warily. She doubted it would hurt her, but it was certainly capable of doing harm if it had a mind to. During the day she and Elisabeth had seen them, with their long black beaks and bright red necks, poking about in shallow water for little fish.

She stopped near the door and watched the stork for a while. What was it doing so close to the house? She'd heard they were shy of people, and dogs. Maybe one of the Shi-vahn-tee had shapeshifted, and still appealed for help.

Smiling at her own fancy she turned to go back to bed, just in time to see an iguana, at least four feet long including tail, dash into her room.

She stopped cold. Dang! Antonio, the ranch owner, had told her to keep her door closed at all times, but she'd forgotten. Should she leave it open now, so the reptile could wander back out, or would it invite all its friends in? She left the door open. *What now? I could make a dash for the bed, but would I wake up with that thing beside me? Sleep is impossible, now. Well, I wanted to see wildlife...*

Sylvia decided to take her chances with the stork. The eastern horizon glowed with light, and the stars were slowly fading back into the cosmos. In the predawn hour all the frogs and crickets had suddenly hushed, and birds hadn't yet found their voices. There was nothing to be heard but silence. *It's better to share the sunrise with an Indian spirit in a giant bird's body; I can rest when I'm old.*

Elisabeth found Sylvia and the jabiru sitting companionably on the fence a few yards apart, when she opened her door at six-thirty to a blaze of slanting rays.

"How do you spell that?"

"*Que?*"

"How do you write that?"

"In English, I'm not sure," Elisabeth laughed and shook her head. "I think it's <u>olivaceous</u> cormorant." She spelled out the first word.

Sylvia struggled to write; they tipped back and forth as Paquito, the old ranch hand, poled the boat along a narrow channel.

"Look at my list of birds we've seen!"

"Eh, yes... you forget the pauraque we saw last night."

"The who? Oh, yeah, the nighthawk."

There had been egrets and herons, rheas and ibises, caracaras and chachalacas. Jacanás, anis, a black-bellied whistling duck... vultures, kingfishers, and others. The waters and the cordilheiras were teeming with avian life.

The days passed gracefully by. Sylvia had shed her watch and the tension in her shoulders as they explored wetlands and woodlands.

On Sylvia's last day a light rain fell, cooling the horses and the women who rode them out into the grasslands.

Elisabeth was chuckling.

"What's funny?"

"You! You're the only American I've met who doesn't care if she gets wet."

"Huh! When the sun comes back out, we'll dry in a flash. It feels good."

They rode for a while in silence.

"You know, you have a good life, a great job," Sylvia remarked at last.

"Eh, yes, it's good for me." The guide gave Sylvia a sidelong glance. "I don't see how you can work with computers all the time; you like the outdoors so much. I mean no criticism— " she added hastily.

"I understand. I think of technology as a set of tools, nothing more. But I have a powerful drive to get out into wild places, often. I need to recharge myself to deal with— well, the snakes and wolves, the city predators, you could say... And I need to be alone, frequently."

Elisabeth shared that need; it required no explanation. She had faced down Antonio and his objections, and let Sylvia take a horse out on her own for an hour or so one day.

"Is he worried about me, or his horse?" Sylvia had asked.

"Ha! The horse, definitely. But he'd also like you to be alive until you pay the bill."

They were only half-joking. If there was a flaw in Sylvia's stay at the fazenda, it was the gloomy nature of the family and their apparent greed. The unfriendliness wasn't a total surprise; she had noticed similar reserve in the first night's pousada owners, and the people they encountered in Porto Jofre. As for Antonio, he was sometimes downright surly. (He had growled at her about the iguana and sent his son to literally lasso and remove it.) Sylvia chalked it up to the isolation of most Pantanal residences; how could they be expected to learn sociability?

Elisabeth pointed out that Pantaneiros were notoriously territorial, so their attitudes may reflect an aversion to having outsiders on their property. "After all," she added, "ninety-nine per cent of the Pantanal is privately owned land, nearly all of it cattle ranches, and it has been so for over 200 years."

"But Antonio tolerates strangers for the money," Sylvia noted. And she couldn't ignore the matter of the drinking water. She had been flabbergasted to discover the family drank bottled water, brought in from Cuiabá.

"In the midst of all this water, and rivers— "

"It seems crazy," explained Elisabeth. "But many Pantaneiros don't trust the water, because of the cattle, and other animals; you know, microbes... Also, in the dry season some of them live in places where the smaller streams dry up."

Sylvia understood a bit better, but she was shocked by the price Antonio was charging her for a small bottle. "I'm already paying him a great deal to stay here. And in this climate I drink water constantly." She was prepared for sticker-shock when she saw her final bill; who knew what Antonio might decide to include?

At noonday they managed to find a grass knoll without too many bugs, overlooking a lovely baia; there they devoured their lunch.

"Oi, look at this!" Elisabeth exclaimed. "La Senhora put in a surprise!" She held up a plastic bag full of small cookies.

"Whaddaya know. She isn't so bad, sometimes."

"She never did this before."

"Uh-oh— the bill is going to be awful!"

Their laughter rang out across the baia, startling a flock of parakeets which exploded from a small cajá tree.

They rode on through the immense grasslands of the ranch. Somewhere a large herd of cattle grazed, but they were nowhere to be seen.

Hours later as daylight waned, from its perch on the garden wall a large jabiru watched as two tired riders moved single file atop a long cordilheira, silhouetted against the deep red sky.

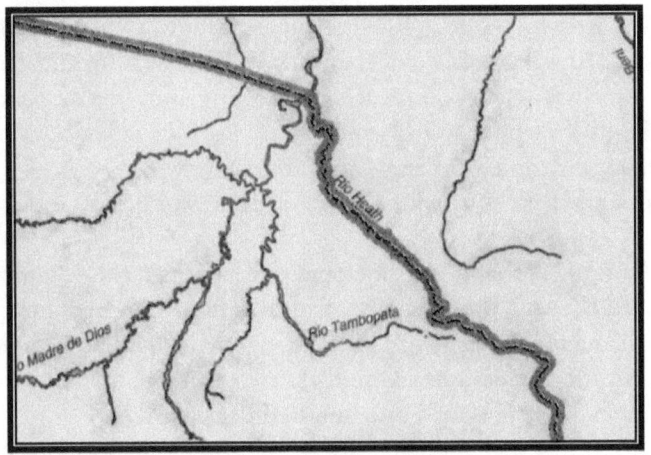

FAWCETT, CHAPTER 6
RIO HEATH

January, 1910 found Fawcett back in England, at "Waterside", the new family home in Uplyme. It was a large house, with an even larger garden, but no property in Great Britain could be big enough for Fawcett now. He had been aching to see his wife and children, but after a month or two the pangs took on a different character and became those of a prisoner, yearning for escape. Everything was an enemy conspiring to entrap him forever: the comfortable house, the civilized, polite neighbors, the tidy lanes and picture-perfect meadows and trees and even the mild, affable sun and rain. In his fancy it seemed a clever plot to soften him with comfort, snare him with guilt.

The panther paced his cage, its walls closing in more surely with every day that passed.

One day, Nina looked up from their morning tea.

"Well, darling, when do you leave?"

"I beg your pardon?"

She laughed. "Oh, Percy, you've been prowling around the house at night like a beast on a short leash. I know you miss it." She held his eyes. Nina always could see directly into his soul.

"Ah, Cheeky... " His shoulders dropped, but he didn't look away. "When I'm there I miss you horribly, and when I'm here— " He shook his head.

"I understand."

"Do you, my love? The wild places seem to have me in their grasp.

217

I wish I were a better husband; you deserve— "

"We are who we are," she interrupted briskly. "If I tried to change you, you'd be miserable and then so would I. With you, I feel as if I have two lives: safe and secure here in England, raising babies close to friends and family, and enjoying a vicarious adventure in South America, with you every step— in spirit, anyway."

He smiled. "You would have made a wonderful explorer, you know."

"Mentally, perhaps, but not physically; I haven't the stamina, by a long shot. And the thought of picking two hundred ticks off my body at the end of each day isn't exactly my idea of good fun! Sometimes vicarious pleasures are best."

"Oh, maybe it was only one hundred ticks per day."

"Ah! In that case, I might go with you sometime."

"Well, in answer to your question, I think I shall soon begin my search for some assistants to go along on the next trip. A pity Fisher isn't available; he's been transferred to Paraguay." The President of Bolivia, Dr. Villazon, had asked Fawcett to survey the Peruvian boundary, which would include exploration of another unknown, unmapped river: the Heath. Up to this point, hostile Indians had prevented penetration of the area.

"Too bad you had to retire, after serving the Army for twenty years."

"Pah! I don't mind, really, that they simply wouldn't 'lend' me out anymore; four years is their limit and they're mindlessly stuck to it. But never mind... the army is no place for a man with initiative; it's for drones, I've decided. If one is at all enterprising, one is quashed immediately, or resented. The army is for wealthy, easily-contented men, and both criteria exclude me. I'm better off working independently."

In a few months, Fawcett again waved good-bye to wife and sons from the deck of a ship, flanked by his new assistants, N.C.O.s from the Rifle Regiment, Corporals Costin and Manley. The familiar mixture of emotions struggled within him: the heavy-hearted dread of a long separation from his family, and the somewhat guilty sense of elation, of freedom from the fetters of the mundane. At these times he felt a particular kinship with Kipling; here was a man who fully understood the need for escape from ordinary, predictable life:

Me that 'ave been what I've been—

Me that 'ave gone where I've gone—
Me that 'ave seen what I've seen—
'Ow can I ever take on
With awful old England again,
An' 'ouses both sides of the street,
And 'edges two sides of the lane,
And the parson an' gentry between,
An' touchin' my 'at when we meet—
Me that 'ave been what I've been?

*

Freezing wind shrieked through the pass and along the trail with a velocity and gusting force that threatened Fawcett's balance on the narrow, icy ledge. If he lost his footing now... He glanced to his left into a yawning chasm, blinking as crystals of ice sprayed from his mustache into his eyes, already near-blind from the wind. He adjusted his grip on the cargo mule's lead, his gloved hand numb, making sure he was not entangled and could release the line in an instant if need be. The reason for this caution was about to be demonstrated, yet again.

An inhuman scream blended in hellish harmony with the wind; a voice cried, "Oh, God!" as a squealing mule tumbled down the vertical mountainside to the river rocks, hundreds of feet below. The line of pack mules, the men, all the party stopped to helplessly watch its descent and death. The boxes it carried burst on impact and lay in splinters about the still, dark body.

Fawcett cringed. "How many is that?" he called to Costin.

"Eleven!" Costin had pulled down his muffler, shouting through bluish lips. "I saw it happening and couldn't do a blessed thing! Its load snagged on those rocks jutting out there and the weight shift knocked the poor beast right off the trail."

The party stood still for a few more moments, gazing bleakly at the scene below while the wind howled in full voice around them. Finally Fawcett, in the lead, turned and slowly, carefully, put one boot in front of the other on the rimy rocks. The mule he led began to walk with shaking legs, dislodging loose gravel with its hoofs. Costin, behind, watched the gravel plunge into the abyss, and the party inched forward: now thirteen cargo mules and four men.

Fawcett, Costin, and Manley had set out from La Paz to survey the boundary between Bolivia and Peru along the shores of Lake Titicaca. When they reached the northwest shore of the lake they were joined by Caspar Gonzales, a young Bolivian officer, and began a triangulation survey requiring three months of sub-freezing Andes treks. The men had reached the source of the Tambopata River near an altitude of 17,000 feet, and were now beginning the descent to Mojos.

After another hour of cautious, nerve-wracking progress the wind began to diminish, to the relief of all, as they descended from the summit; but Fawcett clenched his teeth. The damnable steepness of the trail was as bad as its increasing narrowness, and the risk of rolling uncontrollably on the small rocks made downhill stretches a particular nightmare. Then Fawcett groaned. Ahead, the trail had been washed away, leaving a five-foot gap.

Costin saw it as he caught up. "My Moses! Not again!"

"Get the boards," ordered Fawcett, too tired and cold even to complain. The problem was a common one on Andes trails, and travelers came prepared with some means of traversing such breaks. Everyone knew what to do, and proceeded with fear and trembling to fashion a makeshift bridge and anchor it with the largest rocks they could find. Then came the hard part: coaxing the mules, as sure-footed and brave as any creature alive but thoroughly shaken by the day's events, to cross on the sagging, slippery boards.

With prods, bellowing, bullying, and everything short of outright physical abuse, which Fawcett wouldn't tolerate, the men got one mule at a time across the flimsy span. There was a harrowing moment when the twelfth mule simply stopped dead center of the bridge and refused to move. The creature stood as if frozen in time and space, looking neither right nor left nor, God forbid, downward. Costin, holding its lead, pulled as hard as he dared and cursed mightily. The thirteenth mule became restless as it waited, held by Gonzales, behind the statue-like animal.

"I'm afraid to pull too hard on the rope," Costin panted, almost losing his footing. "I could yank the beast into a skid."

"Just be damned sure you can let go of that rope *fast* if he falls," warned Fawcett. "See here, you have it wrapped round your arm! Free yourself, *now*, and be sure the end is clear of your feet!" As Costin did so, an enlightened look sprang into Fawcett's eyes. "I have an idea," he said.

Fawcett directed Costin to put the rope down, placing the end well to the inner side of the trail. "That's good, put it out of the way.

Now let's go! Everyone, start walking, slowly, and try not to look back; as if we're leaving."

"Well, it's worth a go," said Manley. "We've tried everything else. Maybe the last mule behind it can convince it to move its arse!"

"I hope so," Fawcett concurred with a snort. "I'd hate to have to leave them both behind, and you too, Gonzales!"

"Ho-ho," Gonzales called from the end of the line, deadpan.

The troop, minus two mules and a man, trudged away. They continued until they disappeared around a bend; it had to look as if they were truly leaving. They heard a shout from Gonzales, and Manley ran back to take a peek around the rocks.

"It's across!" The men ran back to greet the mule, which was moving as quickly as possible toward them, and give the beast three cheers. Their hip-hip-hoorahs echoed from the mountain walls as Gonzales hooked the last mule to a long rope and threw it across the gap to Manley.

"Rest your arms, Costin, I'll tug this one over," Manley said. He gave a pull on the rope and clicked his tongue encouragingly; but the thirteenth mule started across the bridge quite readily, not wanting to be left behind, either.

When the slip came, it happened so fast no one could ever say what had caused it; the mule's hind feet skidded out from under it and as the men gasped almost in unison the creature dropped into the chasm and out of sight.

Manley moaned, "The last one! Poor ol' blighter!"

Fawcett had gone to peer over the edge of the trail, and was gesturing excitedly. "Come! Look at this!"

"At what? Another splattered animal?" Costin mumbled grimly.

But four pairs of eyes opened wide at the sight of the mule, a hundred feet below, dangling quite unhurt between two trees where its load had wedged. The beast was looking around, calmly sniffing the foliage, which it began to nibble.

"Will anyone ever believe this?" Manley exclaimed, laughing. "The little bloke likes the eats down there!"

Fawcett shook his head; he had to smile at the scene, but he knew there was no cause for cheer.

"It seems a pity after the stroke of luck the creature had," he told the others, "But unless one of you has some ingenious idea, we have no means of getting it back up here."

After an extended silence, the men agreed it was hopeless.

"Costin, you're the sharpshooter among us," Fawcett said. "Unless you'd rather I do it."

Costin said he would do it, and with a well-aimed rifle shot, one more mule was dead.

Slowly and carefully the group of mules and men wound their way down the eastern slopes of the Cordillera, until it seemed the wind was a trace less bitter and the rocky earth bore more and more tough little plants. At length they reached a broad, flat shelf strewn with boulders and twisted shrubs. Fawcett gathered the group for a meal and an hour's rest.

Manley and Costin were unpacking the edibles when they heard a low whistle. Gonzales was motioning to them as he stared straight ahead into the nearby shrubbery.

"Sh-sh..." he cautioned as they approached. Fawcett reached him first and stood stock still.

In a clearing on the other side of the shrubs stood a circle of some nine or ten dark gray Andean condors. In the middle of the ring were two large black condors and an even bigger white one.

"Díos," said Gonzales softly. "The white one— he's the leader— see how they are all looking at him!"

Fawcett and the others stood transfixed by the scene. *It's a sort of council of condors,* Fawcett was thinking. *What I wouldn't give to understand its purpose!* The grand creatures, among the largest flying birds in the world, seemed aware of the nearby men and beasts but for the most part ignored them as if they were beneath notice.

"The white condor is very rare," Gonzales was whispering. "And that one's wingspan must be near fourteen feet! For many years I have wanted a white for a trophy—" To Fawcett's horror he raised his rifle and fired before anyone could stop him.

"Damn you!" shouted Fawcett, lunging forward to snatch the gun from his hands; but in Gonzales' haste and excitement he had missed the target.

At once the outer circle of birds went into action, taking wing and heading straight for Gonzales, whose eyes bulged from their sockets. All the men ran, but there was no real cover to be found anywhere. The group of birds was interested only in Gonzales, it quickly became obvious; one of them swooped for him, and the man frantically waved his arms to beat it away. Several condors then dived at his head, sending him into a panic; he raced from the clearing and down the trail as Manley floundered about in confusion and Costin ran for his rifle.

"Wait, Costin, don't fire!" Fawcett shouted as he took off after Gonzales down the slippery trail.

Gonzales had fallen and was on his back, flailing his arms at the swooping birds; but he regained his feet as Fawcett reached him, and ran onward in mindless hysteria. The path suddenly steepened. Slipping, Gonzales now clung to the rocks for dear life as two condors beat at him with their huge wings to dislodge him into the yawning chasm. Repeatedly they circled and dove, trying to hit home with wingbones powerful enough to break a man's leg or crack his skull.

Fawcett edged as close to the screaming man as he dared, waving the rifle stock at the birds. But they showed no interest in him; it was Gonzales, the shooter, that they wanted. Fawcett extended the gun and crawled closer. Maybe he could pull Gonzales to a more secure spot next to him; the two of them together might be able to fend off the furious condors.

"Can you grab this? Gonzales!" But Gonzales was beyond listening or thinking, certain his end was upon him.

Just then, a great shadow fell briefly over both men. The white condor floated majestically to a boulder close beside Gonzales, who stopped his screaming and began to weep softly. The other condors ceased attacking and circled quietly above the two men. Gonzales dropped his head to rest on the rock, thinking he may as well let go and have it over.

But the white condor was not looking at Gonzales. With apparent intelligence it considered Fawcett, who met its eyes in fascination. *The man has learned his lesson,* Fawcett silently pled. *Won't you let me get him away from here?*

The king condor's naked white head slowly jutted forward as if to peer into Fawcett's soul. It still had not condescended to glance at Gonzales. Then its wings rose and stretched into their awesome span, as it lifted its great body easily from the mountainside. Powerful wings beat the air with an unforgettable sound as the bird ascended. The other condors followed, disappearing behind the crags.

Gonzales raised his head. "María, Madre de Dios," he breathed.

"Grab my hand, you fool, before I kick your carcass over the edge myself," Fawcett snarled. But as he hauled Gonzales to safety his mind was elsewhere, and his anger quickly faded. He could still see the strange eyes of the white condor and their expression as they bored into him.

Shaken to the core, Gonzales needed help walking back to the mules. As Manley and Costin rushed forward to assist, Fawcett gave orders.

"Eat quickly, and see if you can get some food into him. We won't be resting here, sorry to say." Fawcett raised his eyes to the empty blue vault of the sky. "We've worn out our welcome already, it appears."

"*Bienvenido!*" boomed the friendly voice of Carlos Franck, as the band of mules and men dragged themselves into Pelechuco, altitude 12,000 feet. He introduced himself, saying the entire town had been keeping a lookout for their party. Bolivian officials had sent a message to Franck, requesting that he offer hospitality to the group when they eventually reached Pelechuco. As he led them to his home, he explained how honored he was to accommodate them, as the inhabitants of the entire region saw them as heroes.

"Heroes?" Fawcett stared. "What on earth do you mean?"

"Oh, everyone, particularly the Indians, you know, consider the Boundary Commission to be an instrument of Peru, and nothing less than an effort to invade our country. Silly, eh? But you are representatives of Bolivia, struggling on our behalf! You're helping to save our land from the wily Peruvians, you see?"

Fawcett rolled his eyes with impatience; Costin snorted.

Franck smiled. "Regardless of how some of us see it, it's actually a serious matter. The Indians are on the verge of an uprising over it."

"I know it's serious, you're right," Fawcett conceded. "In fact, I've discovered that Peru's Commission destroyed some of the cairns I put up, for my plane tabling. It's come down to that sort of behavior. But I'll finish this triangulation despite all, and then I will survey the River Heath to its source, as contracted. The two nations can do what they will with the results."

Franck scratched his head. "Nasty business. It might come down to war."

Fawcett tried to put the conversation out of his mind as he and his men settled into the first physical comforts they had known for weeks, but it nagged at him.

The next evening, their stomachs sated by the bounty of Franck's table, the men sat talking over coffee and cigars; all but Gonzales, who bowed good-night and retired to his room. He had kept a low profile since the incident, aware of Fawcett's still-simmering ire.

"He's more afraid of you, now, than the big bird," chuckled Manley after Gonzales had gone.

"What 'big bird'?" inquired Franck with mild curiosity.

"A condor," Manley answered, though Fawcett was shaking his head, wanting to let it go.

"Indeed?" Now Franck was piqued. "Do tell."

Fawcett sighed, and related the story of Gonzales and the condors as Franck listened with keen interest.

"Quite an event, Major," he finally said. "You know, the white condor is considered a sacred sign in these parts. Even to see one is a blessing."

"Gonzales might disagree," snorted Costin.

"Huh! He's blessed to be alive still, I'd say. The local Indians would make much of this story, idolizing you as they do, Major. To them the white condor is not just a creature; it's a spirit. Sometimes it leads people to special places, according to legend, such as gold mines, or ancient cities."

Fawcett's ears perked up. "Cities?"

"There are said to be stunning ruins back in the forests, and even cities where people still live— white people with hair as pale as corn silk, or sometimes red, and sky-blue eyes. But oddest of all, they are Indians. Or so the villagers believe."

"White Indians again," Fawcett murmured. "I'd like to hear more about the cities... "

"Oh, the Indians won't tell you anything. They know where all sorts of treasure and mines are hidden, and over the decades they've been tortured for the information, but they never tell their secrets. They believe outsiders, whites, disturb the spirits, and bring ruin to the people."

"I understand why they'd think so."

"The only detail I can offer," added Franck, "is that the inhabited cities are supposed to be far to the east, in the wilderness beyond the Beni, possibly up in the Serra."

Fawcett thoughtfully relit his cigar, which had gone out long ago. They fell silent. Fawcett watched the bluish smoke curl into fantastic shapes above their heads, wondering if it was an emblem of castles in the air, and nothing more.

"No, no, no, Major, it is impossible! You will all die!" The commander of the large garrison at the mouth of the Heath River faced up to Fawcett, whose jaw was set just as stubbornly as the commander's. "The Indians strike with no warning, using poisoned arrows. Why, the Guarayos have even been bold enough to come downriver and attack the garrison!"

"We are a very small group, commander, we don't look at all like a slaving party. Why shouldn't they let us pass through?"

"Because they are savages, that's why!"

Fawcett persisted. He had completed his survey of the Tambopata all the way to its confluence with the Madre de Dios River, which he had followed northeastward to the garrison. He had a job to do, he reminded the commander, waving his government commission papers at the man. "You are instructed to aid us with whatever we need."

In the end, seeing he could not dissuade the Englishman, the commander let him have three canoes: one to carry Fawcett, Manley, and Costin, a second for Gonzales and another Bolivian officer, Zamora, who had caught up with them at Apolo; and a third bearing five garrison soldiers. After a couple of days of preparations, they set out to map the source of the Heath.

"Over there, sir." Manley gestured toward the riverbank. Fawcett turned to look at a number of footprints where the muddy bank sloped down to the river.

"Yes. There must be another village nearby." Although they had yet to spot a single Indian, they had passed similar areas bearing human prints several times during the day. The soldiers found it a convenient time to return to the river mouth, and since midday the two canoes had continued on alone.

Fawcett was mentally rehearsing a Chucho sentence which an acquaintance in Astillero had taught him, promising the dialect was close enough to the Guarayo to be understood. Now it appeared he would need it: Without warning, the men rounded a bend and encountered an Indian camp. The Guarayos, even more surprised than the travelers, were thrown into a panic; women and children appeared utterly terrified and the men grabbed their weapons in such haste they were bumping into each other. As a hail of arrows surrounded them, the little party hastily pulled onto a sandbar and sought cover behind the canoes.

Fawcett tried the Chucho sentence; he didn't know its exact meaning but assumed it to be a friendly, reassuring greeting. He repeated it a couple of times. The arrows increased in number alarmingly, and Costin asked, "What did you say?"

"I'm not quite sure... "

"Well, I wouldn't say it again, sir," Costin pleaded, ducking lower behind the canoe.

(It wasn't until much later Fawcett discovered that the fool in Astillero thought it hilarious to have him yell, "Greetings! We are enemies who have come to kill you!")

Thunk! A six-foot-long arrow arrived with such power behind it that it pierced both sides of the boat, though its wood was an inch and a half thick. "Good grief!" shouted Manley, who had been narrowly missed.

Clearly, Fawcett saw, the canoes didn't provide very much safety; they had to do something, fast, unless they wanted to give up and retreat.

An insane inspiration struck him.

"Manley! Grab your accordion! "

"Sir?" Had he heard right?

"Take your accordion to that log, there, it's out of range of these arrows. And start playing, anything! Go!"

Manley obeyed, and began playing as coolly and as well as he usually did, under different circumstances, his rendition of "Soldiers of the Queen".

"Sing, everyone!" Fawcett ordered.

In the confusion Fawcett heard Costin singing "Onward Christian Soldiers", a Bolivian drinking song from Gonzales and Zamora, and Fawcett himself was bellowing "Suwannee River" at the top of his lungs. He had no idea what the Indians thought of them, but after a while he noticed Costin singing, "They've... stopped... shoo-oo-ting at us... "

It was true. There were no more arrows. Indian faces, exposed above the foliage, gaped at the intruders with utterly dumbfounded expressions. Fawcett wished he had his camera in hand. He leapt from behind the canoe, showing empty hands to the Guarayo. He walked forward, employing those hands in the sign language which was so widely known throughout Latin America. He signalled a friendly greeting, and then waved both arms over his head, meaning he was coming over to them.

"Costin, come along." As they pushed off in a canoe, he called back: "Manley, keep playing, and all of you keep singing— but with a little more cohesion, perhaps." He picked up an oar.

As they approached the bank they had no idea what sort of reception to expect, having invaded the territory of a people who had been often mistreated by outsiders; but when they attempted to climb the bank, strong arms, painted with square patterns in purple, reached down from the underbrush and lifted them up. They stood surrounded by forty or fifty of the dreaded and maligned Guarayo, and found themselves staring into handsome faces with eyes which radiated intelligence and curiosity. Some wore shirts or long gowns of beaten bark, painted with designs or dyed red, and others were stark naked; all held large bows and arrows, and a few also had shotguns.

They seemed to find the white men and their clothing very amusing, and examined them minutely before taking them about a quarter of a mile into the forest, where stood a group of huts. The cacique, or chieftain, of the tribe was presented, and Fawcett cast about for some way to pay his respects. He reached up and removed his Stetson and placed it on the cacique's head, smiling for all he was worth. The chief at once broke into a large grin, and the others then laughed mightily, which Fawcett later discovered was their standard reaction to every occurrence, even those that were decidedly unamusing.

That evening, a celebration in the visitors' honor followed. Fawcett and Costin rejoined the rest of the men on the sandbar where they set up camp while the Guarayo prepared a feast of bananas and fish.

After the men had gorged themselves on the generous meal, they provided a little entertainment for the Guarayo in the form of an accordion song-fest, more harmonious by far than the first.

*

The morning after the revelry, Fawcett and his men awoke to find six of the Guarayo sprawled among them, fast asleep; the rest had gone away into the forest. Costin, rubbing his eyes sleepily, walked to the river's edge to relieve himself.

"Oh, look here, Major," he called, standing next to a large log. "Looks like they left us some gifts."

One of the Guarayo had awakened. He signed to Fawcett that these were presents from the cacique. Atop the log were bananas, fish, and several tooth necklaces.

The travelers packed up and made their goodbyes to the six Indians who had remained with them. Fawcett presented them with several head veils to protect their faces from the biting flies that cursed the area. One of them communicated to Fawcett that there were Echoca villages ahead, but he taught him a few Guarayo phrases to use which he said the Echoca, their trading partners, would understand, along with the name of the chieftain.

"Hope these words work better than the Chucho," said Manley ironically as they pushed off the sandbar. The Guarayo stood on the bar, waving the head veils, until they could no longer be seen.

There was plenty to eat as the men continued upriver, catching dorado and bagging one of the abundant wild pigs. But rapids also became abundant, causing the men to frequently wade the river, dragging their canoes over the rocks.

"Here's something else we have too much of," complained Costin, as they rested on shore after dealing with a long stretch of whitewater. He craned his neck to look at a festering sore on his shoulder. "Damnable *sututus!*" This tropical curse was a small, flying insect's grub which liked to hitch rides on humans and bury itself beneath the skin. They were extremely difficult to remove and tormenting to endure.

"Ye gods, your back is covered with 'em," said Manley, shuddering. "I've a few, myself."

"Me, too," sighed Fawcett. "All of us. Here now— don't apply that." Gonzales was making a poultice of saliva and tobacco. "That's fine for bee stings, but you heard what they said at the garrison: If you poison sututus and they die beneath the skin, you can wind up with blood poisoning."

"Well, these festering sores we have can turn into the same," countered Gonzales gloomily, nonetheless scrapping his poultice.

After a few days the group encountered eight brown men on a

sandbar ahead of them. "Echoca," Fawcett said. Immediately he ordered Manley and Costin to paddle toward them. As they did, the Indians placed arrows in their bows and raised them.

"Major—" began Costin.

"It's all right; let me out, alone. One unarmed white man can't be too threatening. Where's the sugar? And a big chunk of the pig... "

Fawcett alit from the canoe and walked toward the Indians, gifts in hand, smiling. The eight men kept their arrows trained on him, but their eyes showed confusion. He spoke the Guarayo phrases and laid his gifts on a rock, backing away slightly and standing erect. He waited.

The Indians exchanged a few sentences, conferring, and then all put down their weapons and came forward to greet their visitor with shy but friendly expressions. Back in the canoes, the other men released sighs of relief.

The Echoca were but a small tribe, yet their plantations of maize, mandioca, and bananas were extensive and well-kept. Their friendliness was almost overwhelming; they jumped in and helped the white men with their loathsome chore of dragging the canoes over rapids, until they had come to a large communal hut on the river bank. They insisted the visitors stay the night with them, and at once began preparations for a grand feast.

As Fawcett and the others bathed in the river before the festivities, one of the Echocas eyed the condition of their backs, covered with sututu sores. He gestured for Fawcett to sit on the bank and let him help. Fawcett decided to trust the man. This was their world, after all; they surely had found ways to deal with a problem that seemed all too common.

The Indian knelt close to Fawcett and made a whistling sound with his tongue. Costin, watching, saw the grub poke out its head— whereupon the Indian squeezed the invader smartly out.

"I say!" Costin exclaimed. "Major, the little demon is out!"

The Indian continued in this fashion until all of Fawcett's sututus were gone. But the procedure was quite too unconventional for Gonzales.

"It's witchcraft," he huffed and puffed. "I want no part of it!"

But Costin was more than ready for the Echoca treatment. "If it works, and without risk of blood poisoning, who cares if it's voodoo or hoodoo? I'm next!"

The outsiders sang for their supper that night, astounding their hosts with Manley's accordion, Costin's harmonica, and Fawcett's flageolet. After quite a bit of maize beer, the Indians joined in with their own instruments, and a joyous cacophony ensued.

The next day it was time to hoof it, as the land was going ever steeper uphill and the river was no longer navigable. The men gave their canoes to the Echocas and set out with packs on their backs, accompanied by some of the Indians at least as far as the next settlement of Echocas. With this introduction they were welcomed warmly at every Echoca plantation they encountered and were deluged with gifts of fruit, vegetables, fish, and meat such as tapir.

"So much for the 'dangerous savages'!" laughed Fawcett, as they waved goodbye to the last group of Echocas.

The Heath was now only a couple of feet wide, and getting narrower. The following day the party arrived at the river's source, a spring. Fawcett completed his observations.

"Let's rest here, men. Good job, everyone! Tomorrow we'll retrace our steps until we reach the spot the Echoca pointed out as a good place for our overland march back to the Tambopata. Then we can build rafts and float down to Astillero.

"So far, so good!"

Fawcett awoke that night to feel the soft whir of wings in his face, and was aware at once that he was visited by yet another vampire bat. He knew he should raise his hand and knock it away, but the fanning of its wings was utterly soothing and made him feel quite sleepy, lulled, even hypnotized. This, he knew, was its modus operandi, and he and his men had often awakened to find their hammocks bloody; any part of the body touching the mosquito net was subject to the bite of these clever mesmerists. They had bites on their heads and toes, and one morning Costin complained that every fingertip of his right hand had been bitten. With effort Fawcett roused himself enough to lift a hand and brush away the creature, before he fell deeply asleep again.

The following day, as they neared the spot where they planned to turn toward the Tambopata, they saw several Echocas approaching. These men were laden with food for Fawcett and his party, and they insisted on taking them part of the way. When at last the Tambopata could be seen in the distance, the Echocas made their good-byes.

The little group continued on to the Marte rubber barraca, where they found the people starving. They were met by Señor Neilson, who was in charge of the miserable station. He welcomed them most hospitably, despite his condition.

"You must be hungry after your trek; let me think what we can put together for your dinner... Come, we'll see what I have..." They peered into his storeroom, where he dug the remainder of his maize out of the container. It totalled no more than a quart. "Well," he said, looking at the last of the food, "I'm sorry that this is all I can offer you, but I'll have it cooked up right away."

"No, no, of course not, but you have our sincerest gratitude." It never failed to impress Fawcett how the people of the forests would give a visitor their last bite of food, quite literally. "Good Lord," he burst out, "How have you and your settlement been surviving?"

"The workers have been subsisting mainly on leaves and grass for a good while, and many are sick now, covered with boils... There's no game around here."

"But my good man, on the Heath the fish and game are plentiful, and furthermore, the Indians are friendly; they have large plantations and we found them very willing to share."

The thin, weary man looked blank. "The Heath?"

"Yes, the Heath, that river just beyond those hills."

"Oh," Señor Neilson shook his head, "We don't dare venture far from the barraca; we've heard the opposite, that the Indians are vicious." There was fear, plain and simple, in his eyes. "My men wouldn't go, I'm sure."

Fawcett and his men shared their supplies with Neilson, but later Fawcett said to Costin as they crawled into their hammocks, "The law of cause and effect, once again. The rubber workers have given the Indians such a bad time, in general, that now they feel they have reason to be afraid of all Indians. And maybe they do. Sad, eh?"

At Marte Fawcett and his men built three balsa rafts for a terrifying two-day run down the Tambopata River to Astillero. After the rugged and exhausting tumble down one raging set of rapids after another, the group somehow arrived in Astillero with no loss of life.

"Lord!" exclaimed Costin as they licked their wounds in the home of Angus, a Scot who cheerfully offered to put them up for the night, providing basins of steaming water for a wash-up before supper. "It was no doubt best we couldn't see what was ahead on the river; I would've died of horror. Once we were in it, there was no chance to think now awful it was, one simply fought for one's life!"

"So true," groaned Fawcett, every inch of him sore and battered, as he soaped his arms.

Costin was searching among his dirty clothing in an adjoining room. "I say, Major, have you seen a stray sock anywhere? I seem to have only one here."

Fawcett looked around with little interest. "Can't say that I have."

"Well, filthy or no, I hate to lose it... I was going to give them a wash while we have the warm water."

The two dressed hastily and started for the dining area where the rest of their party had already assembled; enticing aromas led the way and their stomachs rumbled. They passed through the kitchen, inhaling appreciatively.

Costin stopped dead.

"My sock!"

Fawcett turned to him with apprehension, fearing the fellow had gone crackers at last. Then his eyes followed Costin's wide stare. The cook smiled sheepishly as he filtered hot water through the ideal coffee bag: Costin's dirty sock.

Fawcett grabbed Costin's arm and pulled him toward the laden table. "Forget it," he advised, before Costin could make a scene, choking off his own laughter.

After their exertions, the meal was a welcome banquet; their host urged them to overeat, and they happily complied. At length they all sat heavily back in their chairs as Angus passed around his tobacco pouch.

"So grand to have your company, my friends," he beamed. "We'll have a smoke and, let's see... Ah, here it is." He looked around as the cook brought in a tray. Angus breathed in the aroma deeply, with pleasure. "Bless the arabica! Coffee, everyone?"

Fawcett and Costin didn't dare let their eyes meet.

"I haven't a spoonful of free space," declined Fawcett.

"No, thank you," said Costin, politely but firmly.

*

La Paz, December 1912

"So that's it? You're ceding this land to Peru?" Fawcett and the Minister of Foreign Affairs stood before a large wall map. Fawcett pointed to an area along the old border where he had been surveying. "These boundaries are quite arbitrary. My surveys can give you more definitive information, though I had hoped to remap one section, to be sure."

The Minister waved at the map expansively. "Oh, yes, we wish to include the results of your latest surveys as soon as the map can be redrawn and updated. But in the meantime, we had to do something to defuse the situation. The Boundary Delimitation has created quite a stir with Peru; despite the cession of lands, we are still hearing disquieting rumors of Indian uprisings here and there. Ridiculous, isn't it? All for a few square miles of jungle!" He laughed heartily and gave Fawcett's shoulder a little shake.

Fawcett was silent, thinking. The Minister resumed:

"I expect your maps will be accepted as official, in the end. But if talk of war continues, we may have to allow the appointment of a French commission, completely impartial, you see, to decide the boundary, at least for now."

"I see." Fawcett turned from the map to face the Minister, who was relighting his cigar. "Well, you might also find the various other types of data I've collected to be of interest, as well; flora and fauna and that sort of thing, with photographs and drawings... But there's much much more to be obtained— "

"On someone else's treasury, Major; we've spent enough on scientific wild-goose-chases in the past. Besides, there will be more surveys to keep you busy when the present brouhaha blows over."

Fawcett took his leave of the Minister and walked the streets of La Paz for over an hour. It was December 20, a mild summer day. On and on he walked; he could think more clearly when he was moving, and a decision was slowly taking form in his mind.

He was, first of all, uncomfortable with his position squarely in the middle of an international situation. Things had come to a head, he felt, due to inefficiency and delaying tactics on the part of both nations involved, and now lives could actually be lost over the matter. He didn't want to be a part of it any longer. It was a sincere and legitimate concern which had nagged at him for some time.

But there was something else eating him. Sometimes it felt like simple curiosity, a need to explore and answer all the questions that consumed more and more of his mental energy. At other times it took on the glow of a vision: He was beginning to see an image of something he knew existed, somewhere, and it was imperative he find it before he was too old or too burned-out for the quest. This sensation of knowing had begun to move beyond evidence or even instinct, and it almost frightened him; how had he, a hard-headed military man with scientific leanings, become so utterly bewitched by legend and rumor? The dark recesses of the continent of South America made him feel as he had when Miranda knelt before him, her musk filling his senses, offering to tell him stories of her land. His virtuous refusal had been in vain, one might say, because the stories of the forest had nonetheless entered his mind, his heart, his body, and now all parts of him yearned for satisfaction.

He reluctantly admitted to himself he had been further titillated by the recent news of Machupicchu. Yes, its discoverers had been showered with fame and glory. But Fawcett's goal was a civilization far more ancient and mysterious, far more deeply hidden, which might even harbor the living remnants of a lost world. It was a pearl beyond price, far greater than any stack of ruins yet found on any continent.

He sometimes felt he had been chosen to connect that world with his.

He paused at a street corner. *So there it is,* he thought. *I have come to a turning point. Without doubt, I'll resign from boundary work, though I like surveying and I shall miss it. And the sensible man, the good husband and father, should return to home and hearth in England, though what I'd do with myself there I couldn't say. I can't go back to the Army, that is certain.* He drew and expelled a deep breath, standing still, watching the world rush to and fro at the busy intersection.

For better or for worse, I have to follow the path before me, into the forests, or I'll never be content. Forgive me, Cheeky.

And he walked on.

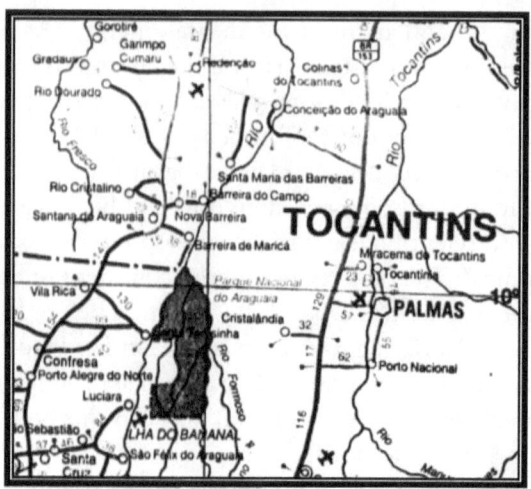

SYLVIA, CHAPTER 6
GOIAS

Once again the lush greens of Brazil passed by thousands of feet beneath her, slowly, it seemed. The drone of the Fokker's engines lulled Sylvia into a semi-trance, drowning even thought in the intense vibrations.

She fumbled in her briefcase on the empty seat beside her; she wanted to re-read Betsy's note. It had taken months to catch up with her, so the news was old. Isabel had brought it along with other mail when they went to lunch, and they both laughed at the picture Betsy enclosed.

"Guess what this is."

Isabel snickered. "That is *your* derrière, right?" She pointed to a bulge at the bottom of a white hammock, slung from slender trees in the midst of jungle growth. The other part of Sylvia that was visible was a long strand of hair hanging over the hammock side.

Without any announcement, the plane began its descent into Brasilia. Sylvia leaned toward her window. They flew over the giant, artificial Lake Paranoá, fifty miles long; the modern capital city sprawled beside it. The layout of Brasilia was often compared to a giant bow and arrow, but to Sylvia it resembled a long, slender airliner with backswept wings. Along the five-mile central axis, Monument Row, were located all the principal ministry buildings and monuments, and most of the city was divided in sections according to their purpose: Commerce Sector, Hotel Sector, Entertainment Sector,

236

Residential Sector, and on and on—there was even a Sports Club Sector. It was probably the most minutely planned and organized city in the world, with every city block numbered or lettered, or both.

Yet Sylvia got lost; hopelessly, frantically lost. It was primarily in cities where her sense of direction seemed to be impaired; on backpacking treks in the U.S. she was like a homing pigeon, as long as she didn't short-circuit her instincts by thinking. She was given maps and directions at the Hertz counter, and all seemed clear: The Bittar Plaza Hotel was in Setor Hoteleiro Norte—the North Hotel Sector—and more specifically, it was then found in quadrant 02, block "M".

"That sector is near the Television Tower, which you can't miss," the smiling agent told her. "Then follow the signs."

She easily reached Monument Row—and there was the Television Tower, couldn't miss it—but once in the midst of the hustle and bustle and cloverleaves at the very heart of Brasilia, Sylvia spun around the hub in a whirl of confusion only to find herself suddenly ejected into the oblivion of one of the "wings" of her airliner. How could she be lost in Brasilia? After more than an hour she accidentally wound up in the correct sector, and at last located Quadra 02, Bloco "M". She dragged herself into the Bittar Plaza, in a foul mood.

"What happened? We expected you to check in much earlier," the desk clerk scolded.

"Sorry." Sylvia smiled weakly. "I took a little drive around Brasilia." As she picked up her key, she added: "I hope you have room service."

Despite being in the driver's seat, she had made it to the Universidade de Brasilia the following morning on time for her meeting with planners of a distance learning station. Afterward, her two hosts, Tomás and Maria, took her to lunch at the nearby tennis club beside the lake, and then for a drive to the opposite shore.

"We'll stop here for a moment; for the view." The driver, Maria, turned down a lane leading to the Shrine of Dom Bosco. "From this side of the lake we can look back and see the entire city."

They walked to the overlook, where they gazed across the water at a spectacular view of Brasilia. Here one could grasp the dramatic scale of the miracle of engineering accomplished in the middle of the vast, empty cerrado, when in the 1960s the new capital of the nation began to rise. The vision of President Juscelino Kubitschek, it was designed by world-famous architects Oscar Niemeyer and Lucio Costa.

From that vantage point, Sylvia could see the circumscription of the city and its background of open space. The haunting sense of Manaus, flaring bizarrely amid the forest, replayed in a new context; but this time Sylvia felt a flash of awe at the constructs of humanity.

"Saint John Bosco was an interesting person," Tomás was saying, gesturing to the shrine behind them.

"Oh?" Sylvia responded politely, dragged from her ruminations.

"Yes, it seems that a hundred years before they broke ground to build Brasilia, Dom Bosco, a monk, had a dream in which he saw the coordinates on a map; and he saw a great lake that would be excavated and would flow forever. And so it was, as it turned out. The lake is man-made, of course."

"Do you think the site was chosen on the basis of Dom Bosco's dream, at least partially?"

"Oh no," demurred Maria. "This location was selected by hard-nosed planners for other reasons entirely. That's what makes the story so interesting..."

Sylvia looked at her map. A number of rivers drained into the area; in terms of abundant water, it was a good place to build a city. And she knew the state of Goiás had been chosen as a central point of the nation, and to draw populations inland.

By the time Sylvia returned to the city center, she was feeling more comfortable with the local layout. Soon, with luck, she'd arrive at her afternoon appointment with Brazil's National Indian Foundation, known by its Portuguese acronym, FUNAI. She was determined to do a little research on Fawcett and possibly gain permission to visit the Xingu River wilderness, now an Indian reserve.

Okay, here it is—Fundaçao Nacional do Indio... let's see, Building A... Right here! She parked the car and put the Fawcett folder in her briefcase. All her research questions were organized and translated into Portuguese; she didn't want to waste anyone's time. She had been pleased by the friendly response she'd gotten when she phoned FUNAI from Rio a few weeks earlier, with Paulo's help.

"It was some years ago that I worked at FUNAI," Paulo reminded her, "so I'm not sure if the same people work in the same departments... But this fellow Artur de Almeida is still the chief of Public Relations, I do know. You should start there. I'll try to get him on the line."

The result of the telephone call was an appointment at FUNAI.

"Oh, yes, I'm familiar with Colonel Fawcett's story," Artur had said in correct but hesitant English. "So tell me a little about yourself, and your job at IDA. " He was relieved when she answered in Portuguese, and after learning more about her he agreed to meet with her when she came to the capital.

Now as she entered Building A, Sylvia expected courteous replies to her list of questions and requests, and then after half an hour or so to be gently escorted to the door with smiles and good wishes. But Artur and his assistant, Gloria, spent two hours with Sylvia, sharing all the printed information they had on Fawcett.

Midway through the afternoon Artur, an amiable man who looked surprisingly young, had sent for coffee.

"You take sugar? No? You haven't yet adopted the Brazilian addiction to cane sugar, I see. Well, Sylvia, now you know everything *we* know about Colonel Fawcett. Gloria, did you give her some photocopies?"

"Yes, we made copies of all the Fawcett materials in our library and archives, what little there is."

Sylvia sipped from the tiny cup. "That's a very good map you have there." She walked over to the large wall map of the Amazon region. "I can see that the Xingu reservation isn't easily accessible, from any side; all forest, with a few dirt roads." She traced over the Trans-Amazon Highway with her finger. "Can you really drive this road all the way across Brazil?"

Artur gave a bitter little snort. "Not if you're sane. It's essentially a dirt road that's washed out in many areas during rainy periods. It was a debacle, and all the grand schemes that went with it—for farms, rice, what-have-you; and it helped to destroy many more Indians. " He waved his hand slowly over the Amazon Basin. "We don't know how many indigenes were here when the Portuguese arrived; anywhere from three to six million, perhaps. Now, there are fewer than one-quarter million left."

"Sounds like the history of North America," Sylvia remarked.

"Similar. The difference here is, some of the more remote tribes— a few—still live as they always did, for the most part. We struggle all the time to protect their cultures from outside corruption; and even innocent visitors are discouraged."

"Postponing the inevitable," added Gloria. "but we're trying to save other tribes from what's happening to the Guarani."

Sylvia gave her a questioning look.

"The suicides. They kill themselves in shocking numbers, even the young people, children."

Artur spoke up. "Their traditional way of life is gone, they're crowded onto reserves and surrounded by cities... All of a sudden they are 'poor', where the concept never even existed before. Then add alcohol to the situation, and they become the walking dead."

Sylvia didn't know what to say.

"But! We do our best. People are even trying to apply new technology to some of the problems. Look at this." He grabbed a black folder from his desk. It bore the name Raytheon, a U.S.-based company, in bold letters on the cover. He opened it to a transparency overlaid on a map of Amazonas, a diagram containing a number of lines and symbols.

"This is a huge project that's underway, managed by Raytheon, for electronic surveillance of the entire region."

"Surveillance? Of the Amazon?"

"It began with a simple need for radar tracking, for air traffic control. Then everyone realized there's a great need to gather data, such as weather and climate data, for environmental protection; also, they can monitor drug smuggling, illegal mining and logging, slash-and-burn farming... and—" He paused pointedly. "FUNAI can keep an eye on our Indian preserves."

"How would they do all this? By satellite?"

"Satellites are one component. There will also be radar units, both stationary and moving; weather stations and data-collecting platforms, and a telecommunications network using computers, the Internet, and plain old telephones."

He put the folder down. "For example: A FUNAI agent like Gloria is in the Xingu reserve, with the right equipment, and she receives a satellite picture—in 'real time'—" Artur used the English words—"Then she can use her computer to contact, let's say, the federal police or an environmental agent if the picture indicates an encroachment into Xingu territory; such as burning of their forests to install a cattle ranch, maybe."

He had Sylvia's attention now. "I see..."

"The picture could be viewed by others on the Internet, as well. Then people can no longer do anything they want because the Amazon is so vast and remote."

"Hmph. It sounds like a gargantuan undertaking."

"So it is. There's no other project like it in the world. The sheer complexity, some say, dooms it to failure... And we all know how rapidly funds can be wasted in a bureaucracy like Brazil's."

"Well, one of the problems I can see, Artur, would be the speed of changes in technology. Designers will have to be very farsighted and flexible, and somehow work this issue into their plans..." Her mind was beginning to churn with the challenge. "They'll have to work tech mutations into both the scheme and the budget."

"You're right. One member of Congress, Senhor Chanaglia, argues it'll all be obsolete by the time it's installed." He was watching Sylvia with keen eyes.

"Does the project have a name?"

"System for the Vigilance of the Amazon: They call it SIVAM, both in English and Portuguese."

Sylvia turned back to the map on the wall. "Interesting." For a few moments she looked over the vast region. "Now, excuse the change of subject, but as far as the Xingu reservation goes, I gather you'd prefer I leave them in peace."

"Well, actually, I spoke with one of the Kalapalo tribal representatives, who said you'd be welcome for a visit, but they require a fee."

"Oh?" She was taken aback; naively, she hadn't expected the Indians to bring up money. It seemed such an "outside" concept. "And how much do they ask?"

"Fifty-five thousand U.S. dollars."

"What?" She laughed with surprise, and suppressed an urge to comment on the tribe's apparent loss of innocence. The world was encroaching on them, and they were quickly learning the power of money in terms of modern survival. Asking a large fee was also a good way to discourage pesky foreign snoops, she imagined.

He spread his hands. "I'm sorry."

Sylvia sighed. "It's okay. I can see the trip isn't feasible, for a lot of reasons. It's just that their reservation is in the vicinity of Dead Horse Camp, one of the areas where Fawcett was last seen. And I've heard there are Kalapalo elders who still talk about him."

Gloria spoke up. "That's true. When I stayed with the tribe for a while, I talked with some who believe Fawcett found the city he went after, but could never leave; they say he and the young men were held captive there by the Xavante."

"The what?" Sylvia stared at her. She had said, "Sha-vahn-tee."

"The Xavante tribe. They live to the north, and legends say they're

241

the protectors of the rainforest. They're to this day often aggressive and unfriendly. People have reported they don't let anyone pass through their territory."

"I— I'd like to learn more about this tribe."

Artur plucked a FUNAI public education supplement, several colorful pages of photos and articles, from a stack of newsletters and magazines. "Here; wait—" He turned a few pages. "Here's a picture of a Xavante. There are a couple more pictures of them inside. You can have this."

Sylvia looked at a photo of a naked, frowning Indian, holding out his hand as if to stop the photographer in his tracks. His body was slender and well-built. His hair was short around his face, in a bowl-cut. The caption beneath the photo read: *Primeiro contato com os xavante.* First contact with the Xavante. And this man, at least, wasn't pleased about it.

"I'm headed up north, later on... " Sylvia said abstractedly. "I have meetings with people in Conceição do Araguaia."

"Maybe she could visit the tribes near São Felix...?" Gloria suggested.

"That's an idea." Artur turned to Sylvia, handing her another cafezinho. "There's a FUNAI office in Redenção, not far from Conceição do Araguaia. It's on the frontier, a rather wild region. There are some interesting tribes in the area, some of them friendly enough. You're getting near Xavante territory, however," he warned. "You'll want to stay clear of them, no matter how interesting they are."

Artur went to his desk and wrote on a pad. "Here's the name of the FUNAI agent there. Call him, say that I sent you."

"But watch yourself up there, Sylvia," Gloria advised. "It's a lawless area."

The church wasn't far from FUNAI's offices, and Sylvia felt like stretching her legs. She deposited her briefcase in the car and rummaged through the packet of Brasilia maps and guides her travel agent had given her, until she found the pamphlet on São João Bosco Sanctuary. In addition to Dom Bosco's monument by the lake, an architecturally interesting church had been dedicated to the monk. After the story she'd heard about him she thought it might be a good place to think for a little while.

She followed the directions Gloria had given her, walked around the block, and there it was. From the outside, the building was simply a big square box with long, peaked windows.

She entered to find an enormous sanctuary, deserted and silent, its very atmosphere awash in stunning blues. The four walls around her consisted of towering, Gothic-style windows, over fifty-two feet high and made of thousands of panes of glass stained in varying tones of blue; sixteen shades, the pamphlet informed her. Sun rays struck the panes, filling the sanctuary with sparkling sapphire lights.

She walked toward the center of the church, her footsteps echoing. A tremendous crucifix was attached to one wall, hovering between two of the windows, and a few long rows of wooden pews faced an altar. Not far from the crucifix, in a corner, there was a white statue of Dom Bosco. Otherwise the remainder of the immense sanctuary was empty, plain, and minimalist. Typical of Brazil, the feeling was one of great space in all directions, including overhead. The polished wood floor reflected long smears of color and light.

The tall, tall windows with their peaked arches swept the eye upward. Their panes were in lighter hues near the floor, then toward the apex of each arch they deepened into royal, lapis, cobalt, then indigo, all the mysterious shades of a night sky still holding onto the last of the day's brightness.

A perfect touch had been added to each corner of the sanctuary: There, the long windows were paned in shades of mauve and violet. Their purples reflected softly on the statue of the monk.

One moment Sylvia felt as if she were at the bottom of a clear, azure sea amid playful sunbeams filtering down from the surface; in the next, she was sailing into a midnight-blue vault of stars. She felt a certain magic only the color blue can create. If the designer's goal— one Carlos Alberto Neves—was to engender both exaltation and profound peace, he had succeeded.

Sylvia sat on the back row of the pews, feeling the day's accumulation of tension and sorting through all the input she'd received since breakfast. But for a few minutes she let go of it all and bathed in the cool tranquility of the sanctuary. After a while she heard soft footsteps, and a man in a business suit went to sit on the front pew, bending his head in prayer.

Sylvia's business at the university had gone well; there was nothing to worry about in that segment of the day. And it was surprisingly easy to brush away her disappointment with the Kalapalo; she wouldn't be visiting the Xingu reservation, period. Oddly enough, she was more intrigued by the SIVAM project. As she left, Artur had given her the Raytheon folder.

"I prepared this for you," he said a trifle sheepishly. "After our first telephone conversation I thought it might be of interest. Though, of course, I know you already have an excellent job..." He let his thoughts unravel, and now Sylvia picked up the thread and toyed with it.

For a few minutes she envisioned a network overlaying the entire Amazon basin, like a giant web as fine as spider silk. When it was touched in one far corner the entire web vibrated, and the Spider rushed to investigate. Yet the Amazon, sheltered beneath, remained untouched, uninvaded.

Quite a different vision from that of Dom Bosco, who'd apparently seen a preview of one of humanity's more drastic interventions in the landscape. But Sylvia found his story reassuring. She wasn't the only one who had precognitive dreams that seemed to serve no specific purpose, other than to hint at little rips in time's fabric, and allow one to peep through and see a bit of tomorrow.

And that brought her thoughts to the Xavante. If she had ever read about the tribe before her dream, she would've seen its name written with initial X but she would not have known how to pronounce it. If she'd simply heard it somewhere, she would've assumed it began with "sh". It was possible, of course, that she had heard of the tribe and it remained in her subconscious until the dream; but there were too many unusual coincidences, especially in light of the role they were said to play as "protectors of the forest."

And of "Z", possibly. She remembered Fawcett's belief that the ancient city was encircled by hostile tribes, barring entrance—or exit. Sylvia remained deep in thought for some time, as the blues slowly darkened. The praying man crossed himself and left, nodding briefly to Sylvia.

All of it, she concluded, all the dreams and coincidences, would've meant nothing more than the fancies of a suggestible mind, except for one inescapable fact: Some of the dreams had occurred years before she'd ever imagined living in Brazil, or before she'd ever heard of Percy Harrison Fawcett.

*

The pungent scent of a mixture of herbs, baking in the sun, swirled through the little car; Sylvia inhaled deeply as she sped along. She was now some distance northeast of Brasilia and had cleared the suburbs. Immediately out of the capital city there was a sense of great space: the Central Plateau, a wide-open land of scrub brush, or *cerrado*, interrupted here and there by riparian woods along the banks of numberless streams and rivers.

She turned onto highway 118, headed for her destination. She had a few days before her appointment in Conceição do Araguaia, and she planned to spend it on the Chapada dos Veadeiros: Deer-hunters' Plateau, about 140 miles from Brasilia. She rolled down the passenger-side window so the fragrance of herbs, mixed with wild-flowers, could circulate inside the car. The Chapada was known for an abundance of wildflowers and medicinal herbs.

She turned off the main road at the charming town of Alto Paraíso, and was tempted to stop; but she was expected at Parque do Lume, a resort, so she pushed on. After asking for directions she turned onto an unpaved road. In a short time she came to a primitive structure of thatched roof and weathered wood, open along one side, all by itself in the middle of the cerrado. A saddled brown horse was tied to a hitching post, and nearby a bicycle was parked. There were no cars in sight other than hers. This was obviously not the resort but, curious, she decided to stop.

It turned out to be a bar, of sorts. Three walls were lined with hundreds of bottles in different sizes, all made of the same dark blue glass and bearing neat, handwritten labels. There was no electricity and no windows, but afternoon sun from the open side illuminated part of the interior brightly, appearing to fill the blue bottles with light. Their contents were liquors made from local herbs, and in one section smaller bottles held herbal potions and remedies. Sylvia bought a couple of concoctions, exchanged a few friendly words with the other patrons, and went on her way.

The rough lane wound through more hot scrubland, then into a wooded area. She went through a tiny village which boasted a very old, wooden church. There were a few houses; in one yard full of flowers two old black men sat outside in chairs, waving as she passed.

The vegetation became denser and the surroundings were wild, devoid of any sign of humans; momentarily Sylvia wondered what she'd do if the car broke down. But before long she reached a driveway and a gate over-arched by a wooden sign reading Parque do

Lume, Park of Light. A young woman came out of a guard shack wearing a welcoming smile.

"*Bom dia.* Are you Sylvia?"

"I am. Hope I haven't kept you waiting."

"Oh, no. I'm Teresa; Marcela said to send you to Shamball-ha. It's the large round cabana. She's expecting you there." She gave Sylvia a map of the park and circled Shamball-ha.

As the sun set, Sylvia drove down the dirt road to a parking area. She had stuffed casual clothing and a swimsuit into her daypack, and shouldering this, she walked up a little path to a large, circular wooden building with a thatched roof. She noticed that every sign and structure was made of wood or other natural materials, and all were simple, humble. The only sound to be heard was a distant rooster.

Shamball-ha appeared to be the center of resort activities, such as workshops and other gatherings, Sylvia assumed. A wide wooden deck encircled the exterior, and the airy interior was brightened by colorful wall hangings, cushions, and here and there a hammock. A lithe, lovely woman with waist-length black hair came to greet Sylvia. She wore a filmy white dress that hung loosely from shoulders to mid-calf, adorned only by a quartz crystal pendant. Her feet were bare.

"I'm Marcela. You must be Sylvia, the American." She spoke in English, and dazzled Sylvia with a smile revealing even, white teeth that contrasted strikingly with her *café au lait* skin. Her eyes gave the same effect; dark brown, almost black, floating in the purest white vitreous.

"How was the drive?"

"Beautiful!"

"Come, have a cool lemonade, would you like that?"

"Sounds wonderful." It was hot. Sylvia's mouth was bone dry.

They moved to a very low, round table which held a pitcher of lemonade. Marcela poured two glasses and they sank into several layers of cushions that enticed the eye with their variety of lush colors, textures, and patterns. Above their heads was a high, domed ceiling and several skylights.

"We grow the lemons here, and this is sweetened with honey from our own hives," Marcela added, raising her glass.

Ah, thought Sylvia, sipping gratefully, *I'm home.*

*

A stroke of luck had led Sylvia to the resort. She'd planned to stay in a pousada in Alto Paraíso, but as she perused a stack of brochures and tourist publications on her hotel room desk in Brasilia, a tour guide caught her eye. Inside was a great deal of useful information about the Chapada, written both in Portuguese and English. It was published by Parque do Lume, an "eco-resort", and included a map of that property. Sylvia was surprised to see drawings of waterfalls, caves, trails, and other fascinating features. There were campsites, and cabanas to rent. It sounded much more interesting than a pousada.

Marcela showed her to a simple, round cabana—they didn't favor straight lines there—with just room for a futon bed, small chest, and a chair, all of plain wood. Just outside the door under the extended roof was a hammock.

"Oh! Would you mind if I slept in this?"

"No, of course, it's fine. I often sleep in a hammock, myself. Use the cushions that are on the futon, if you like." She blazed a smile. "Dinner will be served whenever you come to Shamball-ha. Are you hungry?" Sylvia nodded. "The shower is here." She led Sylvia behind the cabana to a deck where there was an outdoor shower behind a lattice.

"Things are primitive here." She smiled again, and left.

Sylvia bathed away the dust and donned comfortable clothing, mulling her first impressions. It was a little whole-earth-hippie in style; she'd bet money there were workshops on yoga and crystal healing... but it was tastefully done. Small, solar-powered fairy lights were beginning to glow along the pathway, guiding her back to the main building. Torches burned on the front deck, and soft guitar music drifted from speakers somewhere inside. The large interior was dark except for the area where lemonade had been served; here there were many candles, tall ones in candelabra, flower-shaped candles floating in an enormous dish of water, candles suspended by long chains from the ceiling high above.

Marcela appeared out of the dark recesses, carrying a tray which she set on the table next to a brass bowl of fruit.

"Here—" She pointed to the covered dishes on the tray, "is a soup similar to gazpacho, and this is a rice salad full of vegetables, and these are some spreads for the bread." The two women sat down. "Everything except the rice, and the wheat in the bread, was grown on the premises."

"Am I the only guest?"

"Yes. Weekdays are very quiet. We'll have several visitors on the weekend; but the atmosphere is always tranquil, actually. That's one of the reasons people come here."

"I can hardly wait to explore everything tomorrow."

Something about Marcela, an inner stillness, helped Sylvia relax. They talked little as they ate, listening to night birds harmonizing with guitars.

The bowl of fruit was their dessert, and Marcela made it seem like an adventure, introducing Sylvia to fruits she'd never heard of before.

"Try this one; it's sinfully sweet." She cut open a knobby green ovoid to reveal soft, creamy-white flesh, and handed Sylvia a spoon.

"Mmm... It tastes amazing! It's like pudding."

"Let's have our fruit outside, the sky should be very clear tonight. Would you like to?"

Sylvia nodded, her mouth full. Marcela grabbed a few more pieces of fruit and several utensils, blew out some of the candles, and the women went outside. Marcela led the way up a long path behind the building, to the top of a little hill where there was a square deck strewn with cushions.

Marcela pointed out a few constellations, and told Sylvia a little about herself.

"One of my ancestors was among the runaway slaves who established the village of Moinho, you passed through it on the way here. The other side of my family is mostly Dutch." She paused. "And what brings you all the way to Brazil?"

Maybe it was the darkness that made Sylvia open up; she related her interest in Fawcett, and since Marcela was such a patient listener the next thing she knew she was telling her about her dreams, all of them. Marcela heard her in silence until Sylvia finally added,

"I'm not sure why I blurted out all of this. I've taken up your time with something that makes little sense."

"No, no, I believe everything happens for a reason. You mentioned the dreams seemed to be random glimpses of the future, but otherwise insignificant. I don't see it that way."

"What *do* you see in this?"

Marcela collected her thoughts for a moment. "Let's look at the dreams as a whole unit. In one of them, a man, an explorer, convinces you to follow him—to take a chance, just *go*, to an unknown land to seek King Solomon's mines, right? This dream foreshadows your decision to come to Brazil, and you were led here by an explorer, were you not?"

"True, I've thought of that. Go on."

"You'd find a home here, that you like—that's shown in the apartment dream—and a job would appear to be just waiting for you... which might connect to the hotel dream." She paused a moment. "Now, the burning araucária is a powerful spiritual symbol. They're said to be sacred trees, you know."

"I've heard."

"You also dreamed of the giant old tree that's in front of your apartment; so I'd guess trees represent the earth itself, and its importance in your life and your future."

"What about the dwarf?"

"The dwarf. Hmm... maybe its significance lies in the lottery—the Bicho."

"The animals?"

"Right. The animal lottery embodies all the creatures of Brazil, from long before Europeans arrived. The Indians, and also the Africans who came to Brazil, believed in spiritual relationships between people and animals, and other parts of nature; animism, I think it's called in English. These beliefs permeate Brazilian culture, and some people feel this aspect of the *jogo do bicho* adds a great deal to its popularity. "

"Okay. That leaves the Xavante..."

"Ah, the Xavante! They are a special group of people. They are the 'protectors of the forest'."

Sylvia hesitated. Then she said, "My last name, Garth, means 'protector of the garden'—"

Marcela turned to stare at her in the faint starlight.

"—and 'Sylvia' means 'girl of the forest'..."

There was a silence, then Marcela said with a slight laugh, "Sylvia Garth, you have been called."

"What do you mean?"

"You're predestined for a certain role. *That's* why you've been peeping into the future; because your future has been planned for you."

"A future in Brazil."

"Only you can answer that." She stretched. "You're in a good place to contemplate all of this, for the next few days. Time for sleep, *amiga*. In sleep, answers may come from the subconscious."

They stood and gathered up the implements.

"Thanks for listening to me. It helps. I was beginning to feel like some New Age nut-case—"

Marcela's rich laughter penetrated the still night. She put her free arm warmly around Sylvia's shoulders as they walked down from the knoll. "Bless you. All of the chosen ones have felt that way at times."

At Shamball-ha, Marcela paused on the deck to say good night.

"Sleep well, dream well, and whenever you awake come down for breakfast. If I'm not here, help yourself to everything."

As she walked back to her cabana, Marcela's words stayed with her: "All of the chosen ones have felt that way at times..." What a peculiar thing to say. *Maybe it's Brazil, that quality Fawcett wrote about, of openness to the supernatural. I'm falling prey to it, too.*

She was suddenly very tired, and she fell asleep quickly in the hammock. She awoke in the night, drowsily aware she had dreamed of her Shoshone grandmother speaking to her in a language she couldn't identify, but the odd thing was, she understood it perfectly.

The next morning, however, she remembered nothing of what was said.

The next three days were a span of uninterrupted peace. She was reminded of Amazonas, and the two-week smile that was more a feeling than an expression.

In one way the Parque improved on her Amazon trip: Here, time never intruded. Marcela was deliberately vague about meal schedules, and sometimes interesting ingredients for sandwiches and salads were merely made available for her to put a meal together for herself. All day long, from breakfast to dinner, she roamed the resort's acres by herself, her backpack stuffed with snacks.

One unnecessary item, she discovered to her joy, was a swimsuit. In all the daylight hours she glimpsed only one other soul in the distance, a young woman who might've been the gatekeeper she'd met on her arrival.

The Rio Preto flowed through the property and, as promised, there were several waterfalls. Sylvia had expected modest little cascades. On the first day she was quite impressed when she encountered Angel Falls, a powerful flow of transparent water over a drop of some fifty feet, made all the more dramatic by the long, deep pool at its base, channeled between high rock walls.

She sat on a rock for a while, contemplating the pool. It looked safe enough. Off went her clothes and she plunged nude into the cool water. It was a formidable swim up the little canyon, against the flow, and she paused for a rest once or twice, crawling onto one of the many flat-topped boulders at the side. When she reached a point where the water pounded just ahead of her and its current pushed her away, she floated back.

When she'd sun-dried her body, tingling deliciously from the water and the exertion, she put her shorts and T-shirt back on and continued, but she hadn't gone very far when she came to another magnificent waterfall and pool. By midday, she'd given up on her clothing as well as the swimsuit, and she went on her way wearing only shoes and the backpack. She began to feel like a little child, free and playful; water and sun felt marvelous on her skin, as if they were healing agents for something she hadn't even known was ailing.

"I hope you'll return soon," Marcela said as they had lunch. Sylvia's gear was packed and ready for the drive back to Alto Paraíso.

"I hope to. I've been so content here."

"I can see it. You look like a different person, in some ways, from the Sylvia who arrived here. There are no lines of tension in your face, and you walk differently; did you know that?"

Sylvia laughed. "Not hunched over, in a hurry. It's heaven to forget time and schedules for a few days. I think I've found *your* beauty secret."

After a moment, Marcela asked, "Did you find any answers while you were here?"

Sylvia was thoughtful as she ate a small fig-like fruit. "I've been pondering what you said about my destiny... Someone else said something similar to me. I have to decide if I believe in destiny. During the day everywhere I stopped, at the falls, the springs, in the cave, on hilltops, I thought about my life and its purpose, assuming it has one... And maybe I *did* find some answers. You were right about the dreams; they have meaning. And all of them are connected to Fawcett."

Marcela nodded. The second evening the women had discussed

Fawcett in more depth, and Sylvia was surprised to learn Marcela knew a good bit about him.

"That's my feeling, too. Sometime it might be interesting for you to visit the place I mentioned to you, Barra do Garça, near the Roncador Mountains."

"Maybe. But I've heard there are some sects there with fairly outrageous ideas, that practically worship Fawcett."

"Oh, yes, you'll find all sorts of beliefs. But some people there are more grounded, seriously researching Fawcett's disappearance."

"Well, the rumors of a subterranean colony that I found on the Internet intrigue me; supposedly this is connected with Fawcett's ancient civilization. I vaguely recall a dream I had, a long time ago, about a mountain that appeared as solid rock; but it opened in some way, and I entered a cave or crack, and came out in a city—like another world... I'll have to find this dream; I'm sure I wrote it in an older dream log."

"If there's a settlement that's hidden in that way, it might explain why it hasn't been spotted from the air."

"Maybe." Sylvia thought of Poço Verde, how there was no indication of the beautiful pool from the trail; only when she passed through the deep cave had she been able to access it.

But further conversation wasn't possible. Time was once again a factor; there was a plane to be caught. They walked to the parking lot together, where Marcela enfolded Sylvia in a sincere abraço.

"Adeus. If you have a chance, write me, or call, and let me know how things are unfolding."

"I will."

Sylvia drove away wondering if she'd ever see the graceful Marcela again; she intended to keep in touch. There was now much to think about, but her mind kept returning to Poço Verde.

The pilot looked back to see if all three of his passengers had fastened their seat belts; satisfied, he gave the co-pilot an order and the six-seater plane taxied to the runway of Alto Paraíso's small airport. Sylvia had avoided driving back to Brasília by paying an extra fee, a very steep one, to drop the car off in Alto Paraíso.

They flew over many miles of wild, open land, green but not all of it forested, and began to follow the River Tocantins into the state of

the same name. As the time passed Sylvia grew increasingly fascinated by the scope and relative emptiness of the land below. They
were flying over a vast stretch of what appeared to be small mountains
and hills, with areas of plateau grasslands.

What amazed her were the endless miles of dirt roads snaking
along ridges, occasionally corkscrewing down into valleys; tan-colored
threads out in the middle of nowhere, coming from unseen beginnings and heading for unknown destinations. Sylvia figured there
were huge cattle ranches in the region, but she couldn't imagine anyone driving these roads to town. What town? She could see from her
aerial perspective there was nothing, not even a village within any reasonable distance, and they'd been in the air for almost two hours.
But then, she was beginning to see that distance was an altogether
different concept in Brazil. Who had made all these miles of roads,
and how long had they been there? Who lived in such isolation?

They passed over striking examples of deforestation, huge areas
where a perfectly straight line divided the green forest from brown,
naked earth. Near Porto Nacional, they flew over two gaping gouges
in the earth, with dirt roads spiraling down into them and miles of
vegetation scraped away at the perimeter to expose the brownish-red
earth. Mines or quarries of some kind, it appeared.

They landed briefly at Santana do Araguaia, where one man de-
planed and two more boarded. Noticing a number of private aircraft
that bore the names of ranches, she realized people of means moved
around the region by air. Tocantins was a cattle state. The owners of
the great ranches were wealthy, and just about everyone else lived in
poverty. The ranchers wanted IDA's courses in English available to
their youngsters, and in return they were willing to provide the learning station and all equipment, maintain it, and allow poorer students
equal use of the facility. If the ranchers were fair and true to their
word, the station could provide a rare opportunity for the less privi-
leged youth of the area.

During her overnight stay in Conceição do Araguaia she met
with the mayor and a representative of the ranchers who was also af-
filiated with the local school system. They had the usual discussion of
the minimal requirements for the station, and when Sylvia presented
her list of necessary equipment, the ranchers' representative took it.
Sylvia was somewhat reassured by the fact that the station, she was
told, would be located in the public school building.

"It would be my pleasure to invite you to lunch, Senhora," said the mayor, Sr. Carneiro, at the end of their meeting.

"Thank you; but I'm flying to Redenção at 1:00."

He looked at his watch. "Then allow me to drive you to the airport."

"No rooms at all?"

"I'm sorry, Senhora. And the only other hotel in town is full, also. Normally we have plenty of space, but there's a cattlemen's convention in town this weekend."

"A cattlemen's convention!" Sylvia sagged. If only she had called in advance. Now, she was stuck in Redenção with no place to lay her head.

"No one in town rents rooms?"

The woman looked dubious. "Not that I know of... But you shouldn't stay with just anyone." She was beginning to look alarmed at the thought. "Look, go to the restaurant and have a cup of coffee, 'ta bom? And let me see if I can arrange something at our hotel."

"All right. I'm hungry, I'll have dinner."

The clerk pointed her in the direction of Hotel Inacio's restaurant and bar. *Stupid, stupid, stupid,* Sylvia blasted herself as she walked down the corridor. *I've always been lucky with hotel rooms, but now I've landed in this little cow town on its big annual cow weekend...*

She ordered a caipirinha before dinner. Every eye in the room was cast in her direction, most of them belonging to males; but there were a few women in the crowd, laughing robustly along with the boys. She knew everyone was wondering who the hell she was and what she was doing there.

She was pondering the latter question, herself. A glance around Redenção as she'd come in from the air strip, having been offered a ride to the hotel by two ranchers, hadn't promised anything particularly picturesque. The population was around 56,000, and local economy was based on ranching, some farming, logging, and fishing.

She ordered her meal. Another drink arrived, the waiter explaining, "The people at that table sent it for you."

Sylvia turned to see a table full of partying ranchers, one of whom was female, raising their glasses to her. She walked over to thank them and satisfy their curiosity, saying only that she was writing a book about Brazil and wanted to see the area. But their friendliness cheered her. They made room for her and insisted she dine with them.

"Senhora! There you are— " The desk clerk bustled over. "I'm so sorry; I haven't been able to arrange anything. But I'm still trying... "

"Is there a broom closet?" Sylvia asked, smiling feebly.

"What's this?" asked one of the ranchers. The clerk explained the problem.

"Oh, there's no problem now," the man said. "I'll share my room with you!" Everyone laughed, including Sylvia. He added, "Joking aside, I'll share my room with any of you men who's willing to give *his* room to this beautiful American lady who loves Brazil enough to come to this desolate corner."

Immediately one of the men volunteered. "As long as you promise, Luis, not to snore louder than I do."

"Are you sure...?" Sylvia was afraid they'd regret the offer after the hilarity—and the caipirinhas—wore off. But it was settled, and by the end of the meal she realized no one at the table was truly drunk, they were simply in a good mood.

So, my luck held, after all. I'm in!

Ugh. It was hot. There were no fresh ocean breezes, as in Rio, and the waterfalls of Parque do Lume seemed very far away. Sylvia had phoned the FUNAI agent after breakfast and used Artur's name to secure an afternoon appointment; now she wanted to see a little of Redenção in the meantime. So she walked, meandering to the outskirts of town, where she came upon a neighborhood market district. The stalls and shops sold food, herbs and spices, simple clothing, hand-made items, religious candles and paraphernalia. At one door she stopped, and smiled. The shop was made of unpainted wood with a boarded-up window; the open door hung on one rusty hinge. But on either side of the entrance were large, healthy potted plants, and beside the door was a small, factory-printed sign: Avon.

Sylvia walked on until she'd truly reached the margins of town, and found herself staring at mountains of logs behind the fence of a timber yard. She wondered what kind of trees they had been, and where they'd grown.

Footsore, she turned back toward the center of town to find lunch. The main street turned out to be wide and well-maintained, with cement sidewalks and a broad strip down the middle of the street where there were juice and sandwich stands, trees, and benches. Coming toward her was an Indian couple, and Sylvia tried hard not to gape. They seemed straight out of the forest and another century. The male wore only a loincloth of some unknown material, and carried a spear. His body and face bore tattoos and paint. His woman was also bare from the waist up. She carried a large infant who suckled from her breast as she walked. Both adults were frowning and appeared almost hostile, but Sylvia reckoned it was simply the wariness of people who were out of their element. They ignored her, looking straight ahead as if they were the only two people on the earth.

She had seen the Real Thing; "wild" Indians still existed. She stopped at a stand and ordered a sandwich. While she waited, two men who looked like ranchers stomped up to the stand in heavy boots, their shirts open in the heat. Both men wore pistols on their hips. Sylvia reflected back to the morning when a couple of men and a woman had ridden by her hotel room window, on horseback; they, too, wore gunbelts. *Mercy, it's the Old West revisited! Painted Indians, cowboys with six-shooters—and steers.*

She had a shower and a few minutes' rest at the hotel. Then she went down to the desk to procure a taxi; the FUNAI office was too far from her hotel for walking.

"A taxi? Sure," said the desk clerk, the same friendly woman. "But you know, all we have here are motorcycle taxis."

That gave Sylvia a moment's pause. "Okay..." At least it wasn't a pony.

Before long a very young man on a small motorcycle pulled up, smiling broadly. He gestured for Sylvia to hop on, so she sat behind him and held onto his waist while he flew down the unpaved sidestreets of town, eventually arriving at a weathered clapboard structure bearing the symbol of FUNAI, an Indian headdress.

Sylvia got off the bike, windblown and exhilarated, and opened her wallet. One dollar, or the U.S. equivalent, was all it cost.

"That's it? It was kind of a long way," she said.

"Moto-taxi is always one dollar, to anywhere around here," he said cheerily, giving her his card. He waved and roared away before she could fish around for a tip. *They don't expect tips,* she remembered. As in Rio.

She turned toward the building, and got another surprise. A line of Indians stood stony-faced on the porch. All were men, all were nearly naked; most were painted and some carried spears. None seemed to pay any attention to her. They stood as if waiting, silent, gazing from the porch.

She hoped she wasn't cutting in some sort of queue; but she went through the open door and gave her name to the assistant, a young woman, who asked her to wait a few minutes. She sat in a nearby chair. The agent's door was open, and she could see him at his desk, talking, using many gestures. She leaned a little to one side and glimpsed his visitors, two Indians in full regalia as if they were tribal leaders. The agent, it seemed, was doing most of the talking; now and then she heard a few words, in low tones, from one of the Indians who appeared to be interpreting for the other.

After some minutes, the visitors came out of the office. Though they had to brush past her in the narrow space, neither man made eye contact with Sylvia. They went out to the porch and were joined by the others; all of the Indians then left, walking down a road that did not lead to town.

"You may go in now," the assistant was saying.

She was greeted by the tired-looking young agent who still sat behind his desk.

"Please have a seat, Senhora Garth."

"Thank you. I won't take much of your time." She explained her purposes as succinctly as possible, apologizing for the failings of her Portuguese.

"Well," he said when she'd finished, "There are a few tribal lands you could visit, but they're rather far from here. In this immediate region things are... unsettled, you might say; there have been recent disturbances."

Sylvia was familiar with Brazilian usage of euphemisms.

" 'Disturbances'?"

He sighed. "Some tribes are in an uproar over trespasses on their land, and rightfully so. The loggers are felling trees on Indian property; when caught, they always say, 'Oh, sorry! Our mistake!' --as if they'd innocently blundered over the boundaries. Their apologies don't help the trees, which are already down, and any compensation offered to the tribes is a fraction of the loggers' potential profits."

"I see... This is why the Indians were here to see you?"

"They're here to demand FUNAI do something to control the loggers, and others... like miners, and now it's gold prospectors. If there's something people want it doesn't matter if it's on protected land, they'll find a way to take it. But how can I watch every rogue, or police every mile of this territory?"

Sylvia had no answer.

"There's going to be violence," he continued. "And one thing you can bet on: The indigenes will get the worst of it. The extractors will be happy to be attacked, and have an excuse to kill them; they'll be wiping out the *piums* that annoy them with little bites."

"Maybe the SIVAM project can help...?"

"Maybe. But they need to move fast with it." He sighed again. "Now: I'm sorry to put my problems on you. Here, see this map? In this region there's a peaceful tribe, far away from the problems. Sometimes anthropologists visit there, and are treated well."

"It *is* far away. How would I get there?"

"You have to charter a helicopter; the same one FUNAI uses. But it's expensive." He quoted a few prices, and Sylvia gagged.

"That's a lot of money for just a few days."

"So it is. The good news is, this tribe appreciates a few gifts, but doesn't demand cash."

She smiled weakly. "It's nice to hear someone, at least, isn't greedy."

"Indeed. I'm sorry, Senhora Garth, you came a long way to hear discouraging news. But the truth is, this region is plagued by lawlessness. It isn't a good place for an American lady to be roaming on her own. There's really no one to protect you."

She didn't normally think of herself as a person needing protection; but then, she'd never experienced a place quite like this. She was slowly beginning to see how Brazilians had developed so much caution; even today their nation was so wild, especially the immense interior, that most of the population still felt more secure in a crowd.

"One last question: Does anyone ever visit the Xavante? Is that possible?"

"Oh, no *senhora*; they're not at all friendly, and they're farther away. We let them alone."

Thanking him, she took her leave, and asked his assistant to call the moto-taxi; then she went outside to wait on the rickety porch, deep in thought. It was frustrating to realize the difficulties involved in visiting remote reservations or following Fawcett's trail beyond developed regions. *And it's pure fantasy to think I could help the Xavante in some way, since I can't go anywhere near them. Silly. That's one dream I doubt I'll ever see realized.*

She had to admit there was a true element of danger. She remembered Fawcett's son, Brian, had reported that some one hundred people vanished in the wilderness searching for Fawcett, who had foreseen that possibility and tried to prevent it. She didn't think he would want her to be number one hundred-one.

There had been a story in the Los Angeles Times some years back, about an Amazon guide suspected of murdering several of his clients. They were each solo travelers, and no trace of them had been found. It was a reminder that one is in far more danger from one's fellow man than from a jungle full of snakes and jaguars.

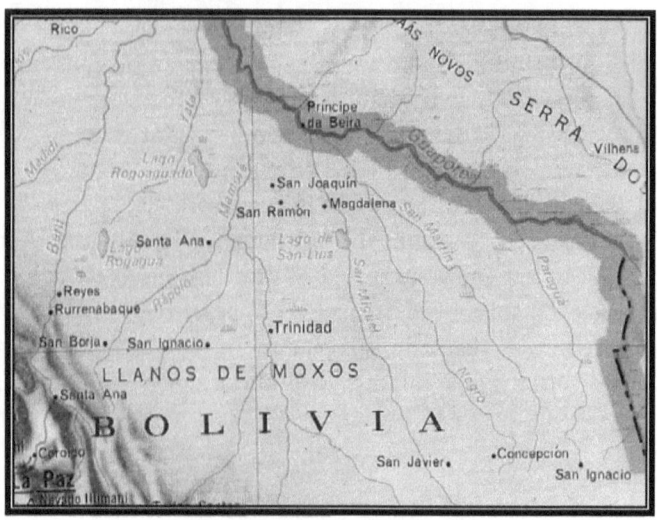

FAWCETT, CHAPTER 7
RIO GUAPORE

"Look out!" Fawcett yelled. Everything happened at once: The bushmaster, which Fawcett had accidentally grabbed as he climbed a steep, scrubby bank, struck in the direction of Manley; Costin and Fawcett threw themselves back down the bank, as Manley pulled the pistol at his hip and fired two bullets into the snake's head. The creature collapsed.

"Did it get you?" Costin asked.

Manley cursed and laughed simultaneously. "I think so— " He felt around his thighs, but could find no injury; then he pulled a tobacco pouch from his pocket.

"I'll be damned!" The men crowded around to gape. On the pouch were two holes that pierced all the way through. Quickly they helped him pull down his pants, and there on his thigh was a wet spot of venom and two slight indentations, but the skin was not broken.

"Were you ever lucky!" exclaimed Costin.

"Guess it wasn't my day to die," agreed Manley.

It was autumn, 1913. Fawcett had spent more than a year and a half at home. He had wanted time, plenty of time, with Nina and the boys, before he returned to what he called his Quest. For all he knew, he might be deep in the wilderness for several years in which he'd be unable to so much as send a message home saying. "I'm still alive!" He devoted himself to his children, and savored every moment his wife's arms were around him. In his ears still rang her final words of encouragement, of faith in him and his motives. With all his soul he wanted to bring home the secrets of the ancients, and hear her say it had been worth the years of separation.

He had had surprisingly little difficulty persuading Costin and Manley to accompany him once more. Costin, who had been found to have the beginning of leishmaniasis, a disease with symptoms similar to leprosy, had mustered out of the army soon after his cure had been effected at the London School of Tropical Medicine. As for Manley, he found the boredom of regular army life to be deadlier than any wilderness threat, and after a few months of it he begged a delighted Fawcett to take him along.

After the New Year the three men sailed to South America, where they landed in Antofagasta, Chile. While roaming the seaport's bazaar one day, they came across an Indian with half a dozen metal figurines, which struck Fawcett, an amateur archaeologist, as Egyptian in style. They were about six inches high and appeared immeasurably ancient. The Indian had brought them into town to sell them, and unfortunately had already done so. He would tell Fawcett nothing about the sale or where he'd gotten the figures, and after allowing Fawcett to examine them thoroughly, he wrapped them in a cloth and hurried away.

Costin, Manley, and Fawcett made their way to Rurrenabaque, which now showed the first signs of a waning rubber trade; there was belt-tightening everywhere one looked. Fawcett wanted to investigate rumors of ruins to the north of that settlement, so the men trekked overland, towards the Heath. Fawcett employed one of the habits he had formed during his years in the wilderness, which was to glean whatever morsels of information he could get from the local people. For every nine bits of useless facts or misinformation there would be one pearl, so Fawcett and his men chatted up nearly everyone who was even semi-rational in the villages of Tumupasa and Ixiamas.

They were kept busy chasing rumors and chimeras, a silver mine, diamonds, ruins— but in weeks of searching, the one true pearl, if it existed, eluded them.

"This is fruitless," Fawcett said one day as they rested on a log beside the Tuiche River. "Let's head back to Rurrenabaque. I don't see any sense in continuing this search. "

Manley and Costin, footsore by now, readily agreed. The new plan was to push eastward to Reyes, at the edge of the Plains of Mojos. But they weren't out of the forest, or the bushmasters, yet. The men had scooted down the bank to fill their canteens in the Tuiche and were clambering back up to a riverside trail when the first snake episode woke them up a bit (and spoiled Manley's tobacco).

As soon as Manley's pants were back in place and his rope belt retied, the men started east along the riverbank. They kept to a brisk pace on the level trail, single file, Fawcett in the lead. Suddenly, he executed a rather breathtaking leap to one side, his legs scissoring wide like a ballet dancer making a lovely arc but a bad landing. He didn't need to explain the maneuver; Costin and Manley saw all nine feet of the bushmaster shooting like an arrow between Fawcett's splayed legs. As he fell, they ran to defend him since a bushmaster rarely gives up so easily, sometimes pursuing the enemy for quite a distance.

But the snake slipped away and lay quietly beneath a bush.

"Leave it," said Fawcett as they helped him quickly to his feet. "Let's go. Keep an eye on it to see if it's inclined to follow."

It wasn't, and they walked on. Fawcett's mind was engaged in interpreting the two amazingly close shaves they'd had. He couldn't have said what had made him jump; as he told the others later by the campfire, he was not conscious of the snake until it flew between his legs. Only his "higher mind", or "inner man", as he called it, had perceived the creature in time to gauge the trajectory of the strike and give the body precise orders for the direction and height of his jump and the rapid spread of his legs.

Costin and Manley marvelled at the power of the subconscious, while privately, Fawcett thought the two incidents could be something other than stunning examples of good luck and instinct. Increasingly in the forests he had felt a protecting presence enveloping him and his men. Surely they could've met with disaster many times, in many ways, yet always they escaped to crow over their good fortune.

"Why so pensive?" Costin asked, stirring up the fire. "Do you count that incident as your eighth life just spent, perhaps?"

Fawcett laughed softly. "Something like that. Without doubt I've had more than my share of what you call 'luck'".

*

The oxen heaved and two solid wooden wheels, six feet in diameter, slowly turned. Their tropical hardwood axles emitted a high, steady whine as the cart rolled along.

"Not exactly music of the spheres, is it?" Costin winced.

"I think I'm getting used to it," said Fawcett. "The owner of this team told me the oxen seem to like it; and it's a good thing, since few people here can afford imported iron axles."

The three men trudged along behind the rented cart as its owner drove the oxen. To start across the Plains of Mojos afoot would have been folly, due to the roving, aggressive herds of wild cattle. The bulls were particularly fierce, and many people journeying on foot had been killed by them; but travelers were generally safe riding a mount or sticking close to an oxcart. Fawcett preferred horses or mules, but had had no luck hiring either in Rurrenabaque.

Costin and Manley had found nothing of interest in Reyes, a small village consisting of Indian huts. But Fawcett observed that it was located atop an artificial mound which was ringed by a wide ditch and rose about twelve feet above the plain. As they left on the eastward trek to Santa Ana, he pointed out signs of an ancient people: wide-ranging earthen ramparts and terrepleins, in some areas interconnected by many miles of raised causeways. To Fawcett it indicated an extensive population which had had reason to erect fortifications. He wondered aloud who the enemy had been.

"The bloody bulls, no doubt," cracked Manley.

The men understood the purpose of the elevated causeways, one of which they themselves were using. The entire vast plain, extending through eastern Bolivia and into Brazil, was subject to summer flooding, as rain and melting Andes snow drained into the lowlands; hammocks of jungle then became islands teeming with animal life which sought refuge from the bañados, or inundated areas.

Slowly the men and oxen progressed. The cart, of course, provided protection only if the men stayed near it. One day, when Manley and Costin repaired to one of the hammocks of forest, as was necessary now and then to hunt wild turkeys or other game, they were followed by a big black bull, sniffing the ground after them like a bloodhound. Since they carried only .22 rifles, they'd been forced to seek flimsy refuge in a thorn thicket and fire at the bull's eyes, blinding it; only then were they able to slip away and race back several hundred yards to the cart.

Fawcett, too, had to learn the hard way. He had left his gun in the cart and lagged some fifty yards behind the others, considerately, to relieve himself; as he started to catch up, out of nowhere came a large red bull to stand snorting and pawing beside the trail, between Fawcett and the cart. The beast lowered its head and glared at Fawcett murderously, on the very edge of charging.

Fawcett glanced around him quickly. There was nothing to climb, nowhere to find safety, but the cart. The other men wouldn't have a chance of stopping the bull with their small-caliber rifles. Then an idea dawned: Maybe two could play the evil-eye game, and it was his only chance. The others hadn't yet seen the bull behind them, nor heard its enraged pawing over the whine of the axles. So, feeling at least glad he'd already emptied his bowel, he mustered all his courage and skewered the bull with the most intensely mesmerizing stare he could manage, while edging smoothly and slowly toward the cart. Sweat poured from his body as he passed the bull, which was now standing stock-still. It flipped through Fawcett's mind how different was this man-beast eye contact from that which he experienced with the condor.

The next thing he knew he had passed the bull and was joining his dumbfounded, petrified companions, who had at last turned to look for him. The bull continued to stand and gape as they moved steadily away.

"Well, I never!" Manley exploded. "I have never seen anything like that!"

"I never want to see anything like it again, myself..." said Fawcett, wiping his brow with his sleeve and realizing his legs had begun to shake.

"At first we thought you were out of your mind," put in Costin, "But by Jove, it worked! What possessed you to think of it?"

"I don't know... just an instinct, maybe..."

"Cool-headed of you, Major!" Costin said admiringly.

Fawcett demurred; he hadn't felt at all cool, but time had seemed strangely suspended as he slowly passed the vicious bull. He shook his head, saying sincerely, "Friends, I'd rather do *jetés* over a nest of bushmasters than to ever need such self-control again!"

They laughed, clapping him on his sweat-soaked back. Saved, once more.

*

At Santa Ana, on the banks of the Mamoré River, Fawcett had felt excitement rise within him; he could hardly wait to get to Santa Cruz where he felt the true starting point of this expedition would be. Beyond was Brazil, and a thousand question marks; unmapped lands north of the Guaporé, forests vast enough to hide entire cities...

Slosh, slosh. When the men weren't wading through muddy water, they were pulling themselves through thick, deep mud, their boots sinking through a surface mat of rotted leaves or grass and into the mire. Then "pulling" was indeed the word for it, as it took effort with every step to break the suction of the mud and free the foot for another plunge. The sound it made had long since ceased to be amusing.

Manley, Costin, and Fawcett, leading pack mules, had had a fairly easy trek from Santa Cruz to San Ignacio, where the bañados— now known in Brazil as the Pantanal— began. They were slogging through low-lying forest which would be completely flooded in the rainy season. Large areas of year-round swamp were punctuated by islands of higher ground where lush forest growth crowded to the very edge of the dry bit of land. These refuges swarmed with snakes and other creatures large and small, particularly during the flood season when a sort of truce took effect among the animals, much as that occurring around African watering holes. Time-out, fellows, wholesale slaughter would be bad form. One's own survival often requires control over greed; if predators destroy more prey than they need, few prey animals survive long enough to reproduce and soon the gluttons would face famine.

Slosh, slosh. For six days they tugged their heavy boots from the sucking mud, making their way to an island to camp at night, ever on the alert for venomous snakes. All the animals tended to avoid them, though anacondas, often of great size in the Pantanal, were a constant danger. In addition to the ubiquitous monkeys, they briefly encountered shy caimans, tapirs, a jaguar, and various wild pigs. The pigs, travelling in groups, were by far the greatest danger to humans of all the other creatures.

Potentially threatening wildlife aside, the clumps of forest beckoned, offering not only a dry place to rest and game to eat, but also shade. Across a bright, wide vista of swamp, dark trees rose against the sky in mysterious silhouette; unnamed species of birds darted and swooped among the branches, but aside from their cries, and the sound of the mud pulling at the men's feet, a primeval peace lay over the region.

Once they encountered a rundown estancia, or ranch, on one of the larger islands, occupied by the dourest group of folk Fawcett had yet come across in South America. They seemed to spend most of their time killing venomous snakes, which may have affected their outlook on life, he reasoned. Other than this poor shred of society, Fawcett's party and the beasts had the island-forests all to themselves.

One morning Fawcett awoke to see a few scraps of glorious sunrise color peeking through the dense canopy high above, and he lay for a long while listening to birds twittering in the distant branches. Manley and Costin still slept. He gazed upward at a tangle of lianas stretching in all directions, horizontally, diagonally, running up tree trunks, twisting around each other, and falling straight down, reaching toward him, it seemed, and he felt like an insect caught in a net.

Nearby, a strangler fig enclosed a large cottonwood tree in its sure, but deadly, grasp. The fig had begun as one of the innocuous lianas, creeping up the tree trunk; steadily it had grown and spread itself like a hand with strong, flexible fingers that reached around the entire girth of the pale, smooth trunk. Over time the fingers would web together and become an unbroken sheath, killing the host tree, which would eventually decay and be replaced by the inexorable fig. In the competition for sun, the fig had not only found a scaffolding leading up to the light, it was also in the process of stealing the cottonwood's place. And all done so slowly that it was almost tender. On this trek Fawcett had seen various types of trees in different stages of the fig's embrace.

A slight breeze stirred the canopy and several little orchids of different colors floated down to the campsite along with a shower of droplets shaken from the leaves above. Fawcett had noticed that it took about five minutes for a true rain to work its way through the umbrella-like canopy to the ground below; conversely, after the rain had stopped falling on the forest, it continued to drip heavily from the sodden bran-ches for the same five minutes, more or less. In this time of year they had only light showers to deal with, and these were usually refreshing.

At length the men reached the San Matías-Villa Bella trail, which

Fawcett knew from his earlier journey to the Rio Verde. They camped beside the Barbados River, where they fired off many rounds of ammunition in an effort to draw attention from residents on the other side of the rampaging river. It took three days before a man from the nearby village of Casal Vasco appeared; when he learned what they wanted, he fetched a canoe and ferried the men across.

"So, we're in Brazil now," said Costin with a slight uncertainty in his tone, as he looked around Casal Vasco, once the home of one Baron Bastos and the seat of his boundless cattle ranch. Ruins of several grand structures attested to bygone glories of the Empire years.

Fawcett snorted. "For the time being, anyway. Next year, who knows? But I doubt if anyone will fight over this area. Perhaps my survey will endure, after all."

The people remembered Fawcett, and he was able to buy a canoe from a man he had known when he was there in '09, Antonio Alves.

"Go with God," said Alves. "It is very isolated where you're headed. Plenty of game available, but about the only people you'll see are Indians, and not all of them are friendly."

"We'll be careful, thank you— " Fawcett shook Alves' hand. Nothing could dampen his excitement, and he maintained an open mind about the Indians based on past experience.

The men's arms had a good workout, as they paddled for eleven days on the Guaporé before they reached a tributary called the Rio Mequens.

"Ah, and here's the German barraca Antonio told me about, at the confluence. Though we'll be expected to pay, we should have some decent food and a chance to rest. We'll strike off overland from here." They were approaching a small dock. A couple of boys helped them tie up the boat and directed them to a small bungalow where visitors could stay.

On the veranda was another guest of the barraca, one Baron Erland Nordenskiöld, a Swede, who seemed delighted to see more visitors. He introduced himself, shaking hands with the three.

"We don't have the pleasure of meeting very many Europeans in these parts, as you may imagine!"

A lovely, very blond young woman standing in the doorway, her smile as wide as the Baron's, stopped Fawcett's party in their tracks for a moment.

"My wife," explained the Baron, making the introductions and ushering the men to the shady end of the veranda.

The Baroness hastily assembled refreshments in the bungalow's little kitchen while the men removed their shoes and made themselves comfortable.

"We are not in the rubber trade, thank goodness," her husband said as he pulled up a chair, "We are scholars, one might say, studying some of the Indian tribes that live along the Guaporé. We usually stop at this barraca when we're passing through the area."

"Ah, anthropologists," said Fawcett, warming to one of his favorite subjects. "Your wife as well?"

"Oh, yes! In fact it was our common interest which brought us together in university some years ago."

"I'm eager to hear what you've learned." Fawcett was practically rubbing his hands together.

The Baroness entered with a tray. "We've learned two dozen ways to remove leeches," she offered, setting the tray on a table.

All the men groaned with familiarity. "We should compare notes on methods," said Manley, accepting a tall glass of fruit juice gratefully.

As they sipped, and nibbled politely on some little nutbreads the Baroness had made earlier that day, Fawcett felt an uncharacteristic stab of— could it be envy?— watching the enthusiasm of the two, describing their forays into the surrounding forests, one or the other of them jumping up from time to time to fetch an artifact or drawing from their baggage, and pass it around the group. The Baroness spoke with lively gestures and great humor, clearly absorbed by their studies and thrilled to find an interested audience. Her husband laughed expansively as she recounted one of their adventures.

As Fawcett watched, her pretty, animated face was overlaid by a vision of Nina, for just an instant, and then it vanished. *What a fine and unusual woman this is,* he thought, *to slog through snake-infested swamps beside her husband, and share his fascination with the natives. Cheeky would've come with me, I'm sure, if she had the endurance and if the children hadn't come along... She may not be as strong in body as the Baroness, but her spirit could equal any human's I know.*

His fancy drifted on and he could see Nina by his side, his surveying partner on the wild rivers; she knew as much about surveying as he did. For a heartbreaking moment, he imagined the completeness of his life in the wilderness if she were with him, in place of the conflict, loneliness, and guilt which so often plagued him...

He snapped back to reality. Of course, he wouldn't trade his children for the world. He couldn't have it both ways. And who could say Nina would truly want such an existence? Sututus and bushmasters and—

The Baron was speaking to him, something about the hills.

"— about twelve miles away, to the east; there are said to be tribes up there that are quite dangerous, cannibalistic, we've heard. The Indians around here are terrified of them."

His wife added, "The men are supposed to be very big, and hairy."

"Are you planning to go see for yourself?" inquired Costin.

"No, no," answered the Baron. "It's far too great a risk, though of course we're very curious."

"We'll let you know if the rumors are true, because that's where we're headed," put in Fawcett.

"You don't say! Oh, Major Fawcett, I'd reconsider those plans if I were you! Why, it's downright foolhardy, if I may say so."

The Baron and his wife were unable, with all their protests, to make a dent in Fawcett's determination. Costin and Manley seemed equally unmoved; after all, the Major had been right about the other Indians they'd encountered, who had not deserved their gruesome reputations.

"Well," said the Baron finally, "if we cannot dissuade you, at least let us share some of the food we've brought. We have an excess of camp provisions in our boat and we won't need to use much of it here at the barraca, where we plan to rest for a while. You can take all you can carry."

And so, well rested, well fed, their stores generously replenished by the Swedes until they could barely lift their packs, the Englishmen made their farewells the following morning.

"You might run across signs of a hermit here and there. Men of all nationalities have found this wilderness appealing, but they'll probably avoid your company entirely."

"And we shall not invade their privacy. Well, goodbye to you both; we can't thank you enough for the stores!"

"If you change your mind and return before we leave," offered the Baron, " You can accompany us to visit a nearby tribe, if you wish. Otherwise, I fear to say, I don't believe we will ever meet again."

On that somber note, the little party shouldered their heavy packs and marched away toward yet more swamps and muck through which they would wade for the next two days.

*

"Up here, Major; it appears to be a river." Manley stood knee-deep in water and mud, facing the northeast.

Fawcett caught up with him. "Ah, I believe you're right. Costin, over here! All right, we'll follow it. Just about any river should give us a good route up to the Serra, where all this moisture comes from!" He clapped Manley on the back, and strode ahead.

For several more days they followed the watercourse, eventually reaching grassy, undulating plains that led into the foothills of the Serra dos Parecis. The farther they climbed into the hills, the more beautiful the scenery became. Lush, virgin forests, green meadows speckled with colorful blossoms, pure rivers and streams. They found giant rubber trees with a few crude slashes, but no sign of the seringueiro or of any other sort of exploitation.

They did see traces of inhabitants. For some time they had been following a well-used path which ran along the riverbank.

"Look, Major, a little intersecting path. Should we follow it?" Costin stood at the head of a narrow trail running beside a clear brook which emptied into the river. "Could be an animal track, but it doesn't seem so, to me."

Fawcett hesitated. Curiosity nibbled at him. "For a little distance, I suppose, and silently..."

The three crept in near-perfect silence up the winding trail, barely a foot wide. Before too long Fawcett, in the lead, held up a hand and his men stopped, peering over his shoulder. Ahead at the apparent end of the path, almost hidden under a heavy bower of tree branches and built partly into a mass of rock, was a quaint, tiny wooden hut. There were no signs of life, but the dwelling was so well kept that it was evidently still occupied. Costin gestured to the right, where a crude basket hung from a branch; it was laden with fresh fruit of various kinds. Beside the hut, a small waterfall tumbled from rocks into the gurgling stream.

With a quick tilt of his head Fawcett signalled the men to go back the way they had come. They didn't speak until they had rejoined the main trail.

"That wasn't an Indian hut, was it," Manley suggested.

"No, you're quite right, I don't think it was," Fawcett agreed. "It looked rather European to me, in fact, though it was so simple..." He looked intrigued.

"I saw a few tools at the side of the hut," Manley added, "Did you notice?" The other two shook their heads. "Well, I'd say they were definitely store-bought."

"We must've found one of the hermits the Baron mentioned, or his home, anyway. He picked a lovely spot, didn't he?" Fawcett became lost in his own thoughts as they continued walking. *Some people,* he mused, *might think these hermits are crazy, or pathetic, hiding away from civilization and all the comforts we think we cannot live without, and its stimulation, its amusements... But in the end they may be the sanest of us all; living a simple, clean life amidst such beauty, requiring little. Would it be better to scrabble in a city for one's daily bread and a room somewhere, fighting for that myth we call security– or climbing society's ladders day after day, always wanting more than we have...?*

It seemed to him the recluses were the wise ones, after all. They knew how superficial the civilized world was. *The true meaning of life is here, I suspect, in the wilds, and I envy them their opportunity to find it.*

He remained introspective as they continued through an Eden-like forest of giant trees and sparse underbrush, making occasional discoveries of unknown fruit, some of which proved edible and delicious.

Three weeks after they entered the Serranian forest they encountered another trail, wide and well-trod, crossing the path they were following.

"Hmm... Looks as if an Indian village is near, Major," said Costin. "Should we try it?"

"I suppose. But in all likelihood either trail will eventually lead us to Indians." They stood, undecided.

Manley held out his hand; a small object lay in his palm.

"What's this?" asked Costin.

"It's a coin, nitwit."

"I can see that, but what are you doing with a coin in the middle of nowhere?"

"It was in my pocket, that's all. Give 'er a flip! Heads we continue, tails we turn."

So they flipped the coin, and this humble oracle directed them to turn onto the new path.

"Very scientific, Manley, thank you," bowed Fawcett.

"Well, it beat standing there going, 'eeny, meeny, miny, moe,' " Manley replied.

After a couple of miles, the men began to see signs of agriculture, small plantations of various vegetables and root crops. They continued more carefully.

Abruptly they came upon a large, bright clearing; this burst of sunlight after the shady forest dazzled their eyes for a moment and they ducked behind foliage. Squin-ting, they peeped through the leaves and straight into a vision from the primeval past.

Slightly off-center in the great clearing stood two beehive-shaped huts, approx-imately one hundred feet in diameter. A small, naked boy squatted beside a flat rock near the opening to the nearer hut, and pounded on a nut with the side of a stone axe. Fawcett stared, feeling transported back in time thousands of years. *The scene is just as it might have been in neolithic days, a peep into prehistory,* he thought.

Reluctantly, he broke from his trance and prepared to disturb the peace of this tribe that time left behind. He pursed his lips and gave a low whistle. The child's head jerked to attention, his eyes met theirs, and all at once panic erupted in the village. Someone reached from the hut and pulled the child inside, where there were shrieks and commotion, and excited voices.

Fawcett seized that moment of confusion to stride across the clearing to the hut; he stepped inside and squatted against the wall, letting his eyes adjust to the dim light. A small fire burned near the center pole, and he smelled maize beer brewing. At first he thought the hut was empty of human life; he saw another door on the opposite side, and assumed the Indians he'd heard had escaped. He surmised the men were out working the plantations, and now the women and children had run to alert them.

Then he saw movement behind the fire. An old woman, partially hidden behind several tall earthenware urns, seemed to say, "Oh, phooey!" or something akin and went to the fire to tend her beer. She was either too old to run away or too old to be afraid. Fawcett smiled and watched her for a moment, aware that she also watched him from the corner of her eye.

He gestured to her that he was hungry, signs which everyone the world over understands. She filled a gourd with something from a second pot and brought it cautiously to Fawcett. Whatever the food was, he couldn't tell, but it was quite good. He took it out to his men, who hungrily agreed.

Thunder rumbled overhead as if the sky were tearing apart, and rain began to pour.

"Come inside, you two. They know we're here now so we may as well be dry and fed." Costin laughed, shaking his head at Fawcett's gall, and all three rushed to the hut.

Fawcett had had the woman refill the gourd twice when shadowy figures of men began creeping through the entrances. They were armed with bows and arrows. Silently the men spread themselves around the perimeter of the hut. The old woman began talking to one of them, whom Fawcett assumed was the chief. The firelight revealed a middle-aged man with long, straight hair. Thrust through his nostrils and lower lip were small pegs, and his earlobes wore shells. On his upper arms were bands of seeds and some sort of carved wood.

Fawcett took several gifts from his pack and approached this man, explaining with signs that he and his men meant no harm and only wanted food.

The chief looked at Fawcett for a long moment, and then held out his hand to accept the gifts. As if this were a signal some of the women came forward bearing gourds filled with huge peanuts and gave them to the three visitors. The chief plopped down on a little stool and opened a peanut shell. Fawcett, Manley, and Costin sat down on the ground near him.

Fawcett cracked a peanut shell, grinning broadly. "We're in, fellows!"

In the predawn hour profound silence reigned in the forest. The nightly clamor of monkeys and insects had ceased, and the birds, residents of the higher branches of giant trees, appeared to be late risers.

The stillness was barely disturbed by an Indian, a young male, walking to a central point in the clearing. He stood motionless for a minute or two, facing east; then, as the first rays of sunlight appeared in the canopy, he began to sing. His voice carried sweetly in the tranquil morning, chanting a repetitive but melodic hymn to the sun.

Fawcett came to the door of the hut where he'd slept, carrying his journal and pencils, and listened to the eerie, beautiful notes rising and falling. Though it was now the tenth time he'd heard this sunrise song, it still provoked shivers of emotion down his spine. Only his beloved Nina could awaken him more thrillingly.

When the song ended, he went to a comfortable spot where the light was good and settled himself to update his journal.

June 2, 1914

Costin, Manley, and I are presently the guests of the Maxubi tribe, in the Serra dos Parecis, Brazil. To say these are a prehistoric people might imply, wrongly, that they are primitive "savages". On the contrary, there seems nothing savage about them.

The Maxubi population consists of some two dozen settlements and a total of about 2,000 souls. Having studied them closely for a week and a half, my conclusion is that they are the fallen remnant, one might say, of a highly developed civilization, rather than a tribe which is evolving from the primitive level. They have a finely-developed sense of morals and manners, and natural gentility. Their bodies are well-formed, their features delicate, their feet and hands small. Their skin is a light copper tone and their hair has a red cast; in fact, in one of the villages I met a boy with distinctly red hair and blue eyes— and he was not an albino.

The men wear a number of adornments in their ears, lips, nostrils and on their arms and ankles; the women wear none, and their hair is short, in contrast to the long hair of the males. Quite the opposite of our customs. The males' ornaments are fine in workmanship, including the red rubber bands (died with urucu) worn around wrists and ankles. Obviously this tribe has learned to tap the rubber trees which surround them, and we have seen the cuts here and there.

The women are skilled in the making of pottery and the brewing of maize beer. All the people smoke tobacco, which is cultivated, and rolled in maize leaves.

The Maxubi stand as an example of the limited knowledge of ethnologists, the very inverse of their conclusions. But to find such tribes one must leave the large rivers and venture more deeply into unknown areas.

These people worship the sun, greeting it every dawn with haunting songs using a pentatonic scale. This is not primitive music, but is subtle and complex, as is their language. They have names for the planets, and some of them are similar to the Incan words. After ten days we can communicate basic ideas in their tongue, but it's apparent there is much to learn in this regard. What a pity I cannot spend more time among them, but we must push on.

They've given us useful information regarding another tribe to the north, the direction in which we're heading: the Maricoxis. They find this group detestable and quite beneath them; cannibals, they say, ignorant and violent.

One day I showed the chief a photograph of my sons, which fascinated him no end; several times he requested to see it again, and show it to others in the

tribe. He told me if I want to see my boys again, I will avoid the Maricoxis.
Yet still, I am curious...

It was time to say farewell. The Maxubi women had loaded Fawcett's little party with bundles of the giant peanuts, their dietary staple. Each long pod contained several nuts, and each nut was at least
three inches long. "One pod is almost a meal," as Costin had said.

"And tasty, as well as convenient for travel," added Fawcett.

The chief approached Fawcett with a string bag containing more
peanuts. "A gift for your sons," he said.

The three white men took their leave and struck off in a northeast-
erly direction— straight toward the Maricoxis, the chief sadly watching
them walk away— making their own path through the forest.

After five days of hacking through moderately dense underbrush,
they came upon a trail.

"Well, men," said Fawcett, looking up and down the path, "to the
north or the south? What would you say?"

"Manley, do you still have that coin, or did you give it to some
Maxubi belle?" Costin asked.

"It's right here, uh— somewhere, just a moment— " Manley fished
in his pocket.

Suddenly Costin's grin froze on his face. "Never mind, Manley,"
he said in a low tone. "We have company."

They followed Costin's gaze to the south trail and their eyes met
those of two men who indeed fit the description of "savages". Their
bows were set with arrows and drawn back by unusually long arms.
They were large men, completely naked but for the thick hair covering their bodies. Their faces were those of ape-men: prominent
ridges over the eyes, sloping foreheads. For a breathless moment everyone stood paralyzed, then all at once the two men turned and disappeared into the brush.

"Good Lord," exhaled Costin. "Maricoxi, I suppose!"

"No need to try and follow them," said Fawcett, to his companions' great relief. "We'll take the northern direction."

"Good move, Major," said Manley.

The men walked on for an hour or more, and just after sunset they
heard a weird sound, like a horn. They heard it first on one side of
them, then the other, and then coming from all directions.

Manley broke into a heavy sweat. "What is it? They're after us, aren't they, the lot of them."

Fawcett kept his voice calm and level. "It sounds as if they fetched the others, all right, and they're blowing some kind of crude horns. Let's just keep going."

"Listen," said Costin tensely. "Voices, now... "

The Maricoxi were nearer, yelling and gabbling to each other with guttural sounds. The brief tropical twilight fades into darkness particularly fast in towering forests. Gathering gloom enhanced the nerve-wracking effect of the wild voices, grunts, and horn-blowing on all sides of them.

"We need to find a safe shelter." Fawcett peered into the dim wood, and spied a tacuara thicket. "Aha! Here's where our clothing saves the day. Those naked savages would be ripped to shreds in here."

The men hurried into the shrubs, their inch-long thorns providing a bizarre haven. Almost immediately, Fawcett began to hang his hammock, eyeing Manley and Costin. "We'll be all right here," he insisted.

The other two men looked unconvinced, as they reluctantly unrolled their own hammocks. But sure enough, though they heard the brutish men carrying on all around them, none cared to risk the vicious thorns; and as darkness closed in, the Maricoxi abruptly left.

"I'd still feel better if we took turns on watch," Manley urged. "In case they decide to burn us out, or something."

"An impromptu barbecue?" joked Costin, with forced levity.

"As you wish," replied Fawcett. "Who wants first watch?"

The men managed to get a little sleep during the long night, and at dawn the surroundings were still peaceful. They hiked on, and late in the day came upon a plantation of papaws and mandioca. They explored the area cautiously but found it deserted.

"Then let's eat up, men; and this looks as good a place to camp as any."

Manley was not in favor of the idea, thinking it all too possible for Indians to visit the plantings, but he said nothing. At least there was food readily available. *We'll be nice and fat for their pots*, he thought ruefully.

When they were fed, and comfortable in their hammocks which were hung close together, Fawcett reached into his pack and withdrew his flageolet.

"How about a little trio?" he suggested. This group needed to perk up a bit; there was no need to creep around, afraid to cough. Any Indians in the vicinity already knew they were there, he reasoned.

"Excuse me, Major, but that seems— ill advised," objected Costin tentatively.

"Translation: 'Are you daft, Major?' " laughed Fawcett.

Manley was suddenly reckless. "No, you're right, sir, it doesn't really matter, does it? And a show of boldness might make us feel stronger. So the Devil take 'em!" And he found his instrument— a comb, much lighter to carry than the accordion— and cleaned it up a bit.

"Don't let me be the spoilsport, then." Costin gamely pulled out his harmonica and blew a few opening notes.

Soon there was a lively performance going on amidst the papaws, shocking the monkeys and bugs into silence. And it met Fawcett's purpose: The men were laughing, at first artificially, but after a while their mirth was genuine.

They slept a little more soundly that night, but they took turns on watch duty.

The next day as they tramped along steadily, they began to see occasional palm-leaf constructions in the lower branches of trees, crude boxes which they guessed were used as sentry posts.

"We must be getting near a village," said Fawcett uneasily.

No sooner had he spoken than they were suddenly at the edge of a wide area of open forest, where all brush was cleared away, leaving only the great trees. Scattered among their trunks were a number of primitive huts; the inhabitants of the village were the same sort of ape-men that had been seen earlier. The rough shelters, and the arrows some of them were making, were the only signs that they were more advanced than beasts.

The three Englishmen watched for a few minutes, and then, following his habit of making a direct, friendly approach, Fawcett whistled.

Instantly the Maricoxi came alive. Great, hairy men fixed arrows into their bows and rushed to surround the intruders, grunting in a pig-like way and dancing from one leg to the other, back and forth. Fawcett attempted to communicate, both with gestures and with a few Maxubi greetings, but it seemed to mean nothing to them. The Maricoxi exchanged only gruff monosyllables and grunts with each other, and kept rocking from foot to foot. Then one of them drew close and raised his bow, pointing its six-foot arrow directly at Faw-cett's chest. He was close enough that Fawcett and his men could see his stained teeth, filed to sharp points, and bright little eyes which were deeply recessed under the projecting, shaggy brows.

"Major, I think he means business!" yelped Costin, his hand on his gun.

"No, wait, hold on, the Maxubis said they give a couple of warn-ings; maybe they want us to run. They like the chase."

The three stood pat. The ape-man lowered his bow and there was more dancing and grunting. Then the performance took place once more, as the same brute raised his bow and aimed it at Fawcett, only to at last lower it with wild whoops and jumps.

The third time he raised it Fawcett said, "This is it." He drew his pistol, a big .38 caliber Mauser, and his companions readied their ri-fles. Fawcett only had to fire one shot into the ground. The tremen-dous roar of the Mauser did its intended magic; all the Maricoxi stood paralyzed with shock, until the one who had been so threaten-ing dropped his bow and hightailed it. The others went into a panic, some hiding behind huts or trees, some running in circles, but many of them were releasing their arrows in the intruders' direction.

Dodging the spear-like missiles, Fawcett fired a few more rounds into the trees, but the Maricoxi showed no signs of coming to order.

"They're beyond listening, Major!" Costin yelled.

"Right; let's go!"

Watching their backs, the three beat a hasty retreat down the path.

"No one seems to be following," panted Manley. The racket from the village was growing mercifully distant as the men struck off northwards from the trail, beating a path through the forest. Later in the day they turned east, hoping they were beyond all of the Maricoxi villages.

But as they set up camp that evening, they realized they couldn't be too sure of that.

"What was that? Listen," said Manley, tense as a bowstring.

Costin froze, cocking his head. "I don't hear anything. Wait—" They all stood rigid, straining their ears.

Finally Fawcett asked, "What did it sound like, Manley?"

"Oh, you know, that grunting sound they make, 'Unh, unh'..."

"Well, there's nothing to hear now. We're all overwrought. Let's try to relax."

Over the next few days, that proved easier said than done. They travelled each day in fear of stumbling into another Maricoxi village, or of hearing the horns and realizing they were being pursued. When they encountered a rotting sentry box above a partially grown-over trail, it sent them into a tailspin of indecision over the best direction in which to proceed from there.

They were getting tired. Walking the forest in a constant state of tension and alertness took its toll on their muscles as well as their nerves. They ate little, not wanting to draw attention to their whereabouts with the gunfire of hunting. At night they slept poorly.

This is no good, Fawcett told himself. *We're becoming too frazzled and exhausted to think, to make decisions, or to save ourselves in a confrontation. Manley is close to a breakdown and Costin's nerves, like mine, are strained to their limits. The Maxubi were right. We're going to get ourselves killed.*

Fawcett realized the constant anxiety had sapped his motivation for the Quest. His usual energy and positivism were sorely challenged.

One morning he said: "Enough of this. Today we turn back."

"Oh thank God," Manley breathed. Costin nodded dumbly.

"You're both quite brave, you know," Fawcett went on, "and I appreciate your willingness. But we must get back to the Guaporé, or at least to the Maxubi, so we can have a complete rest where we feel safe. We can't go on under this strain."

"Do you mean to come back here, sir?" asked Costin.

"I do not." With that, Fawcett rolled up his hammock, and the other two wordlessly began to break camp.

Admitting defeat, for Fawcett, was more difficult than dying with a Maricoxi arrow piercing his innards. But he saw nothing to admire in squandering the lives of his men, and his own. He had promised Nina he would come back to her even if he failed in his mission, and he meant to keep that promise.

The journey back took on nightmarish aspects, at times literally. Horrible dreams disturbed their rest, dreams of hideous Maricoxi faces, dagger teeth and beady eyes; long, hairy arms reaching for them, spitting them over the fire and barbecuing them alive. At times each of them awoke sweating, cursing, or crying out.

"It's as if the bloody Maricoxi have demons in the forest at their beck and call, to wear us down," said Manley one morning after a particularly rough night.

"Stop it, Manley." Fawcett spoke sharply. "We're in bad enough condition without adding the nether world to the mix. We have to keep our heads and our faith."

"You're right, Major; I'm not normally a superstitious man. I just need one good night's sleep, just one, to set me right again."

"Don't we all," murmured Costin, wearily shouldering his pack.

The men went to great lengths to avoid the Maricoxi village, trekking in a wide circle around the entire area, as best they could calculate. By the time they reached Maxubi territory they were indeed nearly exhausted.

"Ah..." grinned Costin gratefully at the sight of a Maxubi village. "Rest, food, friends... we've made it!"

But not quite. Right away the little party noticed a distinct chill in the reception they received. There was a funeral going on, for a warrior who'd been tracked and killed by the Maricoxi. Fawcett wondered if the killing had had anything to do with them, and he was sure the Maxubi were asking themselves the same thing.

"The Maricoxi are after the Maxubi all the time," he said to his men. "But if they believe it has a connection to us— and they're superstitious enough to link two unrelated events— then, this is not good!"

They were given food and were left unmolested, but the night wasn't as restful and cheery as they had hoped. Fawcett thought it best to push on to the next village at first light.

In the next settlement, and the two after that, they found more mourning, more funerals. Every village had lost young men, and the Maxubi were increasingly suspicious that the Maricoxi were venting their anger at the white intruders. They were not hostile to their guests, but their coldness had an unsettling effect on the men's strained nerves.

"What if they decided to end the killings by sacrificing us, as some sort of propitiation? It *could* happen, no?" asked Costin uneasily.

"Unlikely, I think, but anything's possible out here," Fawcett conceded. "Let's thank them for their hospitality, and be on our way in the morning, what say you? This isn't the place for an extended rest, I'm afraid."

So the weary men left the last village before dawn the next day, heading southwest. And soon they faced another challenge: hunger. Game seemed nowhere to be found.

"We're jinxed," offered Manley, careful to use a jesting tone. "The

Maxubi were right, we're bad medicine. All the critters have evacuated."

"Have a peanut." Costin extended his bag.

"All right, men." Fawcett stopped and began counting out nuts. "We're on rations. Let's see... eight peanuts a day. Until we get game, anyway."

The two groaned, but agreed. Somehow they kept going energetically, yet with some anxiety when no game appeared and the peanut supply was running low.

"It's best, actually, that we've killed no game," Fawcett asserted one day as they tramped along.

"How's that, Major?" Costin asked.

"Well, as you see, we're half starved but we continue with strength and energy, am I right?" The other two nodded. "A vegetable diet keeps one going that way, as long as there's enough of it, of course; but if we had a little meat now and then we'd begin to feel quite lethargic. Meat slows the system greatly, under conditions of generally inadequate food."

"You don't say." This from Manley.

"He's quite right. I've experienced it," concurred Costin.

They marched on, all of them aware of the bag of peanuts remaining in Fawcett's pack, the chief's gift to little Jack and Brian. When their peanut supply grew meager, Fawcett at last said:

"Look, you two can have part of my ration, if you need it, but I'd prefer not to touch the gift. It was meant for the boys, and– "

Manley interrupted. "And they shall have it. Don't worry, Major, speaking for myself, anyway, I'm not worried."

"Nor I, " said Costin firmly, and the extra bag was never mentioned again. But unknown to his men, Fawcett had been eating fewer than eight nuts per day, slipping the extra ones into the communal bag to extend the supply for the other two.

As it turned out, before starvation became too serious an issue, following a wide stream they reached the hut of a rubber gatherer, who offered them all the rice and charque they could eat.

"All that we want?" asked Costin. "Are you sure about that? You're looking at three very, very, hungry men!"

But the seringueiro extended the typical unqualified generosity of wilderness settlers, and they rested and stuffed their stomachs for two days; then continuing downstream they at last reached the Guaporé and the German barraca where they had met the Nordenskiölds. No one at the barraca knew exactly where the couple had gone.

"There's a scale on the back porch," suggested Fawcett. "Our pants are falling off, we're so thin. Let's go assess the damages."

Costin had lost thirty-one pounds, Manley twenty-three, and Fawcett fifty-three.

"Well, it didn't seem to hurt us any," observed Costin. "I feel pretty fit, actually!" The other two agreed.

"Our bodies have few reserves left, I suppose... and Cheeky would die if she saw me like this, but I rather like my new size," laughed Fawcett. Still, their appetites seemed limitless.

They bought passage on a boat as far as Porvenir, then journeyed overland to reach San Ignacio on September 1, 1914. There they made the acquaintance of a German businessman who broke the news to them.

"Guess what?" he said, with a regretful smile. "We're officially enemies." And he told them all he knew of the war that had begun in Europe.

"We must start for home right away," Fawcett said to Costin and Manley.

"With what?" asked Costin. "Didn't we determine we have about £4 among us?"

"If we can get to Santa Cruz, the Vice-Consul is holding the rest of my money, then we'll be fine..." Fawcett began.

"Not to worry," the German put in. "I'll lend you whatever money you need. I have an employee in Santa Cruz; you can repay me through him."

"Quite good of you," said Fawcett soberly. The German counted out some currency, and all of the men shook hands.

"Let us hope we meet again some day, under much better circumstances," said their friendly enemy, with a tip of his hat.

Two more weeks of walking, from dawn until dusk; the further necessity for rationing: two hard biscuits for breakfast, sardines and sugar for dinner. Yet they were amazed how well they did on this diet.

In Santa Cruz many Germans were celebrating with beer and parades. Fawcett went to see the British Vice-Consul, who told him that despite the clamor, there had been no violence or "incidents".

Fawcett retrieved his money, paid his debt to the German, and rented mules for the trip to Cochabamba.

In Cochabamba the men were wearily walking down the main road when they heard a hearty "Hallo, Englishmen!"

They whirled around to see the Nordenskiölds beaming at them.

"We couldn't believe our eyes when we spotted you! You made it back alive!" the Baron exclaimed, pumping each man's hand.

"Well, there was some doubt about that for a while," said Manley in his dry way.

"We asked after you at the barraca," Fawcett put in. "Where have you been?"

"We went downriver to stay with the Huari tribe, and then we roamed here and there. The Huari told us what we'd heard from other sources, that there are cannibals to the northeast."

"We found them, it seems!" Costin burst out.

The group spent the evening in a café catching up with one another's activities, at least when the famished Englishmen could stop eating long enough to recount their adventures. It was one of the last carefree dinners the three would have. Soon they were in the tense atmosphere of the Chilean ports, where both Germans and English prowled the piers for one of their own nation's ships to take them to Europe, where they would fight each other.

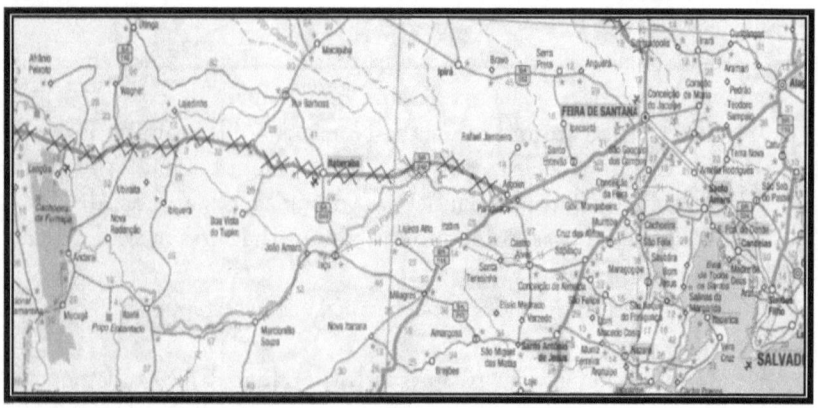

SYLVIA, CHAPTER 7
BAHIA

"*Oi*, Sylvia; *tudo bem?*"

"Paulo! Just fine. How about you?"

"I'm good. Are you busy?"

"Not really. Come on in, please." Sylvia pushed the keyboard tray into the desk and stretched her fingers; Paulo, standing in the door, hesitated a moment before entering.

"It's break time; help yourself to coffee. Can you pour me one, too?" Sylvia had discovered why IDA's coffee was so uninspiring: Brazil exported its premium brands, leaving mostly mediocre beans for its own citizens. She'd finally found one excellent variety, however, so she bought a small machine and brewed her own. Paulo went to the side table. Silently he poured himself a cup of black coffee, and prepared one for Sylvia with plenty of cream.

"Thanks. What have you been up to, Paulo? We haven't talked in a while."

He sipped appreciatively. "This is good; must be Pilão." He winked at her. "You're right, we haven't. I think you've been avoiding me the past few weeks." He looked her straight in the eye.

She took a couple of steaming swallows, stalling for a reply. "I'm sorry. I guess I have been."

"Because of Isabel? But why?"

She drew a long breath. "I suppose things seem a little awkward since you two broke up..." She shrugged.

"I don't understand that. You've always been friends with both of

284

us; why shouldn't you continue to be?"

"You're right, of course." Explanations were difficult. Sylvia felt her face flush with color.

"Isabel and I are still friends, Sylvia; you know that. So there's no reason you and I can't be. You don't have to choose sides, or concern yourself with divided loyalties."

"Thank you, Paulo. I value your friendship more than I can say. But listen, isn't there any chance you two can work things out?"

He shook his head. "We have utterly divergent goals. Our fundamental differences make a permanent relationship unworkable."

Sylvia smiled inwardly at his formal use of English.

"We stopped—as you say, pounding a round peg in a square hole," he added.

An unfortunate metaphor, she thought. "Yeah, I know Isabel's sad, but she says both of you feel a kind of relief."

"That's the word, exactly. So, Girl-of-the-Forest, is there any reason at all that you should feel uncomfortable with me? Or that we should be less friendly than before?" He watched Sylvia's face with sharp eyes. He had not missed the pinkness that rose to her cheeks.

"No, and I'm glad we've talked. Truly."

"Good! Now prove it: Let's go to the Roxy after work; I want to see that movie before it leaves."

"Uh—"

"Come on, no excuses. I heard you tell Ana you're dying to see it."

"Well..."

"Isabel doesn't mind! I told her I was going to have this conversation with you today."

"All right. Okay. Oh, of course she wouldn't mind..."

"See you at six, then. Thanks for the Pilão." He smiled and stood up. "I'll return your cup later; I'd better get back to work."

Sylvia sat for a while after he left, unable to concentrate on her own work. When she returned from her trip to Goiás and Tocantins, she had dined with Isabel and Paulo, who were eager to hear her impressions of everything. Though their continual questions kept her talking, she sensed something had changed between them. A few weeks later Isabel told her they'd mutually decided to call it quits. She was handling it well, and seemed to want to move on with her life now that it was crystal clear she and Paulo had no future. Sylvia followed her lead and left it at that; if Isabel wanted to talk about it, she was available to listen.

*

"Shall we walk?" he asked.

"Yes, let's. I need the exercise. And it's such a beautiful evening." A fresh breeze ruffled Sylvia's hair. It was August, one of the coolest months of the year in Brazil.

"Then why don't we take the beach path?"

The two turned toward the ocean and walked one long block to the wide sidewalk along Copacabana's strand. Sylvia felt a lightness, like a girl let out from school.

"Look at the color of the sky," she waved her hand toward the flaming crimsons.

"Quite a sunset!" Paulo also had a spring in his step. He inhaled the sea air deeply.

There was a juice bar ahead. "Let's stop, Paulo. We have time. "

"'Ta bom."

"Caju," Sylvia told the barman. Paulo laughed.

"You always get caju," he chided her. "There are so many other choices, look: acerola, guava, jaboticaba, maracujá, cupuaçu—"

"I know, but I'm hooked. If they could get it in the U.S., people would go crazy. They've never heard of the cashew *fruit* there, just the nut."

"I think there isn't enough of the juice produced to export."

"Well, Brazil exports most of the best of their other products, like shoes, coffee... I'm glad, actually, there's something's left for only Brazilians to enjoy."

Paulo turned to the barman, who waited patiently for his order. "Caju," he said, smiling at Sylvia.

They walked on. The brilliant colors of the sky were fading in the west, and eastward, stars appeared in the darkening blue background. "Twilight is my favorite time of day," she told Paulo. "What's yours?"

"Oh, I like twilight, too. And I think I'd like sunrise, if I ever saw it."

Sylvia laughed with understanding. "I don't see too well at that hour, myself."

They saw an American movie at the Roxy, a nice-enough theater except for a strong musty smell. Sylvia had been delighted to discover Brazilians prefer subtitles to dubbing; she could hear the dialogue in English and learn a little Portuguese from the captions. She went often to the movies, which helped allay homesickness.

"You Brazilians must be prudes," she teased Paulo, whispering; "They change all the profanities to mild words. And anything that's too earthy is translated into something else entirely!"

"What a gyp! Maybe I should pay more attention to the English."

After the movie, they walked to a nearby restaurant for dinner. A vision of Isabel, dining alone, kept popping into Sylvia's head.

"You look serious," observed Paulo as they sat down. "Are you thinking about Isabel?"

"You're too clever for your own good, sometimes. Or maybe I'm too obvious." That was an unsettling thought.

"Loyalty is a fine trait. I can't fault you for it." The waiter appeared, and they were distracted by the subject of food for a few minutes; by the time they finished ordering, Isabel had vanished from the scene.

"Paulo, what did you do when you worked for FUNAI?"

"I was an Indian agent. I worked out in Rondonia most of the time, out of Porto Velho, where the tribes were dealing with drastic changes in their lives."

"Due to the Trans-Amazon Highway?"

"Generally, yes. The road enabled absentee landowners of the big plantations and cattle ranches to bring in thousands of migrant workers, with the government's help and blessings, and they cleared forest, put up barbed-wire, and basically ran the Indians out. What indigenes are left—because many were killed— have been relegated to a few reservations in outlying areas. There were violent feuds out there... Still are, because now, of course, there are clashes with the *sem terras*."

"Oh, yes, the landless families... "

Paulo nodded. "They're exploited by those holding most of the wealth and property. But there are *sem terras* all over Brazil, not just Rondonia. You might say that's part of our legacy from the Portuguese. From the very beginning the élite were awarded vast tracts of land by the crown, and the workers were either slaves or peons."

"Why did you leave FUNAI?"

Paulo was silent for a moment. "There were several reasons, but I think the primary problem was that I was lonely. As you know, my wife died."

"In an accident."

"She was crossing the road, and a *gato*, a 'wildcat' who worked for one of the big landowners, ran her down in his truck. He didn't even stop. He was drunk."

"Was he arrested?"

"No, he disappeared…" The waiter arrived with an appetizer tray. "*Obrigado.*" Paulo served Sylvia a few items from the tray, adding, "It was a long time ago, and I've let go of my anger. I've even managed to forgive the imbecile."

"Then you came to Rio."

"My family is in Minas, so it isn't too far from them, and I prefer Rio to São Paulo."

"That makes two of us."

He smiled. "By the way, I saw something on the Internet about SIVAM the other day. You know, they're really moving ahead with this project." Paulo had evinced great interest in SIVAM when Sylvia showed him the Raytheon folder.

"You've been keeping up with the news on it?" she asked, a little surprised.

"Somewhat. You know, they have to do something to manage the region better, many problems in Amazonas get more critical all the time; and now they finally have the means. The Brazilian government loves grand projects, so this is in their alley—up their alley? Anyway, maybe *this* scheme will turn out right."

"Let's hope."

"Artur de Almeida appears to be trying to interest you in SIVAM, doesn't he?"

"Hmph. Well, it appeals to me on several levels, I'll admit. But I'm enjoying my life in Rio, and my work at IDA."

Their entrees arrived, and the focus turned once again to food.

"I hope you aren't getting tired of travelling, dear."

"To the contrary, Julia! I get to see Brazil on IDA's dime."

"I'm glad you're making the most of it. All right, here's the information you'll need for Salvador and Lençois. Regarding Lençois, though it seems a long way to go for such a small town, the enthusiasm there is so great we couldn't refuse. But I do wish you'd give up this idea of driving from Salvador."

"People drive around the state of Bahia all the time. I don't see why I shouldn't, just because I'm not Brazilian. I take rentals out on weekend excursions without problems." Julia was the third person to try and talk her out of it, though their cautions were vague and un-convincing.

"I know, you take care of yourself well, and your Portuguese is flu-ent now..."

"See, since I'm renting a car to get around Salvador anyway, I want to keep it and drive around the Chapada Diamantina while I'm over there. I don't think I could rent a car in Lençois."

"No, but that's what guides are for!"

Sylvia sighed. It seemed no one in Rio, with the exceptions of Isabel and Paulo, understood her aversion to sightseeing with guides.

Julia laughed and threw up her hands. "Americans are so inde-pendent! Even women. You know, maybe I envy that. You're cer-tainly a 'free spirit'."

After she left, Sylvia looked over her road map again. Maybe she was overconfident, and Julia and the others were right. It was over 250 miles from Salvador to Lençois, but part of it was a major truck route so it couldn't be *too* bad.

Sylvia stared at the idol; it didn't look at all as she had expected. A smiling male figure, standing against a background of bricks or squares, held a tablet bearing columns of hieroglyphics. He wore a simple headdress and his feet appeared to be bare. *Where is it now, I wonder? Did Fawcett take it back where it belonged, or is it adorning the hut of an indigene, or lying in the mud of an unmapped forest?*

She thumbed through other pictures in Hermes Leal's book, *Coronel Fawcett: A verdadeira história do Indiana Jones (A True History of Indiana Jones)*, recommended by Gloria. She kept returning to the two photos, side by side, of Fawcett and his son Jack. The young man was, as one writer had described him, movie-star handsome in the style of the 1920s. He took after his father. Fawcett's picture showed him as a man of 56 years, in a business suit, beardless, mustached. He emanated strength and vitality in his posture and expression, and to her eye he was even more attractive than his son.

In 1996, trying to retrace Fawcett's journey, Leal had gained per-mission to enter Parque do Xingu; there, he and his men encoun-tered serious problems with the Kalapalo, who were angry because they hadn't been given some sort of payment. The men's lives were threatened, their vehicles stolen and stripped, and other expensive equipment was taken. Sylvia's experience in Brasilia began to make even more sense and she had to laugh, sincerely glad she wasn't rich enough to go to the Xingu region. There was nothing to be learned there, she was sure.

Of more interest to her were the rumors of the Xavante that Leal reported. The city described to Fawcett, near a waterfall forming a lake with a quartz statue of a man in the center, was said to be at the hub of a ring of protective Indians; and these were the Xavante. Leal also recounted rumors Fawcett had a son or grandson with an Indian woman, possibly a Xavante. Nowhere in Fawcett's memoirs could Sylvia find mention of the Xavante, and she wondered if this had been deliberate, perhaps part of his desire to cover his tracks and lead rescuers or followers away from that region.

"Hi, Paulo," she said, as he entered her office. "Look at this."

"Are you working on your lunch break? I came to drag you away for a meal with Julia and me."

"I thought I'd spend my lunch here, translating the book I told you about, on Fawcett. Look at his birthdate." She put her finger on a line of text.

"August 31, 1867. Oh! The same birthday as you."

"Yes! Funny I hadn't come across that fact before, though I knew the *year* he was born. So, we're both Virgos."

"One more item for the list of similarities between you two."

"You think we're similar?"

"You know that you are. Maybe you're his reincarnation. Come on, Julia's found a new place and we're starving."

"Thanks for the invitation, but I have a pizza coming, soon, I hope."

While she waited for her food she perused some of the information she'd gleaned from the Internet, including a physical map of South America. According to geologists, prior to the Miocene epoch most of Amazonia was an inland sea opening to the Pacific Ocean. As the Central Andes rose, this sea became a lake, which eventually began to drain into the Atlantic. Fawcett theorized Brazil was once a large island, and was colonized by people from another island lying either to the west or the north. These may have been the Toltec people, who were said to be of light copper skin color and delicate features, blue eyes, and auburn hair. They wore white or sometimes colored robes woven of fine-textured cloth. He claimed to have himself seen Indians with blue eyes and auburn hair among tribes having no prior contact with modern races of any kind, including the Portuguese or Spanish people.

Many questions of past geologic events, and aspects of current geography, plants, and animal life are open for debate among scientists, she ruminated. *But in short, no one has ever proven Fawcett wrong.*

She was also interested in possible connections between South America and the Middle East. The evidence included numerous Semitic names in Brazil and other countries, such as Solimões, or Solomon, the native name of the Amazon; and inscriptions which were in a phonetic alphabet rather than glyphs. She read of a tradition that the ships of King Solomon, and King Hiram of Tyre, had made voyages regularly to a top-secret location in South America where they obtained valuable resources and much of their fabled riches.

Come with me, and I'll show you King Solomon's Mines. Her dreams were beginning to make more sense now. The mines weren't in Africa... They were in Brazil all the time?

She found intriguing connections with ancient Greece. Amazonas' namesake tribe, for one thing. In the 1500's a Spanish expedition led by Francisco de Orellana explored the Amazon River in search of El Dorado, finding instead a tribe of fierce warrior women bearing bows and arrows and each "fighting like ten men". The Spaniards were impressed by their similarity with the classical Greek "Women Who Live Alone" and who cut off one breast, the better to draw their bows, and named the river for them. A similar tribe had existed in Assyria.

Another subject of her research was the widespread tradition held by many South American indigenes, such as the Tupis, that they had either sprang from or were once under the control of a highly advanced white race. The Incas had built their cities upon earlier ruins and appeared to have restored some of the previously-built structures for their own use. They, too, believed they had descended from a white race of gods, one factor, no doubt, leading to the ease with which they had been subjugated by the Spanish.

She was typing "lost tribes" into the search engine when her pizza arrived. *Food trumps all,* she thought, cancelling the search and logging off. *See you later, Fawcett.*

*

Oh, no! This looks like the same roundabout I've been around about three times! I'll never get out of Salvador... Don't they believe in road signs?

Finally, totally beaten, Sylvia pulled over at the side of the road, turned off the motor, and let her head drop onto the steering wheel. She needed to come to a full stop and recover her calm; she was literally going in circles. Brasilia had been a piece of cake by comparison with the maelstrom of Salvador's traffic.

Then the angel appeared. A young man on a beat-up motorcycle stopped beside Sylvia's open window, and asked if she was all right.

"Oh, I guess so... I'm just lost! People give me directions, but it doesn't help."

"Where are you trying to go?"

"I'm looking for the main highway, 324. Then I'm going to Lençois."

He smiled in a knowing way. "Oh, yes, it's confusing. We need some signs. Do you think you can follow me? I'll lead you to 324."

"You don't mind? Is it far out of your way?"

"A little, but it's okay. Shall we?"

She started the car. For ten or fifteen minutes she followed the motorcycle through a maze of roundabouts and side streets. It was obviously a long way out of his way; he hadn't even been heading in the same direction. At last he stopped and motioned her to pull up beside him.

"You see the large white sign down there?" She nodded. "That's the turn for 324." He started to turn his motorcycle around to head back, with a smile and a wave.

"Wait! This was a long way for you." She fished in her bag for a ten-real bill. "Here, for your gasoline."

He tried to wave it away. "No, anyway, that's too much..."

"Your time is worth something; thank you!" She reached out and thrust the bill into his shirt pocket, and before he could object again she took off toward BR 324, impressed as always by the extraordinary kindness of strangers in Brazil.

Now she entered the hustle and fumes of highway traffic, finally free of Salvador. After the suburbs had been left behind, she passed through many miles of sugar cane, more cane than she had imagined existing in the world. What was here before? she wondered; probably forest, like the small wooded areas she saw here and there. Feira de Santana came up, and at the junction with BR 116 she stopped to buy an icy guaraná, and chatted with the clerk.

"I'm going to Lençois. Is highway 242 easy to find?"

"Oh, *sim*, you can't miss it." (Those four words that struck her with terror...)

A man standing at the counter chimed in. "You can if you don't look sharp. I don't think there's a sign."

"Oh?" Sylvia's alarm bells were ringing. "So how can I spot it?"

"Well, it's at Paraguaçu, and there's a service station there."

"And if you come to Itatim, you've gone too far," the clerk added.

As she walked back to the car, she thought, *Maybe everyone was right; this isn't such a good idea, driving.*

Truck route or no, BR116 apparently didn't qualify for maintenance funds. Sandwiched between trucks, she couldn't see the bone-jarring potholes come up. Tension clutched her shoulders. There was nowhere safe to pull over, and it would've been fruitless; the trucks were legion, inescapable. "Ow!" Another crater. No wonder all the rental cars looked half-wrecked. To her great relief she eventually saw a sign for Paraguaçu, and a service station coming up.

When she made the turn everything abruptly changed. Route 242 had been resurfaced as smooth as silk, and there was no traffic at all. She crossed the Paraguaçu River and flew along, ascending into rolling hills and open countryside, flowers, sweet air. The little road wound through miles of green meadows and occasional farmhouses, and at last she was glad to be behind the wheel of a car.

Despite the scenery, fatigue set in; the road seemed to go on forever. At the small farm village of Itaberaba, approximately the halfway point of her journey, she stopped to rest and eat the boxed lunch she'd brought. Then she drove on and on. It had been a long day, beginning with an early morning meeting in Salvador; and now it seemed as if she would never reach Lençois. Perhaps it had been a mistake to make a drive of this length on unknown roads. Why hadn't she listened to people? She passed no more farms or villages. Night fell, and she was still winding around the hills, feeling as if she were chasing a mirage.

She was now far into the hinterlands, and all around her was darkness; for miles there were no lights of any kind, no other automobiles, no road signs. She had lost track of distance and time, and she fought to stay awake.

Then suddenly there it was, a sign reading, "Lençois 12 km" and an arrow pointing to the left. She slowed down just in time to make the turn. She was now on a straight road through more pitch darkness, and it was the longest 12 kilometers she had ever driven. *It seems so strange, a town this far from everything... Why and how do people live out here?* It was the enigma of Brazil, the remote pockets of civilization; the "how" was answered by the trucks that carried supplies and resources to and fro; the "why" was to be found in history, in the search for wealth and survival. She had read of the *garimpeiros*, diamond seekers who washed the pebbles of Lençóis' river, Ribeirão do Meio, and all the rivers that flowed through the chapada, in search of the special rocks the world would pay good money for.

At long last, she saw electric lights in the distance. After an eternity she drove into the town of Lençóis, population 8,000. She spotted a sign for the pousada Canto das Aguas, Song of the Waters, and pulled wearily into the parking lot. What good luck the inn had been easy to find.

When she opened the car door she heard flowing water. She dragged her suitcase into the stone building. The marvelous sound of a rushing river filled the spacious lobby and at once had the effect of bathing away some of her fatigue. Or maybe it was the negative ions, she reflected, generated by moving water. She felt refreshed, hopeful. She completed the *"chekin"*, one of the adapted English words, and was shown to her room by a teenaged boy. The river's voice overwhelmed all other sounds, flowing through her brain and cleansing away the strain of the long day.

From her window, she could dimly see the Riberão do Meio - May River—racing by, falling down a long, long slope through town. In daylight she'd discover how it flowed as if down huge stair steps, forming pools and then plunging downward to the next terrace. *I'll sleep well tonight, surrounded by the best "white sound" there is.*

The sun was already hot, and it wasn't yet ten o'clock. Sylvia shifted her day-pack and rummaged in it for her water bottle. The trail was well-travelled and easy to follow; she certainly hadn't needed a guide so far, and the only reason she could think of for the desk clerk to urge her to hire one was to enhance the local economy.

She could hear the Ribeirão do Meio on her left, roaring along, and soon she could see it. The trail led to the banks at a point where the river flowed down one of its typical slopes and into a large pool; but the water was roiling with sediment and rushing downward, so it wasn't a good spot for swimming. No matter. The attraction here was on the banks of the river, an extensive, treeless area composed completely of quartz, sparkling in the morning sunshine. Most of it was pink or green quartz, with both clear and milky crystals here and there. The water had carved out hollows of widely differing sizes and shapes and formed small pools, perfect for soaking. Here, the sediment had filtered out and the water was clear as glass. She had read there was so much quartz here that NASA personnel reported seeing flashes of light from the area.

She looked around; not a soul in sight on either side of the wide river. She slipped out of her sticky clothing and settled into one of the more appealing jacuzzis where bubbling water entered at one end and drained from another. Her tub was that of a fairy princess, lined with glistening crystals catching the sun. *Oh, Brazil! How many more secrets do you have?*

She played by the river all morning. Walking downstream where the banks rose higher and became earth, soil that sprouted shrubs and small trees, she found a tiny man-made dwelling nestled back into the bank and half hidden by greenery. Its sides were the natural rock, and it was fronted in rectangular stones, almost as carefully fitted and uniform in size as a brick wall. The roof was partly earth, it appeared, and palm thatch. There was a crude wooden door. In front of the hut was a makeshift bench.

Sylvia was filled with curiosity about the inside of the dwelling, but for all she knew the person who had made it was there, and she dared not approach and disturb his privacy... or hers? It was beautiful, in its way; an exquisitely simple hermit shelter in splendid surroundings. How would it be to wake up here, to bathe in one of the little pools and dry off in the sunshine? She backed away, wistfully.

Colonial Lençois remains in many ways as it appeared in the 1700s; narrow stone lanes, old buildings painted in various colors and covered with red tile roofs. It grew around a river where diamonds and other precious stones were found, and people can still be seen filtering the water into their wide, shallow pans.

Sylvia spent the late-morning hours before her meeting poking into shops and chatting with people. The streets began to bake as the sun reached its zenith, and in the main plaza she noticed a pousada called the Colonial, that looked quite old and interesting. Outside its door was a sign advertising cold beer, guaraná, and sandwiches, so she peeped in; a smiling young woman motioned her to sit down at a table near the door. Through a window she watched the activity on the plaza while she sipped her soft drink, imagining the streets bustling with *garimpeiros* in the town's heyday. Now it was quiet in the midday heat, and the people she saw didn't appear prosperous.

After she ate, with the help of friendly passersby she found the site of her meeting, a tiny pink building with a blue door and a blue, wood-shuttered window, sandwiched between two other buildings, one of them a charming yellow structure with peaked colonial windows. As she stood on the sidewalk admiring the old-style windows, the blue door opened and a grinning young man greeted Sylvia.

"You must be Doutora Garth! I'm Simon Alvorado. The others are inside." He motioned for her to enter. "We hold English language classes in this building in the evenings, for children of all ages, free of charge. I'm their teacher."

With Simon and two of Lençois' leading citizens, Sylvia outlined the arrangements they'd need to make for an IDA distance station. It would be set up in the back room of the building, and would be used by high school students who'd reached a certain minimum level of English proficiency, they told her. As in Tocantins, she suspected the sponsors had their own youngsters in mind, and she couldn't blame them; isolated as they were in the chapada, they wanted to bring the outside world to their kids. And they were, after all, doing something for all of Lençois' children by hiring Simon and providing the building for his classes.

"We'll think about this," one of them finally said. "We can get your television courses by satellite, and we hope to have Internet service very soon."

"Let us know what you decide. There's no hurry."

When she left, Simon walked her to the door, and they chatted for a while about the chapada.

"I understand that you'd like to roam around alone," Simon said. "But there are some definite benefits to hiring a guide. I think you're safe here, but the biggest problem is the lack of signage. You'll waste much valuable time trying to find things. The Chapada is quite large and many of its finest features are far apart."

"Why aren't there any signs?" she asked in consternation.

"The authorities install them, but they disappear."

Sylvia laughed. "I can guess who removes them."

Simon smiled wryly. "Yes, most likely the guides." He shrugged in that Brazilian way, which meant, Oh well, what is one to do? Nothing.

Back at Canto das Aguas for lunch, Sylvia sighed long and hard, gritted her teeth, and approached the counter. The desk clerk asked if he could help her.

"Yes, I'm sure you can. You told me you knew of a reliable guide..."

"Do you have your swimsuit?"

"I'm wearing it, under my clothes."

"You had a good breakfast? You brought a sandwich for lunch?"

"I ate a huge breakfast, and my daypack's full of food."

"And you say you like to walk? And swim?"

Sylvia nodded. "I'm a good hiker, most of the time, and I love swimming in rivers, the sea, anywhere."

"'Ta bom!" Augusto smiled approvingly. "Then let's go; I'll show you some exciting things." From what the desk clerk had told him, this one was adventurous. Pretty, too.

Maybe this will turn out all right, Sylvia was thinking. At least I don't have to worry about getting lost out there, and he probably knows about things that aren't on the tourist map... I can let him take care of all the details.

As they rode along the dusty side roads in Augusto's old car, Sylvia assessed her new guide. He was in his thirties, she figured, of slight build but wiry and strong. He was dark-skinned, of mixed ethnicity. He seemed good-humored, quick, and energetic.

They drove through bizarrely-shaped rock formations and dry scrub brush. The region was blessed with an abundance of rivers and streams, and wherever water was found there was lush growth, ravines, sinkholes, caves. Augusto stopped where the long, rutted road dead-ended near a verdant mountain.

"Leave your backpack here; sunglasses and shoes, too," he advised.

"Really?"

"You won't need anything but your swimsuit; trust me. The other stuff could be a problem." He began to peel off his clothing, leaving only his bathing trunks.

Sylvia did the same. He locked their belongings in the trunk, and they set off down a winding, roller-coaster trail through scrub forest. Sylvia's feet were tender, but the trail was smooth sandstone. In ten minutes they confronted a high, gray wall of rock. It appeared the trail ended there at the mountain face.

Augusto decided he may as well find out what kind of woman he was dealing with, right now.

"Are you brave?" he asked her, with a challenging smile.

"Uh—it depends; what did you have in mind?" She wasn't into rock-climbing.

He motioned her to follow him through shrubbery to a long, vertical crack in the rock. She could see it was possible to enter the mountain through this narrow crevice, but there was one additional element: It was flooded.

"It isn't dangerous, I promise; it's a matter of one's mind." He touched his forehead.

She understood. It was a psychological challenge, in a way. She nodded.

They entered the slit and soon were wading in clear water which became deeper with each step. Before long it was over their heads, and they moved along by grasping the rock on both sides and treading water, in a space only a little wider than their shoulders. The fissure curved, and they lost much of the daylight. Finally they reached what appeared to be the end; the crevice had widened a little and they were in very dim light, facing the solid rock.

"Easy so far, yes?"

"Yeah, I'm fine. What now?"

"You can swim underwater?"

Whoa. Sylvia suddenly flashed back to a lightning-quick review of a story she'd read in a magazine, as a child. It told of a boy who'd become trapped deep in an oceanside cave as the tide came in. Fearing the tiny space would fill and he'd drown, he was forced to swim through the long, low opening underwater, hoping he could reach open air before the tide pushed him back in. He'd had an ordeal of several tries before he made it to safety.

For some reason the story made an impact on young Sylvia, filling her with horror, and she never forgot it. "Well, I can..." she answered hesitantly. She swam underwater, but not in caves.

"It isn't a long swim at all. It's very easy. The opening is right here, at our knees. Watch." He dived beneath the surface, leaving her holding onto the rock in semi-darkness. In just a moment she heard him faintly calling. The water was a good conductor of sound.

"Can you hear me? I'm coming back now." She moved aside, and he reappeared. "Okay? I'd pull you through, but it's too narrow, so you'll have to swim by yourself." He added, seeing her hesitate, "As I said, it's mostly psychological."

If there was one thing that had been the hallmark of Sylvia's life, it was her efforts to defeat all fears that served no useful purpose. This was not, she trusted, a foolhardy thing to do, and it was high time to lay that old cave story to rest.

"I'm ready."

"All right, it's best if I go first. When I call, you can start. You'll see light ahead, just swim to it."

"Do we come back this way?" *Would I have to do this again?*

"No. There's another way back." He added, laughing, before he dived again: "On the route I would take ordinary tourists."

If she had had any more qualms, that erased them.

When he called from the other side of the rock barrier, she took several big breaths and dived underwater deeply enough to clear the rock above her, and began swimming. She could see light ahead; it really was a short distance. Joy replaced fear, unexpectedly. She saw Augusto's legs, and rose to the surface beside him. "Fun, eh?" he asked.

Fun! They were now in a somewhat larger chamber, and the air was fresh; they moved to the side of the widening gap and pulled themselves along a shelf toward the source of daylight. The low ceiling of rock above them rose as they moved into a lofty, bright cave, its walls shimmering with a silvery mineral; it was filled with aqua water as still and clear as a sheet of glass.

"Don't step on the bottom," Augusto cautioned. "There are sharp projections here that can cut your feet." They swam farther, and arrived at the mouth of the cave.

"Oh! It's so beautiful!" Sylvia's reward was a very large pool which extended as far into the open air as it had reached into the mountain. "An indoor-outdoor lake!"

They continued swimming, out into the warm sun; the long pool was ringed with thick forest, and no sign of mankind whatsoever. They swam to a sandy beach and came ashore to rest.

"The lake's called *Pratinha*, which means 'little silver'," Augusto said.

Sylvia could see why. The turquoise water seemed lit from below. "The bottom must be lined with the same mineral as the cave..."

"Yes, mica, or some other silica."

They lounged in the warm sun; the sky was sapphire and puffs of white cloud drifted by. Augusto did handstands on the flat rocks, showing off for Sylvia, and eventually he said, "Time to go see something else! We'll take the 'ordinary' route back." He winked, and she hopped up and followed him into the brush.

"If you like caves, I have a couple more."

"Uh-oh—"

"Ha! No more swimming, don't worry." He spun the car around a turn, its gears slipping. "There are many, many caves on the chapada," he went on, "and there are even some places that were only discovered by going through caves, because the undergrowth had hidden them for centuries."

Sylvia nodded, thinking about Poço Verde.

"You know, we have UFOs here; they've been seen by some people, seeming to fly out of the earth... They must be coming from hidden caves." He looked embarrassed. "Well, if you believe in that sort of thing..."

"Anything is possible."

Augusto took Sylvia to a cave called Lapa Doce, at the end of another long, dusty road. "There are no lights in the caverns," he explained as he readied an old-fashioned gas lantern. "I also brought two flashlights, in case the lantern fails."

It was quite a contrast to caves Sylvia had visited in the U.S. and Europe, with their electric lights, paved paths, handrails; even elevators. They walked the sandy bottom of the cave, Augusto carrying the heavy, hissing gas lantern and pointing out stalactites and strange, pale life forms that existed in the cave's shallow pools. They played Ghost with the flashlight: Extinguishing the lantern, they sat in darkness until their eyes had forgotten the light; when Augusto said "Now!" he jumped into the air as high as he could while Sylvia flashed the light on and off quickly, once. The instant of light, followed by utter blackness, formed an eerie, long-lasting image of Augusto floating in the air.

"My turn to be Ghost," Sylvia said, fumbling in the dark to hand

Augusto the light. They competed to see who could look the scariest, laughing hysterically at some of their poses, and were soon covered with fine sand from falling.

"Hey, if you don't have to rush home," Sylvia said as they drove back to town, "I'd like to buy you dinner." He had earned it.

"Sounds great, thanks!"

"And by the way, you said there were some terrific waterfalls on the chapada...?"

Augusto put his thumb up in the ubiquitous Brazilian gesture. "You bet! Would you like to see them tomorrow?" he asked hopefully.

She leaned back in the lumpy old seat of the rattling auto, tired but content. "I would. Let's have some more fun."

Augusto grinned. He would show this American lady his very best, secret spots on the chapada. She had earned it.

There was an unholy racket as the avalanche of garbage fell down, down, down Cantogalo Mountain.

Oh, no. Not again. Sylvia was having breakfast on her veranda when the trash began raining down on Copacabana. The first time it had happened, she was speechless. She had been crossing the courtyard, heading to her apartment, and when she ran to investigate the clatter she was aghast to see a cascade of trash of all kinds falling through the air, bouncing off the granite mountain, and coming to rest somewhere behind the apartment building.

"What's going on?" she had asked the moço on duty that evening.

"What, the trash?"

"Yes!"

"Oh," he shrugged distastefully. "It's coming from the favela. They have no city garbage collection up there."

"Why not?"

"Well, for one thing, there are no roads that a truck could use. And even if there were, no one would want to go up there to collect it, I think."

Holy cow. What a situation, Sylvia considered. They had to do something with their trash; and what irony that they could simply dump it upon the well-off residents of Copacabana Beach, and let them contend with it! But it disgusted her to see the trees adorned with plastic bags. She was beginning to see plastic bags as a modern curse; they swam in the sea, sprouted from trees and shrubs, strangled birds, blew down the sidewalks. And now they were falling again, along with dirty diapers, cans, glass bottles.

She dressed and walked to work. In a few weeks, she would celebrate one year of living in Brazil. She was comfortable with the language and most of the customs, but there were some things she'd never get used to. She stopped for her newspaper at the usual kiosk, exchanging a few friendly words with the seller.

At the next block a small crowd had gathered, an unusually quiet, somber-looking group. She paused to see what they were looking at, and immediately wished she hadn't. Two policemen were loading a dead body into the back of an official pickup truck. It was a man, his chest covered in dried blood, his legs stiffly bent in rigor mortis. He was young and poorly dressed, and she assumed it was a gang-related killing; like the majority of violent deaths in Rio. Now and then an innocent bystander caught a stray bullet, but for the most part it was intra-gang warfare that claimed most of the lives in Brazil's cities. That didn't make people feel much better. Life was cheap in Brazil, everyone said.

At work, she told her assistant, Ana, about the morning, though she tried to make light of it. Isabel had once said Brazilians suffered from an inferiority complex, sometimes despairing of their country ever realizing the "eternal potential" everyone talked about. But their day will come, Sylvia reckoned.

Close to lunchtime, the telephone rang and Ana answered it; soon she hung up and leaned her head around the glass divider.

"Oi, Sylvia; Julia wants you to come down to the conference room, if you have a moment."

"Sure."

Sylvia walked into the conference room and found everyone who worked on the floor crowded around the large table.

"Surprise!" They shrieked. *"Feliz Aniversário!"*

There was a big sheet cake on the table, some bottles of soda, cups, plates, chips, the works. She hadn't mentioned it was her birthday, thinking it would be a little childish; she'd forgotten Cariocas made a big fuss over birthdays. For the first time that day, she genuinely grinned as the group sang the familiar birthday song, in Portuguese and then in English, especially for her. They lit the candles.

"We put thirty-six candles; that's right, isn't it?" Ana, who had materialized behind her, asked mischievously.

"It's enough, thanks!" As she leaned over to blow them out, and the others drew in their breath to help in case she failed, she noticed the words iced onto her cake:

Feliz Aniversário, Sylvia & Fawcett

She looked quickly at Paulo, still holding her breath. He smiled.

"Did you make your wish?" someone yelled. Quickly a desire crossed her mind and, flustered, she released her breath on the little flames, missing a few which her friends rapidly extinguished.

Ana handed her a huge slice of cake. "You can save it for after lunch if you'd like," she said, "But we Brazilians eat our sugar at any time of day."

"Happy birthday, Sylvia," Paulo said. "I hope *all* your wishes come true."

Julia hugged her. "If you don't have plans for lunch, Paulo and I, and a few others, would like to take you to the Internacional. Remember that place?"

"Oh, how quickly a year has passed..."

"We hope you will spend many more years in Brazil," Paulo said.

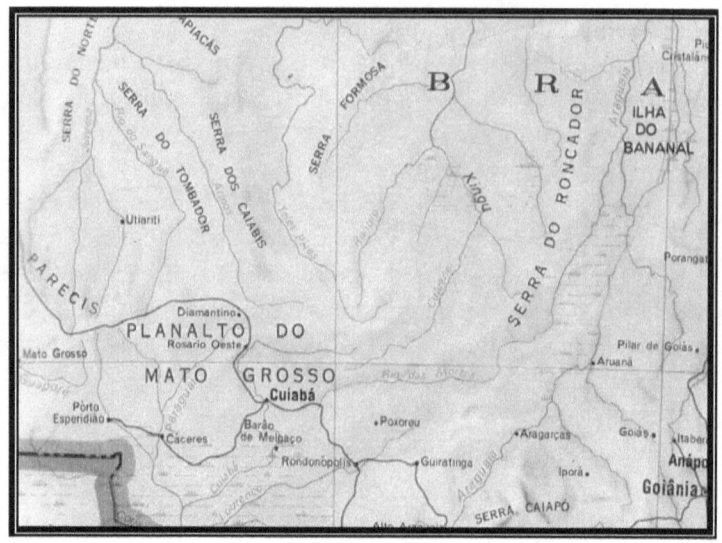

FAWCETT, CHAPTER 8
RIO CUYABA

February 8, 1920
Rio de Janeiro

From my vantage point atop the British Embassy's roof, this jewel of a city extends before me in all its sparkling beauty. By comparison our English cities are dull and grey. The coastline undulates from steep, dramatic rock formations to sand beaches and perfect coves with blue-green water, all of it dressed in tropical foliage and flowers. Even the people are arrayed in vibrant colors and gay smiles. And why shouldn't they be? If I could live here forever, I think I would also beam, and wear bright hues.

In fact, I've hatched a plan, sitting here over the Beira Mar Avenue: Assuming our finances will allow, when I've accomplished the goals of my exploration I shall bring Cheeky to a lovely home overlooking Rio's blue bay, where we'll live out the rest of our days together. How I wish she were with me now, but she is settling into a new home in Jamaica, and I do not expect to be here very long before beginning my next expedition.

My viewpoint may be jaundiced by the years of war, but Europe now seems to me a gloomy place, its glory days finished. It is no place to raise youngsters. Feeling so strongly, Cheeky and I decided this was the time to break free, and my little family is now enjoying the sunshine of the Caribbean. I invest my hopes in the Americas; their culture has a robustness and optimism which ours appears to have lost. In particular I place my bets on South America.

When I arrived last week I stayed in the International Hotel, and liked it very much until I realized it was beginning to fill with Germans, seeking refuge. Try as I might, no matter how I lectured myself, I could not overcome a visceral aversion; pure prejudice, I'm aware. The illusion we call "patriotism" has infected me as well as the next man, and it seems a millenium ago that I was friends with many Germans. The wounds, I fear, are simply too fresh, and I left the hotel with sadness and a sense of shame.

Sir Ralph Paget, Britain's Ambassador to Rio, insisted I stay with him at the Embassy residence, a lovely place, and here I find it easier to begin to let go of the past. Now that I'm once again in South America I wish to think as little as possible about the war.

I have enough of a challenge before me, which is the usual difficulty: that of financial backing for my expedition. I had no luck in England. As a Founder's Medallist of the Royal Geographic Society, I at least was heard, but it was obvious the elderly gentlemen who hold the purse-strings found my accounts too incredible. Ah, and such was the very existence of the Americas, incredible, until the voyage of Columbus! But we tend to learn little from the past, which is downright frightening sometimes.

Having connected with Brazil's President Pessoa when he visited London, and receiving his encouragement, I now pin my hopes on the ministers of his Cabinet whom I expect to address soon.

In the meantime, I'm savoring the magnificent vistas all around me, the wide boulevards, and an occasional jaunt by motorcar along the coast highway. I'm alone. Costin was with me during part of the war years, but he has since married and prefers to remain in England, understandably. Poor Manley made it through the war, but succumbed to a heart attack after everything was over.

As it happened, Fawcett remained in Rio six long months, trying first to see President Pessoa again, then to be heard by the ministers of the interior regions, and finally, awaiting their decision. But he filled the time to his advantage, researching the Brazilian wilds and talking to as many people as he could. Little by little he gleaned a great deal of intriguing information.

He discovered through talking to the Ambassador that the late British Consul at Rio had told of being taken by an Indian to see the ruins of a city, which was completely hidden in dense jungle. The Indian claimed that few people outside his tribe knew of these ruins. The Consul described the remains of a once-sophisticated city center, including a crumbling statue on a pedestal of black stone, in the city square.

The Ambassador also steered Fawcett to national archives located in Rio, where he thought it possible something of interest might turn up. And indeed it did.

After combing the dusty books and drawers for hours, Fawcett came to an eighteenth-century document written in Portuguese. Due to the similarity of Portuguese to Spanish he could decipher most of it, and an archive employee who spoke English helped him with the details. What he read sent a thrill down his spine.

In 1743, the unnamed author of the document, whom Fawcett decided to call Francisco Raposo, set out to find legendary gold, silver, and gemstone mines said to have been discovered over two hundred years earlier by a shipwrecked Portuguese mariner. With a party of about eighteen Portuguese and their slaves, he journeyed northward from the state of Minas Gerais; with no maps and little idea where to go, the group wandered about for a decade, finding nothing.

One day, traveling eastward through miles of alternating grassland and swamp, the sharp pinnacles of a mountain range appeared in the distance. Raposo determined to scale them to gain a wide view, and from atop a ridge the men were astounded to see a large, walled city, which at first they feared was a Spanish outpost. After hours of observation, followed by the cautious forays of scouts, it was determined the city was uninhabited.

The party proceeded to the city's grand entryway of three arches built of immense blocks of stone, blackened with age and reminiscent of other ancient South American ruins. Stricken with awe, the men stopped. Unknown characters were carved into the central arch. All was peaceful and still, but for the cries of birds. They walked into a ruined city of wide streets, tumbled blocks of stone, and broken columns, everything overgrown with vegetation. Some structures still stood intact, and many were constructed of huge blocks fitted together with precise mortarless joins. There were two-story buildings, A-shaped porticos, and carvings of people and animals which retained bits of color here and there. Some buildings had collapsed to rubble.

Farther along what was evidently the main avenue, the party reached a very large square. In its center on a column of black stone stood a statue of a man. One hand was at his hip and the other pointed straight ahead, to the north. Who was this person, and what did he mean to the inhabitants of this place? they all asked themselves. Carved obelisks occupied each corner of the square, and along one entire side was a stately building fronted by square columns and finely decorated with frescoes and carvings.

It was evident the city had been destroyed by a cataclysmic earthquake. The group encountered places where the earth had literally opened up and swallowed entire structures, leaving bottomless crevices.

Then one of the group found a gold coin, engraved with images that reminded them of Greece.

"So there's gold here!" Raposo's eyes lit. He divided the men into small parties and sent them in different directions to see what other surprises there might be, and to make maps, including landmarks to help them find the city again. He intended to return with a well-equipped expedition, suspecting there was tremendous wealth hidden in the rubble.

One of the groups returned with news of a silver mine, but another scouting party had something quite strange to report: a canoe on one of the lagoons, bearing two white people— the men were adamant on this point— with long, dark hair. They were wearing clothing, furthermore, of an unfamiliar design. When they saw the intruders, they rapidly disappeared down a creek.

Raposo and his band crept away as quietly as possible, edging their way eastward. Months later they arrived at the São Francisco River and continued on to Bahia. Raposo sent the document Fawcett was now reading to Viceroy Don Luiz Peregrino de Carvalho Menezes de Athayde, but nothing more was known of the story afterward.

Almost a hundred years later, Fawcett discovered, a government official came across the document and launched an investigation, but the expedition had no success in finding any ruins.

At last Fawcett was able to present his proposal to the Cabinet ministers, and after a long delay, he received good news: The Brazilian government would fund an expedition, including equipment, two Brazilian officers, and another officer of Fawcett's choosing; however, no salary for Fawcett himself would be provided. He happily agreed.

The months he had had to wait had proven invaluable, for after his discovery of the Raposo document he had continued to comb all the archives he could get his hands on in Rio and in the state capital of Niteroi. He had unearthed enticing tidbits of information from various sources, archival and human, finding his habit of friendly conversation worked as well in Rio as it had in the wilderness.

Best of all, the reports he had ferreted out tended to corroborate what he'd learned while in the forests. The pieces of the puzzle were coming together in a most satisfying and exciting way, but he made a decision to keep most of it to himself. If he had learned one thing in the wilderness, it was that a small party of men with stamina and the right attitude had a much greater chance of success than a large group of oafs stampeding through Indian villages; and as far as survival went, often the forests supplied enough sustenance for a few men, where a large group might starve. He had no use for adventure-seekers tagging along, or following, so he became close-mouthed about his sources and conclusions.

Fawcett had a British officer in mind who was his first choice to accompany him and who had expressed his willingness when the two spoke back in England. But an exchange of cables brought the disappointing news that the officer was no longer available. A friend of Fawcett's in Rio came to the rescue with a fellow named Felipe, whose cheerful enthusiasm helped to quell Fawcett's concerns about going into the wilderness with a man about whom he knew so little.

Meanwhile, General Cândido Rondon, known for his aid to the 1914 Roosevelt expedition to the Rio Duvida, began making arrangements for two Brazilian officers to rendezvous with Fawcett and Felipe in Corumbá. The General had a great deal of useful advice for Fawcett.

"If I were you, I'd take two horses and two oxen; you can ride the horses as far as possible, then beyond that point the four animals will still be useful for carrying your gear... at least for a while. When large animals can't proceed any farther through the growth you'll have to carry your gear on your backs, but by then you'll have eaten most of the food, anyway."

On August 12, the two men left for São Paulo. They wanted to make a visit to the Butantan Snake Farm, where a wide variety of venomous snakes were used to manufacture antivenin. Fawcett had been told that the sera produced there were life-saving after bites from even the deadliest snakes. He and Felipe left with a copious supply, hoping they wouldn't need any of it.

They journeyed by rail to the Paraguay River, and by steamer to Corumbá, where Fawcett received a telegram and another disappointment: A government official apologized, but the officers would not be able to accompany him due to "governmental finances".

"This is very serious," Fawcett murmured, running his hand over his head. It meant that if Felipe, for any reason, would not or could not continue, Fawcett would have to give it up and return, once more stymied. But what could he do? Sit around and wait until Brazil resolved its financial pinch?

So Fawcett and Felipe continued on to Cuyabá, resigned to carrying on as a party of two. Fawcett tried to impress upon the young man something of the commitment he was making.

"We will be in the forests for a minimum of eighteen months," he stressed, repeating the terms specified when Felipe was hired on. "We're headed into unknown, unmapped regions, beyond the headwaters of the Cuyabá River. We won't attempt to come back the way we came; my plan is to return via one of the other primary rivers, which we should eventually run across."

"I understand, Colonel."

"And remember that at some point the animals will be unable to continue, and we'll be carrying our gear on our backs."

"Yes, yes. I'm quite prepared. And I'm most excited about the birds we'll encounter in these wild lands; surely there are new and unknown species! I hope you'll allow me a little time to observe, and sketch...?"

"Of course; you should have ample opportunity to study birds, as long as you keep in mind our overriding goal."

"The ancient cities, yes, Colonel."

Fawcett regarded the young fellow, whose enthusiasm seemed to exceed his strength. He suppressed a sigh, deciding to hope for the best. If he turned back now the money already spent was wasted, and he was unlikely to receive further funds from the Brazilian Government; at least not any time soon.

The two men headed north from Cuyabá, on a trail following the river of the same name. They rode horses and led two oxen which carried their supplies, as General Rondon had advised. Along the way they found no shortage of hospitality— or rumors.

"If you keep going north you'll run into the Morcegos," stated Colonel Hermenegildo Galvão, at whose ranch they were spending the night. "I don't think you would find *them* very hospitable," he added ominously.

"Morcegos?" echoed Felipe. " 'Bat People'?"

"So they're called, because they only come out at night. During the day they live in holes in the ground. They're primitive brutes, like apes, who'll kill you on sight."

"We'll try and steer clear of them," said Fawcett politely, privately wondering if the Morcegos were cut of the same cloth as the Maricoxi, or if the stories were as exaggerated as most of the other tales of savages had been. But with the Maricoxi still fresh in his memory, (despite the intervening horrors of European-style warfare) and given his doubts about Felipe, he'd play it safe this time and try to avoid trouble.

He was far more interested in the Colonel's account of local rumors concerning Indian cities beyond the Xingu River, cities containing temples with baptismal fonts, and buildings lit by "stars" that never burned out. This mysterious form of lighting described by Colonel Galvão provided further corroboration of tales he'd heard from other sources. Legends widely repeated by far-flung groups of people who could never have made contact with each other probably had, he reasoned, at least some bases in truth.

After a number of nights spent along the river at friendly estancias, Fawcett and Felipe arrived at the headwaters of the Rio Cuyabá. With the last cattle ranch behind them, they prepared to strike off into a wilderness populated only by little-known Indian tribes of dubious reputation.

The terrain was shot through with small rivers and streams, often creating immense bogs in between. The first inconvenience they encountered were anacondas, which seemed almost as numerous and pesky as the myriad ground ticks and tiny flies, or piums. Then they entered the domain of the wasp, and the other pests seemed like butterflies by comparison.

"Deus!" screamed Felipe, as a legion of inch-long wasps stung his face ten, twenty, thirty times. Fawcett, gasping with pain, was busy beating the little demons from his own face and neck. Even worse was the very small variety which preferred to attack the eyes.

"Try not to panic," Fawcett yelled, as Felipe, crashing madly around in the brush, stirred up even more of the furious insects. "Remain calm!"

The animals began to tire. There came a day when Fawcett decided his horse was too weak to carry his weight, and after shifting some of the cargo to the horse's back he continued afoot.

During the sixth week one of the oxen collapsed, and had to be shot. The dwindling supplies were divided among the other animals.

In the seventh week, the two men awoke one morning to see that Felipe's horse was not where he had tied it.

"I'm not too surprised if it pulled free, I must say," Fawcett remonstrated. "You can't just casually loop the lines— "

"Uh, oh." Felipe's tone stopped Fawcett mid-lecture. He was looking off into the bog, where lay a large, dark hump protruding from the water. The two men dragged themselves through hip-deep water to find the poor beast drowned.

"Looks as though it got stuck in the mud and sank deeper and deeper," said Fawcett. "Wonder why it made no cries of distress? Maybe we could've pulled it free."

"If it sank quickly enough, its head was under before there was time to squeal, perhaps. Anyway, what now?"

Fawcett looked at him. "Obviously, you'll be walking, as I am."

Felipe's expression made it plain what he thought of that idea.

"Go on without me, Colonel. It's all right, leave me, or shoot me like the ox..." Felipe moaned, holding his head in apparent agony.

Fawcett stood over the young man, concern mingled with intense frustration. He had to bite his tongue to keep from saying, "Don't tempt me!" Ever since Felipe's horse had died, he'd developed one complaint after the other. When his legs became stiff and sore from the unaccustomed exercise he was convinced a serious childhood ailment had returned which, he said, had affected his muscles. Now his head felt as if it were splitting apart, he claimed, and his heart was threatening to quit on him.

What had quit, Fawcett felt, was Felipe's spirit; though he had no doubts the fellow suffered various pains, their origins were, in Fawcett's opinion, psychological. He had lost all motivation to be there.

"Let me think for a moment." Fawcett walked away from Felipe and sat on a log, swatting at the eternal biting flies that went after the same spots on one's skin until the area was red, raw, and burning with pain. His mouth was dry, and he knew thirst was one cause of Felipe's pounding head, as his head ached, too. In this exceedingly dry, hot forest they had found no water for thirty-six hours and had had to strictly ration the little they had left.

Earlier in the afternoon, as they had made camp early to allow Felipe to rest, Fawcett's horse collapsed, dying, and he shot it. Now only one ox remained, a clever animal that had an instinct for the best route; the men had learned to let it take the lead through the maze-like bogs. Perhaps losing another animal had been the last straw for Felipe, Fawcett mused; they were not only on foot, they were forced to carry more and more of their equipment.

Fawcett sat with heavy heart; another failure stared him straight in the face. He considered his options: He could let Felipe rest, then rouse him in a day or so, kick him in the rear and push him onward. But for what purpose? What use was Felipe to him now, in his weakened state, if danger arose? Another option was to send the young man back and keep going alone. He would have liked very much to do so, but he knew Felipe would never make it; he didn't have Fawcett's wilderness training or sense of direction.

That left only one choice. He would have to take Felipe back. Another expedition aborted, abandoned, wasted.

The two men had turned southward and were once more in the bogs. The abundance of water was a mixed blessing, as their feet were always wet and chafed, the raw skin falling away like onion layers. And still the piums bit and the wasps stung. But Felipe's mood seemed to improve with every mile closer to home that they covered.

Then as they crossed a stream, the faithful ox, its legs quivering, suddenly dropped into the water.

"Get it up! Pull it up!" shouted Felipe, tugging at the lines frantically.

"It's no use," Fawcett said. "The poor creature is dead."

The ox lay like a boulder in the stream, motionless.

There was nothing to do but stuff the load the beast had carried into their own packs, and struggle on. The next few days were grindingly hard, but Felipe was happy to know civilization was just around the bend, even when he nearly collapsed from sunstroke.

At last the two reached an estancia where there was plentiful food and a chance to attend to their feet, which were in serious condition. After a couple of days they limped on, until they came to a ranch where they were able to borrow mounts for the remainder of the journey to Cuyabá. It was over.

*

Bahia. At least here there was something to look forward to, something that might lift his depression. Having made his goodbyes to Felipe, who was happily off to his mother in Rio, Fawcett now turned his steps toward the Consulate. There he picked up his mail.

When he was settled into his hotel room he at last sat down to sort his letters. He took the pile that was from Nina and the boys and arranged them by postmark date. Finally he began to read, starting with the earliest letters. Only when he'd finished the stack did he delve into the other pieces of mail. Then he read the letters from his loved ones once more.

He longed for his family, yet he couldn't go back to them with a total sense of failure hovering about him like a cloud of gloom. What next? he asked himself for the hundredth time since Felipe fell apart. He sorely missed Costin, and Manley, the only two companions he'd ever been able to rely on for the physical and mental fortitude to bear the rigors of exploration. How he wished his firstborn, Jack, now eighteen, was old enough to join him; now, there was a strapping young man! With an attitude to match.

Serious doubts began to surface, uncertainty about the very existence of any hidden cities. It could all be based upon the quivering sands of myth, a mirage, and perhaps he should admit defeat now. If his own faith was waning he could hardly expect to motivate other men to risk their lives chasing a chimera.

Fawcett's stubbornness came to his rescue, dragging him from the doldrums. He would *not* leave Brazil without some gain in knowledge to show for the time and effort spent here, and then he *would* put together another expedition, the next time a proper one. To reach the first goal he'd take a step he had many times threatened: He would set out alone. And high time. Better to take the risks involved in solitude than to once more curtail his plans in order to bring someone back. But he didn't blame them. Exploration sounded glamorous until you got out there where reality chipped away at your resolve.

The Brazilians had a saying, the gist of which was that it was better to be alone than in bad company. He couldn't agree more.

Fawcett knew he was not invulnerable. He knew he could fall ill or injured, and he had discovered what a case of "nerves" felt like. But he had several personal qualities, to begin with, which most other men lacked. He was a lone wolf by nature, and this self-sufficience gave him the psychological and spiritual strength needed to spend long periods far from civilization. He was also extremely disciplined. Men accustomed to self-indulgence, whether in drink, food, or women, found it hard to bear the deprivations of the wilderness; but Fawcett, by nature sparing and abstinent, had been further toughened by his grueling years in the forest. He had never had much of an opportunity to be softened by comfort or security.

Having made his decision, his first step was to order lightweight versions of the instruments he'd need for navigating the wilds, since he would be carrying them by himself and he couldn't depend on having pack animals throughout the journey. After the cable was sent, he used his waiting time to research a route and pick the brains of the locals.

He now had arrived at an opinion of the general location of the city he called "Z". There was more than one way to reach the area, and this time he wanted to avoid the long trek to Mato Grosso and approach his goal from the east.

He had turned up some intriguing reports of strange inscriptions carved into rock, and fine ceramics found deep in the forest. He was told of an old man who had become lost somewhere near Conquista, and later described an abandoned city he had found which sounded a great deal like Raposo's city, right down to the statue in the square. The locations didn't tally, but Fawcett had learned how vague and unreliable local accounts of regions and distances could be. The people, particularly Indians, often had little idea what was to be found outside the area where they lived. Tales of other places had been passed down, but their estimates of distance, measured by number of days' walking it would take to reach them, were often wildly inaccurate.

When the instruments arrived Fawcett set out from Bahia, using a railway which pierced the interior as far as the diamond fields where people were madly washing the gravel, most of them wasting their lives in a craze for stones. As he travelled inland he gazed at miles upon miles of forest, thinking what fine timberland it was; Brazil, he saw, held a wealth of resources such as the oil deposits he had noted near Cobija, waiting to be exploited.

The line ended in Bandeira de Mello, where he spent the night; and the following day he chartered mules to the town of Lençois, beside a rushing river lined with banks of pink and green quartz. The diamond trade was lively in Lençois, at the west end of the conglomerate mountain range; garimpeiros, most of them desperately poor and many diseased, roamed the streets.

Fawcett explored the cobbled lanes of the colonial village, with its charming structures painted in various pastels, until he found a tidy-looking inn on the plaza, aptly named Hotel Colonial. After checking in he again ventured out to purchase one mule for a mount and another as a pack animal.

When he struck out alone with only a rough idea of his route or when he would return, a sense of freedom filled him, rejuvenating him in body and mind. He realized that although he would have no human help in a tight spot, and no witness in the event of a discovery, for compensation he would have no drain on his energy from prodding or reassuring a failing companion, no need to explain or justify his decisions; and no worries about his responsibility for the health and safety of another man.

Initially he was keenly aware of his solitude, even a bit lonely. It took some getting used to. But once he had adjusted, he liked it. He found profound peace in the wild land, with only himself for company, and his patient mules.

After several days' journey beyond the frontier, he found an interesting thing happening. The best word he knew for it was "attunement". For the first time he could imagine how, for example, the ox had known the best routes, and how birds have a sense of what berries might be safe to eat. His own senses were beginning to tell him things. He tested them constantly, for when he acted on his instincts the results were favorable, and when he deliberately ignored the urges, there were difficulties of one type or the other.

The best examples of this were in the paths he chose. Rarely did he have to backtrack when he followed his intuition. He also seemed to find game quickly and easily by suspending thought as much as possible and arriving at a quiet place deep inside himself. Then he was able to sense where an animal might be hiding. He was reminded of the incident with the bushmaster, when his subconscious mind had taken over to assure survival. He decided human beings have such instincts buried within, but have lost touch with them due to the "noise" of their complex thoughts and concerns, and other distractions, such as speech. It was a valuable lesson; even if nothing else had come of the trek, this newfound insight would have made it worthwhile.

*

Fawcett stopped, dead still. It was not his imagination; after more than two months of roaming, he was weary, but not hallucinating. And the tremor he felt through his body wasn't fatigue, it was excitement. Without taking his eyes from the sight before them he fumbled in his pack and extracted a small telescope, paper, and pencil. He had been afoot, leading the mules through dense brush to the top of a hill. Now he left the beasts where they stood and hacked his way through the scrub until he had a clearer view. Then he began to sketch what he saw.

One month later, a bedraggled Fawcett approached the outskirts of Lençois, with his two mules. Now, his conviction was complete, his determination boundless.

He made his way back to the Colonial where he had stored the rest of his gear. After he bathed and put on fresh clothing, he went down to the little café for maté and a bowl of soup. He sat at a small table near the entrance and stared out the window at the quiet plaza. His mind was buzzing.

Now that I've seen the evidence for myself, I'll take whatever risks necessary to find what I know is there. "Me that 'ave seen what I've seen" *must follow this road to its end, or my years in the wild mean little. I've been spared, protected, and led for a purpose, I'm sure of it. Somehow I'll find the funds, the companions— and the precise route through the forest to "Z".*

There will be no more failures.

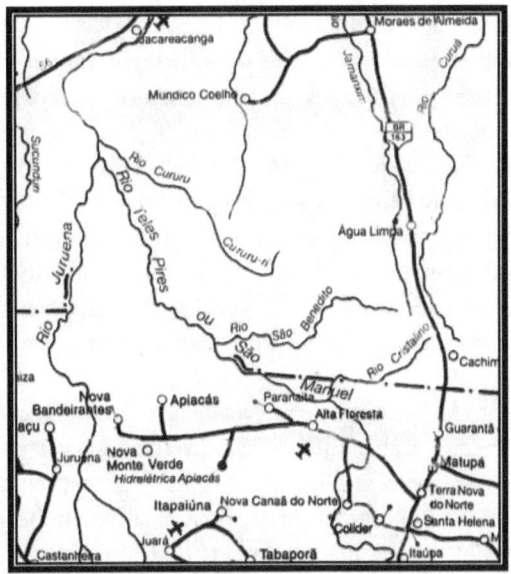

SYLVIA, CHAPTER 8
PARA

"May I speak to Doutora Garth?"

"This is she."

"*Boa tarde*, Sylvia, this is Artur de Almeida, from FUNAI."

"Artur! How nice to hear from you. How are you?"

"I'm fine. And you?"

"Very fine, thank you." *...And all the necessary civilities, etc. etc.; now, why is he calling?*

"How is your work on Colonel Fawcett going?"

"Oh, okay, I guess. Progressing slowly." *Should I mention I'm tearing my hair out in confusion these days, regarding the eminent Colonel?*

"Well, you're probably wondering why I've called. I'll be in Rio next week for a few days, and I wondered if I could make an appointment with you, perhaps take you to lunch...? There's something I'd like to talk to you about."

"Sure; lunch sounds great. My schedule's wide open next week. May I ask—"

"If you don't mind, I'd like to wait until I see you to explain what it's all about. How's Tuesday?"

So. He doesn't want to reveal anything. Maybe one question would lead to another, and that isn't the way he wants to handle it, whatever "it" is.

"Tuesday's fine. About 1:00?"

She hung up and wrote the appointment in her calendar. She tried to concentrate on work, but her curiosity was distracting. *It's either about Fawcett—he did ask how my work's going, though that may've just been courtesy—or it's about SIVAM. What else could it be?*

She finished for the day and walked home. There were no more business trips planned for the next few months; most of the distance stations currently practical to develop had already been covered. Most of her future work, for a good while, anyway, would involve site-support duties and curriculum management, done from her Rio office.

She spent the evening poring over her research on Fawcett. She had recently reread his memoirs, and she was still reckoning with some of her discoveries. Midway through her reading, she put a map of Brazil on the wall over her worktable. On it she began placing white sticky-dots at the places Fawcett had been, or along the general routes he'd taken. Then she added a number of red dots, representing her own travels in Brazil.

The first time she had read Fawcett's memoirs, worlds away in Los Angeles, most of the Brazilian place names meant little to her and therefore hadn't found a place in her conscious memory. But when IDA work was done and she had free time to roam, she'd coincidentally, or subconsciously, chosen to visit many of the places where he had been, without any recognition of their names. Only when she reread his memoirs did she realize how close to his footsteps she'd been treading; many of her red dots sat side by side with the white ones.

There was Cuiabá and the Pantanal, which was nothing unusual for a visitor, but there was also Porto Jofre and her spin up the Cuiabá River, an area far from the beaten tourist track. She'd followed his trail through Santa Ana do Araguaia; and to Lençois, even to the very same spot in the Hotel Colonial. Did he pause beside the quartz-lined river, as she had done, and bathe in one of the little pools? And of course, there was Rio. She'd wound up living in the city where he had hoped to retire and live out his days with Nina.

But the most intriguing fact had come to her attention soon after she planned her vacation. She had four weeks coming to her, and she was long overdue in taking it. Her destination had been a tough decision; she felt she should be using the time to research Fawcett's routes, or see some of the areas where he had been in western Brazil, but she was discouraged. Some of these places were not a good option for her due to issues of accessibility or expense; others had changed so drastically in the intervening years that she wasn't sure what could be gained in seeing them. After living in Brazil for more than a year, it was clearer why there had been so little written about Fawcett and so few new discoveries.

She toyed with the possibility of a trip to Barra do Garças, but she was turned off by the idea of UFO cults and the like. She sometimes felt as if she heard Fawcett's voice in the distance, calling her, and he wasn't to be found in any of these places.

"I want to spend at least part of my time in the Amazon, but in a completely different area from my previous trip," she told her travel agent, Inez. "Where are the huge trees, the buttressed kapoks?"

"Ah," Inez said, her eyes lighting. "You want to go to Pará; but first to Alta Floresta."

"High Forest?"

"Yes. So named because of the big trees, of course!" She grabbed the map on her desk and pointed out a small town in the north of Mato Grosso, just below the border with Pará state. "Alta Floresta is the jumping-off spot for the forests of Pará. I've never been there, I'm not as adventurous as you, but I've heard it's beautiful."

Sylvia did some Web research into the area, and talked to anyone she could find who had been there; since this turned out to be only one person, she was hooked. Her favorite places tended to be those which drew the most cautions from her Brazilian acquaintances, reflecting fundamental differences between them: They liked safe, well-trod places, she sought out the wild and untamed; they were highly social, she eschewed crowds. With Brazilians, "the more the merrier" is the rule of the day, and those who don't fit that mold wind up in the Pantanal, she thought with an inward chuckle. The remote, undeveloped High Forests of southern Pará might give me a better feel for Fawcett's love of the Amazon than visiting Indian tribes who wear flip-flops and have Sony plugged into their ears.

The Internet research on Fawcett had turned bizarre.

For starters, cults and societies had sprung up all over the world, some of which virtually worshipped Fawcett in semi-religious rituals. Instead of dying out over time, the legend and mystery of Fawcett's quest had grown into an obsession for thousands of people.

One researcher claimed the coordinates Fawcett gave for Dead Horse Camp were deliberately false; the actual location of the death of his mount was farther south. And the route he took on his last journey was *not* to the northeast, into Xingu territory, but northwest, toward the Rio Sangue—River of Blood—and the Juruena River.

Right into the south of Pará, she saw by her map. Once again, was she accidentally, as it were, following Fawcett?

Some believed Fawcett was actually searching for an advanced race of people called the "Earth Guardians", and was bringing his son, Jack, to these people for special initiation and training; it was this select destiny, as a member and leader in this group, which was predicted by the Buddhists of Ceylon at Jack's birth.

Whoa. So these Guardians are supposedly the elusive white race glimpsed in uncharted wilderness from time to time, providing the stuff of legend for countless years? It's crazy.

One modern-day explorer, an anonymous intelligence official from the United States, reported seeing a luminous flying saucer coming from an opening in a tunnel which led to a city inside a mountain. He claimed he had entered the tunnel and heard the *canto galo*, the crowing rooster, supposedly a symbol indicating subterranean cities in Brazil, of which there are said to be many. Other researchers described the accumulation of evidence for numerous hidden entrances to subterranean cities.

On one website she read of the Buddhist belief in a subterranean world they called Agharta; its capital was named Shamballah, which sounded familiar to her. Then she thought of Parque do Lume's circular building. Ah, yes... Did Marcela believe in Agharta?

She came up with an account by a BBC producer of a lost settlement he found in Colombia in 1988. The inhabitants wore white robes and told him they were the Kogi, or Earth Guardians, and their mission was to educate mankind in spiritual living and care of the earth. There were stories about UFOs and civilizations beneath the ground, many of them attributed to Theosophists from all over the world who believe in the cities, and who have gathered in Brazil.

And there was the matter of an unlikely number of Hebrew names in Amazonas, and in Brazil in general, as well as stone inscriptions bearing characters identical to others in distant parts of the world.

(One minor point she stumbled across: Apparently Fawcett hadn't liked either of his names very much, and preferred to be known as "PHF". Since the beginning, Sylvia had referred to him by those initials in her notes and in her mind. Funny.)

Sylvia didn't know what to make of any of it. She had seen Fawcett as a dreamer, and yes, a mystic, who believed he had gathered legitimate evidence for the existence of a pre-Incan civilization which may have been Atlantean. That, in her opinion, was far enough "out there" as it was. All the stuff about Jack as an advanced spirit and Earth Guardian initiate seemed over the line.

What to do? Ignore it? Try to work it into her story? Research it with an open mind? *As they say, Keep an open mind, but not so open that your brains fall out.* It would take time to wade through all the static of the current obsession with Fawcett, a phenomenon she didn't fully understand. Yet she was part of it, one of the growing legion who had a peculiar fascination with the man.

The portly man with Artur was introduced as Harold Wilman, of Raytheon; he was from the United States. Artur was using his English, so Sylvia assumed Mr. Wilman didn't speak Portuguese. She was glad. It was an unexpected relief to speak English with the two men; she always felt at a disadvantage when she had to think about grammar and vocabulary, though her new language was becoming more automatic with every month.

"Did you select a restaurant for us?" Artur asked.

"I thought we might go to Vin Santo; most people like it and it's close enough to walk."

The three strolled down to Rua Constante Ramos, which crossed the Avenida. Sylvia now was certain, upon meeting the Raytheon executive, the topic of discussion would be SIVAM; they wanted her to work with them. She was filled with consternation. *I should've prepared myself, mentally, for this; I have no idea how I feel about SIVAM, beyond a casual professional curiosity... No, I'm lying to myself. I'm interested, but there are many factors to consider besides the job.*

She was right. As soon as they'd ordered their meals, Harold Wilman launched into his proposal. Artur would've waited until they had eaten, but Harold correctly presumed his fellow American didn't want to waste anymore time with chit-chat; they could get to the point of the luncheon.

"... And so that, basically, is the position we offer," he concluded. "We know you have a satisfying job here in this gorgeous city, and we're asking you to drag yourself over the far corners of the Amazon Basin; to make it more palatable we'll triple your salary with IDA. Whatever it is, and I have no idea. We'll pay you in U.S. dollars."

It wasn't as dramatic as it sounded; he knew she was paid in Brazilian currency, which would convert to a good bit less in dollars.

"We need you, Sylvia—" She had made him drop the "Doctor Garth" business right away— "We need your ideas, so the position we're offering you is one with a great deal of control and responsibility. It helps that you speak both English and Portuguese and you're already culturally acclimated to Brazil. Bringing in a Raytheon employee from the U.S. would be a gamble; culture shock can be a big issue."

Sylvia nodded. She well understood the challenges of dealing with a new job, language, and culture simultaneously.

"What we're doing has never been done anywhere before," he stressed, "and we need someone who can help us build this network from the ground up."

He had intuited how to win her over. Nothing got her creative and intellectual juices flowing like the prospect of starting something from scratch, especially something novel and untested.

Artur spoke up, and his input was most welcome at that point. "We realize you'll want to think about it; it's a big decision."

"Um, yes, I'd need to sleep on it—"

"And you'll no doubt think of many questions for us," added Harold, "after the initial idea has sunk in a bit deeper; we'll try to answer them, if possible. But although we don't want to pressure you, in which case you'd probably give us a big 'no' right away, we do have to get moving on this."

"What's your deadline?"

"Well, I'll admit there are very few people we know of who'd be right for this job; so we don't have a line-up of candidates to interview," he snorted ruefully. "But if you aren't interested, we need to get cracking and come up with a list; we do have people searching for Brazilians who might qualify."

She nodded. "Well, I'll think hard on this; I am interested. From the first minute Artur described SIVAM, I was caught up in the concept. But there are many issues to consider..."

For the remainder of the time, they dined and talked about the project in general terms. Sylvia did think of more questions, and the very dearth of answers piqued her interest even more.

*

"Don't worry, I won't say anything to Julia, or anyone else for that matter." Paulo had closed his office door and asked his secretary to take telephone messages. He leaned back. "Okay, if I understand it, you would be setting up and monitoring ground stations, or coordination centers, to sort and relay information acquired by satellite and other means, right? In a nutshell?"

"Yes. There are so many different categories of data that'll be gathered, from climate info to trespassers, and organizing it all will be critical to its rapid dissemination—" She paused. "Also, I'd be involved in selecting and configuring some of the communication systems. We'd have to consider flexibility as a prime goal, to accommodate rapid changes in technology, as well as infrastructural limitations in certain areas of the Amazon. Oh, I almost forgot, it's possible I'd also bear the responsibility of training key personnel in use of the system."

Paulo laughed. "In other words, they haven't actually written a job description, since they don't know what might be involved until they do it!"

"I think you hit the nail on the head."

"The nail... oh, yes." He looked pensive. Sylvia waited. Finally he said, "Well, Sylvia, you have a lot to think about. It's an interesting offer." He stopped, sighed.

She stared at him. "That's all you have to say?"

"What else can I say? It's all one big question mark; but I'm sure it would be an adventure. The decision has to be yours."

"Of course it has to be mine, you ninny; but I was hoping you'd have a few ideas I could chew on." She was astounded that that was all the input he could offer.

"Well, I'll think about it. It's all pretty sudden for me, too, you know." He shuffled some papers on his desk as if he needed to get back to work. Feeling she had almost been brushed off, she retreated and went to her office to brood.

At the moment there was no one else to talk to. She was glad Ana had gone to lunch before Artur and Harold arrived; if she'd seen the American, she would've had a thousand questions, and Sylvia didn't want anyone at IDA, besides Paolo, to know of the offer.

Especially since she knew she would most likely turn it down.

*

Isabel was considerably more forthright than Paulo had been. She cleared the table after dinner; Sylvia jumped up to help.

"When I have a tricky decision to make, I usually use the old method of listing the pros and cons on paper. Have you done that?" Sylvia shook her head in the negative. "Do you want to?"

"It can't hurt. Might help."

Isabel fetched paper and pens. "Maybe we should each make up separate lists of both pros and cons. You know, some of the things I would think of as disadvantages might be on your list of advantages. It might give you a different perspective."

"So true, Isabel. One thing I've learned in life is that something that at first appears to be a plus is the very thing that later drives you up the wall."

"There's always another side of the coin, isn't there?"

They looked over each other's lists when they'd finished. Working in isolated reaches of Amazonas, not surprisingly, was a positive for Sylvia and a drawback for Isabel.

"You loved being in Amazonas when you were camping; but living there is another matter," pointed out Isabel. "You won't enjoy many of the advantages you have here in Rio, like the beaches, mild climate, safe food... There's illness in some of those places: hepatitis, malaria, even typhus. But the main thing I'd worry about would be social isolation. All the travel appeals to you now, but it can be isolating."

"Those are good points, and I'll admit I hadn't thought of it that way."

"But—" Isabel went on, "Balance all that with the benefits. You didn't write on your Con list that you might be getting a little bored with your job at IDA." She regarded Sylvia. "Are you?"

"You're perceptive. I still enjoy my work, but most of the challenge has worn away... From now on, I'll have to find ways to make it rewarding." She paused thoughtfully. "I've always looked for purpose in my life, or, well, a mission of some kind. Maybe that's just a childhood dream."

They talked until late into the night. If there was one thing Sylvia hated, it was decision-making when there were too many variables and unknowns to use pure logic; yet the instincts she often relied on were stubbornly refusing to kick in. She slept on it, again and again, awakening to the same mental dickering, back and forth, every morning. A change of scene might help; her vacation was coming at the perfect time.

"It's all arranged, Senhora; you leave at 7:00 tomorrow morning. Your guide will be Celia Martins, and she'll be here at six in the morning for breakfast. 'Ta bom?"

"That's fine. I'll be ready." Sylvia nodded at the manager of the Floresta Amazonica Hotel, who stood beside her table on the hotel's veranda.

Sylvia turned back to the menu. Now she could enjoy her dinner, knowing things were finally set for her journey into the forests. Inez had sent her off to Alta Floresta with the vaguest of information about the excursion, asssuring her the folks at the hotel were putting something together for her. They didn't have too many requests to send a single American woman as far back as possible in the wilds of Pará.

But as usual with Brazilians, they had a way of working everything out. They knew of a highly qualified guide, they promised her, and the guide had radioed a remote lodge used by ornithologists from all over the world; the manager agreed to accommodate the visitor as long as she understood how primitive it was there. The lodge had no electricity and few other amenities; sleeping hammocks were provided, but there was only one room with a bed. The food was wholesome, but limited.

Thinking of that brought Sylvia's attention back to the menu in her hand. The hotel was much to her liking. It was a low and rambling structure, made of beautiful Brazilian hardwoods and furnished in luscious tropical colors. The décor was rustic but tasteful, including ceiling fans and huge urns filled with ferns and palms; all quite appropriate for a resort surrounded by jungle. There were dining tables on the long, wide veranda which ran along one entire side of the building and overlooked a swimming pool bordered by lush vegetation.

She was hungry after a long walk down one of the beautiful trails through the forest, where she'd been surprised by a two-foot-long iguana that popped out of the bushes. Why couldn't she be satisfied to stay here, in comfort and safety?

But no. The next morning she ate a very early breakfast with her guide, an ornithologist who lived in the nearby town and was working on her Masters thesis in the area.

"You realize I have some limitations when it comes to creatures other than birds," Celia explained. "I usually take birders out. But I've learned enough about the flora and fauna of the area that I think I can make it interesting for you."

"I'm sure you can." Sylvia thought she'd like Celia, a petite young woman of part-Asian heritage, soft-spoken and delicate in her mannerisms.

"It's a long trip, with few comforts; but from what I understand about you, this won't be a problem?" She brought out a map and traced their route with a pencil. This pleased Sylvia, who constantly pored over maps, but found her interest was not matched by many people in Brazil. Sylvia had a need to visualize her surroundings with a birds-eye view, and orient herself on the globe's directional grid.

The Teles Pires River, also called the São Manoel, is a long watercourse that begins in the Mato Grosso highlands east of the Pantanal. Joined by smaller branches as it winds northward, it grows in volume and eventually passes near Alta Floresta, forming part of the border between Mato Grosso and Pará. It's then joined by Rio Juruena from the southwest, creating the immense Tapajós, which flows directly into the Amazon River.

Sylvia and Celia would be heading northeast on unpaved roads to the point where the Cristalino River, a tributary descending from the Serra do Cachimbo mountains, pours into the Teles Pires.

"After we reach the confluence, we still have to drive upstream for a way. There are some nasty rapids on the Cristalino as it gets near the Teles Pires. Above these, we'll be met by the lodge's boat, which will take us upriver to the lodge. It's a noisy little motorboat, and a long trip, but it'll be worth it once we're there."

Though on the map the overland leg of the trip appeared to be twenty-five miles or less, as the crow flies, it was grueling. They had soon left the paved road behind; the dirt track was winding and sometimes washed out, and Celia struggled the little red Jeep across ditches and around sinks with expertise. They careened through dense forest, branches shrieking along the sides of the vehicle and whipping into the windows to slap their faces.

At length they reached the riverside, where they found a man from the lodge who looked as though he had been dozing while he waited in the gently rocking boat, tied to a tree.

"*Oi, Celia, como vai?*"

"*Bem, Eduardo, e você?*" The two exchanged obligatory pecks at the air surrounding both cheeks. As they loaded their gear, she heard Eduardo tell Celia he had left the lodge at sunrise, and he hadn't been waiting very long; it was now almost 9 a.m., so it looked as if they had a long trip, indeed, ahead of them. She noticed he had brought extra gasoline.

Butterflies were everywhere, in the air, perched on the shrubs. For a while there was one on Sylvia's shoulder; butterflies—or moths—that she had previously seen only under glass or in photographs: the spectacular blue Morpho, as big as a man's hand, and colorful Sunset moths with their shimmering greens and blues on one side, red and white figure-eights on the reverse.

The two women sat on the veranda eating a simple dinner of beans and rice, the South American staples, followed by local fruits. There were bananas hanging from the lodge posts, and great suspended baskets, roughly made, full of fruits Sylvia hadn't yet encountered. She could deal with beans and rice every day if she got to sample a few new fruits.

The lodge, which bore a hand-made sign reading "Canto das Aves"—Birdsong—was indeed primitive. There was one large room in the primary wooden, thatched structure, and a shed behind it for food preparation. The manager, Carlos, cooked on a wood stove part of the time, and in a long, strange-looking wood-fired oven; occasionally he made sparing use of a propane camp stove. He produced excellent bread and beans that were seasoned with herbs he grew in a small, enclosed garden. He caught fish almost every day, but Celia said he never served fowl when guests were there, even though he raised chickens.

"Why?"

"Because some of the birders look at the dinner suspiciously, as if they're afraid he shot one of the wild fowl they came here to study," Celia answered with amusement. "The type of chickens he has don't resemble what the guests are used to, so I can understand why they wonder. But most of them eat the eggs he serves! When you think about it, it's a little odd to be a bird-lover, and yet eat chickens, and eggs..."

Sylvia laughed. "I have to agree."

"So, Sylvia, truthfully, what do you think of the place?"

"It's perfect."

A short distance beyond the main building was another shelter; part of it was enclosed and the remainder was covered, but open on the sides. A few hammocks were strung on this veranda, and Sylvia had noticed many more hooks where others could be suspended. In the enclosed space there was a long table, a few wood chairs, and a double bed. Mosquito nets were bundled up near the ceiling, both indoors and out.

"You can have the bed, if you want," offered Celia.

"No, thanks! A hammock out here'll be fine with me."

"Me, too. It's cooler."

They spent the long evening in the sitting room, going over nature books and maps Celia had brought until their eyes tired in the light of hurricane lamps. The absence of electric light had a relaxing effect on Sylvia.

"Bright light at night isn't normal, so who knows how it affects us?" she mentioned to Celia. "Maybe that's one reason people take so many sleeping pills."

Celia nodded. "I don't miss electricity all that much; there are no machine sounds here, no refrigerators droning, blenders..." She yawned broadly. "We should get up around dawn or before," Celia suggested. "That's when we'll see fantastic birds and other animals moving around. We can take fruit along, and then we'll come back and have a real breakfast with pancakes and avian sex cells. I mean eggs."

"Sounds good."

Miles and miles of trails surrounded Canto das Aves, and over the next few days Sylvia felt they must have covered most of them. The two women were good hiking partners, walking in perfect silence, the better to spot shy birds and beasts. Celia's footsteps were usually soundless, and Sylvia watched her until she learned to tread delicately, also. Celia reminded her of the heroine of Green Mansions, the D.H. Lawrence tale of a sylph-like girl who was raised by her hermit father in a rainforest. The High Forest of Pará was similar to the description of Lawrence's tropical woodland; there were enormous buttressed trees spaced widely apart, and between them the ground was open, mostly clear of underbrush, though graceful tree ferns were common. Easy walking, in most areas.

Celia appeared perfectly comfortable in the wilds, and her fearlessness made Sylvia relax.

"We're animals, too," the guide said one day. "We just need to use our senses and our wiles, as the other creatures do."

Celia used all of her senses, especially her nose. She detected the fragrance of a fruit she said was rare and delicious and she kept sniffing until she found it. She didn't recall the Indian name for it, and it had no other. The two ate the nameless delicacy sitting on a wavy bench formed by one of the buttresses of a giant kapok tree, and stuffed a few extra in their backpacks.

"Let's leave many of them behind, to be sure their seed is spread. Greed results in shortages, in the long run."

One day, the guide stopped stock still with her head raised and motioned Sylvia to freeze. Sylvia saw Celia's little nose working as she sniffed the air, then she led Sylvia quickly and wordlessly to a kapok whose lower branches had sent down long, thick supports which reached the ground, some of them twisting in bizarre shapes and folds. She climbed up into the contorted wood, as easily as mounting a stairway, and Sylvia followed, mystified but suddenly frightened. "Shh..." Celia gestured.

Then Sylvia smelled them, and heard their hooves. The most feared creature in the rainforests was not the jaguar, which preferred to avoid humans; it was the wild pig. The pigs travelled in groups and attacked almost anything with vicious strength, and one could be trapped by them in places where there was nothing to climb, no place to hide.

The herd ran through the woods, snorting and pausing to smell the ground. They obviously had the humans' scent, and for a few minutes they ran circles in the area. But they never seemed to track them to the tree, and they never looked up. In a while, they were gone.

"We should sit here a little longer," Celia whispered, "In case they come back. They do that sometimes." Sylvia nodded, shaken. She didn't know if she'd ever come down.

They sat in silence for several minutes. Finally Celia motioned for her to climb down. Sylvia hung back. "Are you sure it's all right?"

"We can never be sure about anything," Celia replied honestly, "But we should move on, leave the area. Lucky for us, they headed off in a different direction from our return route."

"What would we do if they hadn't?"

"We'd wait a little longer up here," Celia said calmly. "Now, let's go." The last words had a touch of firmness; she didn't want Sylvia to succumb to paralysis.

Sylvia reluctantly descended.

"No wonder they lost our scent; they trampled all over the place until they'd confused themselves thoroughly," Celia observed. "See, that's what happens when you get too excited."

"But what would we do if pigs came when there's nothing to climb?"

"Run like hell until we find something. They're fast, but we can outrun them if we have a head start. That's where one's senses count. But don't worry; there's usually something to climb. We've never lost a birder to pigs, that I've ever heard of. Though some of them choose to carry Carlos' shotgun."

Not a bad idea, Sylvia thought. Then she remembered the big machete hanging from Celia's waist, which was infrequently needed on these trails. Perhaps it had another purpose.

Sylvia's hearing and olfactory sense sharpened considerably on that one outing.

"Eduardo, can you bring the chest?" The man nodded to Celia, and went back to the kitchen where Carlos had packed a picnic chest full of food: a fresh loaf of bread, bean salad, fruit, cucumbers from the garden, cakes, a bottle of wine. A veritable feast. "I think there's first aid kit in the canoe..."

"I saw it under the life jackets," Sylvia answered. "Do we have bug spray?"

"We'd better go; it's getting late. Eduardo! *Trago o DEET, 'ta?*"

Eduardo came to the dock carrying the picnic hamper with both hands. He glanced back at his rear pocket, where a bottle of bug repellent protruded. Celia grabbed it. *"Obrigada. Vamos!"*

The women boarded the long canoe, tethered to the motorboat. The paddles safely stowed, Celia raised her thumb in the "okay" signal, and Eduardo started the motor. He turned the boat in a wide arc and began to slowly tow the canoe and its occupants upriver. The afternoon sun flickered through the trees as they made their noisy way up the Cristalino.

"How far are we going?" Sylvia hollered.

"Several miles," she replied vaguely. "We'll go as far as we can, until we reach a cascade. It's very pretty. We can tie up there, swim, and have our dinner. Then we'll float back down at our own pace."

Earlier, she had told Sylvia of the tow-and-float plan:

"This is one of my favorite things to do. Sunset is the best time to be on the river; we can see so many birds and other wildlife from the water. Be sure you have the faster film in your camera, since we'll be losing light quickly."

They had taken the canoe out several times during the week. It was good exercise, but no matter how quietly they tried to paddle they scared away many of the shy creatures they wanted to look at. The downstream float would let them relax, observe silence, and take pictures from the open perspective of the river.

If there are any animals within five miles left to see, after this racket, Sylvia thought as they roared along. After an eternity of the motor, she heard another sound over it: the cataract. She had been expecting a series of rapids and small cascades, as on the Bariaú, so she was surprised to see a ten-foot-high waterfall stretching across the width of the river. She could see the motorboat straining against the increased current. Eduardo turned the boat expertly until the canoe made an arc toward the north bank; then he unhooked the towline from his boat.

"Okay, paddle," Celia said, and the two of them propelled the canoe toward the riverside, where the guide grasped a low branch and pulled them firmly to the bank. Sylvia hauled in the line and gave its end to Celia, who tied the canoe to a small tree trunk leaning over the river. Then she waved to Eduardo, who had been holding his boat steady against the current. He waved back, and accelerated downstream. Slowly the drone of the motor died away, as the women maneuvered themselves to a spot where they could disembark.

"There's a little pool over here where we can bathe without getting pulled into the current, if we're careful," Celia said, as they picked their way through the riverside vegetation, watching for snakes. The pool was lined with ferns and moss-covered rocks, which seemed to attract masses of golden butterflies. There was a huge kapok where monkeys played, throwing debris down onto the intruders who laughed at the antics as they arranged their picnic. After a quick dip to cool off, they broke bread and poured wine, and talked, as the sun slanted low through the forest.

Sylvia released a long sigh. "If I thought I could go to enchanted places like this now and then, I'd take the SIVAM job." During the week Sylvia had told Celia something of her life, and the crossroads she faced; in turn, Celia had discussed her own career, as she would complete her thesis soon.

"Why couldn't you?"

"Oh, I don't know. I'd probably spend most of my time in grubby little towns in the hinterland, or in larger cities like Manaus or Belem, or Santarem. They haven't yet decided where I'd be based."

"All of these places are in Amazonas, don't forget. I'm pretty sure I'll take the job I was offered in Manaus, and I intend to find many places as lovely as this around there." She looked at the sky and frowned. "You know, it's getting late. I think we'd better pack up."

Once they'd begun their leisurely downstream idyll, serenity took gradual hold of Sylvia. With the waterfall out of hearing the peace of the river and voices of its inhabitants ruled the day. The women kept their canoe near the north bank most of the time, in order to drift more slowly and spot wildlife.

The sun disappeared completely as they floated along; the high forest closed in on them and they were soon enveloped in a brief tropical twilight. Birds rioted in the trees, and monkeys collected into screeching bands of delinquents, quarrelling over territory, bullying each other. Animals crept down to the river to drink or dip themselves: an armadillo, a few pigs, a large rodent. The canoe glided by so silently in the dusk that some of the creatures never noticed it.

They drifted past a low-leaning tree, its branches sweeping the water's surface, and suddenly both women froze. They were staring into the equally startled eyes of a spotted jaguar crouched for a drink, not three yards away. Neither of the women moved a hair as the craft slowly, slowly—it seemed to Sylvia they weren't moving at all—passed by the mesmerized beast, which also never stirred. And then they were out of sight behind more branches.

For a few more moments they just looked at each other, then both of them exhaled with a rush.

"Oh!" exclaimed Celia, "in all my time out here that's the first one I've seen! And so close!"

"Maybe *too* close, huh? It could've plunged in after us?"

"It could've, they like to swim, but I think a canoe is too strange for them to comprehend. Too bad we didn't get a picture."

As they chattered on, darkness fell like a curtain, as it appears to do at nine degrees south of the equator. The sky had slid from cerulean to indigo; stars were peeping out. Sylvia realized she couldn't see Celia's expression anymore.

"We'd better move along a little faster," the guide said. "I'm sorry, we should've started back sooner..."

"Should we paddle out to midstream? Step up the pace?" In midstream, the current moved more quickly.

"For a little while, yes; but we don't want to pass by the dock..."

They floated on, faster now. The monkeys still screamed, but birds were quieting. Celia didn't talk at all; she was straining to see the shore. But it was impossible; the only light was in the overhead sky, and a faint glow reflecting from the water. The riverbanks were plunged into deepest black.

"We'd better move nearer the bank," Celia said, paddling. "I'm not sure how far from the lodge we are— can you find the flashlight, quickly, please."

Sylvia didn't like the new edge in her guide's voice. She rummaged in Celia's pack. "Here." Surely things would be all right, if they stayed near the bank until they ran into the dock; that seemed simple enough.

It wasn't. The flashlight was not up to the task of piercing the darkness to find a small wooden dock that blended into the surroundings even in daytime. And the trees, reaching low and far over the river, impeded their progress when they tried to hug the bank. They remembered the jaguar, another reason to avoid the very edge of the water.

"Won't we see some lights from the lodge?"

"That's the problem; we won't. It's far back in the trees, and the kerosene lamps aren't usually seen from the riverside... Unless Carlos gets worried and puts a lamp out for us. Yes! I'm sure he'll think to put a lamp on the dock."

"Maybe he'll be out there, waiting for us."

"Maybe; we should make some sound." The two began hallooing, their voices echoing in the night, causing the monkeys to hush momentarily.

Carlos, ironically, was taking advantage of the solitude to drown his sundry sorrows in cabernet, a gift from Celia for accepting the visitor at short notice. Eduardo had gone to bed at twilight, by habit, and the manager strummed his guitar and sang dolefully to his pet parrot, Pele.

Meanwhile, the Cristalino was uncooperative, snaking its way through the night, sending the canoe into midstream currents with every curve of its bed.

"Paddle! Paddle! We're going out into the middle again!" Celia was trying to paddle and scan with the inadequate flashlight at the same time.

Sylvia caught her breath and asked, "What happens if we pass the dock?" It must be bad, she thought, to rattle this normally sanguine person.

"There's nothing out here but the lodge. You saw, when we came up here. Nothing; we're in wilderness. If we think we've passed it, we'll have to tie up on the side and wait till they come looking for us...which might not be until morning."

"Morning?"

"Yes, well, they might not miss us...You know, if they're asleep or something." The "or something" concerned her. She was kicking herself for giving Carlos, a known tippler, the bottle of wine. She should've waited until they were leaving the lodge. "Anyway, it's too risky to go searching for us in the motorboat at night—you can barely see underwater snags in daylight—Darn!" She shook the rapidly dimming light and tried to keep it trained on the bank while Sylvia paddled.

"The trouble is," Celia went on while she peered into the gloom, "it's easy to get disoriented. We might be getting close, then again, we could've already passed it! But we can't take a chance and keep going; we could get to the place where the river speeds up beyond our control, and then goes into rapids."

Sylvia understood what she meant about disorientation. Even with daylight, there were precious few landmarks and those had been passed long ago; one stretch of river looked the same as the one before it. There was no means of judging by elapsed time how far they had come or when they should be nearing the lodge, since they had paused many times, and the canoe travelled at a different rate from the motorboat. The little dock, made of unfinished wood from the surrounding trees, was the only indication of shelter.

Swept along on a river they could no longer see, their light failing, the only thing clearer than the stars appearing above them was the fact of human fragility in the wild world. How quickly their larks can turn serious! Even the crickets were more comfortable in their world, more confident, singing boldly in the black forest.

"We just have to keep our heads," Sylvia said, feeling suddenly calm. "Let's tie up now, and sit tight. We won't be hungry; there's plenty of food left."

"You're right. We'll get out of this." But she was thinking they should throw their food overboard before tying up; its scent could attract animals. She moved the light along the waterside, but saw nothing.

"Oops! Watch those branches!" Bang! Overhanging branches tugged at Celia's hair, but a solid one caught Sylvia hard across the temple as the canoe swung around. "Are you okay? Sylvia?"

Warm blood trickled down Sylvia's forehead into her eye. She felt dizzy. "I'm okay... Damn, we can't see anything out here!"

There was a shout from somewhere in the forest. Celia gasped and waved the fading flashlight.

"*Celia! Aqui!*" It was Eduardo. Something had awakened him, and he had decided he might as well step outside and take a leak. He wasn't aware the canoe hadn't come back, but when he saw a weak light on the river, he knew instantly what was going on.

They had passed the dock; the voice was coming from upstream.

"Paddlepaddlepaddle," Celia yelled. "Eduardo!"

They paddled to the riverside and grabbed the first thing that came to hand, hoping it didn't have snakes twined within. "Shine the light while I try to pull us along," Sylvia said. But the light was dead. Alternately paddling and pulling the canoe through the branches, they progressed upstream.

Eduardo made a snap decision to run into the lodge and fetch a light, feeling his way with cat-eyes. "Carlos!" He called, but the lodge was dark and its manager was nowhere in sight. He returned in record time with a lantern burning brightly, and raced down to the dock. "*Aqui!*"

The women emerged from the shrubs and saw Eduardo and his lantern, and paddled with renewed strength. Sylvia threw him the rope.

"Well, talk about going with the flow!" Sylvia joked over breakfast, offering a bread crust to Pele. She sported a white bandage on her forehead.

Celia moaned; she was taking it hard. She had apologized repeatedly until Sylvia finally begged her to stop.

"I was enjoying myself too much," Celia insisted. "It's a guide's duty to stay vigilant, and always on the safe side—"

"So you made a human mistake," Sylvia said for the umpteenth time. "We would've been all right even if we'd spent the night in the canoe."

"Or you could've floated on down the river," Carlos put in. "*If* you make it through the rapids it's a nice ride, until you come to the cataract on the Teles Pires, that is." Now that it was over, he appeared to think it was a hilarious tale.

"Look, Celia;" Sylvia repeated. "We made it back to our hammocks, thanks to Eduardo— by the way, why did you wake up in the first place, Eduardo?"

He shrugged. "I don't know. I had a dream, someone was calling me, and I woke up."

"Well, anyway," Sylvia resumed, "It turned out okay, and I learned something."

"Not to trust Celia Caterina Martins," the guide said ruefully.

"No. I learned I could keep my head when necessary."

"You are very generous, my friend."

"Not at all. I'm fully prepared to put all the blame on Carlos." The two women, joined by Eduardo, turned their gaze on the manager, watching his grin begin to fade.

"Me?"

"All you had to do was put a lantern on the dock, Carlos." Sylvia said it; she knew Celia didn't want to point the finger at anyone else. She pretended to be serious; the man shouldn't get off scot-free.

He shuffled around for a moment, mumbling grumpily. He was hungover and didn't need this. "Look," he finally said, "You can say that you learned yet another lesson, Senhora Sylvia."

"And that is?"

"Not to rely on anyone but yourself."

The airliner banked over Brasilia, and the attendant scurried around, picking up cups and pushing trays back in their places. The cabin air was dry and sterile, and the paper on the headrests, stale peanuts in plastic packages, all was odious and alien to Sylvia; but she was back in "the world" now, and would soon be careening through the national capital in a rental car. It was no Shamballah, that was plain.

Brasilia had not been on her itinerary. It was an impulse; she had been doing some hard thinking, and she wanted to speak to Artur in person, and talk things through: the pluses and minuses. She trusted Artur not to give her a sales pitch. He cleared his schedule, cancelling a couple of "non-essential appointments", as he put it, to make time for her. If she wanted to speak with Harold, he was in town.

"Maybe later," she told him. "For now, I'd just like to get your perspective." She had learned Brazilians often saw things differently from her own countrymen, and the view from that angle might shed light on her own way of thinking.

This time she zipped straight from the airport to FUNAI. After an hour and a half with Artur, during which time he never glanced at his watch even once but patiently discussed every concern and query Sylvia came up with—all of the pros and cons—she left, feeling drained.

It was time to digest everything. She didn't have a hotel room; she should deal with that, first. But her feet disobeyed her. She walked, without thinking about it, around the corner and down to the Sanctuary of Dom Bosco.

As she walked in, she was a trace disappointed to see there was another person, a man, sitting in one of the back pews. *Can't expect to have the place all to myself... Anyway, he won't bother me.* She drank in the serene atmosphere of the sanctuary. It was about the same time of day as it had been the first time she was there.

She stood for a while in the great empty space behind the benches. Then she walked toward the altar, intending to sit on the front bench. Her hard-soled shoes echoed on the floor, though she tried to walk quietly.

"Sylvia!"

She whirled in surprise toward the man in the back pew. He stood up.

"Paulo!"

The two stared at each other in mutual amazement.

"What are you doing here??"

"I thought you were in Pará!"

Their voices reverberated through the sanctuary. They met in the middle of the section of benches.

"What happened to your head?"

"Nothing much. You should see the other guy."

"Pardon?"

"Never mind. I'll tell you about it. I came here after my stay in the lodge, to talk to Artur about SIVAM. And you?"

He stalled. "Sylvia, we need to talk. I've been making some decisions of my own."

"So, talk! I'm listening."

"We could go someplace..."

"What's wrong with right here?" She moved to a pew and sat down.

He looked down at her for a moment. "All right." He joined her. She waited as he collected his words.

"I'm leaving IDA."

"What? Why?" The bottom of the world seemed to fall away.

"I've accepted a job at FUNAI." There was a brief silence.

"Paulo, have you been planning this?"

"Not exactly. But I've been thinking about it for a long, long, time."

"Well—why now, then?"

He ran his long fingers through his hair and dropped his head thoughtfully. "It came to a head after we talked about SIVAM, your job offer. Two very strong feelings took hold of me; one of them involved my own life and was sort of like—envy. You were offered a chance to do something that could make a real difference. When we hear about all the troubles in Amazonas, the destruction, conflicting human needs, most of us feel frustrated because we can't think of much we can do about it. There are lots of little things, like buying sustainable rainforest products, but they seem like drops in an ocean." He met her eyes. "But now we have the means to be proactive on a large scale, and you were asked to be a part of it."

"So you wanted the job for yourself?"

"Not really... My qualifications aren't so ideal as yours. My background is quite different, though I'm also a technophile. I've had a standing offer from FUNAI to come back any time—"

"I didn't know that."

"No, I thought it best not to mention it, though Isabel knew. Anyway, I phoned my former boss and asked him what sorts of opportunities might be open for me, now. He started talking about SIVAM; and next thing I knew, I'd been offered a position as

FUNAI's field liaison to SIVAM."

"Paulo! That's—that's, at least it seems, perfect!"

"It does appear to be an almost perfect fit. I'll be able to do something for the indigenous people of an area I love. I'll be drawing on my experience in the agency, and connecting it to the technology that interests me and the project that holds so much promise."

"Have you told Julia yet?"

"Yes. I'll be continuing with IDA until they find a replacement for me, but the board of directors gave me a few days off to come here and work out some details with FUNAI. I've been there all day, meeting with various people... Oh, and I met Harold Wilman."

"I don't believe it. Then we've been in separate offices in the same building all afternoon."

He nodded, smiling. "And now, Sylvia—"

"Wait. You said two feelings took hold of you; what was the second?"

He wasn't sure how to begin. "It involves you."

She was silent. Sunbeams pierced indigo panels of glass, setting dust motes in the air dancing; a ray of blue light fell across Paulo's head.

"Tell me, first," he went on. "How did you leave things with Artur? Have you decided what you'll do about Wilman's offer?"

"No... I told him I hoped to reach a decision before I left Brasilia."

"Which is when?"

"A couple of days. I have no firm plans. I was going to go wherever the spirit moved me after Pará; I thought I might go to Barra do Garça—you know, check out the wild stories around there, regarding Fawcett."

"How are you feeling about the offer?"

"I don't know, Paulo! I go back and forth in my mind, constantly. When I flew here this morning, I was thinking I'd take the job. The time I spent in Pará had me feeling—well, as if I'd seen my true self. It's hard to put into words. But after going through all the advantages and disadvantages, all the unknowns I'd face, now I'm vacillating again. Artur was very honest with me, and I appreciate it. I can't walk away from everything I have at IDA, and in Rio, without knowing the difficulties I might confront out there."

"Isabel told me about the lists of 'pros and cons' you two made. Was that exercise helpful?" There was an undertone to his voice. Sylvia wasn't sure what it meant.

"Yeah, it made many things clearer... "

"Ah, so it helped you make a decision?"

Her shoulders dropped. "No. What are you getting at, Paulo? Spit it out."

His laughter rang incongruously in the church. "You and your expressions. Maybe we should switch to Portuguese."

"No, your English is far better than my Portuguese."

He looked at her closely. "Sylvia. Weighing the pros and cons can work for some decisions. But you and I both know the point where logic leaves off and our hearts step in. Something like the SIVAM position is more than a job. Tell me, did you make up such a list when you were thinking of coming to work in Brazil? Or when you were offered the job at IDA?"

"No. It just felt right. That is, I took a leap of faith. That's what it felt like."

"Why are you hesitant to leap once more?"

She took a moment to search her own mind for the truth. She found a half-truth.

"I don't know. I think it makes me feel lonely..."

"I thought you once said you were never lonely."

She was quiet. He wasn't going to let her off the hook so easily. She became acutely aware of his eyes, seeing through her like glass.

"Maybe I'm losing my nerve," she said finally.

"To be afraid to take chances isn't like you, Sylvia; it isn't *you*, at all." He shifted uncomfortably; this was not easy. "The other emotion that overwhelmed me that day was a conflict about you. I didn't want you to vanish, just when I was getting to know you, but I also wanted you to grab that job! After our discussions about destiny, I couldn't understand why you were so hesitant. It seemed clear to me this offer was no simple fluke, but what mattered was how *you* saw it.

"You know," he continued, "Isabel had the best intentions, having you weigh the decision judiciously, but that is *Isabel*. And maybe most people, in fact. And it lies at the core of the differences between Isabel and me. She plans rationally, step by step, her career and her life goals; first you do this, and then you'll wind up with that. I may appear on the surface to think that way, but I don't; my instincts and spirit steer me, and I can't live my life according to a rational plan. I don't think you can, either."

No, she thought, *I never have...*

"Accept their offer, Sylvia; let's both do what we can out there.

You won't be alone."

"But—where will you be based?"

"Manaus. The same as you."

"How did you know? I just found out this afternoon it would be Manaus."

"I asked Wilman today." He smiled.

A priest entered the sanctuary, with another man and a woman. The three stood talking softly at the rear of the building. Shafts of sapphire streamed from the windows; the statue of Dom Bosco had turned a deep mauve.

"Where are you staying?" Paulo whispered.

"I hadn't even thought about a hotel yet..."

"Come on. Let's leave these people in peace. I think we can get you a room where I'm staying, at the Nacional." He pulled Sylvia to her feet and, nodding to the other visitors, they left quietly.

"So, you almost got a free trip to Santarem!" Paulo was chuckling over the canoe fiasco.

"I was told we wouldn't have gotten very far on the Teles Pires... Though our remains might've wound up somewhere along the Amazon, eventually." She turned pensive. They'd finished their meal at the hotel's restaurant; now she gazed into the garnet depths of a wine glass. She'd been unusually subdued throughout dinner.

"When Celia and I were out there in the dark, I had one of those moments when you feel you've risen out of the situation, up high somewhere looking down on yourself— It's probably a stress reaction of some kind— Do you know what I mean?"

"I think so; sort of a meta-conscious experience."

"Yeah. I could visualize the Cristalino, carrying us toward the Teles Pires, as I'd seen it on the map, flowing into the Tapajos and then to the Amazon River itself... and out to the sea. We were moving down one branch, or connection, of a great network. I could see the whole of it, the 'Big Picture'! What I'm getting at is, often I feel I'm just drifting, wherever life takes me, until I make one of those occasional leaps of faith we were talking about. I started to suspect that I came to Brazil looking for something besides information on Fawcett." She paused.

"Looking for what, Sylvia?"

"You said it yourself, that thing about destiny. Maybe I've been gathering experience in various areas, all these years, for a purpose."

Paulo's expression was somber. "In my life, too, I begin to see a pattern in some of the 'coincidences'..."

Sylvia nodded. A few moments passed before he spoke again.

"Is this your way of saying you're coming with me to Manaus?"

"No. It's my way of saying I'm sure, now, I'd be going to Amazonas even if you weren't there."

Paulo's brown eyes twinkled in the candlelight. "That, Girl of the Forest, is what I've been wanting to hear all along."

They sat in silence as the waiter approached and poured the remainder of the wine. Paulo cleared his throat a little awkwardly, and said:

"Tomorrow we both have a few more details to handle at FUNAI, and then what? Did you say you wanted to go to Barra do Garça? May I join you, or would you like to be alone for a few days?"

Sylvia leaned forward, looking at Paulo and through him at the same time; she was far away from the Hotel Nacional at that moment.

"I don't need to be alone... And I have a better idea. I know just the place where we should go."

Their dusty rental car rolled to a stop in the gravel parking area; Paulo set the brake. They grabbed their gear, Sylvia leading the way.

Marcela met them as they approached Shambal-ha, and enveloped Sylvia in a great hug. "I was so surprised and happy when you called me," she said, embracing Paulo next. "You're both setting out on a wonderful adventure."

"Most of the bits and pieces of our lives, our pasts, are starting to fit together," Sylvia replied.

"The big picture, as you said on the telephone." Marcela tilted her head as an idea struck her. "And speaking of that, maybe you'll find Fawcett's city out there, with the help of your satellites; and even King Solomon's Mines." She winked.

"Or another sort of treasure," Paulo said. The three of them went inside, where an icy pitcher of lemonade was waiting.

FAWCETT, CHAPTER 9
BEYOND the XINGU

"Let's see, beans, potatoes, carrots, leeks... peas, um, garlic..." Nina rummaged through the larder while Brian looked on, sharpening knives on a whetstone. "Oh, there you are!" Nina turned to her husband, who had appeared in the doorway. "How does a nice stew sound?"

"Just fine." He yanked off his boots. "You have a way of making everything tasty, my dear."

Jack entered the kitchen behind his father, in time to hear the last sentence.

"No meat, right, mum?"

"No meat. Don't worry." She smiled up at her son, who was even taller than his father.

Brian stood up, several kitchen knives in his hand. "Here you go; just watch out, they're razor sharp." Nina smiled her thanks at her younger son as he slipped the knives into their block. He turned to his brother.

"How did the lesson go?"

343

Jack laughed. "I don't know, honestly. The theodolite takes some getting used to."

"Perhaps the problem is the teacher," said Fawcett wryly. "Cheeky, you made everything so easy when I was learning, maybe you should take over this part of Jack's training."

"I would if you didn't keep me so busy trying to come up with vegetarian meals. How is your energy level, by the way?"

"More than adequate," her husband replied, slipping one arm around her waist and giving her a pinch their sons didn't notice.

"I feel great, actually!" offered Jack, "Better than before. Dad's right, I'm sure, that with conditions of scarcity we're likely to be in, a vegetarian diet keeps one's energy high. I'm sticking with this regimen until it's all over."

Nina turned away to her work, afraid her face might reveal her feelings. "Until it's all over..." How she longed for it to be over, to have her husband home for good after a final expedition that vindicated his beliefs...

It was early in 1924. She had had him with her for over two years now, and her contentment had been marred only by knowing how hard it was for him, struggling to arrange finances for his expedition while fearing he was getting too old and out of condition to trek the forests. Time had indeed become his enemy.

There were dark days as Fawcett's frustration grew. He was determined not to take it out on his family, who had sacrificed so much, so willingly, over the years. But he would have spells of withdrawal and at times become silent and morose; then, filled with remorse, he'd rebound and dive into family activities, playing on a cricket team with Jack, attending church with Nina, sharing Brian's interest in locomotive engineering.

Now at last things were falling into place, funds were forthcoming. Fawcett and Jack, now twenty-one, began to prepare in earnest. The only other member of the expedition would be Jack's school chum, Raleigh Rimell.

And, of course, Nina yearned to have her son safe again; at least for a while. He was his father's son in every respect, born to tempt fate. She'd always known Jack would quite literally follow in his father's footsteps. He idolized this man who swept into their humdrum lives after years of absence, bringing tales of adventure and discovery, lighting fires of curiosity in all their minds.

If she herself was not immune to the contagion, how could she expect her impressionable sons to be? One doesn't plead with the wind not to blow.

Besides, she and her husband had been attracted to each other because of the traits they shared. He was what she would've been, she often thought, if she'd been a man. In some ways she lived through him, and he through her. Now she had to let their son live the life for which he was born and raised.

Jack deposited an enormous load of firewood he'd brought in. He never seemed to tire, glorying in physical challenges, the tougher the better. Much of his devotion to fitness had sprung from watching his father and, later, absorbing the accounts of expeditions which depended so heavily on the health and strength of each participant. In the back of his mind a steady resolve grew over the years: He would accompany his father one day, and *he* would not let him down.

Life for Jack hummed along pleasantly enough with Mum and Brian when Dad was away, with occasional spates of letters from the wild places, read by all until they were tattered. Then he returned, and Jack's routine world would melt into the background, replaced by a vision of colorful birds, Indians, brooding forests slashed through with silver rivers and ruins half-hidden under jungle creepers, filling the very rooms of their home and his nightly dreams.

He was indeed his father's son, iron-willed, abstemious— he had never touched liquor or tobacco— and as virgin as the day he was born. He required no physical or mental conditioning for the planned trek; his body was lean and muscular, his eye single, his vital energy channeled toward the purpose. The young women of the area had long ago given up any idea of distracting him.

If he had a fault, it was that he was over-serious for one so young. In this respect his friend, Raleigh, was the perfect foil. Raleigh was a natural cutup, the class clown, and his zaniness helped Jack loosen up. Jack, for his part, kept Raleigh's antics somewhat in check, and for this Raleigh's father, a physician at Seaton, admired Jack and encouraged the friendship.

Somewhat to Fawcett's dismay, Raleigh was in Los Angeles with his mother and would be joining him and Jack in New York, at the start of their journey. He would've liked to have had him there for training, to make sure of his conditioning and give him lessons in Portuguese and surveying. But Raleigh was a quick learner and there would be time aboard ship for crash courses, which would have to suffice. More important, Jack vouched for his friend's general fitness and health, and that was good enough for Fawcett.

"Cheeky," asked Fawcett, poking around in the pantry, "How are we stocked for oats? I'll soak them for porridge tomorrow."

"There's another sack, there, dear— see it? But I wish you'd let me get breakfast for a change... "

"No, I'd rather see you lolling in bed. Besides, I enjoy cooking. Why don't I take over all of it; then you can help Jack with surveying. What do you think?"

Nina laughed. "You have made yourself a deal."

Jack, stoking the fire, glanced up at his father. "I don't know how you find time, or energy, to do everything, including writing. When do you sleep?"

"I get enough sleep," answered Fawcett, measuring oats into a pot.

"How is it going, darling? The book, I mean," Nina asked.

"Almost done! For what it's worth." The subject of Fawcett's memoirs was quickly dropped. Everyone knew the writing of it had served dual ostensible purposes: to give him something worthwhile to do while he sought funding and sat out the delays— patience for the waiting game never being his strong point— and to present the complete background for his convictions. But lurking in the back of their minds was the awareness he might never return from this final expedition; now might be the only time to record his story.

Fawcett felt a peculiar sort of assurance he would reach his goal; what he discussed with no one but his family, however, was an intuition of the most difficult part: returning to tell of it. If "Z" was inhabited, as he suspected, its residents could have many reasons for wishing to remain hidden. All the indications of his research and experience pointed to a place within uncharted forests, where the remnant of a once-numerous people lived encircled and shielded by primitive tribes. Fawcett might penetrate this barrier, but escaping from the protected center was another question entirely.

Though he wrestled with the fear he was slipping into superstition, which he'd always detested, he felt the figurine might function as a sort of key, allowing passage through the filter of Indians.

When he was discouraged he sometimes took it from its case, allowing its strange current to vibrate through his body. That more than one psychometrist had given essentially the same reading was a vital confirmation of all the bits and pieces of evidence he'd gathered over the years, and he clung to it. Thank God he and Nina were in perfect accord in this area; in fact, it was she who had located the psychometrists.

The readers had each seen a large continent, where no continent exists today, in the Atlantic Ocean between Northern Africa and South America. This body of land appeared to have distinct differences between its east and west sides, the two regions being divided by mountain ranges in which live volcanoes were evident. The eastern side was sparsely populated. The well-built people had bright, piercing, dark eyes, and high cheekbones. Their structures, including temples, indicated a reasonably advanced civilization; their religion appeared to be a type of demonology.

The western land was far more heavily populated, its cities crowded. The terrain was hilly and lushly vegetated. The society was divided into a sophisticated, graceful ruling class, a middle class, and a large number of the poor and enslaved. There were many beautiful temples carved into the rock cliffs, but here, too, the people practiced the black arts and their worship centered around blood sacrifice. In some of the temples, priests paid homage to an icon of a large eye, placed over the altar.

The high priests wore breastplates comparable to that seen on the figurine, which appeared to be a representation of a certain eminent priest or leader. Similar carved figures were seen by some of the psychometrists occupying special niches in the temples.

As one reader said: "The effigy I now hold was entrusted to a priest, a guardian of the earth, who was charged to preserve it carefully and pass it to others until, in the course of generations of time, it would fall into the hands of a person who is the reincarnation of the priest it depicts. At this time in the affairs of mankind, all that was forgotten shall again come to light."

With slight differences in detail, the psychometrists then saw the violent end of the two societies. One reader heard a voice declaring the time had come to demonstrate the weakness of the people, who had lived without humility, as if they held dominion over both Creation and Creator. "Now, hear the cries of the powerless!" said the voice.

The land suddenly shook, and a sound like thunder issued forth as the earth heaved and pitched. Volcanoes roared like dragons, spewing fiery lava and poisonous gases. The seas rose; great walls of water swept over the continent, flooding all but the highest mountains. The earth's seizures continued as chaos reigned among the small portion of the populace that survived the waters. In the midst of the tumult a few people managed to climb into the mountains, including the priest who safeguarded the figurine. Some of the inhabitants were able to escape in boats, though many of these capsized in the churning sea.

Those who lived looked back from their boats to see the continent inundated but for the central ranges, where refugees cowered in terror. The mighty voice spoke again. "Behold the judgment of Atlanta!"

None of the readers could give Fawcett an exact date for the disaster, but most of them discerned a time long before the dynasties of Egypt. None could state precisely what had happened to the figurine.

In the long winter days, Fawcett and Nina had researched and discussed the stories of Atlantis, and the arguments for and against its existence. They approached the issue as amateur geologists, anthropologists, and archaeologists. Both had sufficient intelligence and education to evaluate the evidence objectively, but they could not ignore the role often played, in many great discoveries, by intuition and inspiration. In the end they concluded the wide collection of clues Fawcett had brought back from Brazil, including scientific evidence such as heiroglyphics, weighed heavily in favor of Atlantis as fact, rather than myth. It explained so many enigmas and anomalies that it was almost irresistible.

After much deliberation and discussion with Nina, he had decided to include the psychometrists' revelations in his memoirs. They both felt strongly that the importance of speaking out courageously justified the risk of ridicule.

"Things have already reached a point where people are dividing into camps: those who credit my accounts, or at least maintain open minds, and those who've decided I'm daft," he told his wife, watching her brush out her long hair at bedtime. "I may as well tell it all. Either I *have* succumbed to nonsense, or I'm ahead of my time. One or the other."

"It's our particular society, darling. Remember, not all cultures draw such a rigid distinction between the material and the unknown..."

"Yes, quite right. Perhaps I should've approached the Chinese for funds."

They both laughed.

"At any rate, Cheeky, one thing I *won't* be including in my memoirs is the exact route I plan to take."

"You're concerned people will try to follow."

"That's one reason. Another group barging in on us could spoil everything, especially any hopes we have of acceptance by the Indians. But another worry has been nagging at me... though I hesitate to bring it up..."

She sighed. "You may as well. I'm sure I've already confronted every possible fear that I have for you."

"Well, in the event we should not return in a reasonable length of time, say, three or four years," he began, watching his wife's face, "The very last thing I'd want is a search party trooping off to my rescue. I mean, if we can't make it to 'Z' and back, with all my years of experience in those regions, it's highly unlikely a rescue party would survive, either. I don't want anyone risking their necks on my behalf."

Nina nodded slowly, crawling under the covers beside him.

"Cheeky, I mean it. Do everything you can to discourage them. And that includes Brian."

"Oh, I will, I promise; but you know how people are. I can't stop anyone who's determined... "

"At least tell them that these are my wishes, all right?"

He held her close to him, feeling her heart beat, and kissed her hair, as he continued.

"You know I'll do everything in my power to see that Jack returns safely to you, and Raleigh to his family. As for you and me, we have a beautiful retirement ahead of us in Rio... Ah, my dear, you'll love it there, just keep that vision in mind while we're apart!"

"I'll try; but my mind'll be busy, as always, visualizing guardian spirits around you. There might not be much space for Rio."

"Huh! I won't interfere with whatever you've been doing, because something's always seemed to be protecting me and my men." They were quiet for a few moments.

"Cheeky," he began, "Another thing: The more I've thought about it, the more I think it's important for you and me to work out some sort of signals between us, including fine-tuning our efforts at telepathy."

"What do you have in mind?"

"Well, I truly believe you'll be able to receive a general message that I'm alive, or that I've found 'Z'... But you might need something a bit more concrete in order to convince other people."

"Why should I care? People believe what they want to believe, anyway."

"What I'm getting at is this: Let's say I've reached 'Z', and now I'm ready to bring the evidence back to the world-at-large; I might need some help protecting, or even transporting, this evidence. I mean, it's quite likely I might have some great slab of stone bearing inscriptions, that sort of thing..."

"Yes, I see."

"All I know is, this problem of *proof* concerns me more and more. We could make our goal, discover something fabulous, get out safely— and come home to find no one believes us! And if 'Z' is deserted and in ruins like Raposo's city, there may be no other evidence than what's carved in indestructible stone. We can't depend on getting something as delicate as photographic film back safely, especially in that climate."

"Right, and you can't depend on turning up portable objects like coins or engraved metal plates..."

"Exactly."

The two were silent for a few minutes, thinking. At length Nina said:

"Is it remotely possible you could do something on the order of the message-in-a-bottle idea? Write a message, enclose it in a metal container or otherwise protect it from the elements, and get it to an area where someone would come across it before too much time has passed?"

"Mmm... Maybe. But we have to assume I might not have the materials for that; the paper to write on, nor a proper container, even. Cheeky, you can't know what it's like there. Sometimes everything is wet, either from constant rain or from falling into the river... You know how many times my sketches and journals have been destroyed; and this trip promises to be even worse. There are so many ways we can lose our belongings, or have to jettison certain things."

"Ah! There's an idea, actually." Her husband turned to glance at her quizzically. "Leave behind some sturdy object, perhaps something on which you could scratch a brief message...? Would this be more feasible?"

Fawcett rubbed his chin. "You're on the right track, my dear, let's see... Some of my surveying equipment bears my initials, either engraved into the metal itself or inside the case. And anything that's weighty, such as the theodolite, would have to be left by the wayside if we lose pack animals, say... How's this: If possible I'll leave some sort of written message in the case or with the object, but if I can't do that for some reason, the item itself will stand as the message!"

Nina digested this for a moment. "But how will I know, if there's no written message, whether this object is a signal or was simply jettisoned?"

"Perhaps by the location in which it's found, or other clues indicating we'd lost our animals, and dumped other heavy items as well. In that case, it's not a signal."

"Hm, all right..."

"And Cheeky, your intuition will undoubtedly play a role in the interpretation of any signals; we can't get away from that, I suppose. As you said, people will believe as they wish. But back to my original problem: having something real and concrete, and our prearranged signal, might help to convince others *and* lead them to the area where I can meet up with them as I come out. And I repeat. This would *not* be an SOS or a clue for any rescue party!"

"I understand," Nina said solemnly, sinking back against her husband's chest.

"Brian, where is the lunch I made you?"

"It's right here, Mother; don't worry, I wouldn't leave *that* behind!" The family stood on the platform, waiting for a train that would take Brian to his ship at Liverpool and the first leg of a long journey to Peru. The March wind made Nina shiver, and she suppressed an impulse to close the top button of her younger son's coat.

It was the cruelest blow that eighteen-year-old Brian would also be leaving home; but he shared his brother's passion for South America, equalled only by his dedication to a career in locomotive engineering. When he sought and won a railway position in Peru and joyfully dove into a textbook in beginning Spanish, Nina had to admit it had been inevitable. In a few years, she silently prayed, let us all be reunited in Rio at our housewarming party...

Warmed by that future scene, when the train chugged into St. David's Station she was able to smile at Brian's obvious excitement as his family went aboard to help him stow his belongings and settle at his seat.

"Here's one more parcel to worry about." Brian took the package from his father and untied its string. "What's this? Books? Ah, a Spanish dictionary... but Dad, this is your own."

"Yes, from my Bolivian years... But you take it, son, you need it more than I do, now. My Spanish grammar is in there, too. The books you're taking along are insufficient."

"Excellent; I never did have enough time to study, but now I'll have nothing but time on the trip out." He hesitated. "I wish we were at least going as far as New York together."

"We'll be right behind you," Jack put in, crossing his fingers. He took Brian's hand in a firm farewell grip. The brothers looked into each other's eyes for the last time. The warning whistle blew.

Fawcett stepped forward. His years in South America had taught him there were times when a British handshake wasn't enough, and he clasped his son in a warm, Brazilian abraço.

"I'll see you and Jack in a few years, in South America," Brian said, a little huskily.

"That you will!" Fawcett moved aside to let Nina kiss her son, and the family hastily debarked as the last whistle shrieked in their ears.

Brian leaned from the carriage window to wave at them all, standing on the platform, and caught his mother surreptitiously wiping away a tear. Jack saw it, too, and as the train began to pull out he escorted his mother into the station house. But Fawcett remained rooted to the platform, and Brian watched from the window until the tall, straight form of his father could no longer be seen.

*

January 22, 1925
On board S.S. Vauban

Aside from observing the pleasure Jack and Raleigh are finding in this long voyage, I am so bored my teeth itch. I count the days and hours until we land in Rio.

But— at least we are actually on our way! When we saw Brian off for Peru, I never dreamed Jack and I would still be cooling our heels in Stoke Canon six or seven months later. Tthere were funding delays, postponed sailings, problems too tedious to retell. It was late October before we could sail for New York.

In that city, I contacted every scientific organization that would hear me in an effort to raise more money, with success in several of them, but the greatest coup was an agreement with the North American Newspaper Alliance for newspaper rights to the story. I am now a "special correspondent," and owing to the various articles covering our departure, upwards of forty million people have read of our quest. There may be quite a large gap of time in which NANA will hear nothing from me or of me, but I hope the eventual outcome of our expedition will sell many newspapers and return their investment many times over.

Though the stresses of the past three years have taken their toll, I feel physically and mentally ready for my last venture. It appears to be preordained. I recall how I had hovered on the edge of giving up my belief in "Z" or any such ancient places after the failed trek with Felipe... But something prodded me to take my solo journey, and there I found the evidence I needed. That this happened by sheer luck is improbable.

The city we will be seeking may or may not be the same that Raposo found. I believe it's located in the region north of what I call Dead Horse Camp, the site of my horse's collapse in 1921. I've publicly stated that we will continue northeast to the Xingu, and somewhere east of that river we'll turn northward. Then according to our announced plan, when it's time to return home we'll follow the watershed to Santa Maria do Araguaya, continuing eastward to the Rio Tocantins and eventually reaching Bahia City on the seacoast.

This scheme is partly determined by my research and the many reports I've heard from Indians and others; and partly based on the ruins I spotted on my solo trek. These appear to be the remains of an outpost of Z, and include what looked in my spyglass like one of the towers described by others. But I've been deliberately general and vague, hoping to discourage anyone from following or attempting a rescue. In addition, the plan may change considerably as we proceed; only a fool would try to plot a precise course when searching for a needle in a haystack. We will be following clues as they present themselves, attempting to communicate with native tribes, and, as always, heeding our intuitions.

I'm eager to land in Rio, where I intend to show Jack and Raleigh around the high spots. Since many hardships await us, I want them to enjoy their week in this lovely city. Then we'll be off to São Paulo, then Mato Grosso and Cuyabá.

While I'm in a writing mood, I'll dash off a letter to Brian. I've had him on my mind a great deal lately, as we'll soon be on the same continent, at least.

February found the three men en route to São Paulo, from which city they began the long journey by rail to Corumbá. From there they continued via river launch to Cuyabá where Fawcett acquired two horses, eight mules, and two dogs, and hired two peons to accompany them for part of their trek.

In mid-April things were going as well as could be expected, for that region. There were endless delays, and the tail of the summer season proved even wetter than usual. The intense humidity took its toll on Fawcett; he wasn't sure if the weather was actually that much worse than he remembered it, or if he was simply that much older. But they were now truly on their way and Jack was in his element, at last living his dream.

To Raleigh it was a wondrous adventure; "But I could do without the ticks," he said one night, as they sat by the campfire assessing the day's bodily damage wrought by insects. He had taken off his shoes and socks, and was having a good scratch.

"Ugh, I'll agree!" exclaimed Jack, removing another tick from his underarm.

Fawcett cast a practiced eye at a large red spot on Raleigh's left foot. "I say, Raleigh; that doesn't look good..."

"What, this? It was a tick bite. Now it's rather sore, I admit."

"And swollen. We'd better take good care of that. The smallest injury to a foot can become a great problem in the wilderness, especially in this climate. Don't scratch. Don't even touch it." Fawcett went into his first-aid kit for salve and a gauze dressing.

"There, that should do it." He sat back, watching Raleigh carefully replace his sock over the small bandage. "Good thing we're riding; it'll have a chance to heal."

The next day the men found themselves in the Land of Invisible Demons, as Jack called it. Clouds of piums, which could only be seen in direct sunshine, attacked with merciless bites having toxic effect far out of proportion to their size. Every inch of exposed skin was covered with welts from these creatures, who could fly easily through protective netting. Even the ticks in this region were too tiny to be removed, and during their sojourn in the skin they caused intense itching.

In a few more days they reached the ranch of Colonel Hermenegildo Galvão, Fawcett's old friend.

"So you received my letter?" Fawcett asked, as Galvão's men relieved the mules of their packs.

"Yes, miracles do happen, sometimes the mail gets through in timely fashion! Come in, come in... I am so delighted to at last meet your son, and his friend!"

While Jack and Raleigh went off for a bath, Fawcett spoke with Colonel Galvão. "I hope you won't mind if we linger here a few days; Raleigh's getting a nasty sore on his foot, worsening with each day. I'd like to see it healed."

"I'll be happy if you stay a month! We have years of talking to catch up with. His foot, eh? That can escalate to something serious, as we well know... One of my men is very good at doctoring such things; I'll get him on it right away. Ah! And by the way, we were speaking of mail, a letter arrived for you bearing the return address of Senhor Donayre."

"Donayre! Capital! I wrote him of my plans for this journey, as he's always been interested in my quest."

Galvão opened the drawer of a small table near the entrance and handed Fawcett the letter.

"Thank you, my friend. Oh, it is good to be here again!"

That night, an herbal poultice having been applied to Raleigh's ulcerated foot, the men savored a hearty meal.

"Whatever you need while you're my guests, simply ask one of the servants," their host said graciously. "I assume you two young fellows can make your wishes known in Portuguese by now?"

Raleigh laughed. "Jack will have to do the asking for me. He gets by all right; I can't utter a sensible word!"

"True enough," concurred Fawcett. "Raleigh has multiple talents, but Portuguese isn't among them."

"Photography is his forte," put in Jack. "He'll be helping my father with that task, if we can keep the equipment dry enough."

Galvão leaned over, pushing his empty plate aside. "Well, then, I have something in mind that you might be interested in photographing..."

He described a long, rectangular rock he had found in the Rio Paranatinga. Someone had bored three holes through it, sealing the middle opening at both ends with a sort of cement. On the back side of this rock were inscribed fourteen characters which were completely unfamiliar to Galvão.

Fawcett was intrigued. "It will be interesting to see if any of these characters are similar to those I've collected." He was thinking of the figurine. "Perhaps tomorrow? And I'll be the photographer, myself... Sorry, Raleigh, I want you to stay off that foot for a few days."

"Tomorrow's fine!" Galvão laughed. "I'm infected with your curiosity."

"There are many oddities waiting to be examined. Some distance north of Dead Horse Camp, I believe we'll come across a short, squat, stone tower, lit from within by an unknown source that never burns out. Since it's in Morcegos territory, no one has wanted to investigate closely, it seems. But Donayre's letter confounds me a bit... I'll go over it with you later." He turned to Jack and Raleigh. "He sends new information we'll need to digest."

"How do you know of this tower?" asked Galvão.

"From my Indian sources. I estimate the distance from their descriptions of their journeys, the terrain, and the number of days they walked."

"Well, it reminds me of something I was told by an Indian from a very remote tribe... I mean, the back-of-beyond! I took him to a great church in Cuyabá— expecting to awe him, you know— but where he came from, he said, far back in the jungle, were much bigger and more ornate buildings! And in some of them, on a central column a large crystal is mounted, which emits light bright enough to flood every corner."

"Ah," said Fawcett, "I wonder if you could point out, on my map, the general vicinity of this man's tribe... I'd like to see if it tallies with other information I have."

"Of course!" The two men retired to Galvão's office where Fawcett was able to spread his maps on a large table. Jack and Raleigh remained at the dining table, sipping their coffee, listening to the older men compare notes in the next room.

"Sorry about your foot," Jack said in a low voice. "It looks as though you won't be rambling the woods with us tomorrow."

356

Raleigh shrugged. "It's all right. I'm not going to argue. More than anything I want this foot to be set aright. Nothing, but nothing, is going to keep me from continuing to the goal." His twinkling eyes had taken on a steely glint.

"Good man." Jack raised his coffee cup. "Here's to 'Z'!"

"All the way."

"This *is* rather perplexing." Colonel Galvão scratched his chin thoughtfully. "May I have another look at the map Donayre sent?"

"Here it is." Fawcett fished around beneath one of the maps for a small, creased sheet of paper.

Donayre had explained in his letter that an Indian, whose tribe lives near the Juruena River, came to work for him. He told Donayre of an ancient highway running east and west; small, ruined cities are found along this road, he said, flanking a large capital in the center of an area where many rivers flow. The elders of his tribe tell of white Indians living in the capital, part of which was built underground. The tower Fawcett sought was near the Juruena, Donayre had written, not the Xingu.

"See here, now," Fawcett said, "I'm not surprised that there might be more than one of the towers and other ruined outposts; it quite tallies with accounts I've been given by people in widely separated regions. But Donayre's map— I should say, the Indian's map; he drew it, Donayre only reproduced it for me and labelled a few things— well, it conflicts with some of my ideas..."

"Let's see," said Galvão, picking up a pawn from the chessboard on a side table. "It shows a tower here... " He placed the pawn on one of Fawcett's maps. "Right? Possibly another here— "

"No, wait; use this map, the broader view of the entire region." Fawcett swept aside the other maps. "Now, replace the pawns... And the ruined tower I saw from the east was about here..."

Fawcett looked through his notes and diagrams, positioning more pawns on the regional map. "There were reports of a stone building with perpetual light in this general area, here... "

"What are we making, a spiral?" asked Galvão.

"Not quite."

After a while Fawcett stood back from the table with pad and pencil, rapidly diagramming what he saw on the map, which at first glance appeared to be a confusion of pawns.

"Have you a straightedge?"

Galvão fetched the item from a desk drawer, and Fawcett drew a few lines on the pad. Then he put down his pencil, a look of wonder dawning in his eyes.

"Extraordinary. Beyond anything I had imagined."

"Does it affect your planned route?"

Fawcett looked at him. "It changes everything." He handed his diagram to Colonel Galvão, adding:

"I trust you will never share what you see with anyone, aside from my wife."

"These are wonderful," said Fawcett, fiddling with his camera. "But I don't know if I'll be able to photograph them clearly... " One of Galvão's men, Manoel, tried to hold the boat steady while Fawcett snapped a few shots.

"Difficult, isn't it?" agreed Galvão. "The characters are almost hidden, as if they weren't meant to be readily seen; and with the movement of the boat— "

"The biggest problem, actually, is poor light. But at least I have a copy of them, on paper." Fawcett had been pleased to find several characters on the rock which were familiar to him. He took photographs, and carefully examined the holes, particularly the material used to close the middle opening. It was as hard as the rock, but didn't look like any cement he'd seen.

They returned to the bungalow to sit in the relative coolness of the veranda.

"I'll send a copy of the inscriptions back to my wife to analyze," Fawcett said. "Ever since I was posted to Ceylon, I've been fascinated by carved hieroglyphs, and I've made a study of it. I find that a great number of the characters, from all over the world— Ceylon, Malta, North Africa, Ireland, and here... match perfectly."

"From one distant place to another?"

"That's right. And many others are too similar to be coincidental. The conclusion I draw from that, and other connections, is that civilization originated from one central source."

As they lounged on the steps, discussing Fawcett's theory and refreshing themselves with cups of maté, Manoel and another Indian approached.

Shyly Manoel told Galvão that his friend had some information which might interest the English Colonel.

"*Sim,*" Galvão nodded at the man, motioning him forward. The Indian spoke in a dialect which Manoel translated as best he could.

"He lives on the *chapada*, you see, the high land over there— " Manoel gestured to the north.

"Yes," Fawcett put in, "I know of the plateau, once part of an ancient island."

"Well, up there are skeletons of giant animals, he says, and more scratchings on flat pieces of rock... and the stone floors of great buildings— " He listened further, then interpreted: "In the middle of a plain there is a huge rock carved like a mushroom."

"What?" asked Galvão. "A mushroom?"

"That is what he said."

"Can he describe it further?" Fawcett asked.

Manoel said a few words to his friend, and the Indian picked up a stick and drew a simple, clear shape in the dirt.

"Well, that's a typical mushroom," said Fawcett. "Strange object for a carving! Anything else?"

No, said the Indian from the chapada, only fallen trees made of stone rather than wood.

"Petrified trees," murmured Fawcett.

Galvão offered the two Indian men maté, and after they had drained their cups, they left. Galvão turned to his guest.

"What do you think?"

"Interesting," Fawcett said, smiling.

Four more days of rest and herb poultices brought improvement in Raleigh's lesion. The three men were restless to continue, and said farewell to their genial host.

"We can never thank you enough," began Fawcett.

"Tush! For nothing, it was such a pleasure to have you here. Jack, Raleigh..." He embraced the three in turn. "Go with God. I hope we will meet again, before too long."

The party moved down the trail, the two peons, the mules, the riders on their horses; Fawcett turned back once, to wave. Galvão watched until they were out of sight and, though not a religious man, he crossed himself and murmured a brief blessing.

The miles and the days passed in a continuing round of damp, chilly nights, sweltering days, unceasing insect attacks of one species or the other, and frequent difficulties with the mules as they sank deeply into the mucky streambeds or balked at crossing altogether. They reached a small settlement of Bacairy Indians and spent a couple of days resting there, talking to the people.

Jack and Raleigh were excited when several naked Indians from the region of the Xingu showed up at the Bacairy's post.

"These are truly wild Indians, untainted by civilization," Fawcett said as he set up his camera, having secured permission to photograph them.

"Our peons are looking rather terrified," noted Raleigh.

"Yes, I see," said Fawcett, glancing up. "They will be going back soon, I'm sure... "

"Look," Jack interrupted. "Isn't that the Bacairy chief you wanted to talk to? The one who speaks Portuguese?"

"Ah, yes! Roberto. I'm almost finished here. Get a bottle of wine from the packs, would you? I want to offer him a gift... I'll be right with you."

Later, the men sat in the shade of a tree, watching the chief refill his cup with wine and become quite talkative. The sun dipped lower and lower, flickering through the branches as they stirred in a gentle breeze.

Fawcett had asked Roberto if he'd heard of ancient cities in the region, or rocks with strange carvings. Immediately he responded by saying he had known of several cities, one in particular.

"My grandfather had been to this place, many days' journey from here, that way." He pointed northwest. "He said our ancestors built it. I used to beg him to take me there; I wanted to see the waterfall."

"Waterfall?"

"A powerful river runs beside the city, and there are enormous falls that can be heard far away, he told me. Below them is a wide lake, and in it, near the waterfall, is a man made of shiny white rock. I always wanted to see and hear this roaring water, and see the stone man, who moves back and forth a little in the powerful current."

"Why didn't you go?"

"My grandfather was too old to take me, and my father said there were many bad people living near there... And now, I'm too old for such a journey. I will never see it." He sighed, and sipped from his cup.

Fawcett looked at Roberto intently. "That could be the Rio São Manoel." Roberto shrugged. "Go on, what else did your grandfather say about this place?"

"Many strange things. The city has stone buildings set along straight lines, like this." He crossed a finger from each hand to show streets crossing at right angles. "Most buildings were low, not higher than that tree, there— but he saw some very big, high buildings, one that he thought was a temple, and he never forgot it because inside was a large round, flat crystal that made light."

"Did he see any people in the city?"

"He didn't tell me, if he did. But I remember something else... On the way to this city, there is a small building of stone that also has a light in it. Some of my people have seen this, too, and all are afraid of it."

Jack, who had been listening quietly and jotting a few notes, spoke up: "Was it like this?" He flipped back through his notebook a number of pages until he found a drawing his father had made. He showed it to Roberto.

"Uh! That looks like it, from what people have told me. Have you seen it?"

"No," Jack replied in hesitant Portuguese. "Others have described a similar place to my father."

Just then the group was startled by a sound, something between a hiss and a whine, coming from the north. The sound seemed to rise high above the forest and then diminish as it fell slowly downward, like a roman candle. Then there was a rolling, thunderous boom.

"What on earth— " began Raleigh, sitting up straight.

They all looked at Roberto, who was placid enough, having paused only a moment before taking another sip. He chuckled at the Englishmen's wide eyes.

"We hear that sometimes."

"Have you any idea what it is?" asked Fawcett.

"Nobody knows. Some people are afraid, but it's never hurt us, so... " He shrugged. "What scares people even more is this sound: " He mimicked a deep, snoring sound.

"And that sound also comes from those forests?" Fawcett gestured to the north. Roberto nodded.

"How long have you heard these sounds?" asked Jack.

"For many years, most of my life. But maybe they happen more often, now."

"Hm, perhaps it has a volcanic explanation," Fawcett speculated.

"If you go there, you might find out," said Roberto, as he rose unsteadily. "And you might see the city, and the waterfall. I will ask my ancestors to show you the way." He turned toward the group of huts.

"Thank you, Roberto," Fawcett called after him. "We might need them."

May 29, 1925
Dead Horse Camp
My dearest Cheeky,

Though we've encountered both common and uncommon difficulties along the way, at last we've arrived at Dead Horse Camp. I hope you, and Brian, have received the letters we sent from H. Galvão's fazenda. This, my darling girl, will be the last you'll hear from me for quite some time... Tomorrow I'll send the peons back— they are increasingly eager to return— and trust they'll take care of our letters. I have also sent dozens of photographs, of wild Indians and various artifacts, to NANA with a request that you will be sent copies.

Jack tells me he has written an account for you of our time spent with the Bacairys, so I won't repeat it; my hands are covered with stings from little bees and other insects, and they're so swollen it's challenging to write. Don't you wish you were here?

Jack is also well-bitten, but otherwise he seems stronger every day. I envy his youth; I'll admit I'm feeling my age somewhat.

Raleigh is the one who worries me. His foot is once again swollen and ulcerated, with clumps of dead and dying skin falling away. We're still riding saddle mules and will continue with five cargo mules as well, but this can't last; eventually there may be little for the animals to eat. I do not see how he would be able to continue afoot, but he is absolutely determined to go on. His perseverance is admirable, but I'm anxious about him.

Cheeky, the plan I outlined to you has changed dramatically, due to

*new information I received while at Galvão's. He's aware of everything
that transpired, but he can be trusted to keep quiet about it. I think it best
I write nothing further, since for all I know our correspondence might be
tampered with at some point. All I will say is that many of the riddles and
inconsistencies that plagued me are now resolved, and my eyes have been
opened to the magnitude of this enigma which has possessed me for so long.*

*We should come upon Indians in a week or two, and a waterfall spo-
ken of in all the tales. We still hope to reach Z by August. If I'm able to
accomplish this goal at long last, my love, it will be to a great extent because of you. You have been my steadfast partner on so many levels, practical as well as spiritual, ever believing in me and boosting my spirits when
I faltered. In long separations such as we've endured, the one left behind
bears the greater burden.*

*The only means I have of repaying your sacrifice is to see to it that
your confidence has not been in vain.*
All my love, P.

Fawcett sealed the letter and placed it in the pack with the
other letters, reports, and photographs the peons would take with
them the next day. Raleigh and Jack were napping, under head
veils that did little good, and he stood for a moment looking down
at their fresh, young faces. The peons, gone to hunt for game, were
nowhere in sight.

He walked down to the stream, where his horse had fallen and
still lay. He gazed at the white bones, some of them scattered
about by animals.

Suddenly assailed by doubts, he thought of sending Jack and
Raleigh back with the peons; he'd go on alone, responsible only for
himself. He dropped his head. He knew they wouldn't hear of it;
and he knew he needed them.

He removed the figurine from a small pack he wore when travelling, and kept always near his person. Some of the characters on
the effigy's chestplate had found their match on Galvão's rock.
How he wished to know their meaning!

He gripped the figurine firmly in his inflamed hand. *It's time
to take you back where you belong. We should be there very soon.*

363

EPILOGUE
Madeira, 1936

Nina sat in her usual chair by the window, where she could look up from her reading or sewing now and then to rest her eyes on the flowering vines outside. She folded Brian's letter and put it back in the envelope. She sat peacefully for a while, watching a raptor lazily circle in the blue heavens.

Her son had written from London, where the experts of the Royal Anthropological Institute had affirmed that the bones found near the Kuluene River were not his father's. She could've told them so. Where their assessment was made on the basis of height, however, hers was formed according to intimate knowledge of her husband's habit and character.

The Kalapalo Indians, she assumed, had come up with both story and bones to collect the reward NANA had offered for "the truth". Though she, too, wanted the truth, and she had tirelessly pursued it and pressured NANA, and anyone else who would listen, she had from the beginning felt the reward was a bad idea; she knew Puggy would've laughed at it. The story the Kalapalo gave— of multiple insults to the tribe, resulting in the murder of the offending white men— in no way matched the personalities of her husband, son, or Raleigh. Fawcett, who wouldn't fire on any group of Indians even when they sent a shower of arrows his way, would never attack a chief; and her virginal son would be the last man on earth to force himself on the chief's wife. It was ludicrous.

Scarcely two years after the Fawcett party had left Dead Horse Camp, the rumors and "Fawcett sightings" had started to come in, most of which were investigated and found to be unlikely. In 1928, NANA organized a rescue expedition led by Commander George Dyott. This party had found Fawcett's metal uniform case in the possession of an Anaqua Indian chief. The chief said the case was a gift from a white man who was travelling with two younger men, both lame; the three had crossed the Kuluene River and continued east. It sounded believable, but for one detail: The case was one Fawcett had discarded in 1920.

Dyott believed the party had been killed, but had no proof of it. He finished his journey with the feeling that if a lost civilization existed in Brazil, it would likely be found somewhere between the Xingu and Araguaya Rivers.

Fawcett's concerns about rescue efforts were justified. Journalist Albert de Winton's 1930 search party, for example, reached the Kalapalo village through which Fawcett had apparently passed before crossing the Kuluene; but the de Winton group never returned.

There were others, some claiming, as did Swiss trapper Stefan Rattin in 1932, to have seen an old white man held captive by the Indians. Some of them, including Rattin, attempted to return to the tribes and rescue the white man; but they, too, were swallowed by the forest and never seen again.

Nina still had the letter Senhor Galvão had written her, dated July 8, 1932. Galvão insisted Fawcett had outlined for him on a map his intended route, but though Galvão shared the information with search parties, they usually did not follow this route. He offered to lead an expedition himself, "to find out the real truth".

Nina didn't take him up on his offer; she felt her husband would not have approved. After all, as Commander Dyott said, it had seemed to him as his expedition tried to follow Fawcett's trail that he had purposely obscured his route. Though she knew Galvão had the best intentions, her husband's last letter to her had made his feelings clear.

Then, a year after Galvão wrote to her, the compass portion of Fawcett's theodolite was found near the Bacairy outpost by Colonel

Botelho, deputy of Mato Grosso State.

To Nina, the significance of the find was clear. But now she confronted the very problem she had discussed with her husband: How to get people to believe her? How could she convince others she'd been receiving telepathic messages from him, simply to the effect that he was alive, but his freedom was restricted. There was more, more of the communication, but she couldn't seem to hear it or see it, though she worked in concert with several psychics whom she trusted.

Even Brian didn't fully believe her. She had written him of her assurance that the compass was a message to her, that his father found what he sought and now needed help in coming out from the interior. Brian responded with skepticism, and when he returned to Europe on leave they'd argued the matter.

"Brian, listen: Your father knew Colonel Botelho was often in that area as part of his duties. The compass has identifying numbers which the makers have traced to the theodolite sold to him in 1913."

"I know, Mother, there's no question it's his instrument– "

"He knew it would be identified as his, and he had all hopes Botelho would find it, *and* he knew I would understand its meaning. We talked about this very thing!"

"Yes, so you said in your letters... But to be realistic, Mother, it's far likelier it was one of the articles he had to leave behind in 1920, when the pack animals all died; or it might've been given to someone who offered him hospitality on that trip."

"Ah!" Nina threw up her hands. "My dear son, if we are to be 'realistic', as you say, your argument is far from the mark. There is every indication, don't forget, that he'd never been near the Bacairys until the last trip. The compass would not have been left behind in that vicinity in 1920."

Brian said nothing.

"Also, look at this." She turned to the table where the selfsame compass lay and thrust it into her son's hands. "Is it not in tip-top condition? No corrosion at all. I have done nothing to refurbish it, nor did the Brazilians; this is just as it was found, minus a bit of mud and debris, no doubt."

"I see where you're heading– "

"Yes! I know this instrument well, remember, and it could not have been in the weather long before it was found, I assure you. Besides, Brian, there's something more: *This* is the compass he had with him when he left; he didn't take a new one."

"You're quite sure, Mother?"

"Quite. I packed it for him, myself." There was a silence. Nina gently took the compass from her son and replaced it on the table.

"There's one more thing," she turned to face him, "for you to think about, son. Your father wrote in his journal that the Bacairys' primary settlement was far to the north, and more or less along his route, which is one reason he wanted to glean information from Roberto, right?"

"Yes, and so— ?"

"The point being, we can explain how the compass came to be near the southernmost Bacairy camp: The Bacairys themselves brought it there, at his behest."

Brian sat, thoughtful for a moment.

"If you're right, Mother, then the Bacairys were in contact with him even after he became— a captive, or whatever has happened— "

"Detained, let's say."

"Detained... and therefore they might still know where he is, and even be able to contact him now."

"Perhaps. But he *might* have given the compass to the Bacairys before he was restricted in his movements."

Brian sighed. "You do make a good case, I admit."

"Yes, it also squares, somewhat, with the Nafaqua woman's story. "

Soon after the compass had been found, Virginio Pessione, leader of an expedition to the Kuluene River, had encountered a woman of the Nafaqua tribe who had a story to tell, which he duly recorded and sent to the Royal Geographical Society. She'd been asked to repeat her story several times, by different interlocutors, and had remained consistent.

She told of three white men who descended the Kuluene in a canoe to her village. Her physical description of the three, and their relative ages, tallied with that of the Fawcett party, including details such as Fawcett's beard and bald head; and further, she stated that one of the younger men was the son of the elder. The approximate year they had shown up in the region was determined by the present apparent age of her son, whom she said had been a babe in arms at the time of the white men's arrival; this, too, conformed.

They were, and still are, she insisted, living with the Aruvudu tribe; in fact, the elder white man is now a chief, and his son is married to the daughter of another Aruvudu chief. When asked why the white men remain with the Aruvudu, she answered to the effect that they were watched constantly and were not allowed to leave. "Nearby tribes are very dangerous, the Suyas and Cayapos, and would kill them. They have no more bullets for their guns. And anyway," she added, "The Aruvudu want them to stay; they are greatly valued."

She described how the white men were allowed to visit all the Aruvudu villages, always under escort. They would draw in the sand, and teach the children. They spoke the languages of friendly regional tribes.

At this point Pessione wrote of having previously seen, along the Kuluene, what looked to be letters of the alphabet cut into the tree bark about two years ago, he estimated by their appearance. At the time he hadn't seen any particular significance in the finding, and so had not copied the markings.

Nina and Brian were struck by many parallels between the white men described and Percy, Jack, and Raleigh. In addition to physical correspondences, the detail about drawing in the sand hit home with them.

"They were both artists," Brian had said, trying to suppress his excitement— it wouldn't do to get one's hopes too high— "They always drew when they explained things; and Jack, you remember, absolutely could not resist picking up a stick and doodling on any smooth sand or dirt he came across!"

"I remember," Cheeky said, her eyes misting.

"It also makes sense," Brian added, "That they would've taken to the river if Raleigh's foot worsened, and they no longer had mounts." He paced, thinking. "Or it could be they found something momentous at the waterfall, causing them to use the river trying to get back immediately to report their find."

The woman's account of their captivity was all too credible, for several reasons. There were other known cases of detained whites who had become highly honored members of the tribe; they were sometimes wanted for their skills in medicine, and for the distinction of possessing a person from another race and culture.

The problem lay in convincing someone to try and reach the Aruvudu settlements. When Pessione had asked the Nafaqua woman how a group of white people could get to them, she launched into a long account of the numerous tribes, mostly unfriendly, that lived between the Kuluene River and the Aruvudu.

Nina persisted in trying to find someone who would help. Her husband was alive, that she knew in her heart regardless of the world's sympathetic disbelief. Then came developments which both reinforced her intuition and dampened her hopes.

She received in 1935 a letter from a Mr. Patrick Ulyatt, who had just returned from Mato Grosso. He and his brother, Gordon, had come across information about which they preferred to reveal no detail, that had persuaded them Fawcett, or at least one member of his party, was alive. Furthermore, the two brothers were now convinced that the lost city sought by Fawcett did exist.

Patrick and Gordon had set off in search of Fawcett's party, or any information they could find. After paddling up a tributary of the Madeira they made their way to the forest lining the Rio Machadinho, where they surprised a group of Boca Preta Indians. They were not allowed to pass onward, and in fact there was some doubt they would be allowed to turn back. The Boca Preta appeared to discuss among themselves what the fate of these travellers should be. At last, making it crystal clear they were not to continue their journey, but could only return the way they had come, they were spared. The Indians confiscated the Ulyatts' packs but left them their rifles, which seemed less a matter of thievery as it was insurance that without equipment or stores of food, they would be less likely to attempt to circle around the Boca Preta settlements. They then escorted the brothers for several miles of the return trip.

Why, the brothers wondered, had these Indians been so determined to halt the Ulyatts' passage through their territory?

On the way back, Patrick and Gordon spoke with rubber gatherers who spent their lives roaming the woods. From their remarks it was obvious they knew of Fawcett, his movements in the area, and his encounters with Indians. He was reported to have gone into a region which was encircled with hostile tribes; how he had penetrated these, the bushmen didn't know. The Ulyatts wondered the same.

But the brothers were now throughly drawn into the magnetic mystery that had captured Fawcett. They suffered greatly on their trek, he wrote, yet they were positively committed to go back. "I can't explain it, it may seem madness," Patrick wrote, "*But I must go back.*"

Yet more lives will be lost, Nina had thought, fearing for the Ulyatt brothers. *This is precisely what Puggy did not want; yet he said he might need help coming out... How to reconcile the two requests?*

The following year she received a letter from an Irish medium, Geraldine Cummins, with whom she had been in correspondence. Mrs. Cummins said she had received several telepathic messages from

Fawcett, who wanted her to tell Nina he had found relics of what appeared to be Atlantis but was now ill, drifting in and out of consciousness. In the past, Mrs. Cummins had relayed messages that convinced Nina the communiqués were genuine, since they contained personal meaning which only Fawcett and Nina would have known. The psychic appeared to have true talent; perhaps she was a better receiver of Fawcett's messages because she wasn't emotionally involved.

So he was alive, as she herself had sensed; he had made it through the belt of hostile, perhaps protective, savages; he had found proof of his theories. But as he had warned, the chance of his return was slim, indeed. There was now a compelling collection of evidence that the three men were virtual captives, with little hope of a rescue party having the skill and good fortune to both reach them and bring them out.

And now, he was ill. He was sixty-nine years old. Escape was most unlikely.

He had always belonged to the wild places, she knew; they had at last claimed him, brought him home.

Geneva, 1948

Nina Fawcett sat by the window, a different window in a different nation, the family Bible on her lap. Below her husband's name, she wrote 1948 as the date of death.

After communicating through Geraldine several times in the late 1930s concerning his discoveries and his illness, there was a long silence. This year, however, he notified them of his own passing at the age of eighty-one. With no other information, Nina could only assume, or hope, Jack and Raleigh were still alive.

Her husband was gone; she had known it even before the telephone call from Geraldine. She put the Bible on the table beside her, and her eyes fell on the compass, which always rested there. She picked it up. He had passed over, but he had not been killed by an Indian, or by anyone else. He had died peacefully.

Holding the compass, its cold metal slowly warming in her hands, she looked out at the tall conifers of the Swiss countryside. When the time was right, when his discoveries would be most meaningful for mankind, someone would find her husband's remains, and his city "Z". Someday, the end of his story could be written.

*

Upper Xingu region, 2005

"All right, how many is that in all, Michael?"

"Nineteen. We've found nineteen settlements so far, and at least four of those are good-sized residential centers."

"Could I see that satellite image again?" The visitor, journalist Evelyn Kelly, fumbled among the documents on the large table.

"Here it is. Compare it to the master diagram I made; see the pattern? So far we've uncovered two large clusters of villages. In each cluster, the settlements were integrated into a gridlike system; picture an enormous grid encompassing the entire area. Straight roads, about the width of our four-lane highways, link the settlements every two or three miles. Their version of our interstate highways, you might say, except that there were no vehicles that we know of. But in other words, there was quite an elaborate regional plan."

"How many people in each cluster, would you estimate?"

"Up to five thousand. And now, from a wide perspective, look at the entirety and we can see the roads and settlements were laid out in a wheel-like or galactic pattern, like a basic representation of a star system."

"Incredible."

"You know, we've been digging since the early 1990s, but it took forever to cut each survey corridor; we weren't really able to map the roads until '99, when GPS technology became available. *Then* we moved ahead quickly and uncovered a larger pattern."

"The Big Picture."

"Right. And with the new radar we have, which can penetrate the ground to locate buried ruins, we might turn up some very interesting sites in the future..."

Evelyn scribbled in a notebook while the archaeologist pulled another drawing over the others. "Here's something else for your article." He pointed to what appeared to be the hub of a wheel.

"In this simple diagram, you see an example of one community layout. All of them follow a similar plan. It's built around a central, circular plaza, with roads going straight out from this hub like a big X, forming the *same mathematical angles*. The supposed roads— with curbs, no less— continue in straight lines from one point to the next, leading to other, evenly-spaced villages. All of them interconnect and form the larger pattern."

"The implications are rather boggling, Mike."

"Well, yes; for starters, the people who created this complex had to be able to reproduce angles on a large scale, over great distances."

"What was in between the settlements? Forest and jungle?"

"No, in fact all those areas were apparently managed lands. Some of it was under cultivation, some was set aside as parkland. They cleared large areas for farms or orchards, and preserved other sectors as sources of wood, game, and probably medicines."

"How did you determine this?"

"Look again at the satellite image. Except for the preserves, the vegetation in these inter-settlement areas doesn't look at all like the forest in the areas outside the grid... that, you see there, is older forest. See the difference?"

"Oh, definitely." Evelyn pointed. "And what are these symbols?"

"Those represent bridges, these are canals or moats. We found these wherever the settlements abut wetlands. Some of them are still in use by the Kuikuro."

"They're a subgroup of the Xinguano Indians?"

"Right. They've been helping with our research. Interestingly, they're familiar with the rich soil we've found in the agricultural areas, which to us indicates past management of farmlands. They know certain plants grow well in this soil."

"This is the *terra preta* I've heard about?"

"That's it. There's no other soil like it, as far as I know. Not only is it super-fertile, it's also self-renewing, not needing the addition of any other organic material; and it never needs to lie fallow. Also, crops grown in it are very rich in nutrients."

"Most Amazon soils aren't very fertile, are they... And this was enhanced by humans, somehow?"

"We assume so. It's full of ceramic fragments, and charcoal... I'd say it's mad-made, all right, but we don't know how they made it! And we're finding areas of this soil all along the Amazon, the Tapajos, and other rivers, which suggests this region could've supported many more people than previously thought. People who made pottery," he added with emphasis.

"Any sign of dwellings, or what they might have been like?"

"No... In this area, people didn't have many sources of stone, like the Maya did, for example, to use for great cities or pyramids; that sort of thing. We assume their equipment and building materials mainly consisted of wood, and bone; and these don't last long in the Amazon.

In fact, it's the lack of stone buildings that caused all of this to stay hidden for so long. That, and their pattern of small integrated communities, rather than huge population centers."

"The jungle obliterated most of it, over time."

"Exactly. And the entire network hasn't yet been revealed."

They were interrupted by several beeps, and the archaeologist excused himself, turning to answer a satellite phone.

"Oh, hey there. I'm just giving the interview I told you about... Yeah, the data came through nice and clear; it looks like there are quite a few more sites, doesn't it? ...Okay, we'll talk more when I'm in Manaus. Thanks, Syl." He hung up and turned back to the journalist. "Where were we?"

"I'm going to let you get back to your work, Mike. You know, as my editor and I were saying before I came down here, your discoveries challenge many of our beliefs about the Amazon, don't they? We have some mental adjustments to make. It apparently wasn't the primordial wilderness we thought it was, before the Europeans came..."

"Yep. And what's even more intriguing, the inhabitants obviously possessed sophisticated knowledge in agriculture, math and astronomy, perhaps equal to the pyramid builders."

"Leaving all kinds of questions about what happened to them and their complex society. Oh, I love a good mystery! Listen, one more question that's been nagging me: You mentioned there were no vehicles. Why were the roads so wide? About 50 yards or more. Didn't they have carts of some kind?"

"They didn't have wheeled conveyances at all, apparently."

"But– "

"It must've been the design, itself, that had meaning for them, like a monument. It was an image of the cosmos, maybe... " He smiled enigmatically.

"Let's just say it's another mystery for you to think about, Evelyn."

BIBLIOGRAPHY

Constable, George (Editor), Time-Life Books, *Mysteries of the Unknown* (series): *Mystic Places*, Alexandria, Virginia, 1987.

Cruttenden, Walter, *Lost Star of Myth and Time*, St. Lynn's Press, Pittsburgh, Pennsylvania, 2006.

Dyott, George M., *Man-Hunting in the Jungle*, Blue Ribbon Books, New York, 1930.

Fawcett, Percy Harrison, *Lost Trails, Lost Cities*, Funk & Wagnalls Company, New York, 1953.

Fleming, Peter, *Brazilian Adventure*, Alden Press, Oxford, 1933.

Frantz, Douglas, *Searching for Heart of Darkness*, Los Angeles Times, July 29, 1990, p. 1, 38-39.

Leal, Hermes, *Coronel Fawcett: A verdadeira história do Indiana Jones*, Geração Editorial, São Paulo, Brazil, 1996.

Lee, J. Fitzgerald, *The Great Migration*, Skeffington & Son, Ltd., London, 1932.

Page, Joseph A., *The Brazilians*, Addison-Wesley Publishing Co., Reading, Mass., 1995.

Strange Case of Colonel Fawcett, Life Magazine, April 16, 1951, pp. 95 - 102.

Wilson, Colin, and Rand Flem-Ath, *The Atlantis Blueprint*, Delta Trade Paperbacks, 3rd ed,. New York, 2002.

Z: Beyond the Xingu